A FEW OF THE GIRLS

Also by Maeve Binchy

FICTION
Light a Penny Candle
Echoes
The Lilac Bus
Firefly Summer
Silver Wedding
Circle of Friends
The Copper Beech
The Glass Lake
Evening Class
Tara Road
Scarlet Feather
Quentins
Nights of Rain and Stars
Whitethorn Woods
Heart and Soul
Minding Frankie
A Week in Winter
Chestnut Street

NONFICTION
Aches & Pains
The Maeve Binchy Writers' Club
Maeve's Times

A FEW OF THE GIRLS

Maeve Binchy

ALFRED A. KNOPF

NEW YORK · 2016

Doubleday Large Print Home Library Edition

This Large Print Edition, prepared especially for Doubleday Large Print Home Library, contains the complete, unabridged text of the original Publisher's Edition.

THIS IS A BORZOI BOOK
PUBLISHED BY ALFRED A. KNOPF

Copyright © 2015 by Gordon Snell

ISBN 978-1-62953-950-8

Jacket illustration by William Low
Jacket design by Carol Devine Carson

Printed in the United States of America

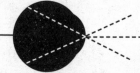

**This Large Print Book carries the
Seal of Approval of N.A.V.H**

Contents

Your Cheating Heart

Relatives and Other Strangers

Work and No Play

Holidays

A FEW OF THE GIRLS

Foreword

Maeve's mind was always full of stories. In all the years we sat writing, at each end of the long desk in front of our study window, I never saw her gazing at a blank page, wondering how to start.

She plunged at the keyboard, like a swimmer into the sea, typing at breakneck speed, and without pausing to correct any errors in punctuation or spelling. If the devilish machine suddenly disappeared a page or two of text, she didn't spend any time on technical fiddling. She said it was quicker to write the whole section again, there and then.

And the stories and characters emerged, shaped and described with her smooth, straightforward, and sensitive style. It seemed almost effortless, as if she had sat down to tell you eagerly about something that had just happened.

Maeve always said that she didn't write any better if she wrote more slowly—and she talked in the same way, the words almost tumbling out in their haste to be said. Storytelling was her natural and magical talent, and as well as her novels and books of short stories, she wrote stories for newspapers and magazines. I knew that her many devoted readers would be delighted to see in book form so many stories they hadn't come across before.

So here they are in this new collection, **A Few of the Girls,** selected and gathered together by her agent Christine Green, editors Juliet Ewers, Carole Baron, and Pauline Proctor. The stories are just part of the truly extraordinary output of Maeve's powerful and compassionate imagination, and the great storytelling legacy she has left to us all.

—Gordon Snell

Friends and Enemies

Falling Apart

When they were young, they went to school together, their schoolbags on their backs, and their mothers smiled at them. They held hands as they went along the road. Solemn dark-haired Cathy and laughing blond Clare—they would be friends forever. And at eighteen, they went together to Spain to be nannies in nearby families. They struggled to laugh and joke in Spanish, but of course they drank strong black coffee and smoked and laughed together about the future. Cathy was going to study for a degree and get a great job. Clare was going to get a job, make money, and have fun.

Back in Dublin, everything changed. Clare's father died. Her mother, unable to cope without him, began to drink heavily. Clare's notion of having fun seemed a hollow promise to herself. The money she earned at her office went to keeping the house going. Her mother had looked after her for nineteen years—she couldn't abandon her now.

Cathy worked hard at UCD, but in her third year at the university things took a different turn and she found it hard to sit her degree examination since the morning sickness was very bad. Bad too was the pain in her heart because Martin said he was far too young to be tied down. He would, of course, acknowledge the child and pay what he could towards education or whatever. Martin got a First Class degree, Cathy got a Third. Cathy's parents were far from supportive; in fact, they were downright disapproving. Why couldn't she have been more careful? Why did she have to make a fool of herself?

And, as always, Cathy and Clare had each other.

There were too many cups of strong coffee, too many cigarettes, but long, consoling chats about the strange ways of the world. About the alcoholic mother in one house, the new fatherless baby about to be born in the other. The dreams they had talked about so confidently in the Spanish café were gone.

"We're too young to be falling apart," Clare said, with one of her survival laughs. "We're only twenty-one. This is meant to be **our** time, you know, when people look back and talk about in **their** day. This is meant to be **our** day, for heaven's sake, and look at us."

Cathy pushed her long dark hair out of her eyes; there were circles under them. She had never been able to laugh as much as Clare, whose face was set in a smile. These days, Cathy looked like the Mother of Sorrows in some painting; her mother was very annoyed about the new arrival. Nothing would console her. No, she did not look forward to being a grandmother.

Yes, she might have sometime in the future, perhaps, when she had a married daughter and a son-in-law, not under these circumstances. Nor was she pleased that her daughter's career had been cut short. Or that Cathy had been made to appear so foolish and abandoned. Let there be no belief that Cathy would find a built-in babysitting service. This house had to continue its own way and Cathy should consider herself lucky her father was doing up a room over the garage for her and the infant. They sighed, Cathy and Clare. It had turned out very differently indeed to how they had hoped.

"At least your mother remembers your name," Clare said, looking for a silver lining.

"But she says it with such a sour taste in her mouth, I'd nearly prefer she didn't."

"I bet Martin will go mad with excitement when he sees the baby." Clare was always full of encouragement.

"Aren't you lucky you never loved anyone? It saved you a lot of trouble," Cathy said enviously.

Clare puzzled about this afterwards. Why was it assumed she had never loved anyone? She had loved Harry at work for a year, but Cathy hadn't understood. Clare and Harry hadn't had an affair, so apparently this didn't count as love. Not in

Cathy's book. And Clare sort of loved Michael at work now, but kept him at arm's length because it wasn't fair to involve him with all her problems at home.

Michael knew of her mother's drinking, but Clare's optimism kept telling her that perhaps it might all sort itself out, then she and Michael could meet as equals without all this drama hanging over them. Cathy assumed that Clare and Michael were just friends, mates, in fact. There had been no full sexual relationship: how could love be involved?

Cathy's waters broke in Clare's house. The timing could not have been worse. Clare's mother was singing rebel songs in the next room and cursing almost every race in the world including, rather illogically, the Irish race, which she was purporting to praise in tuneless song. She hurled abuse at the two girls as they left in the ambulance. Cathy's mother came to the hospital but managed to say to Clare in three different ways that if Cathy had a more reliable friend with a better lifestyle, all this would never have happened.

Cathy had a baby boy and, as predicted,

Martin fell in love with the child and with Cathy all over again. They would marry soon, he said, as Cathy lay in bed, the child in her arms, her dark hair held back with a ribbon, a serene smile on her face. She looked like a contented Madonna. Everything was turning out all right, she told Clare, maybe they weren't all falling apart after all.

Clare tidied up the house, washed her mother's clothes, put the bottles in a box for the bottle bank. If things have to run amok, she would say, let them run amok ecologically. Look on the bright side, lots of bottles to be saved and recycled.

When her mother was asleep, she went in and trimmed her hair. It looked very bedraggled these days. It was better to cut it and remove the cut bits while she was asleep. Wielding a scissors in front of a flailing mother was not a good idea. Clare sat and thought about Cathy, the new baby, and Martin and the wonder in his eyes when he saw his son.

Would that ever happen for Michael and herself?

She looked at her mother's lined face.

Clare turned off the light and left the door slightly open so she could hear the snores and know all was well. She had some work from the office. She was doing very well there in spite of everything at home, and Michael was so encouraging. She sighed and decided not to think about being twenty-two next birthday and having the odd feeling that her life was over.

Martin's parents put a lot of obstacles in the way when he said he wanted to marry Cathy. Too young, not started in his career, too much responsibility. And anyway, the girl seemed quite happy to bring up the baby herself. So Cathy had many a long tale to tell of how the world had treated everyone so badly. Poor little baby Dan, poor Martin, and, most of all, poor Cathy herself.

During all this, Clare worked on and minded her mother. Michael said he couldn't wait forever so Clare let him come home. Somehow her mother sensed this was dangerous, something that might change things. So she behaved worse than usual and insulted Michael to his face while also telling him that Clare had brought home a string of strange men to stay the night and all they needed these days was a red light over the door.

Then Cathy rang up to say she and Martin would marry on baby Dan's first birthday, wasn't that wonderful? Would Clare be bridesmaid?

She had to pay someone to look after her mother that day. The thought that Clare was going to a wedding made the older woman uneasy. It was as if she feared Clare might want to get married herself once she was at such close quarters to a ceremony. Michael came to the wedding. He asked Clare to marry him that evening.

"You know I can't," she said with all the regret in the world.

"I just know you won't," he said, turning away to hide his hurt and disappointment.

"I can't throw her into somewhere, I couldn't live with myself."

"We wouldn't throw her; we'd **put** her and visit her often, that way she might get better." This had been pleaded so often, so persuasively, but it had never worked.

"Michael, I'm the worst person in the

world for you to get involved with. I beg you don't," she said.

"It's too late, I am. I love you."

"And I love you..."

"No you don't, Clare. If you did, then you'd..."

Clare looked at him in despair.

It had been a long day; she had been coping with Cathy, with baby Dan, with Martin, with Martin's mother and father, and Cathy's mother—now she was going home to her own mother and she knew not what situation. It was just unfair to be told that, if she loved him, she would turn her back on all this. People were always being blackmailed this way. If you loved me, you'd sleep with me. If you loved me, you'd give up your job for me. If you loved me, you'd lock up your mother and throw away the key.

"If you loved **me,** Michael, then you'd either wait until things sorted themselves out or you'd move in with me as they are."

"I can't move in! She orders me out of the house, she is hysterical if I come near the place. And things will **not** sort themselves out, **we** have to," he said.

Funnily, Cathy had said that to her the night before when she had called round to the bride's house for the last-minute fuss and preparations.

"You'll find someone too," Cathy had said to her.

"I have someone, I have Michael," Clare had protested.

"Of course you don't. You can't love him, otherwise you'd have done something about the situation," Cathy had insisted.

She had not thought it worthy of discussion. They had gone back to the speeches, the seating plan, the flowers in the church. Now, on the night of Cathy's wedding, Clare was turning down a proposal.

"Everything's falling apart," she said to Michael, tears in her eyes.

"Only because you're allowing it to," he said.

He drove her home. His eyes were very hard. He kissed her on the cheek and didn't even look up at her mother's bedroom window to see the figure sitting at the window, her hand on the curtain, waiting.

"How did the farce go?" her mother asked.

"The wedding was fine, Mother. Cathy's father is a bit long-winded, but, you know, it was nice. Everyone seemed very happy."

"What's happy?" Her mother sneered.

"I don't think I really know, Mother. Would you like a hot water bottle before I change?"

"Change?" her mother asked suspiciously.

"I have two hours' work to do, Mother. I don't want to do it wearing lime green satin," Clare said.

She knew her voice was lifeless. But she had not the energy to put on an act. Even though she knew her mother was less drunk than usual tonight, she would not allow herself to have any hope. Perhaps it was the presence of the retired nurse, who had looked after her, perhaps it was just anxiety to ensure that Clare had returned to her.

Clare would hope no more. Michael was right: if things fell apart, it was because she had let them fall. Funny Clare, thinking everything would somehow get better.

Michael was always nice in the office but he did not ask her out anymore. They sometimes had lunch and talked about work. Once he had reached across and laid his hand on hers.

"I wish things were different," he'd said.

"God, so do I," Clare had replied. She tried to grin the old grin but it did not quite work. She felt the muscles of her face twist awkwardly. She must be becoming as peculiar as her mother.

Cathy rang that evening. Clare was pleased. Cathy, at least, had remembered. Nobody else had acknowledged that Clare was twenty-four today. Her mother had not known about birthdays for five years. Michael probably did not think it appropriate since they would not be sharing birthdays from now on.

"It's great to have friends, Cathy," Clare said, a genuine smile coming back to her face.

"Hey, that's my line," Cathy said.

Clare was surprised. "No, come on, you rang me, you remembered, no one else did."

She could hear Cathy fumble.

"Remember? Well yes. Yes, sure."

Then Clare knew her only friend had not remembered at all. She felt an ache of self-pity. She had remembered Cathy's birthday every year since they had been seven. Two long decades of sending cards and gifts; she sent things to baby Dan, she prepared feasts for her mother, which largely remained uneaten, she had bought thoughtful presents for Michael. She felt a strange coldness come over her. Like being numbed. Instead of chattering on, Clare remained oddly silent. Cathy spoke, of course.

"Yes, well, it's great to talk to you and of course I'd ring you...but..."

Clare waited.

"I wonder if I could ask you to babysit tonight, it's a last-minute thing."

"Not tonight. Sorry, Cathy."

"But why? She can be left, you often leave her."

"No, it's got nothing to do with Mother."

"Well, if it's Michael, can't you ask him to come round here—have a bottle of wine and a cuddle or whatever it is you do by the fire."

"No, it's not Michael, I don't see Michael anymore."

"Well, then?" Cathy asked.

Clare couldn't **believe** it. This was her friend. Her best friend. She had told Cathy she loved Michael, Cathy knew everything and all she could say was "Well, then?"

Cathy had not even taken time to notice Clare had said those terrible words "I don't see Michael anymore."

She had not cried out in disbelief, demanded to know what had happened, rushed to give reassurance as Clare had done so many times over Martin. She did not try to hold a friend's hand over the phone, she did not want to know every heartbeat. All she had said was "Well, then?"

Clare stood in the hall of the house she cleaned for a mother who appreciated neither her nor the cleaning. It was her twenty-fourth birthday and this was all she had to show for her life. She held the phone a little way away from her and could hear Cathy's voice pleading. Some long tale about Martin saying she was never free to go out anymore and about Cathy's mother refusing on some kind of principle.

"I **know** you'll do it, Clare," Cathy begged. "We've been through so much together and my life is falling apart."

"Only because you are allowing it to," Clare said.

Her voice sounded alien in her own ears. But what she said was true. Clare went upstairs slowly and opened the door of her mother's room. Despite her best attempts to clean it, the room smelled stale and close. Her mother knew immediately something had changed. Fearful eyes looked up at Clare from the low chair where she lay slumped most of the day.

"Do you think you understand me, Mother? Because I'm going to say something quite important. I'll say it twice today and twice tomorrow and I'll write it down but I'd like you to know how serious I am."

Her mother began to bluster in the usual way, but, when Clare's voice cut across her, it had a steely ring. Her mother stopped midsentence to listen. Without any anger or recrimination, Clare explained there were three choices open to her mother. She could try a rehabilitation program in which Clare would support her every step of the way. She could be admitted and possibly committed to a psychiatric home on the grounds that she was unable to look after herself, or she could stay here on her own for the few short weeks it would take for the neighbors to report the unsanitary conditions and the risk to health and safety.

Clare's voice was steady and unwavering; there was affection and concern, but no beseeching. It was clear that, whatever her mother's decision, she would go along with it. She sat calmly while her mother ranted and attacked her and came up with a list of reasons why nothing was her fault, that it was all Clare's. Then, when there was finally silence, Clare, as she had promised, repeated the options clearly and without any hint of Last Chance Saloon.

"Why are you saying all this?" her mother wept.

"Because it's my birthday. You gave birth

to me this day twenty-four years ago and you didn't remember."

Clare closed the door quietly behind her and left the house. She arrived at Michael's flat some twenty minutes later. He came to the door and stood there, surprised to see her. Pleased to see her too, she decided, a little watchful, but pleased.

"You were right," she said simply.

"About what?" He was definitely cautious.

"My life doesn't need to fall apart. Do you still love me?"

He opened the door wide.

"Are you coming in...just for a bit?" he asked. He **did** love her still. She closed the door behind her.

Clare was coming in for the night...and she hoped for a great deal longer.

Picnic at St. Paul's

Once, a long time ago, ten years ago, Catherine had spent a week in Suzi's smart Washington apartment. About four times a year for ten years she had reason to regret this, even though it had been pleasant enough at the time. But every three months or so, she got phone calls from Americans sent to torment her by Suzi.

"Hi, Catherine, I'm Mitzi Bernbach. I'm a friend of Suzi's. She said I mustn't come to London without calling to say hi. Suzi's sent you a little gift. When can we meet so I can give it to you?"

Suzi's little gifts ranged from totally un-usable, absurd toys like an elephant that held a pencil in its trunk to a map of some walk that Catherine had taken by the Potomac River in the distant past. She had to put on a show of enthusiasm for whoever had transported the gift, but always ended up feeling resentful, buying some ridiculous souvenir of London in return, and feeling under an ungracious obligation to entertain whatever wandering American had landed friendless in London. More than once she considered changing her address, but it seemed ridiculous to be hunted out of where she was happy by a vague threat from across the Atlantic.

Through all these penniless Mitzis and Jerrys and Chucks she had learned the course of Suzi's life. Suzi was still an ambitious young Washington host, for the younger set. She gathered people who were not yet successful but who had potential. She no longer ran her flower shop; instead she ran a contract flower hire service. Apparently, she visited the homes of rich people and advised them on what flowers to buy or rent for occasions: she then got commission from various florists for the orders that were put in. Only Suzi could have seen the potential in using the same set of expensive cut flowers for three separate occasions in a single day. She had been known to arrive in her van after a christening at one house to collect the flowers and rearrange them for someone else's bar mitzvah party, and taken them on to a twenty-first all on the same day. Everybody paid slightly less for the flowers; everybody was happy.

But Catherine, though she admired Suzi's well-organized mind from afar, did wish that one day Suzi would lose her address where Catherine was filed under "Contact, useful, Britain." The last visitor had been a real pain. He had telephoned from the airport with some terrible tale about his friends not being there to meet him and Suzi having said that he must call Catherine if he was in any trouble. He had slept on Catherine's sofa for four nights. He never seemed to change his socks and her house smelled of feet for a week after he left; he had no money, no interests, and no charm. He had even eaten the thoughtful gift of a jar of ginger that Suzi had sent Catherine this time.

So it was with a heavy heart that she greeted the voice on the phone, which told her yet again that Suzi had asked it to call. It called at midnight, just after she had gone to sleep. She thought it was morning and was bitterly disappointed to find that it wasn't. Catherine hadn't been sleeping well and she now regarded getting off to sleep as a kind of achievement. This new Suzi person had committed a great crime.

"I think I ought to tell you," Catherine said with tears in her voice, "I really don't know Suzi Dane at all well. Ten years ago—yes, ten whole years ago—I spent six nights in her apartment in Washington, while you were still at school. I knew her only because of a complete accident. I found her purse at a telephone kiosk and returned it to her. She invited me to stay for a week. I am not, as she claims, a lifelong friend. I have no room for anyone to stay. I have no time to take you to the Changing of the Guard, or to the Tower of London. I do not want to hear what Suzi is doing now, and how rich and successful she has become. I'm sorry, I know I'm taking it out on you, but really, I've had quite enough of Suzi's friends, and I think it's better to tell you that straight out. Besides, I'd just got to sleep, and I haven't slept properly for weeks. Now I'll never get back to sleep."

To her horror she burst into tears.

There was a kind of silence interrupted by a few soothing noises at the other end of the phone. Catherine could hear them as she put down the receiver and went to hunt for some tissues. Twice, as she blew her nose hard, she made a move to hang up—she had been so rude, there was no saving the conversation now. Twice she didn't in case she thought of some way of rescuing it.

After a final blow, she picked up the receiver cautiously.

"Are you still there?" she asked.

"Yeah, I'm still here," said the voice, which didn't sound hurt, sulky, or even surprised.

"Well, as you can gather you caught me at rather a bad time," she said. "Perhaps I should ask you to ring again. Tomorrow lunchtime, maybe? I'll be fine by then. I'm very sorry for getting upset. I must have still been half asleep."

"That's okay. I shouldn't have called so late."

He didn't sound like Suzi's usual friends. He hadn't said yet how broke he was, how he had nowhere to stay, how he had carried over this little gift. Also to his credit, he didn't sound apologetic. Catherine couldn't have borne him to be sorry; it was, in fact, her fault: five past midnight wasn't too late to call someone.

"What was your name again? I'll telephone you when I'm awake," she said, trying to be cheerful.

"It's no use trying to go back to sleep if you've got insomnia," he said calmly. "The damage is done now. You must get up, have a shower, get dressed, and pretend it's day. Do whatever you'd do during the day. Vacuum the house, write letters, cook a meal, go for a walk, listen to the radio, read a book, but don't go back to bed, no matter how tired you feel."

"And how will I feel tomorrow?" she asked.

"Rotten, but you'll feel rotten anyway so

why not get something done instead of lying there trying to go to sleep?"

"But we **need** sleep," said Catherine with interest.

"Not nearly as much as we think. In two or three days, you'll just drop off somewhere and sleep soundly. Listen, I'll leave you to get on with it all, and call in a few days."

"Get on with what?" asked Catherine in amazement.

"Whatever you're going to do," he said and hung up.

Startled at her own obedience, Catherine got up, washed, and dressed. Then she made scrambled eggs and had a cigarette. She certainly felt more relaxed than she had at eleven o'clock, when she had been worrying whether she would get to sleep that night. She took out all her old silver and polished it and she put on some Strauss waltzes, which she liked but which Alec had said were impossible to listen to. She had pretended to Alec that she only kept them because they belonged to someone else.

When the silver was shining at her and

reflecting her busy face bent over it, she decided that she'd put it out on a shelf rather than hide it in the back of a cupboard. Alec had thought it was vulgar to exhibit silver; the cottage mentality, he called it. He also said it was an invitation to burglars. Catherine put the silver on shelves around the room and stood back to admire it. Each piece had a story. The teapot was the first thing her parents had bought when they got married; they had hardly enough coal to light a fire but they thought you weren't properly married without a nice silver teapot. The silver rose vase was a gift from the office where she had worked happily for six years but which Alec said was a nonjob. She had left it a year ago, but often wondered why she was no longer there. It had been happy, so it had been cheerful going to work on Mondays. Most people didn't have that at work. She certainly didn't have that now.

The silver napkin ring had been a present from her sister Margie. Margie had saved for a year, putting a pound a week aside to get something in solid silver. Margie was innocent and simple. Alec thought she was very sweet and wondered whether she had had brain damage as a child. He thought that they should get her to see a specialist. Catherine knew that Margie was just slow and loved working in a hotel kitchen where they fed her, looked after her, and tucked her up at night in return for days scouring and scrubbing and washing up. Catherine thought that people should be left where they were if they were happy. She went to see Margie every week. It was two bus journeys and a taxi at the other end, and took up most of Sunday. Sometimes that irritated Alec if he wanted to spend the day with her. He only went once to the hotel. He had stayed an hour.

It was nearly three o'clock, Catherine realized, when she glanced at the digital watch Alec had given her for Christmas. She had never got used to the way the figures changed on it; secretly she would have preferred a watch with hands. Where had the hours gone? No wonder she felt so tired! Perhaps she should go to bed now—she would definitely sleep. But that odd Yank on the phone had sounded so certain that he was right in his plan, she didn't like to disobey him. She made more tea, found a program on the World Service, and started some knitting, which she hadn't taken out for weeks. It was to be a big chunky sweater for Margie, red and white. It would make her look very fat, but it was the color scheme she wanted. Several Sundays now Margie had asked how it was getting on. Peacefully until dawn Catherine sat there knitting, finishing the sweater, and then she had a stretch, took a walk down the quiet streets and then back home to finish the sweater. She felt tired but, as the American had said, no more tired than she normally felt after a night of little snatches of sleep and long periods of looking at the patterns on the ceiling made by the light that came through the windows.

She began to wonder about this American, what she would do when he called. She half wished that he would ring now; she felt able to go out and wander around London in the sun on a Saturday morning. She wouldn't resent having to do her unpaid London guide act today. In fact, she would take him to the Albert Memorial. Tourists loved that, and they could walk around the park for a bit. Of course he would want to go to Harrods; even penniless Americans liked to tour the great store, which they seemed to regard as a sight to be seen rather than a shop where you bought things. Perhaps she would take him to St. Paul's. Yes, she'd like that, and they could walk for a bit along the Embankment; they might even take a boat trip, but mainly they would walk around St. Paul's. Catherine liked St. Paul's; it wasn't as fussy as the Abbey, and it seemed to have a confident life of its own.

The flat was clean and shining after her work through the night and the sweater was wrapped up and ready to take tomorrow to Margie. Had Saturdays always been a bit empty since she and Alec split up or was it just today? Outside the world was waking up, and she wanted to be a part of it. She would like to put on her nice leather jacket and her good tartan skirt and walk with someone who didn't know London. Why didn't this friend of Suzi's ring? She hadn't been that rude to him, had she? The morning dragged and she couldn't think of anyone she wanted to telephone or to meet. Three years of Alec had cut her off from a lot of friends, and Catherine was too proud or too something to ring everybody up and ask if could she join the party again just because the affair was over.

In the afternoon she went to the cinema and felt sleepy on the bus coming home. The phone was ringing as she let herself into the flat, but stopped before she got there. Tired as she was, she felt furious, because she was sure it had been the American.

He was beginning to assume quite extraordinary proportions in her mind. It had something to do with sounding cool and unruffled. Unlike any of Suzi's other friends, he appeared to be able to look after himself, and to give advice to hysterical strangers on the phone. Catherine planned a night program for herself. She would stick all her photos into albums, she would make herself an autumn skirt in nice autumn colors, she would methodically remove from her vision anything that reminded her of Alec, and she would restore the things she had liked before he came along because the sight of the silver cheered her up. By four a.m. she was too exhausted to do any more, but she refused to go to bed. Out into the silent streets, and a long, long walk, but not nervous. London was her city, she was never nervous here. Right up to the steps of St. Paul's.

She wished they left churches open at night; many people might like to wander around them when they couldn't sleep. Of course, many more who had nowhere to sleep might use the pews as beds. But would that matter? If it was meant to be the house of a loving God, then surely he would like that sort of thing? As she sat on the steps she remembered a day when she and Alec had come here. A military band was playing and the tourists had loved it. Alec had said it was a form of prostitution to change your city to make it appeal to tourists so that they would spend their money there.

She must clear her mind of Alec in the

same way that she had cleared her flat of memories. He was no good for her, he had never loved her—he had never loved anyone—he had made her feel inferior, he had brought little laughter into her life. Why had she loved him? Chemistry, perhaps, if that wasn't too ridiculous an idea.

She walked home, tired, legs dragging, but her mind awake.

At eleven o'clock, when she was just leaving the flat on the first stage of her journey to Margie's, the phone rang.

"Am I talking with Catherine?" he asked.

"I'm glad you rang. You know, I didn't even get your name the other night," she said breathlessly.

"I'm Bob," he said. "Look, I was wondering, could I take you to lunch somewhere today? You must be feeling a bit too tired to fix yourself lunch, and you'll probably want to sleep tonight."

Catherine was surprised that he seemed to assume she had followed his advice. Today was bad, she explained. She had to go and see her sister miles away. Could they make it one evening during the week, when she'd be happy to cook him a meal?

Maybe they could meet on Tuesday; she could leave work early, they might stroll up to St. Paul's, if he hadn't already seen it, and then she'd be happy, really happy, to make dinner for them.

"No," he said. "I'll be gone by Tuesday. Would your sister like it if I took you both to lunch?"

Catherine thought for a moment. Perhaps Margie wouldn't mind all that much if she didn't go to see her today. There was no hard-and-fast rule that she must turn up every Sunday. Margie was so easy to please, just a telephone call and some explanation, and she would agree to the visit being canceled.

"It's nothing very concrete with my sister," she said, feeling a little treacherous, "no, nothing that can't keep. Let's meet for lunch."

"Are you sure your sister wouldn't like to come, too?" he asked.

"She's miles away, she'd hate to make the journey," said Catherine, and they fixed to meet in a pub.

"I know a nice place for lunch," he said, which was more than Catherine did.

Nobody who lived in London knew where to go for Sunday lunch.

He said he was tall and would carry **The Sunday Times,** and she said she was small and dark and would carry the same thing. All giggles, overexcited and over-tired, she rang Margie at the hotel.

"Something's come up, love," she said. "I can't make it. I was just ready to leave, and I have your sweater finished. Next Sunday without fail."

"Right," said Margie glumly.

"You're not upset? I really have to meet this man from America; he's a friend of Suzi's and he has nowhere to go."

"**I've** nowhere to go," said Margie.

"I know, Margie, but you're there, and you have all your friends. He has nobody."

"I have nobody on a Sunday either," said Margie.

"Nobody has anybody on a Sunday," cried Catherine in exasperation. Why, oh why, of all days, could Margie not be sunny and cheerful? Why must it be today that she was low?

"Could you bring him here for lunch?" asked Margie. "You could book a table and we could all have lunch in the dining room. I'm allowed to do that you know, on Sundays, if there are guests."

"No, he has to stay in the center of town," lied Catherine. "Listen, I'll give you a ring later tonight. Okay?"

"Okay," said Margie doubtfully.

Catherine changed her clothes; she put on the good leather coat and nice tartan skirt, she put on makeup, and splashed on her best perfume. She spent so long doing it that she had to take a taxi to the pub. She recognized him at once, tousle-haired, intense, reading **The Sunday Times,** looking sensitive.

"Bob?" she said confidently, disturbing him from his half pint and his reading.

"No, but I wish I was," he said in a Geordie accent.

Annoyed, Catherine went to the bar and sat on a stool.

"A large vodka and ice," she said to the barman.

"On no sleep?" asked the elderly man beside her, a man whom she hadn't noticed before.

"I'm Bob Dane, Catherine," he said, like

a family doctor who had been asked to take someone away quietly to the asylum without upsetting the neighbors. "I'm very pleased to know you. Shall we take our drinks to that corner over there?"

He was in his late sixties, at least. Damn him, damn him, why did he have to pretend to be young, and eligible, and some kind of Lancelot to her on the phone? He was an old, old man.

She hadn't even taken in his name.

"My little Suzi said that I mustn't leave London without seeing you and I'm very glad we're seeing each other," he said, carrying the drinks to the table he had pointed out.

His name registered.

"You're Suzi's...?" she asked.

"I'm Suzi's father," he said.

"I didn't even know she had one. I hardly know her, you know," gasped Catherine.

"We're not very close. Suzi lives her life; I live mine. Since Suzi's mother died, when she was eighteen, she's been very much her own person," said the man. "I'm not surprised you didn't know of me. In fact, we've only got together recently. I was quite shy of approaching her. But now we meet like friends, and as you so rightly said, Suzi has a lot of friends. She likes them. She regards me as an interesting new addition to her collection."

Catherine drank most of her vodka.

"How about the sleeping?" he asked kindly.

"I did what you said. I stayed out of bed since midnight on Friday. My legs and back feel tired but the rest of me is awake."

"You'll sleep tonight," he said positively.

Catherine nodded. "I'm sure I will."

There was a silence.

"You said something about wanting to go to St. Paul's, Catherine, so I took a little liberty. I packed a picnic, it's such a lovely day I thought we might eat it on the steps, or nearby."

Catherine looked at him, a nice confident face, gray hair, light tan, heavy gold ring on his finger. He was a successful retired American businessman and there seemed no reason to hurt him—he didn't look like someone who would hurt her.

"A picnic would be lovely," said Catherine.

"You mustn't feel that you have to take back anything you said about Suzi to me on the phone," he said, just as Catherine was wondering how she might possibly do this. "I know only too well what a burden some of her lame dogs can be. I had a great hesitancy about calling you because of this. I felt sure you had been stuck with Chuck and Mitzi among others."

"Well, yes," agreed Catherine, laughing.

"Yet we mustn't be too hard on Suzi. She has this odd cosmic theory that the people of the world should all get to know each other, and that some of us are too timid to go up and say hi, therefore an introduction helps."

"Oh, in theory she's right," agreed Catherine enthusiastically. "I suppose, selfishly, I feel it's all one-way traffic. You see, I don't know anyone going to the United States much, so I don't send my friends to **her**."

"I know. I understand that, but you must never underestimate Suzi. She may indeed be overbusy, oversuccessful, and very haphazard about who she deposits on whom, yet she does care about people

It's not just a wish to be at the center of some web, you know."

"Oh, I never thought that," cried Catherine insincerely.

"I'm sure you didn't," said Bob gravely. And Catherine knew he saw through her.

They walked in the autumn lunchtime sun to the steps of St. Paul's; it had become autumn overnight. Catherine didn't need to do her guide-to-London act, because Bob had obviously been to Britain several times. It turned out that he was a doctor, but he had retired earlier and organized medical conferences instead. He was in Europe a great deal.

"Why didn't Suzi ever give you my address before?" asked Catherine.

"Well, as I said, we've only been close in the last couple of years."

"But since then?" she persisted.

"Oh, I don't think she thought the time was ripe," he said mysteriously.

They walked around the building, they chatted to each other amicably about Wren, and what he thought he was at, and what other people thought of him in his time. Bob told her about the cathedral at

Rheims, which was overpowering in its detail, and about temples in Salt Lake City, which were equally startling. They both felt they could cope with St. Paul's.

As they had their picnic he told her about a woman he had loved once. When Suzi's mother died, he had contacted her again and the woman told him to get lost. He said it was hurtful to be told that at fifty you were finished and no use to anybody; he had been very lost in those days, but now, at sixty-four, somehow he felt more secure. He said he didn't feel old enough to have a daughter of thirty-two, and that when he heard of the older generation he never included himself in that category at all.

Catherine told him how she had been in love for three years and only very recently had stopped. She said she tried hard not to feel bitter but this man had really hurt her a lot, and it was hard to take up the reins again.

The evening shadows came and they talked, and then they walked along the Embankment, and she told him more, about how she couldn't sleep because she kept wondering did other people manage relationships better than she did. She had worked out one day that she was happy twenty percent of the time with this man and decided that it wasn't enough so she had ended it. He had been surprised and annoyed. She had liked him feeling that way.

But sometimes, as she was going to sleep alone, she wondered about the rest of the world. Perhaps twenty percent was average for happiness with another human being. Maybe she had wanted too much and didn't know how to compromise. What did Bob think? How much happiness had he enjoyed with Suzi's mother, say?

"Oh, about ninety percent," he said. "You were right to finish with Alec. What we must do is make sure that the cure isn't worse than the disease."

"I didn't say his name, how did you know?" asked Catherine. She made a point of not mentioning Alec's name, ever. It made him seem like more of a person if his name was allowed to occur in conversation.

"Suzi told me," he said calmly.

"But how could Suzi possibly know? I send her a Christmas card once a year. I send her a note of three lines thanking her for whatever she has sent me by one of her ghastly friends. I never mentioned Alec to her, not once. I haven't seen Suzi for ten years. Nobody ever seems to believe that."

"Chuck told her," said Bob.

Chuck? Chuck! The man with the smelly socks and no money; the man who had eaten the jar of ginger, the man who met Alec twice. How dare Chuck mention Alec's name at the other side of the world? She was speechless with rage and shock.

"Chuck told Suzi that it was a bad scene, and Suzi asked me to see if I could help you straighten your problems out. I guess I arrived just in time. At least I'm able to fix your sleeping problems. That's better than talking you out of Alec."

"You couldn't have talked me out of Alec, nobody could," Catherine said, stunned by his intrusion and confidence. "I don't know what makes you and Suzi think you have any right to interfere in other people's affairs. People you don't even know. It's outrageous!"

"Yeah, but you were agreeing earlier that we are all too buttoned up about getting to know people, the British particularly."

"But it's **my** business, nobody else's."

"Your friends care," said Bob simply.

"You're not my friend. Suzi's not my friend. I've no friends who care."

"Margie might care if you talked to her about it," said Bob.

Catherine felt weak at her thighs, as if she were going to fall. She didn't know whether it was tiredness or the sense of unreality. How did this old, old American man know about Margie? She never told people about Margie, only Alec had known, for all the good he had been.

"Mitzi mentioned to Suzi that you had a sister who was a problem to you. She said she was in a hotel somewhere and you were ashamed to include her in your life. That's why I was so anxious we should meet her today and talk, all three of us."

Yes, Mitzi had been told about Margie. That's because Mitzi had stayed three weeks in Catherine's flat, and had asked where she went every Sunday. God damn

Mitzi and Suzi and whatever other transatlantic spies she had harbored.

They were passing a seat and Catherine sat down. Bob talked on in his calm voice. "I've rented a car; we could ride out and see your sister. I could act as an intermediary, you and she could discuss how she could participate more in your life. You would feel the benefit, **she** would feel the benefit."

Catherine spoke slowly and carefully. "I know you mean well. I know Suzi means well. I know Americans are thicker-skinned than we are; they are also more friendly and they risk insult more easily out of kindness. I also know it's foolish to make generalizations about my nationality. Now given all this, can I thank you for your interest, and walk back to a bus stop with you, and part friends in some sort of way? I won't begin to tell you how impossible I would find it to thrash out my whole life and problems with a stranger, however kind."

"But you were very frank about your relationship with Alec."

"Because I thought you were someone

who hadn't much interest and whom I would never meet again!" said Catherine desperately.

"You mean you'd prefer to talk to someone who could be of no help?" asked Bob.

"I don't want help," she said, choked.

"You do, my dear Catherine, you do, you're just afraid to admit it. This British reserve may have got you all through national crises but it's no good for a young girl all by herself."

"Please don't say any more," begged Catherine.

On shaking legs she rose and ran haltingly down the Embankment towards a bus stop. Behind her, Bob was calling, "Catherine, Catherine, we must talk, you need to talk." Behind her, St. Paul's towered knowingly over it all.

Someone's Got to Tell Her

Oh, we could tell each other **anything** when we were fifteen, Angela! Couldn't we? You and Maggie and I. You two could tell me that white lipstick was tarty. We two could tell you that the short skirt gave you thunder thighs. We could both tell Maggie that the frizzy perm didn't work. We were always together, Maggie, Angela, and Deirdre. They used to call us MAD back then. We thought it was a scream.

And when we got a bit older we could tell each other **almost** anything. Like we told Maggie that the fellow Liam she was seeing was also seeing a lot of other people. We only told her because she was actually starting to talk about weddings and we couldn't let her go down that road.

And we told you that your boss Eric that you fancied was a con man. And we had to tell you because you were about to invest all your savings in some scam. And you both told me to go back home and live with my mam because my lovely bedsit that I was so proud of was actually a room in a brothel.

And back then we never really minded being told that we were wrong or foolish or silly or whatever. We didn't **like** it now, but we didn't get upset or sulk or anything. It was what friends did for each other. So why has it become so difficult now that we are twenty-eight?

It's not that twenty-nine is old. Or that the dreaded thirty is creeping up on us... We've lost something along the way. I don't know what happened, but we seem to be walking on eggshells with each other. And there's no reason for it.

We've all done fine. Well, as regards work anyway. Not quite so well in the Men Department. But then, people marry much later nowadays. And some don't marry at all.

It's not like it was back in our mothers'
time where they still had the notion of
being old maids or spinsters or whatever.
And of course we'd all like to have children,
but when we're ready. Not like half the
kids we were at school with who had kids
of their own just to get out and have a flat,
and now they're tied down and can't go
anywhere.

And I mean, you have to admit we're
not doing badly. You run a hair salon on
your own. And you go out to movie sets
and meet the stars and do their hair.
You have your picture taken with them.
That's pretty good, Angela, by anyone's
standards.

And I'm doing okay as well. Nobody in
my family had even heard of a career in
marketing, and yet here I am in a consultancy doing very nicely thank you. Away
long from the classroom when poor
Miss O'Sullivan said that we would all
end up in the gutter because we had no
get-up-and-go.

And of course Maggie's doing fine too. In
a way. You know. Considering everything.

And really **her** family was much more

difficult than ours were so she more or less **had** to help out all the time. And she couldn't get any real money together for a training course like we did. When we all worked stacking shelves and serving tables, back then. And honestly, Ange, we **did** try to tell her.

Remember when we said we'd all stand up to her father when he came down to take her wages from her? We said we'd speak to him straight out and tell the authorities that he was taking every penny his daughter slaved hard for, but Maggie begged us not to, said it would be worse for her mother if we did.

So we did nothing.

And then when her mother got sick Maggie said she **had** to stay at home and mind the younger ones. Who else was there?

And we did say to each other then that someone should tell her we didn't get all that many chances in life and she should have gone to college. She was brighter than all of us. She could easily have got a place.

But would she listen?

Instead it was all this about the young ones wetting the bed, what with her mother being so long in hospital, and her father being so drunk. And somebody had to be there and do it and she was there and did it.

I mean, Maggie's marvelous, and what she did for those sisters and brothers was fantastic. Some of **them** are actually in college now. And she was tough, too. She got her father into some alcoholics' program and he did stop eventually, I think. Didn't he?

Anyway, it was all too late for Maggie and somebody should have told her that it's not so easy to go back to studying when you're older. And they want babes, nowadays, not mature women. But it was getting harder to talk to her. All the old easy feeling had gone.

And that's what has her where she is now. Not that there's anything wrong with it; working in a tacky kind of shop like that, selling all kinds of rubbish. But you know the way Maggie goes on. It's lovely. She meets great people, they get marvelous bargains, it's near home, one of

the younger sisters has asthma or something and she likes to put a good meal on
the table for her father. And honestly, she
doesn't seem to remember that we are
all out for each other's good. And that
since we were the group they called
MAD back at school, there was literally
nothing we couldn't say to each other.

You get the feeling she's become touchy.

We never did touchy before, did we?
But I didn't like the way she reacted when
I offered to give her my old jacket. It was a
million times better than anything she had.
A million. But Maggie said she wouldn't
have a call to wear it. What a strange
phrase, instead of saying thank you and
being delighted with it. Like we all would. If
we were in a position to, I mean.

And remember that time we went to
have lunch with her in the posh hotel. It
was almost embarrassing. Well, it wasn't
really embarrassing, what with her being
Maggie and everything. But she seemed
so out of place and asking could she take
home the little sugar packets and paper
napkins with the name of the place on them
to her sisters. They were giving us such

pitying looks. Did you notice?

No? But then, Ange, to be honest, you are as blind as a bat these days.

Anyway, it was impossible to get a thing out of Maggie about her own life and her plans or anything. She just kept saying she'd see what happened, as if that were any way to get anywhere.

I don't know whether you noticed, but she never answered a direct question. I know I asked if her father was still off the sauce and she said something totally waffly about him being marvelous, all things considered, which is neither a yes nor a no, so I asked again and she said that to some people drink was as natural as breathing. Where does that leave us?

Then she was asking all about **my** mother and father and whether I should tell my father that my mum had been for tests. He might want to know. I said he had wanted to know very little else about her over the years since he left. She remembered everything, Maggie did, about when he left. More than I do. We were all twelve then. You'd swear it was her own family. Honestly, it was spooky. And she's been to see my mother more often than I have.

And it wasn't only me. She knows all about your family, too, Angela. She said she heard from your brother who went to jail in Australia. I mean, I know you told us all about it at the time, but Maggie actually sends him postcards and things because he'd be lonely so far from home. She knows the name of the jail and all. And apparently he's got very interested in birds, like in that film with Burt Lancaster. He writes to her about spangled drongos and galahs and things you'd never have heard of...

Oh, he does to you, too? You keep in touch with him?

That's great. Great. Well, he **is** family, of course.

No, I was just surprised that Maggie would.

Yes, of course it's kind of her.

Maggie **is** kind. That's what she does. And of course if you wanted **me** to write to him, I would. I just didn't think you had anything in common with him anymore.

No, indeed, you're right. He probably

wouldn't remember me. And too much water under the bridge, really. But that wasn't what I was talking about. I was saying that someone should tell Maggie for her own good that this kind of thing can't go on any longer. It's not fair, not on herself, not on anyone.

No, Angela, I **know** what you're going to say, that we should never try to come between lovers, no matter how star-crossed they are. Look, I know there's a point in that. I know that you often end up with egg on your face when it turns out to be a long-lasting affair. But be honest, you were glad when we turned you against Eric, that con man who was going to take your money, weren't you?

What do you mean it was only money? You had **worked** for it. Saved it.

No, that's ludicrous, Ange. You know it is. He couldn't have loved you. You couldn't have been the only one he didn't con. You were so well out of it.

It's not like you to look back and regret. Not like you at all.

And going back to that time—at least you'll admit that Maggie was lucky we pointed out that her fellow Liam had so many other girls. Look at the fool she would have made of herself and she had more things to worry about with her sister with asthma, her mother not well, and her father drinking.

Oh, come **on,** Angela, how could that Liam have helped her with any of those problems? If he had been around he would have made things much, much worse.

But now it's really serious that someone says something.

This guy Hanif. I mean, Angela, he's an African. An Algerian. From Africa.

Oh, I know Maggie says he's a French citizen but it won't work.

Well it **can't** work. I mean, marriage is hard enough anyway. Look at all the disasters we see around us and that's even when they're from the same culture and background and race and religion.

I mean, what does Maggie know about Hanif's life before he came here? He could have lived in a hut in the desert.

No stop it, Angela. Stop telling me he's from Marseilles. That's not what it's about. He can't go in and live with Maggie in her house with her father poised to go back on the drink, with her sister whooping with asthma, with poor, daft Maggie going to see **my** mother, writing letters to **your** brother. It's just ludicrous.

I know it's hard to do because we all like Maggie so much and we go back such a long way, but honestly, someone should tell her before she starts organizing a wedding.

She **has** organized a wedding? I don't believe you!

You're serious? When?

But that's only six weeks away. It can't be!

Angela?

Angela, have you been invited?

And are you going?

I see.

I see.

Okay. I haven't been invited, but I suppose you know that.

What do you mean, when did I see her last? She's our friend, for God's sake. I'm **always** seeing her. I saw her that time we went to the smart hotel where she took the sugar packets and paper napkins.

And then I saw her when we went to that weepy film and had a pizza afterwards.

No, of course I haven't been to Maggie's house.

Angela, listen to me. Who could go to that house with the chance that her father might come reeling in and the sister wheezing away in the corner?

You do. I see.

Okay, I know she asked me, but honestly...

And so that's true, I haven't sat down and talked properly to Hanif. But what's the point? What would there be to say?

Oh. You do? You have? Good, good.

No, I mean it. I'm **glad** you like him. And that you've found plenty to talk to him about.

No, that's nice, really it is. It's just that... Oh, come on, Angela, you and I, we don't have to talk politically correct to each other. It's just that no matter how nice he is, he's an immigrant. He'll bring Maggie down. Whatever hope she had before, she'll have none now. And suppose she has children? Well, I mean...

But she's not seriously going to marry

him, is she?

She is.

And did she think I would never find out? I mean, was she ever going to tell me or anything? Was she going to wait until I walked into her one day when she had a brood of children by the hand?

What do you mean, that's what she said?

She said she wouldn't be likely to run into me because I never suggested any meetings! That is **so** unfair! That's **so** Maggie for you.

No, Angela, don't take her side.

Didn't I go along to that excruciating thing at the hotel and the movie and pizza in that place with plastic tables? You say nothing because there's nothing you **can** say.

I wouldn't want to go to her wedding anyway, even if she did ask me. It's all so petty, isn't it?

When you think what friends we all used to be. If I were getting married I would have asked Maggie. Probably...

And where are they having it anyway?

In a registry office. I see.

And you're going to be a witness. Oh, I

see.

And are they having a reception?

Oh really? **Really?** That's rather a nice restaurant. What made them choose that one? Won't they feel a bit out of place?

Oh, they both work there. I see.

And will he have anyone there, coming over from Algeria?

Oh, France. I see. Thirty of them. Good heavens! Well, well, well.

And does she know you're telling me about this or is it to be forever a secret?

She **asked** you to! Maggie asked you to tell me?

She said what?

She said: "Someone's got to tell her!"

Those were her actual words?

The Foul-Weather Friend

Whenever I look at my telephone answering machine winking at me as I come in, I think of my friend. I bought the answering machine once because of a friend. A good friend indeed, but a foul-weather friend.

She stood by the bus stop the day that I met her first, so thin, so frail, that I thought a strong gust of wind coming around that corner might brush her and make her hit her head against the shelter. Her head seemed very large—a lot of very frizzy brown hair, not an Afro cut, but as if someone had gone around it shaving little bits off like those pom-pom tassels we used to make at school. I looked at her hair for a long time, not realizing I was staring.

Probably a lot of people stand at that

bus stop not realizing they are staring. It's just outside the hospital. I wanted to think of anything except the face of my friend Maria, who wouldn't see me, who sat in her room—they won't call it a cell—dealing and redealing those cards. Not ordinary playing cards, but Tarot cards with swords and cups and pentacles. Hour after hour she sits there, laying them out in the shape of a cross and mumbling to them.

John didn't know I had been. He had begged me not to go. "We made her this way," he had said so often. "This is our punishment." I had tried to laugh him out of it. I am the Irish Catholic, I told him; if there is a sense of Sin, I should have it.

He was brought up in a house where nobody talked conversationally about Hell like we all did. Yet he was the one with the huge guilt that ended our love. We had betrayed Maria, he her husband, I her best friend. I stood staring at the big fuzzy head of the pale woman who hugged her arms around her thin waist as if she were trying to hold the top half of her trunk in some unsatisfactory way to the rest of her body.

She spoke to me without smiling.

"My name is Fenella," she said.

"I only read that kind of name in school stories." It was true; Fenella was always the plucky one, or the tomboy even. Nobody back home was called Fenella.

"You're very upset, aren't you?" she asked.

She had so much compassion in her voice I could have reached out and touched her, helped her to hold that thin body together for fear of its breaking and one half being swept away. She hadn't made a bus stop remark about there never being any kind of transport when you needed it. She hadn't made a hospital remark about having to be grateful for having your own health. She looked at me and saw my hurt and unhappiness; they were so clear for her to see that she had spoken of them.

I thought it was only the sharp, cold wind that stung my eyes as it whistled around the high walls of the hospital, but it was her sympathy that made my eyes sting. No stranger had ever reached out and spoken to me like that before. Not even back home, where they often spoke almost too directly and came too far into your life. But in England of all places. In the manicured leafy lanes of the Home Counties outside the well-pointed walls of a private mental hospital, a complete stranger had said that she could see my upset. I felt like a fool as the tears rolled down. She put out her arm and I thought she was going to embrace me so I flinched a little. But no, it was just that the bus was coming.

"It's a request stop," she said gently. "You have to ask it nicely otherwise it will just pass by."

She was trying to make me smile, I think, to look less like someone who had escaped from behind those high walls.

She paid my fare on the bus and came into my life.

In the town she knew a place where they served homemade soup and lovely whole-wheat rolls. It was comfort food and the tables were far apart. Nobody, except Fenella, had heard my tale of John and Maria, and how it had all been her fault, how she had a perfectly happy life until she took off in hot pursuit of Carlos, how it had unhinged her. I told her of the lonely days and nights and how John and I had consoled each other in the only way great and good friends could do, by loving and giving. And how I had hoped she would find happiness with her Carlos and her mad quests. But John wanted things tidied up, so he broke it off with her—he hated loose ends. And now they were tidy all right. John a workaholic, Maria mad as birds in a place she would never leave, and as for me...It's odd, but I never remember telling anyone as much as I told Fenella, not only that afternoon in the warm restaurant with its crackling fire and its crusty rolls and its deep, warming, reviving, steaming bowls of good things.

Later that evening, on the train back to London, and that night, when she said it didn't seem wise to leave me alone, she came back to my flat. She sat in a chair and her hair was like a halo. I thought she was indeed some kind of saint, ready to listen, and listen. Always wanting to hear more. Never a word of blame.

And what was so wonderful was that she

never once tried to cheer me up. There was no point where she said I would get over him and find someone else. She never warned me that all men were some variety of louse and that time spent weeping over them was time wasted. She didn't offer me hope that Maria would die, that John would come to his senses and beg me to return to his side, she just accepted that things were utterly terrible and shared the burden with me.

Soon I felt a great, great tiredness, I welcomed it like you'd welcome rain when it has been a close day. It had been so long since my shoulders and eyes had been tired. Normally I sat, awake and tense, smoking for most of the night. In the staff room at school I knew they must have noticed how short-tempered and irritable I had become. A wave of resent-ment towards them all came over me. These were my colleagues and indeed friends for nearly a decade. How had none of **them** spotted my grief and been able to listen, to understand, to be such a great friend? I smiled sleepily at Fenella, who said she must leave. She refused the offer of the spare room. She said she would ring me tomorrow. It would be Saturday, known to be a very low time when people were unhappy.

As I drifted off into the first proper sleep I had known for months, I remembered that she didn't have my telephone number. Well, maybe I could find her again, I thought. Fenella can't be a very usual name. I couldn't think what her last name was, or what she did for a living, or where she lived. She must have told me. Surely? We couldn't have talked about **me** all that time. But sleep was stronger than puzzlement. I didn't even turn off the light.

I was on my second cup of coffee when she rang. She had taken down the number, she said. I was too distressed to be bothered with trivialities. Would we go to the park? It was such a lovely day, we could walk and talk without anyone disturbing us. I felt a little twinge that surely I had talked enough, but she seemed so caring it would almost have been throwing her friendship back in her face.

And indeed that sunny day while lovers entwined, and mothers talked between screaming for toddlers, when old men read newspapers and told each other about things that had happened years ago, Fenella and I walked the length and the breadth of one of London's big parks.

And sometimes we sat, and she had brought small sandwiches and a flask of coffee so that we didn't have to leave until my legs were tired and my eyes were aching for all the tears they had wept as I told her of the first night with John and of how he had always loved me even before Maria had gone to this clairvoyant, which had tilted her mind and sent her in search of unsuitable love and unreachable dreams.

Fenella remembered everything. Every single thing.

"It must have been hard for you both when Maria took up all this card business herself. You know, dealing and redealing," she said.

I had forgotten that I told her about Maria and the Tarot cards. By Sunday I felt strong enough to go to see John, this time without making a scene. I had known two good nights' sleep. I had talked out every heartbeat of the thing. There would be no emotion, no drama, no terrible recriminations.

On the way back from John's house, through the blurry tears I wondered what kind of self-absorption had allowed me to let Fenella go without asking her where she lived, or for her phone number. But when I got to my flat she was sitting in the courtyard. It was a warm evening and she sat, calmly unhurried, on one of the rather folksy carved benches under the old cherry tree.

"I thought you might need me," she said.

"You must think I'm very weak," I sobbed as I sat on my bed drinking the honey, lemon, and hot water that she said was soothing. Fenella sat in a chair.

She was so good to me, Fenella was; she had all the time in the world. Of course I did take her address and her phone number and found out that she worked in a book rights agency. It sounded fascinating, but Fenella didn't talk much about it—she said she didn't want to bore me with the technicalities of her job. They just acted as brokers between literary agents in Britain and on the Continent. They suggested books that might be translated into Greek or Italian or whatever, and they got a commission on them. Did she meet a lot of fascinating people? I wondered. Not many, they didn't deal with the authors directly, you see. I saw, and asked little more about Fenella's job. Because I talked so much about my own.

I told her what stick-in-the-muds they were at school and how they never tried to set up anything new for the children. How I longed to invite authors in to tell them what it was **really** like to write. To let them meet living writers instead of assuming that anyone who wrote was long-buried. I had been hoping for the woman who wrote **Open Windows.** Not really a children's book, of course, but surprising how many of the Sixth Form had read it and identified with the rage against mothers that went through it. But I had not been able to find out where the author lived and was sure that the publishers would never forward a letter, especially if it was a speaking request.

"I can give you her address," Fenella said

surprisingly. It turned out that they had handled deals for the translations and European sales.

"Is she nice?" I couldn't believe that anyone knew her.

"I used to know her quite well when her mother had a horrible hip injury; we talked a lot in those days. But she's too busy to chat now." Fenella's voice was cold.

She was not too busy however to come to the school. And they liked her enormously. She didn't talk down to them. She said, quite truthfully, that she did have a dreadful mother herself but then so did most people, including her own children. They liked that; it made them think. It made me think, too. I thought about my own mother, long dead now, in Ireland. I had never visited her grave. Did that make me a dreadful daughter? She had been a dreadful mother in many ways, wanting me to live at home in the country and marry a man who owned a pub. She said it was fast to travel as I did, that no man would want me. Perhaps she had been right, after all. I talked about it for hours with Fenella.

The children wanted Louise Mitchell too, the one who writes those so-called historical sagas. For once I saw eye to eye with the principal that they were, in fact, pornography. I wondered, was I becoming more conservative or was the principal becoming more aware of the world? We did have Maxwell Lawrie at the school, the creator of Vladimir Klein, Master Spy. He was marvelous with children, told them how to write spy books and thrillers by beginning on the last page and working it out from there. It was like a problem, he said, just see who couldn't have done it and eliminate them and then find an improbable motive for who could have done it and start at the beginning.

He stayed for coffee in the staff room and he seemed to be giving me the eye a bit. Said that he'd like ten children at least, wouldn't I? I say yes, I agreed totally, might as well have a brood: they'd be company for each other and more fun, but if we were going to do it we'd better set about it fairly soon. He suggested that night. I think he was ninety percent joking.

Fenella said he was sick, and it would have been madness to get involved before my wounds were healed. It was funny, that was when I realized that my wounds **had** healed. I rarely thought of John now, and that Maxwell Lawrie—which wasn't his real name at all, he was Cyril Biggs—he did seem interesting. I didn't think his approach was sick, I thought it was jokey. It was just a way of speaking. I mean, I'm twenty-eight and he is a great deal more; you don't say things like "would you come on a date with me?" when you get to our stage. Do you? You make jokes about having to start soon to create ten people or whatever. Fenella's lips were pursed. I let it go. I didn't want to upset her.

Cyril had told me that we should have Mavis Ormitage to talk at the school. A wonderful woman, he said, she is enormous, wears white just to make herself look a little larger still, people used to call her Moby Dick. She wrote true romances, hundreds of them, Cyril knew her because they met every summer at a writers' school. She had a real gift in talking about life, made it all seem quite simple and easy to handle, somehow, and a great laugh like a roll of drums to go with it. I had thought that the principal mightn't go for the Queen of the True as she was called. Cyril said he'd have a word; it was easy to make a superficial decision without meeting the person. Mavis would be good for those kids about to set out on Life—she knew it all, somehow, without being preachy. That's why she was such a success. She drove around everywhere in a Land Rover, wearing a white raincoat and a white lifeboat man's hat when it rained. She kept her books in plastic bags because she liked open cars and the feel of rain on her face. That sort of thing had to be helpful to children, Cyril said.

Fenella knew Mavis Ormitage. I couldn't believe it. In a city of twelve million people, she had known two people that I had come across too. And Mavis wasn't even a client. Fenella said that there was no way **her** sort of writing would translate—it was amazing enough that it sold here.

No, Fenella had met Mavis Ormitage in real life, oh, it must be about five years ago now. She had a daughter who was totally incapacitated and she had given her life to this girl. Well, she wasn't a girl; she was a woman. The daughter must have been in her forties when Mavis had been forced to put her into a hospital. Fenella had a friend, Ruth, who worked in the hospital.

I had never heard of Ruth.

"Where is she now? Ruth, I mean."

Fenella had no idea. Ruth had been very depressed in those days—she had this really diabolical mother, talk of the mother in **Open Windows**! This one dressed like a teenager and was totally pathetic, going around accosting men in the street. Poor Ruth had been very low indeed, but in order to drag herself out of it she had taken up voluntary work in the hospital. And by chance Ruth had been to a writers' course that Mavis Ormitage had been lecturing at, must have been the same one as that Cyril.

I felt Fenella disapproved of that Cyril. And Mavis. And in some way her friend Ruth.

Anyway, it was all very briefly told. Fenella didn't ever go into much detail about herself. But Mavis recognized Ruth, who was working taking round trolleys of books and magazines, and they all used to talk in the hospital corridors and in the canteen and in the nice big garden of the hospital. I could see it very well. Mavis talking about her dying daughter and Ruth telling of the mad, groping mother. Both of them leaning on Fenella's interest, her phenomenal memory for the minutiae of their stories.

"Those were good days," Fenella said. "We had good conversations under a tree in the hospital garden." Her face looked far away as she thought of the good days, when she heard about the grossness of a mad old woman and the slow lingering death of a disabled girl. I felt a shiver and wished that I had gone out with Cyril Biggs that night.

It wasn't a question of procreating ten or indeed any children. He was a funny, self-deprecating kind of man, who didn't take himself or anyone else seriously. Had I told him about John and Maria, which would have been highly unlikely, he would have dismissed it briefly. He would not have asked what Maria said when she first found out about John and how we had betrayed her.

Mavis Ormitage was undoubtedly the most talked-of visitor the school had ever known. From the moment she roared up the drive in her open Land Rover and stepped, in billowing silk, into the school hall they loved her. She demanded questions afterwards and only when the school security men said it was time to lock the gates could she be prized away.

Mavis Ormitage had a small brandy flask and she topped up everyone's coffee in the staff room. Even the principal seemed enthusiastic about the celebration, something that had never been known. I brought myself to mention Fenella, though it wasn't easy. For two reasons. It was hard to get Mavis alone for one thing and also, I was almost afraid that it was disloyal. It was like probing a sore tooth: ask about Fenella and I will hear something bad, I thought. Why do I want to hear something bad about a woman who has been so kind to me? Am I looking for an excuse to stop seeing her?

Mavis had small beady eyes in the middle

of all the creases of good-humored flesh.

"One of the kindest people I ever met," Mavis said. "At the time. There's a time for Fenella, like the old psalm says, there's a time for being born and dying and a time for Fenella."

"And when the time is over?" I asked.

"You'll know, but Fenella will never know. She is like a doomed ship, always encountering other stricken ships, helping them and then being abandoned by them."

It was a bit flowery and it also made me feel guilty.

I was feeling better now. I didn't **want** to talk about John and Maria or not having visited my mother's grave or sleepless nights or uncaring colleagues. Things were looking up. Only Fenella was looking down.

"What happened to Ruth?" I wanted to know.

"Marvelous things," said Mavis, wobbling with pleasure. "Her mother got heavily involved with three handsome young men from the market—nobody knows which, if any of them, is her lover. She has calmed down totally and is a businesswoman extraordinaire. Ruth met this wonderful man who works in the museum—they're doing that big dinosaur exhibit, you know, the one that's getting all the publicity?"

"And they're getting married! I saw it in the papers," I cried excitedly. "They're going to have the ceremony in the Prehistoric Hall."

"She invited Fenella but Ruth knows she won't get an answer."

There was a little silence. I had to speak quickly lest someone take Mavis Ormitage away from me.

"Was it when you got better, you know, stopped being a stricken ship, that you felt it a bit..."

"She was a wonderful person for her time," Mavis repeated.

"Will I give her your love, say you were asking for her?" I knew it was a hollow kind of thing.

"No, no. Wiser not. Anyway, the ocean is full of stricken ships, you'll discover that later...I mean, before me there was that marvelous woman who wrote **Open Windows,** who had that devil of a mother, and then there was Ruth and then there was me, and between me and you there were plenty."

A few weeks later, the phone rang and I hoped it was Cyril, but my heart sank when it was Fenella. I listened to the message.

"Oppressive day today, I suppose it's brought you down," she said.

Then I deleted the recording.

I remembered something Mavis Ormitage said to the principal about her answering machine. "You can't get brought down by a recorded voice on a machine, like you can by a live voice. A voice whose time is past."

The principal had nodded vaguely and confusedly, unaccustomed to the tot of brandy in the coffee. But I knew now what Mavis had meant. And anyway, Cyril said he loved leaving messages on machines. It made him feel inventive, creative, and even, when the mood called for it, it made him feel loving.

Giving Up Men

When Eileen decided to give up men she did it in style. She was also going to give up her home, her country, and her job, she said. Her friend Katy thought that this was very extreme.

"You could still give up men here and keep teaching," she said.

Eileen was adamant. No, the school was full of danger. This was the second father she had fallen in love with. The second rat that had promised the moon and delivered nothing at all. No, she must get well away from deceiving fathers who pretended to be serious about the parent-teacher association and then suggested wine bars.

"Couldn't you change your job and still

stay in Ireland?" Katy begged.

No, apparently the whole country was filled with villainous men who would be her undoing.

"Where are you going to go?" Katy would miss her friend dreadfully and she also had this dark foreboding that wherever Eileen went she would, like a heat-seeking missile, find the rat and the bounder waiting for her. It was more a question of changing attitudes than locale, but there was no persuading her.

"I'm going to Scotland," Eileen said triumphantly. "Tomorrow!"

"Scotland?" Katy was dumbfounded. "Who on earth do you know there?"

"Nobody. That's the point. I can start afresh."

Eileen's eyes were shining. She looked like a child instead of a teacher. No one would have thought she was twenty-six. She looked like a typical illustration for a brochure about Ireland with the freckles on her nose and the long, red curly hair.

"And what part of Scotland?" Katy was resigned now.

"Which is nearer, Glasgow or Edinburgh?

One of them is on this side."

"Glasgow's on this side." Katy felt the outing was doomed.

"That's where I'll go then. I'll get on the boat from Dun Laoghaire to Holyhead tomorrow."

"That's Wales, you fool!" Katy said.

"I'll take a train up the map."

"You could go up the map here to Northern Ireland and take a boat straight over to Stranraer—that is, if you're set on going."

"I **am** set on going, and I daren't risk any more journeys in Ireland. It would be safer to get off the island as quickly as possible."

"Why Scotland? Just tell me that so that I'll know in my old age when people ask me whatever happened to you."

"They always seem reliable, practical, down-to-earth when you see them being interviewed about anything on television."

"Don't be ridiculous! You can't understand a word they say any more than I can." Katy was outraged to lose her friend on such a frail premise.

"I can understand a lot of it—and anyway, it's probably better if I don't."

"Don't walk out on your job, Eileen, you'll never be employed again."

"I'm not walking out. I've found them a substitute. She's better than I am. What I'm doing is a favor for everyone, including myself. I've got to mix with sensible, taciturn people who say **aye** instead of coming out with a stream of romantic baloney that would break your heart. A year or two of nice morose **aye**s will see me right."

Katy looked at her friend sadly. She knew that somewhere in Glasgow at this moment there was a romantic, kilt-wearing knave waiting to promise Eileen the earth and the heavens. She assumed that Eileen would probably meet him as soon as she got off the train.

Eileen's letters were a surprise. There seemed to be no Jock or Andy or Alastair creeping out of the Scottish woodwork plotting her downfall. Not a Jimmy or a Sandy had sworn that he was going to leave his wife for her. Instead there were tales of job hunting and outings to Loch Lomond and excursions to castles where Mary, Queen of Scots, had lived. Scotland was full of scenery, apparently. Katy read this bitterly, thinking that Ireland had its fair share of mountains, rivers, and lakes, but she had never been able to drag her friend Eileen from the wine bars and the secret and doomed assignations to see any of it.

Eileen had worked in a supermarket, at a gas station, and was now in a bookshop. She had found a bedsitter in a house with quite a lot of people in it, but obviously because some of them were men she just kept her eyes down and shouted "Aye" at them if they began to speak.

It was mostly women in the bookshop, and she kept conversations with the customers strictly on the subject of books. Oddly, some of them found **her** accent a bit hard to understand, which was hilarious since Eileen didn't speak with any accent, she wrote cheerfully. **She** spoke perfectly normally.

Reluctantly, Katy began to believe that her friend Eileen had made the right move. Perhaps the sudden change of environment had been just what she needed to shake her out of the Romantic Distressed Heroine role she had managed to get fixed in while she was in Dublin. It needn't have been Scotland. It could have been Chicago or Birmingham. She just had to break the spiral.

Perhaps one day she might feel really cured and come home. Katy hoped so. She missed her redheaded friend and all her madcap adventures. Katy would love to have had her around to talk about the new man in her own life. Michael, he was called—very, very nice, honest, trustworthy, no hidden wife and kids. No false promises. But Katy didn't really feel it would be kind and tactful to talk of love. Not when Eileen was so busy curing herself of it. It would be like dangling a martini in front of an alcoholic, or blowing cigarette smoke up the nose of anyone trying to give up smoking. No, she would keep quiet for a while about Michael. And if there was anything dramatic to tell, which there well might be, then she would go over to Scotland and tell her friend all about it personally.

As it happened, it was Michael who went to Scotland first. Katy had debated going too, but then she wasn't a serious rugby follower, and in a way it looked a bit silly to go as a hanger-on. She thought it would be more mature to let him go on his own with the lads.

Murrayfield was a great outing, Michael said. They always loved the years when Ireland played in Cardiff Arms Park and in Murrayfield. Two great weekends— win, lose, or draw. So Katy thought she would not try to intrude into his culture, his traditions. But it seemed a long, lonely weekend while he was gone. Katy hadn't realized how fond she had grown of this man.

She found the time hanging heavily on her hands, and she wrote a long, long letter to her friend. She knew that Eileen would not be in Edinburgh. Apart from anything else the thought of so many Irish deceivers arriving on package deals would keep her firmly where she was. Katy wrote about how great it was to have discovered real love at last. She said that she hadn't intended to tell it all, but there was something about the fact that her true love and her dear best friend were in the same land that made her want to write.

Michael didn't ring on Monday when he got back, but Katy didn't mind because the plane was probably late and he had to rush to work. She was startled, however, when he didn't phone on Monday evening. By Tuesday she was really alarmed and rang him at work. He was with a client, Katy was told. She had never been told that before when she rang the solicitor's office. She had always been put through, even for a couple of seconds.

On Tuesday night she called to his flat, and his flatmate said that he had been called away but would definitely be getting in touch with her on Wednesday.

Hurt and frightened, Katy went home. She hardly slept that night and had a headache on the Wednesday morning when she went to pick up the letter on the mat from her friend Eileen.

Katy sat on the stairs and read how Eileen had gone suddenly to the great match. She had got a ticket at the last moment and it seemed a waste not to go. She had met this really nice guy.

Now Katy was not to think, Oh dear, here we go again. This man was truly different.

He had been very up-front. He did have a sort of relationship going on in Dublin and he was going to sort it out with the girl there. No lies, no double-dealing. He was a solicitor, after all. He was called Michael.

Oh, **please** believe that this is the real thing, Eileen begged her friend in closely written pages. This time at last it was going to work out.

And as Katy sat on the stairs and her own life seemed to end, she knew that for Eileen, who had never liked rugby, who had said that solicitors were dull, it very arguably was the Real Thing at last.

Living Well

When I heard that he had left my friend Orla, I began to panic. She loved him so much, trusted him, believed everything he said.

You couldn't tell Orla that Eddie was a man who moved on. She would say that, of course, that had been the way in the past, but not now. Now he had found what he had been looking for everywhere —and thank the Lord he had gone on looking until he eventually found her.

He had moved into her flat four years ago. With all his gear. They made the spare guest bedroom into a dressing room—nobody had as many clothes as Eddie. Orla got a carpenter to make a big closet, with a hanging rail the length of the room and a little angled shelf for his shoes. She had an ironing board in this room and a full-length mirror so that he could admire himself.

She put a new shelf in the bathroom for his various colognes and aftershave products. She changed the furniture around in the sitting room to accommodate his exercise bicycle—Eddie liked to cycle as he watched television. She removed some of her marvelous paintings from the walls to put up his posters, and her own CDs and tapes were stacked out of sight, while Eddie's were all displayed.

As Orla's friends, we rarely went to see her at the flat anymore. Even I, who have the reputation of knowing the right thing to do, or being overbossy, as my enemies might put it, didn't feel at ease going to see Orla. She was too anxious. She was always looking at the door in case he came back; when he did, she would start fussing over him. And then we had to be quiet in case Eddie wanted to work.

There was little sign of Eddie's work around the house.

He was always in the middle of a deal

with someone; a project was permanently getting off the ground, or an opportunity being explored. It was restless and uncertain, while Orla went out regularly each morning to work on a women's magazine.

So, if we wanted to meet Orla it was at our own places or in a restaurant. Out of loyalty we didn't talk about her too much, only an occasional sigh or a raising of the eyes up to heaven.

I was surprised that he stayed four years. I thought he would have gone long ago.

So on the morning when Julie texted me to say that the dreaded Eddie had gone, bags and baggage, I was genuinely upset about what Orla might do. And if anyone could help her to see things clearly, I could. I mean, so much so that I told them at work that I didn't feel well and went straight around to Orla's place.

She was sitting, white-faced, at the kitchen table and she showed me the note he had left.

It was brief. I'll give him that.

Dear Orla—and you will always be dear to me—it's time to end

it. It's run its course, what we had is over. Let's not fight and squabble about who was right and who was wrong. Let's just remember the good and forget the bad and the upsetting.
Good luck always.
Eddie

I made the coffee, wishing I was grinding his evil, horrible head with the coffee beans, and when I was pressing down the plunger on the coffee I wished it were a stake going through his faithless heart. Her face was empty, as if someone had reached in and turned off a light inside.

"I didn't know there **was** any bad or any upsetting bits, Gina," she said in a bleak voice. "I thought it was all good, all the time."

I made meaningless sounds. It wasn't like speaking, actually it was like gurgling or something, it was an effort to be soothing and sympathetic like the way you might talk to a baby. It didn't really matter. I could have been saying the alphabet, quoting a psalm, reading a shopping list. Orla wasn't listening. She was puzzling and regretting and wishing she had behaved differently.

I looked around, just in order to stop looking at her shell of a face.

He had taken all his framed posters from the kitchen walls and the wok that he liked was gone. Through the door in the sitting room I could see that his exercise bike had been removed. Presumably every stitch of clothes in what had been his dressing room had been lovingly packed and taken away. It had taken him a day and a half to unload all his gear into Orla's flat with all of us helping.

How had he got everything out himself?

Orla was weeping now. "It happened on Sunday. I was at one of those 'meet the readers' events all day. When I came back, this is what I found." Her sad eyes looked around the near-empty flat and the note on the table.

"Did he take any of your things as well?" I asked in a voice that was like a hiss.

"No, of course not." She was shocked in his defense.

"Where's the microwave then?" I snapped.

"That was **his,** Gina, I gave it to him for his birthday."

"What do you want, Orla? Do you want us to kill him?" I asked. I felt I would be able to do it easily. Not anything that involved blood, but something slow enough for him to realize just why he was meeting his end.

"I want to find him and beg him to come back," she said piteously. "If he'd only tell me what I was doing wrong I'd change it."

Years ago my mother told me that Living Well is the Best Revenge. She said that it was a wonderful philosophy. You didn't waste time sending poison-pen letters, dialing his phone in the middle of the night; you didn't need to humiliate yourself by making a scene in public, you were not an object of pity for your friends to worry about. You simply lived well.

That was the sweetest payback.

She was absolutely right, I had done it myself a few times, but what could we do with Orla? It wasn't a question of talking her out of some petty revenge. She didn't want **any** revenge: she simply wanted the louse back.

The one bit of good news was that she didn't seem to know where he had gone. She knew of no rival for her affections. But he could never have moved himself unaided from her apartment, I told her.

His friends, his male friends, must have helped him, Orla said.

"But had he any? They were never mentioned," I said sternly.

"His colleagues, then."

"But he **had** no colleagues," I pointed out, "he lived and worked off a mobile phone—talking of which...I am dialing the phone now." **Big surprise. It wasn't working anymore. Out of service.** "Had he family?"

"None he ever spoke of. Things had been difficult for him," Orla explained.

I had to be very clever. If I were to get my friend Orla to live well and to forget him eventually, it must all be disguised as an attempt to get him back.

"Right then," I said, amazed at my own dishonesty. "We'll get him back for you." I hated the deception, but it was the only way to go.

First, I suggested she have a makeover.

She could do it for the magazine and report on every step of the way. That way it wouldn't cost anything. Together we booked the various parts of it, the slimming session, the tanning bed, the hair restyle, the manicure, the pedicure.

"Not that you aren't lovely already," I said. "You just need to be even lovelier for Eddie when he comes back." She smiled at me trustingly and I knew she'd feared I would be brisk and urge her to forget him.

Then we approached the work side of things. She should go for promotion. Head of Special Features section.

Yes, **of course** she could do it.

I would help her by giving her a free holiday as a competition prize from my travel agency; Julie would give her a prize of a digital camera and photography lessons from her place; Laura, who was a history teacher, would organize a readers' outing to a place of historical interest.

We would all come round and paint the flat for her next weekend. Bright, classy colors.

"You won't move the wardrobe for Eddie's gear?" Orla pleaded.

"Of course not," I said with gritted teeth.

And then began the summer of Orla's flowering.

She got the job as Head of Special Features, and we all delivered on our promises about the prizes, **and** we painted the flat, which all looked terrific except that we painted the louse's dressing room in entirely unsuitable pastel shades of blue and pink.

Orla got slimmer and prettier and wore really smart clothes for the first time in ages as she didn't have to support Eddie's lifestyle and pay his phone bills anymore. And we went round often to the flat, which was happy again.

Of course we put up with a lot of nonsense about how wonderful it would be when Eddie came back, as he would, and what great friends we were to her. Whenever she puzzled a bit about where Eddie might be now and what he might be doing, we did everything to head her off at the pass.

One day she would realize he was never coming back and by then she would be so confident and busy and happy she might be able to face it. She was very different to that ashen-faced girl who sat at the table the day after he had disappeared without a trace.

We wondered who would hear something about him first. And, as a matter of fact, I was the one to walk slap into him.

It was six months after he had gone, and it was at a travel fair. Eddie was there, doing deals, following leads, and chasing up projects about snowboarding.

"Gina!" he cried, as if I had been the one person he was looking forward to seeing there. We talked, if you could call it a conversation. From my side it was a series of staccato barks, until he asked about Orla. He actually asked about her. How was she getting along these days?

That's where I burst into information. Orla was just **fine,** she looked wonderful, she had a promotion at work, she had been traveling a lot, she had painted her apartment, wonderful warm, glowing colors. He nodded, pleased.

"It was a little bit drab all right," he agreed.

And I told him how she had lost nine kilos, and had beautiful window boxes stuffed with flowers and held parties on Friday evenings, and had joined a gym, and was going to be on afternoon television the very next day, talking about women and self-esteem. And every word I said gave me such pleasure, I couldn't keep the smile off my face.

Eddie nodded and seemed pleased for Orla.

And eventually I wore myself out singing her praises and listing her successes and asked him how were the deals doing in snowboarding.

"You know me, Gina, play it close to the chest," he said.

I deliberated whether I would tell Orla or just conveniently forget that I had met him. But I didn't have to make the choice.

She called me excitedly. Eddie was back.

He had moved back in last night, had decided to the moment he saw her on television. Imagine, he had seen her and thought she looked so well that he had come straight back to say he had forgotten the bad times and the upsetting times and could only remember the good.

I was hardly able to get the words out

from sheer rage. **This** was not the revenge of living well. This was the most cruel punishment.

"And what does he think of his dressing room?" I almost whispered.

"He just loved it! He says that we should think of it as a nursery in waiting. Oh, and Gina, thank you **so much** for everything. I used to wonder whether you were too bossy to me at the start, you and Julie and Laura. But you were quite right. It worked like a dream and I'll never be able to repay you. Never in my whole life..."

Chalk and Cheese

She had just slightly sticky-out teeth, Linda thought. Which was quite unusual for an American.

"I thought you'd have had braces on them as soon as you could speak," she said to her. Nothing sounded rude when Linda said it. She had such a sunny and interested way of approaching things. There wasn't a hint of criticism. Alice Chalker took no offense.

"Anyone else's parents would have paid money for braces, that's true," she said ruefully. "Sadly, I got the kind of parents who paid money for another shot of rye— you win some, you lose some. At least they left me alone to live my life."

Linda's beautiful face looked sad for a

moment. Then it cleared. She could always see the silver lining. "And if they had been proper parents then they'd never have let you travel the world. We might not have met, and you could have missed out on England entirely."

"And that would have been bad news," Chalkie said.

She had always been Chalkie, ever since Linda had met her out on a Greek island and told her about a little restaurant in London, and suggested she come and work there for a while. That had been just over four years ago.

Chalkie worked in the background. She didn't come out front much. Linda was the one with the charms and the looks and the personality. Chalkie was the one who kept it all going, behind the scenes.

They were great friends. Chalk and Cheese people called them, so unalike were they. Linda, with her dimples and huge blue eyes, her long blond hair shining and tossing like an advertisement for shampoo. Chalkie, with her nervous smile, her long neck, and her long, shapeless cardigans.

They laughed so happily together and would sit for hours drinking coffee that some people assumed they were more than just friends, that maybe Chalkie and Linda were lovers. But that was before they got to know them. Of course, it couldn't possibly have been true—not with Linda's record, not with the long line of broken hearts and confused males that stretched from the restaurant door. Linda's loves were legendary.

"I'd really like to settle down, to be like you," Linda would say to her duller friends, birds of much less exotic plumage, who often felt drab beside the lovely, laughing Linda with her shiny hair, sparkling eyes, and bouncy ways. They felt good for a while when Linda said that. It made them seem like winners for a moment. Not that Linda would ever settle for their men and their lifestyles. Still, it was nice that she appeared to envy them.

It was very hard to keep track of Linda's loves because none of them ever went properly away.

Dan, the accountant who had rescued the books in the early days, still came back to keep a friendly eye on things, and if he looked at Linda longingly as he spoke of VAT and turnover, then Linda never seemed to notice.

There was Roddy, the artist, who had done the menus and some of the paintings on the walls. He looked in a lot, always on the excuse that he wondered if his pictures were selling—actually he never cared whether they sold or not. He just wanted to see Linda laugh and pour him a coffee, then look at him with her big blue eyes and hope he was happy.

Then there was Derek, the man from the health food shop, who surely didn't have to check on the menu twice a week, months after his fling with Linda was over. Yet he still felt the need to come in and talk lentils and cauliflower bake.

And then there was Brian from the tourist board, who could just have delivered his thirty-two tourists for their morning coffee and carrot cake without coming in beforehand to check if it would be all right. It was always all right, but he loved to hear it from Linda with her huge warm smile, no matter how many times she had already said so.

None of them seemed to resent having been replaced, Chalkie thought wonderingly, as she sat in Linda's kitchen and chopped and grated and shredded, moving from work space to sink, washing and scrubbing all the saucepans, clearing up behind Linda. For Linda was the chef as well as the front of house. Nobody knew how she did it. Not even the men who sat praising her to Chalkie really knew how she did it, not even as they watched Chalkie wash and polish and put away.

They all sat and sipped and spoke of Linda, a girl in a million. And Chalkie agreed. Dan and Roddy and Derek and Brian said she was a great friend, a tower of strength and easy to talk to. Chalkie was pleased. It was good that people liked her and accepted her.

She blessed the day she had met Linda in that taverna. She often said so, and Linda always smiled one of her great, warm smiles. But Linda never said that she, too, blessed the day that she had found someone to take the entire workload off her shoulders, to keep the place running smoothly and to support her throughout all the various crises. She didn't say it because there was no need to say things like that to Chalkie. She was above compliments and being humored.

Chalkie gave great advice to the four men who buzzed around her friend Linda, but only when they asked for it.

She told Dan, the accountant, that Linda loved the ballet, so he went out and bought two tickets for **Swan Lake,** and the evening was a great success.

She told Roddy, the artist, he should do a portrait of Linda as a birthday present, and she had been right. Roddy was back in favor again overnight.

Chalkie suggested to Derek that he should talk less about nut roast and more about how much he liked Linda's new hairstyle. And, to Brian, she said that Linda was probably not quite as interested in the incoming tourist statistics as he obviously was.

Linda told everyone that Chalkie was simply wonderful about giving advice. She listened and she listened and then she gave her carefully considered opinion.

Chalkie had been able to warn her when Dan was so infatuated or when Roddy was cooling off. Chalkie was the best friend imaginable. And no, she never had any romantic problems of her own. But then some people were just like that, weren't they?

Andy arrived at the restaurant one evening in October. He was a tall, easygoing schoolteacher. He took to dropping in on his way home from school. He would bring his exercise books with him and correct them at the table. Sometimes they would see him shaking his head sadly over the things that the children had written.

"Don't you think it's strange that he hasn't asked me out yet?" Linda said with a toss of her hair.

"Don't worry. He soon will," Chalkie reassured her.

"Do you think so? Really?" Linda's eyes raked Chalkie's face for confirmation. Andy had managed to interest her by his very lack of interest.

Two weeks went by. "Perhaps he's married," Chalkie offered as an explanation.

"That has never stood in anyone's way

before," said Linda. It was true. Roddy the artist certainly had a wife lurking in the background.

"Be patient," said Chalkie. Linda was patient. After all, Chalkie had never been wrong before, had she?

They discovered that Andy taught English. "Should I sort of catch up on my poetry—seasons of mist and all that stuff?" Linda wondered.

"A bit too obvious, don't you think? Anyway, he probably wants to get away from all that. He has it morning, noon, and night."

"You're right." Linda looked at Chalkie admiringly. The woman was a genius. For a fleeting moment she wondered why Chalkie had never applied all her wise strategies to herself. Why hadn't she got her teeth fixed and been clever with men? Instead she was sitting in the kitchen in a long cardigan peeling onions into men's faces.

But it was only for a very fleeting moment that Linda thought this. There were too many other things to think about, like the new menu. She must try to get Chalkie to dream up something different, something that would make Linda's even more the place that everyone wanted to go.

Andy sat in the kitchen talking to Chalkie as they all did, sooner or later. "How did they teach you poetry in the States?" he asked. "Did they make you learn it by rote? I wish I knew the answer. I want them to love it, but how can they love it if it's a torture for them to learn chunks every night..."

"How would they ever remember it to love it later, if they didn't know it by heart?" Chalkie asked.

He wasn't convinced. "That's for later. I'm thinking of now," he said.

"But surely that's the point. You should be thinking of later. That's what teaching is all about," she argued fiercely. She sat curiously still as her hands were busy, chopping tomatoes very finely. She had long, narrow, white hands, he noticed.

They talked on companionably. Her hands never stopped, but yet she seemed so calm. After the bedlam of school she was restful. After spending all day with people who threw themselves around the place with an excess of energy, she seemed mature and peaceful.

Linda came bouncing into the kitchen. It was all movement. It was dashing here and back, it was dipping her finger in this and that. It was rushing in to get a cup of coffee and rushing out again. When she left the kitchen, things returned to the way they were.

"Wonderful girl, Linda," Chalkie said automatically.

"Yes...I'm sure she is."

Chalkie looked up. She was about to list some of Linda's qualities to this warm, kind man who sat beside her, but the familiar words just wouldn't come to her. She didn't say anything at all.

Andy seemed apologetic at having slighted her friend. "I'm sure she is a great person when you get to know her," he said. "It's just that she's got that off-putting cheesy smile. You know, it flashes on and off. It's as if she were always saying cheese for a photographer who's about to take her picture."

"That's what they call us, Chalk and Cheese," Chalkie said sadly.

Andy reached across and touched her long, narrow, white hand. "In my business, chalk is much more valuable you know... No teacher would ever be without it."

Chalkie would have advised Linda to play hard to get, but she didn't give herself any such rules. She smiled a big, wide smile. When it was something this important, there were no games that had to be played.

A Few of the Girls

When they heard that Nicola was coming back to sell the family home they all said they simply **must** have a gathering for her. Nothing fancy, just a few of the girls. It would be marvelous to see Nicola again; she never changed. It was such a pity that she didn't live in Dublin. She'd liven things up, she always had, remember her at school, for heaven's sake? They all had a dozen tales of Nicola.

Mary thought of it first, so it was to be in her house. Just a simple supper, she said, no fuss. All they wanted was to sit and natter anyway.

They contacted Nicola through the auctioneers. She was never great at keeping in touch but she sounded delighted when she rang and said she had got the letter.

"Supper with the girls, how great," she had said in a voice of wonder, as if it was as unusual a thing to do as flying to the moon.

For some reason Mary felt unsettled after she had put the phone down. She decided to go on a diet. You could do a lot in ten days, firm up a little, that's all, nothing drastic, and heavens it wasn't a question of going on a diet to impress Nicola. How silly. She had been a school friend. One couldn't impress school friends.

"I don't think we'll have the husbands," Mary said to Nora. "I mean, it's a bit silly, isn't it, having to explain all the do-you-remember bits. Better just have the girls— what do you think?"

"I think just the girls, certainly," said Nora, whose husband would never have come home from the pub in time for any supper party.

Mary was relieved. It wasn't that she didn't trust Gerald, but he did have a flirtatious way of going on, and if he directed it all at Nicola, she might think it was very stupid and put him down—or then again, she might think it was quite attractive and encourage him like mad.

"Yes, just us is better," she said. "It makes it easier on Angie too, doesn't it?"

Angie had a husband, but he wasn't her own, he was somebody else's, and so he didn't come to many parties with her. It was only fair to think of Angie and be a bit sensitive.

They all wondered what it would be like to see Nicola again.

Angie noticed that there was a big paragraph about Nicola's home in the papers amongst the auctioneers' and estate agents' ads. It was described as a very unusual property full of character. How had she got that? Angie wondered. How on earth had Nicola, who lived in another country, been able to make a property correspondent describe a perfectly ordinary terraced house as unusual? Her father had died a long time ago and the house had been let to Italians. Only Nicola could have found elegant Italians. But now it appeared Nicola's brother was in some kind of trouble and she needed cash to bail him out. So the home had to go.

Nicola had always called it the Family Home as if it were Brideshead or Castletown. Other people would have called it the house or number eleven.

Angie hoped Nicola wouldn't ask too many questions about Brian and the setup. Nicola had a disconcerting habit of saying things straight out, things better unsaid, or half said. Angie bought a new handbag and had an aromatherapy facial. She didn't want to seem pathetic to Nicola. She didn't want to look like a loser.

Nora remembered the last time they had all gathered for Nicola's return: it had been in a restaurant nearly seven years ago. They were all still in their twenties — well, just. It had been a strange kind of evening. Nicola's father had been buried the day before and her brother hadn't turned up for the funeral. With anyone else there would have been talk, but not in Nicola's case. It was an arty, bohemian sort of affair, one of the many things that set her apart from other people.

They hadn't meant to talk so girlishly that

night, brimming with confidences. It was the wine, and the fact of a funeral that did it. Mary had wept into her veal Milanese and told them that Gerald was seeing another woman. Angie had not got involved with the dreadful Brian at that stage, but she had confessed rather too openly that she was thinking of the Lisdoonvarna Matchmaking Festival or an ad in the papers if Mr. Even-Sort-of-Right didn't turn up soon. Nora also remembered, with shame, telling Nicola about how much Barry drank.

She had wished the next day that she could have had the evening over again. She remembered Nicola: small, dark, alert and interested as always, but nowadays trying to hide her mystification. Why don't you leave him? That was the question. It was so obvious that Nicola wondered why it had to be asked. Of course Mary should leave a two-timer. Of course Nora shouldn't sit around watching a lush drink away everything they'd worked for. Angie must need her head examined to set on this husband-at-all-costs crusade. These were all smashing women, they didn't

need the aggravation of such men.

Nicola had always been right about everything at school; she had said they couldn't get expelled if the whole class just went to the disco. No convent was going to risk the publicity of expelling twenty-eight girls three weeks before their leaving certificate. And she had been right, of course. Like she had been right about everything else. They should all learn typing the summer they left school so that they couldn't be sent off for a dreary year to learn it in somewhere as bad as school. They shouldn't worry beforehand about what their mothers would say if they dyed their hair, got their ears pierced, disappeared to music festivals. Do it first, think about the explanations later. And amazingly, of course, the world did not come to an end, none of them were thrown out of their homes, and, oddly, nobody ever knew or would have believed that this small, dark girl, Nicola, was the spirit behind the rebellious, mutinous teenage years of their daughters.

Would things have been different if Nicola hadn't gone away?

Perhaps Mary might have had the courage not to marry Gerald when everyone around her said she must and held shotguns to them both all the way to the altar. Perhaps Nora would not have covered for Barry's drinking, lying to bosses and friends and family alike. Surely a shrugging Nicola would have given her the courage to see that it wasn't **Nora's** shame, it was his.

And maybe with Nicola as a playmate, Angie wouldn't have had to settle for the cliché life of being the girlfriend of a married man. Nicola would definitely have made her see that Brian could and should treat her far better, even given the situation.

Nora was pleased that the party wasn't in her house. The house didn't look great nowadays and Barry could always lurch home during the evening. Nora bought herself a pink tracksuit and white runners. She wanted Nicola to think she looked independent even though she wasn't.

The room was overheated; it felt stuffy for a spring evening. Mary decided to open the window and knocked over a vase of flowers on the piano. As she mopped up she hoped Nicola wouldn't ask who played the piano in the household and, on hearing that nobody did, would not further ask why on earth they had one.

Angie arrived. She felt awkward with this new handbag and carried it like a toddler carries a dolly bag. She was used to a briefcase. She felt overmade-up; the beautician had asked whether she wanted full evening or daytime makeup. Unwisely she had chosen the former and she thought she looked like an unsuccessful tart. But perhaps that's what she was... She prayed that Nicola wouldn't ask her why she just didn't charge for it if she needed sex, instead of creeping away like a terrorist on the run to meet Brian whenever he felt it was possible and/or desirable.

Nora had hoped that none of the family would see the tracksuit, but her ten-year-old son had dragged his father away from the television to laugh at the sight of Mother in her gear. It was one of the few nights of the 365 allotted to the year that Barry had come home early. He corpsed himself laughing so much that she felt he would shortly have to go out again to a pub in order to recover.

"No, honestly, love, you're sweet," he had said when he saw the hurt in her eyes. That was even worse than the laughter.

She had caught sight of herself in Mary's hall mirror; she looked like a young elephant with a face prematurely aged with worry.

They often met—Mary, Nora, and Angie—or two of them met; they thought of each other as friends. But there were things they didn't tell each other. Friends don't have to know everything.

They weren't schoolgirls anymore, they were grown-up women of thirty-six. Imagine, they shrilled, our ages add up to 144; they thought that was funny for a moment and then somehow didn't.

The simple supper had, of course, turned into a six-course dinner. Nicola ate hardly anything; she was so delighted to see them all, she asked about this and about that and she held it in her head so that when she asked the next question it was obvious she had remembered the answer to the one before.

Mary and Nora didn't know that the awful Brian's wife was called Shirley and that she was expecting another child; they had no idea that Brian liked Angie to stay in all evening so that **if** he had the chance to ring her then he would find her there. They hadn't known that Angie couldn't ring him at the office in case his secretary might become suspicious.

Angie and Nora hadn't known that Mary's Gerald had been named as the father of a university student's child, and that he was paying support for a baby girl. Since he and Mary had produced only boys he said he had a soft spot for this child, whom he referred to as "my daughter" in tones of great pride. Mary told this tale quite simply, in between carrying groaning platters to and from the table. She would never have told that story if Nicola hadn't asked the questions that produced the answers that made the tale.

Nora could hear her own voice telling

them how Barry had had his final warning from the office: get dried out or else. He wouldn't get dried out. Nora was sussing out jobs for herself, property jobs—she had been doing temp work for months now. Angie and Mary hadn't known that.

Nicola told them little of herself; her brother was caught up in drugs, very messy. None of them had the right sympathetic questions to find out what kinds of drugs and how caught up. Was he victim? Dealer? Pusher? They would never know because the moment passed.

They all wanted to know how much the house went for, and somehow that moment passed too. All they knew was that the sweet Italians had left it simply perfect, and the new people were Greeks and darlings and loved gardening.

And was it because they weren't interested enough, or didn't have the vocabulary, that they never discovered whether Nicola had found anyone else after the simply marvelous but utterly impossible American she had married and had left? And was it because they didn't know the vocabulary and the jargon that they never learned exactly what she did in design? Was she a couturier, a secretary? Did she have her own office? Did she work in someone else's? Did she think up bouquets of spring flowers for duvet covers or did she make ashtrays with steel and chrome?

And she said she had to go at ten-thirty because Tommy was picking her up. They remembered Tommy, didn't they? They did. The boy that everyone fancied the summer they left school and Nicola had said he wasn't worth running after because his head was swelling to the size of a balloon—they should wait until he became nice and normal, then he'd probably be easy to catch and very nice. And he turned out to be both. Nicola had been right again. He came in for a drink, remembered them all, spoke words of praise. Angie, Nora, Mary, all of them as lovely as ever, how great that they and Nicola all kept up together. Women were so much **nicer** than men, really.

And they were gone and the girls sat there and the light had gone. Mary apolo-gized for the meal, said it had been too heavy and said that, of course, her children were never to know about Gerald and all that business...And Angie said she quite understood, but of course she hoped they realized that Brian and Shirley had to live a normal life and she didn't mind one bit. That was the other side of Brian's life. Totally. And Nora said that in a way it might be a blessing having to go out and get a job, might be the makings of her.

And suppose Nicola didn't come back for another seven years. They'd all be forty-three. Imagine. Just think of it...what would they learn about each other then.

Love and Marriage

The Bargain

When Cara met Jim at a party the rest of the world seemed to disappear; they stood looking at each other with delight and listening to each other in fascination, as if they were old friends.

When the evening was over, they knew they would meet again and everyone else knew as well.

So they met the following day for lunch, and that turned into a walk beside the canal, and they spent so long over a cup of coffee that the waitress had to ask them to order another one or leave.

They were both aged twenty-eight, they loved travel and jazz and cooking and dogs.

His mother had died three years ago. Her

father had died at the same time.

Jim knew the fellow who was giving the party because he had been on the same hurling team as him, way back when they were kids.

Cara knew him because he was a driving instructor and he had helped her to get her test.

Cara was a short story writer. She had gone to the party to celebrate having finished her latest collection of stories.

Jim sold agricultural machinery. He had come to Dublin to celebrate a big sale and his father making him a partner in the business.

Finally, they hit one problem.

Cara lived in Dublin. Jim lived two hundred miles away in the country.

He was going back home the following morning. So they talked nearly all night about what they would do and finally, exhausted, they agreed that Cara would make the journey to Jim's part of the world the next weekend.

They made a bargain.

If Cara hated it she was to say so. If she thought that she could manage to write her stories there, and that she wouldn't miss her Dublin life too much, then she would say that and they would get married as soon as possible.

That's how sure they were in less than forty-eight hours.

So they both waited nervously for Cara's visit.

It involved a train journey, followed by a bus trip. Jim was standing there waiting at the bus stop. Cara's heart leaped when she saw him look anxiously at the bus in case she might not be on board. She saw the smile light up his face. He was so generous and warm.

Please may this not be a desperate place, she prayed silently.

Jim couldn't leave his father and the business they had both built up. She knew that. And she would be the one who should move. She lived at home with her mother and a big family of brothers and sisters. Her younger sister would get Cara's bedroom. Life would go on without her. But Jim could not possibly leave home. His father and his four sisters depended on him to keep the business going.

Surely it couldn't be too bad a place? It had produced Jim, after all. But the countryside looked very wild and woolly as the bus had hurtled along. Frightening-looking goats, or sheep maybe, but probably goats. They had terrifying curvy horns. Small, rough fields divided by stone walls...It was very far from anywhere, anywhere normal. But she nailed a smile on her face and he held her in his arms for a long time.

"I was afraid you might not come," he said.

They drove together down one of the four streets in the town and out into the countryside.

The house where Jim lived had old roses in the garden and sweet peas, and the grass had been freshly cut.

"I did that this morning," Jim said. "I was too excited to do anything else. They wouldn't let me near work in case I gave the machinery away."

His father was stooped over a stick, standing at the door to welcome them.

"He told me that you were a lovely girl,

Cara, and he didn't exaggerate," he said with a big, broad smile just like his son's.

Jim's sisters were in the kitchen, trying not to look too eager to examine her. The eldest one was Rose. The bossy one, Jim had said. She was married to a rich man about twenty miles away. A miserly man, Jim had said, who didn't like Rose wasting his earnings on things like hair-dos and clothes. She was very forthright, he said, sometimes too forthright. Rose looked Cara up and down.

"We don't often have visitors," she said, "but we've prepared a room for you. It will be separate rooms, I'm afraid. This is my father's house and we have standards."

"I'm glad to hear it," Cara replied with spirit. "It would have been extremely embarrassing if it had been otherwise. Jim and I don't know each other very well yet, and certainly not well enough to share a room."

The other girls giggled. And even Rose looked at her with some respect.

Cara had won that round.

Jim had said that he would build a house nearer to the town. He had the land already and she would help him choose what kind of house. They would have a big studio where Cara would write, a small office where Jim would do his accounts, and plenty of rooms for when the children came along.

Together they would plant herbs and vegetables and flowers.

She looked around the table as they sat down for a late lunch; a lunch in her honor, with a full turnout to inspect and welcome her. Would these be her closest friends and contacts from now on if she were to make this giant leap and live here?

Could she bear trying to keep Rose in her place and to encourage the awkward, shyer younger ones, who seemed hesitant of themselves and doubting that they had anything to say unless it was drawn out of them?

Would she become involved in the machinery that Jim and his father were buying and selling?

Would she find anything to write about in this empty landscape and the small town with the four streets, one church, seventeen shops, and five public houses?

It would be ridiculous to make a decision on the basis of one weekend.

And anyway, Jim would have to come and meet **her** family and get to know them too. They didn't need to rush things, did they?

Then she looked across the table at him, his face beaming with pride that she was there, and she knew that there was no point in hanging about. This really **was** the kind of man she had dreamed of and never met. What did it matter where they lived, really?

They would not let Cara help with the washing up. Cara noticed that Rose filled a container with leftover food. "Waste not, want not," she said when she saw she was being observed.

"Oh, you're so right. Very sensible," Cara said hastily.

The younger girls took her on a tour to show her everything: the hens and geese, the old donkey, the orchard and the cow in the far field.

They loved this place where they had grown up.

They also loved their big brother.

"He never brought anyone home before," said one.

"So we knew you were special," said another.

"He talked about you all week," said the third.

Then Jim came and drove her into town. They walked around and he saluted almost everyone he met.

"We'll have a drink," he said.

"Which is your local?" Cara asked.

"In a place like this, with a job like mine, they're **all** my local," Jim said and he brought her into Ryan's.

He had obviously told everyone in the place about her. Cara realized that they were all expecting to meet her. She shook hands with a dozen people who all said to Jim that he had done well for himself up in Dublin. Amazing in the fumes of traffic and all the noise that he had managed to find such a lovely girl.

Then they went to Walsh's pub and the other three.

In every place they had heard she was coming and Cara began to get edgy, as if she was some kind of traveling exhibition instead of a girl down from Dublin for the weekend.

Jim had a lemonade in each place and so did Cara. She felt full of fizz and bubbles. Only the café and the garage to call on and then they could go home.

"They all think you're wonderful," Jim said, "and so do I."

She felt trapped and imprisoned by this marvelous man. She felt that it was all happening too quickly.

In a moment he would introduce her to the priest and they would set a day and then she would spend the rest of her life in this small, faraway place.

"It's too soon, Jim," she said, almost in tears. "You're lovely. It's **all** lovely. But it's gathering too much speed, like something rolling downhill."

"We had a bargain," he said sadly. "If you didn't like it you were to say so."

"I can't say yes or no in twenty minutes," Cara begged.

"So it's no then..." His face was lined with disappointment.

They drove back to Jim's home in silence.

His father and the girls were waiting inside eagerly. Rose had gone home to her mean husband, taking a plastic box of supper. Cara realized she hadn't known any of these people a week ago and now she was expected to come and make her life with them.

It wasn't fair. She **had** to have time to get used to it.

The supper wasn't as jolly as the lunch had been. Jim said nothing at all and one by one the others let their chatter die down.

"I'm sure you must be tired, Cara," Jim's father said. "You'll be needing an early night."

She looked at him gratefully.

"It has been a long day. Wonderful. But it had a lot of people in it," she said, and there was a chorus of good nights.

Jim looked like a child who had lost his lollipop.

In her bedroom Cara sat wretched on the side of her bed. It had been such a mistake to have rushed across the country after so short a time, giving rise to expectations that couldn't be realized. Just as she was about to climb the stairs, Jim's father had given her a big folder.

"You might like to read this, my dear," he said. "It's my late wife's diary. She wrote it every day."

"But I can't. It's too private. Too personal," Cara began.

"No, she would have liked you to read it," he said.

So she began at the start, when Maria had first come to this place. She had marveled that anyone could live so far from the bustling city where she had been born and grew up. She could not believe that it was possible to be so far from the theater and art galleries. How could anyone look out at those stony fields and go along the narrow roads without losing part of their soul?

But as the pages went on, Maria began to love the place, to know the seasons, to go hunting for mushrooms, to finding sheep that had rolled over on their backs and couldn't get up again. Maria wrote on how she started a mobile library. She had learned to drive and took books and art books to faraway farms and villages. She got to know everyone who lived within miles around. She wondered what she had been doing in a city of strangers, walking past people whose faces and life histories she did not know. And all through the story was a thread: even up to the very last weeks was her love for Mikey, Jim's father.

How she had been nervous of his certainty in the very start, how he was so sure she was the one for him and she feared it was a decision too quickly made.

She wrote on and on about Jim's birth and how proud she was of him and her hope that he might be like his father before him and find the right one before she died.

Cara didn't know what time it was. She looked out the window. The moon seemed high in the dark sky.

The orchard looked beautiful with the old trees casting curled shadows.

The old donkey was asleep, standing up with his head on the gate. Cara had read how Maria had rescued him from people who had been ill-treating him when he was just a foal or whatever you call a young donkey. He had never done any work, just given the children rides on his back for years.

Down in the farmyard the hens and geese were clucking contentedly behind the mesh doors that kept the beautiful red fox away from them.

Cara could not understand now why she had feared this place. It was very like home already...

She blessed her future father-in-law for giving her the diary. She wished she had met Jim earlier and she would have known her soon-to-be mother-in-law.

Yes, of course she would marry Jim.

She remembered counting the hours after she had said good-bye to him in Dublin last week.

Now she was counting the hours until morning when she could tell him that they should see the priest while they were at it. She was going to live here—she might as well get married here.

After all, that's what Maria had done all those years ago, and she had never known a day's regret.

The Afternoon Phone-In

It was amazing how quickly "Fiona's Phone-In" took off. Fiona was very different from any of the others. She wasn't concerned with issues and welfare and lifestyles like Marian and Gay and Pat and Derek and Des. Fiona specialized in one thing: her forte was getting people out of whatever ludicrous trouble they had got themselves into.

If you had invited your future mother-in-law to afternoon tea and you had no idea what to serve, a listener would come to the rescue and advise.

To make her phone-in on her part of the **Afternoon Talk Show** exciting, there had to be an element of urgency about it. The mother-in-law had to be coming today, the boss and his wife tonight, or the drunk you had agreed to go greyhound racing with would have bought the tickets for Shelbourne Park.

Fiona was great at communicating the lurking danger. **Unless someone phones in now, this poor person is up the creek!** And, from all over Ireland, people began to phone their advice, showing the country to be utterly devious and cunning and able to get out of almost any situation, no matter how terrifying.

For a radio personality, Fiona kept a very low profile. You never saw pictures of her at art exhibitions or theater first nights. She never opened supermarkets or presented prizes at schools, and nobody ever remembered seeing her in a fashionable restaurant or a country hotel. A small picture appeared from time to time in the RTÉ Guide. She had a lot of curly—well, frizzy—hair and wore huge glasses. It was impossible to guess her age. No papers ever said whether she was married or single. Fiona was one thing and one thing only: the frenetic excitement and drama of her own program.

She sounded anguished about the problems that came her way twice a week. This boy who had intercepted his school report because he knew it would be bad. Now his parents were going to the school tonight to check. What should he do? There were only a couple of hours left before he had to act.

This girl who had told her friends she knew all about boats had been invited out on a yacht this weekend. There were only two days for her to become an expert.

And people rang in inviting the would-be yachtswoman out on their boats or getting the report stealer to repost the envelope and it would be delivered eventually.

Fiona's ratings were high. The station considered putting the program out more frequently but Fiona said there would be a danger it would falter and flag, better to leave them wanting more.

If you asked anyone in RTÉ about Fiona they were always a bit vague. She was a freelance they said, she was always rushing in and out. No, she didn't sit in the canteen much, or indeed ever. Did she drive a car? Well, it was hard to say; no one had seen her driving one or riding a bike. Most people found it hard to remember her second name. And still the program went from strength to strength.

A woman who was afraid to go into her house because she thought that there might be intruders inside rang Fiona. She said she didn't want to bother the Gardai in case it was a false alarm. In minutes she had a posse of people to escort her, and it turned out that there **were** burglars inside, who were caught red-handed.

There was a lot about Fiona and her program in the papers on that occasion, but her only quote was to say that it was further proof that it was the listeners who made it all such a success.

Rory had always been very interested in Fiona and her program, as he had been one of her very first callers. His ex-wife had suddenly decided to let him have their nine-year-old daughter for the whole weekend. She would be arriving in two hours. Having only been able to see the little girl for three hours on a Saturday up to now he had no idea what a nine-year-old girl would want for a whole weekend. The airwaves were swamped with advice, all of it marvelous.

His daughter, Katie, had an unforgettable weekend, and even been invited to two children's parties. It had formed the basis of all her future visits to him. He had written to thank Fiona and got a business-like little postcard in return.

He listened to her phone-in regularly and twice he was able to help people who called in. He minded a cat for a weekend for an old woman who wouldn't have gone away to a wedding otherwise, and he had faxed clear instructions on how to program a video for someone who needed desperately to set the timer and couldn't manage it.

Rory had always hoped that Fiona would remember him when he called in, that she would say, "You're the man with the nine-year-old girl! How good of you to come back to us." He even fantasized that she might ring him and suggest they meet for a meal so that she could say a proper thank-you. He would be wonderful and lively and restless, and the meal would be interrupted from time to time with calls on her mobile phone and requests from other tables and waiters asking for her autograph.

In his dreams she would wear a black dress and a simple gold chain. Her frizzy hair would stand like a halo around her head and she would take off her glasses, showing big dark pools of eyes.

But Fiona never thanked him personally. At the end of her program she thanked all the good, kind people out there who proved that we were really all one big community ready to help each other if given the opportunity. And then, breathlessly, she would say good-bye, rushing her words at the end to be finished before the time signal and the next program started.

Rory envied her so much—busy, active, caring, rushed off her feet.

Wasn't it amazing that some people had those kinds of lives while people like him had hardly any life at all?

Perhaps it was just as well that he would never meet Fiona. She would scorn him as his wife, Helen, had eventually scorned him. A man without passions, without interest, without any sense of living, that's what she said he was when she left with their daughter, Katie.

"Why did you marry me, if I am all those things?" Rory had asked.

"Because I didn't know you were like that, I thought you were just quiet."

Helen had thought there were depths there, depths that apparently didn't exist.

Rory was philosophical about this; it was probably true. He didn't support any causes, he was on no committees, he had never carried a placard, he didn't always vote at elections, he was not a member of a trade union. He read a little, watched some television; he cooked simple meals like lamb chops or else bought convenience foods. Rory thought of himself as Mr. Average.

Friends had introduced him to other women since Helen had left. But somehow he never followed anything up. He thought that people might describe him as perfectly pleasant. Which was fairly damning these days. It was funny that he could not get Fiona and her phone-in show out of his mind. He would love to do something to impress her, something where she would have to take notice of him. But he couldn't think of anything. Not anything that didn't need an accomplice.

Like suppose he had a friend…He could say to her that she should pretend to be burning to death in her house and that Rory would run in and save her. There wouldn't need to be a fire at all. And he would be a hero.

But that wouldn't work, even if he could find an accomplice.

Fiona had fleets of people checking that calls were genuine. He would be unmasked at once. Maybe if he could meet her socially and tell her that he had minded the cats and set the video…but they didn't seem very brave things to have done. In fact, they seemed a bit wimpish. Yet he would dearly love to meet her. He might get some more life in him just by talking to her, some sense of purpose, a share in her electricity.

It was perfectly possible that he could meet her. This was Ireland, not New York; he could say hello to any celebrity in Grafton

Street, thinking he knew her and she had said hello back.

Why shouldn't he meet Fiona of the afternoon phone-in?

Rory worked from nine to five so he couldn't lurk outside RTÉ at four-thirty when Fiona's show ended. But his holidays were coming up and Rory had nothing better to do with his time. He had painted Katie's room for her since she now stayed over at least one night a week. He had toured bookshops and even gone to children's book events to know what normal nine-year-olds would like.

He didn't like going off to a hotel for a holiday by himself since he always looked odd, he thought, and if he did approach people he seemed to do it wrong and they thought he was making advances or trying to go home and live with them. He really was a sad sack, Rory admitted to himself. Helen had been right to make her own life without him.

Three days hanging outside the entrance to the radio and television station did him no good. There wasn't a sign of Fiona. He watched the cars, the bicycles and pedestrians come in; he saw a lot of famous faces but nowhere the frizzy hair and big glasses of Fiona, solver of the nation's dramas.

He didn't like to ask the security guards or people at the information desks. They might suspect he was some kind of pervert or nutter. And there was no point in writing to her saying he was a constant listener and would she like to join him for a supper one evening. No, it would have to be an accidental meeting or nothing. But what kinds of places did she go? She sounded as if she must know all sorts of people in every different class and age group. Nothing was alien or difficult to Fiona. She might be having a hamburger or she could be in a big posh restaurant. Was she at the theater or the cinema? At a party with her boyfriend? He didn't think of her as married—a husband had never been mentioned.

But then he began to wonder if he was becoming fixated on her. It was bad enough to be dull and sad and ordinary— he didn't want to end up like something from **Psycho.**

He had half his holiday left and he would go around Dublin as if he were from a different place altogether and he might well bump into her somewhere. He went to gyms and leisure centers in the early mornings to ask for brochures. Lots of these broadcasters did workouts, he heard. Maybe he might see her in the foyer or something. He saw a lot of glowing healthy people, but no Fiona.

She might have breakfast in health food places or lunch near Donnybrook. She would be invited to poetry readings or art exhibitions. It wasn't hard to get invited, if you went about it cleverly. Rory had a full week and indeed a happy week, even though he never laid eyes once on Fiona of the **Afternoon Talk Show.**

"Are we looking for anyone?" Katie asked him one Saturday afternoon in St. Stephen's Green when her father's eyes roamed all around the place.

"Often I look, Katie," he said. "I look for someone who will make me more lively and exciting, more interesting than I am."

"I think you're nice the way you are, Daddy," his daughter said. "I wouldn't want you different, I feel safe with you."

That's because she's nine, he thought, when she's fourteen even she'll realize what a shell I am. The visits will be shorter, the impatience very obvious.

Rory was invited to a colleague's wedding. Brian, the bridegroom, sat beside him at work, and he had been through all the highs and lows of the romance with Maureen, the dramas of the courtship, the on-off nature of the engagement. The throwing away and retrieval of the diamond ring. Now the day was almost here.

Normally he would have made an excuse and got out of it, but not on this occasion. He couldn't let Brian down.

"You know, I owe it all to that girl Fiona on the radio," Brian had said unexpectedly the day before the wedding. Rory blushed as if he had been found out. Fiona was **his** secret—he didn't want her shared with everybody. Not in a personal way.

"Did you phone her show?" He could hardly believe it. Rory thought he was the only one in the office who listened to Fiona on his earpiece.

"No, but my fiancée, Maureen, did. She

rang her last week and said she was so nervous of giving up everything, and changing her name and becoming a chattel, all the usual crap, and Fiona was great to her."

"What did she do?"

"Oh, she sent some mousy woman round to talk to her and the two of them got on like a house on fire. The mousy woman said that Maureen didn't have to change her name and she and I should be partners and friends, and suddenly since last week everything is just magical."

"Good for Fiona, then," croaked Rory.

"No, good for the Mouse, I say. She is coming to the wedding, by the way, but don't tell anyone."

At the wedding the groom, Brian, red-faced with happiness and drink, introduced his friend Rory to this quiet, slim woman, with short, straight, shiny hair and a slightly diffident smile.

"This issh the woman who saved my marriage," he said, and left them together.

"I'm Fiona," she said simply.

It was the same voice, the one off the radio, not so urgent and strident, but it was the same woman.

"But I thought you were the Mouse? The Mouse who came to sort out Maureen."

"I'm both," she said.

He had seen her before, several times, walking quietly into RTÉ or leaving. But where was the hair, the glasses?

"I wear them as a disguise," she said. "You see, I'm actually not that sort of person at all, but someone I loved—or used to love a long time ago—said I was so dull and ordinary that I should try to get a job as an actress or something to liven myself up. So I invented this personality..."

Rory looked at her in amazement.

"Was it a long time ago?" he asked.

"That I got the job?" she wanted to know.

"That you loved the other person, the one who said you were ordinary."

"Oh, ages ago. I don't love him anymore. I didn't have the show and the false personality and everything just to get him back; I just thought he might be right that maybe I **am** very dull and ordinary."

"No, you're not, you're terrific, you sorted Maureen out." He waved at the dazzling, happy bride.

"Oh, that was easy. I do a lot of other things—I often get involved in a sort of quieter way myself to sort out people's problems. I quite enjoy it."

He wondered for a moment had she known the women who had asked Katie to the birthday parties. Did he dare to ask her?

Yes, of course he could. He knew it was a long shot but he was right. One invitation had been from Fiona's sister Angela, who just loved little Katie, and in fact Fiona had met Katie at the house when she was doing her conjuring tricks.

"You were the conjurer?" Rory cried. Katie had talked of nothing else for weeks.

"I bought a book of conjuring; it was part of trying to be less dull." Her eyes were big and anxious. He reached across and took her hands authoritatively.

"You're not dull, you're marvelous," he said, pure admiration shining from his eyes.

"I never told all this to anyone before," she said in a low voice.

"I'll trade you," he said. "I took two weeks' holiday just trying to find you. I liked you so much I hung around outside RTÉ looking for someone with hair and glasses."

"And?" she asked hopefully.

"And it's even better than I dared hope," he said.

It was quite a drunken wedding and the bridesmaid did an entirely uncalled-for striptease, which she would probably regret for the rest of her life. Brian was rather too appreciative of the brides-maid's displayed charms, and there was an argument about trade unionism that did no favors to either side but alienated a lot of people permanently. Three of the pageboys were sick, and the bride's father got into a poker game where he lost five hundred pounds.

But in the middle of this and all the music, Rory and Fiona celebrated the fact that nobody is, or ever has been, ordinary. Not since time began.

Audrey

When old Miss Harris died, her black-and-white cat, Audrey, didn't know where to go.

Audrey knew that some kind people thought it would be best if Audrey were put down too, but Audrey wasn't nearly ready to go so she knew she must act swiftly. Choose somewhere to live and make herself indispensable and part of the household. The trouble was that she didn't know people all that well in the area. Living with Miss Harris had been easy and pleasant: Audrey had had no need to look at the alternatives. But now she must decide.

She didn't want to live with the Wilsons next door. The wife had a very sharp voice and the husband had been known to aim a kick at Audrey when nobody was looking. The Wilsons had not been good neighbors to poor Miss Harris when she got old and frail. It wouldn't have killed them to bring her in a mug of tea in the morning. Audrey had longed to be able to make the tea herself, but cats somehow couldn't do this so she watched glumly as Miss Harris dragged her aching limbs from the bed and slowly and painfully got the whole show on the road.

Audrey considered going to Eric. He was a pleasant man who had once given Audrey a whole fillet steak. But that turned out to be because he was drunk. It had been a mistake; he got the steak ready for himself and then left it on the floor, so naturally Audrey had eaten it—and been very grateful—and couldn't understand why he was going through the house searching for it high and low.

But even though Eric was good-hearted —and he had been kind to Miss Harris— he might be a poor choice because he was often drunk and was therefore unreliable. He could easily lock Audrey in the house and go away for six months and she would be a cat skeleton when he returned.

Audrey didn't really know many of the other households so she went on a tour of inspection.

No to the family who said "shoo **shoo**" before she came in the door. No to the retired couple who spelled out to each other that Audrey might have f-l-e-a-s. Imagine! Apart from the fact that Audrey **never** had fleas, why would they think that if she understood the word she might not also know how to spell it?

No to the three girls who said a cat would be too expensive and they must not encourage it. No to the drummer who made the most alarming sounds unexpectedly with the drums and would unsettle even a calm cat like Audrey. No to the family with toddlers who were inclined to pick Audrey up by the throat and squeeze the breath out of her.

Audrey wished that Miss Harris hadn't died and left her. She had been such a nice lady, always digging in her garden and talking to herself. She used to say to Audrey, "You're the only one who will really miss me when I'm gone. But I can't leave **you** my treasure, because Henry would have me pronounced insane."

Miss Harris hated her nephew Henry with a great passion. He visited her once a year and seemed displeased that she was still alive. He would jangle his change in his pockets and look around Miss Harris's house as if planning serious changes there after her time. After Henry's last visit, Miss Harris had been very upset. She went into her garden with a shovel and went digging at a great rate.

Audrey had joined her to be companionable. It was a great pity that Miss Harris didn't know Audrey could understand everything she said and was trying to answer her. All Miss Harris and anyone else heard was the one word **miaow.**

It was hugely irritating.

Miss Harris had dug and dug, muttering that even Henry and a fleet of detectives would never find this. Audrey watched with interest as the good silver candlesticks and great plastic envelopes of cash were buried near the delphiniums. Then Miss Harris went back to the house and rested.

She rested more and more after that, with Audrey lying in her lap, until the day she stopped breathing.

Audrey hung around for long enough to know that Henry was livid with rage.

"My aunt **must** have had more in her estate than what she left in her handbag," he spluttered. In the will, Miss Harris had asked that the house and contents be sold and the proceeds go to an animal charity, with the rest of her estate going to her nephew Henry in gratitude for his annual visit.

The rest of the estate turned out to be minimal. Very minimal. But everything was in order. Miss Harris had made the will in sound mind and she had regularly been taking money out of her savings in cash. That was her right. And no trace of this cash had been found.

Audrey hugged her secret to herself as she walked along the road in great doubt about her future, and when she reached her street she saw a furniture van unloading at number twenty-eight. Miss Harris's few belongings had already been sold in aid of the animal charity.

Audrey watched carefully from under the hedge as the goods were unloaded. No kennel—that was good, they didn't have a big barking dog. No birdcage, good also; people with caged canaries or budgies were afraid of cats. No toddlers to take Audrey by the throat.

The people moving in seemed to be a young couple, and this was going to be their first home. They were exhausted from the move, excited about the future, and worried about whether they would be able to meet the payments every month. Suppose one of them got sick? Suppose there was a recession and there was no extra work?

Then they would reassure each other with big mugs of tea and walk around Miss Harris's house patting the walls and trying to summon up the energy to unpack the boxes. They were called Ken and Lilly, and the more Audrey watched them through the window the more she liked them.

But she must not move in too quickly. They were tired and anxious. They wouldn't want another four legs around the place, another mouth to feed. She would do it gradually. Until then she could sleep in Miss Harris's shed.

Audrey found a sparrow for lunch one day and a field mouse the next, but she was anxious to resume the nice meals that Miss Harris used to give her: a bowl of cat food that would build up her bones and make her glossy.

On day three she thought it was time to join them. She groomed herself carefully in preparation for the visit. She knew she must not frighten them, and she mustn't try to talk because they wouldn't understand; they would think she was a whining cat or a hungry cat or a lost cat when in fact she was actually interviewing them to know whether this was a good place to stay.

If **only** there was some way to communicate, to tell Lilly and Ken that she would be no trouble, that in fact she had lived in this house for three years, that she would show them round the neighborhood. But the language didn't exist. They would think she was a hopeless stray instead of a new and helpful member of the household. Then suddenly Audrey remembered the collar that Miss Harris had given her. It said

AUDREY and there was an address.

When Miss Harris had died Audrey had asked two passing cats to help her get rid of the collar. It would be pretty pointless if kindly passersby kept delivering her back to an empty house when she was in the middle of finding a new home. But now, of course, it looked as if her old home could become her new home if she played her cards right. Audrey found the collar in the back of the shed and brought it with her when she went calling at Lilly and Ken's house.

They were astounded to see a black-and-white cat waiting patiently at the door, holding a broken cat collar in its mouth. They were more astounded by the address.

"Audrey?" they said uncertainly, and so Audrey snaked around their legs and purred like an engine and offered her paw for a pawshake the way humans liked.

"We should find out where it lives," Ken said.

"Well, according to the collar she lives here," said Lilly. Lilly was the soft cop, Audrey decided, the easy touch, even.

Ken was more anxious. "We'll have to

buy it food and we've barely enough to buy ourselves food." Ken was the one Audrey would have to convince. She tried to make herself look small, a creature that would hardly need any maintenance. She purred louder and louder. He was stressed and anxious and it seemed to calm him.

"All right, we'll give the thing a week," he said. Audrey was home free. No one ever gets rid of a cat after a week.

They were very nice but, oh, Lordy, they were a very worried young couple. They were in a panic about repayments. Every night they went around patting the walls of Miss Harris's house, saying how nice it was and how it had seemed like home from the moment they saw it. Then Ken's firm stopped giving so much overtime, so Lilly said she would take in ironing. She had all the leaflets ready but didn't like to approach the neighbors. So one day Audrey, tired of the dithering, took the leaflets herself and pushed them through people's doors or left them under flower-pots and the ironing business began.

Lilly was astounded that so many people had heard of her—she said that word of mouth was incredible. Audrey knew it was mouth of cat, but it was pointless to try and tell anyone that. There had been no mention of Audrey being asked to leave after a week. They were very fond of her and she slept on their bed like she had with Miss Harris, a comforting presence in the night.

And then Lilly told Ken she was expecting a kitten. Well, a human kitten. And Ken got so upset and said they couldn't possibly afford it yet and went out of the house banging the door behind him. And Lilly cried and told Audrey all about it, said they would have no kitten ever. They would never have enough money. They had been foolish to take on this lovely house.

Audrey didn't understand; either you were having a kitten or you weren't. Somebody had done something to Audrey and she couldn't have kittens: she would have liked one or two litters but she thought that either you did or you didn't, she didn't know it could be changed midstream. But it was all making Ken and Lilly so tearful and Audrey knew she had to do something fairly speedily.

So she led them to the garden with a great deal of mewing and meowing and agitation and she scraped at the earth where she had seen Miss Harris burying the treasure. With her little paws she scrabbled at the ground.

"She's like a dog looking for a bone," Lilly said.

"God knows what we'll dig up," Ken said. "Maybe some awful carcass of a long-dead bird."

"No, I'm sure there has to be something important," Lilly said, so Ken dug on and found the box and the wallets of money. A fortune that would mean they could go on living at number twenty-eight.

They could afford a kitten of their own. They could afford even cat food for Audrey. She looked at them, beseeching them to do the right thing.

They went into the kitchen and looked at the money. They said it must have belonged to the old lady—poor old dear, she must have gone mad and buried it out there. Then they remembered Henry, the old lady's horrible nephew.

Yes, of course they would keep it. You couldn't possibly let him have it.

Audrey relaxed a little.

But then they felt guilty. It wasn't theirs to spend. They must give it to the authorities. Audrey tensed up again and asked them what the authorities had ever done for Ken and Lilly, but naturally they didn't hear her. And then she saw them kissing, which was a good sign, and she was sure they had come to the right decision.

And Ken went back to the garden and filled in the hole so she knew that they had.

And she didn't tell them about the silver candlesticks because then they **might** have started to feel guilty. She would wait until their kitten was old enough to be demanding and they needed extra cash.

Audrey settled down and enjoyed a bowl of expensive cat food. She wished she could tell Miss Harris that there had been a result.

A great result.

Kiss Me, Kate

At every family wedding they said to Kate, "You'll be next."

She never knew whether it was said as a consolation or a threat. She always gave the same rueful little smile, the sort of look that said that she'd never be so lucky as to marry anyone. But in her heart she didn't want any of the trimmings that she had been through so often with her sisters and her brothers. For Kate had never been in love. At twenty-five that was a shameful thing to admit, so she didn't admit it.

People had loved her, or had **said** they loved her. Kate had read all about it, wept over love at the movies, listened to tales of love from her friends. She knew she would recognize it when it happened.

But she nearly didn't.

Because it happened, of all places, in Birmingham. At a big trade fair in the exhibition center. And his name was Paul and he was an Englishman. This made it both inconvenient and unlikely.

Kate was a Dubliner and her job was there, and her life. All Kate's family had married great, rangy-looking, loud people like them-selves, many of them with red hair, all of them with opinions. Paul was small and dark and quiet, and had a habit of letting the other person have their say, which would be looked on with great suspicion by Kate's family.

They were both embarrassed by how quickly each of them seemed to recognize a kindred spirit in the other. They kept apologizing.

"I know it's none of my business but is there...I mean, do you...are you...have you anyone else?" he said after ten minutes.

"Nobody at all, no one in the world. And you, tell me, tell me. Sorry to be so impatient," she answered.

They went to lunch and to dinner. They

went to the pictures. They went on a bus tour. They went to bed. Then they went back to their offices in London and Dublin with little understanding of what they had been sent to inspect and learn. They spent days and nights writing to each other but, because letters took so long, they spent hours standing by faxes trying to send off their very private thoughts at exactly the time when the other would be there to intercept them at either end. They were practical.

"It may have been just a few days out of time," Kate wrote. "Perhaps we shouldn't build on it."

"I'm possibly a bit of a dull chap," Paul wrote.

Kate hugged the fax to her for days. Apart from school stories she had never heard anyone called a dull chap. After six weeks they couldn't bear it anymore. "Come to London," he wrote in a letter.

It crossed with hers saying, "Come to Dublin."

"I've never been to Ireland," he said on the phone. So that settled it. He would come for a long weekend. The letters and faxes changed. They were full of longing, and eagerness. As well as dying to see her, he was dying to see Ireland. Kate wasn't sure if Ireland would live up to the expectations. She knew that she would be fine, like they had been fine in Birmingham, talking, learning, understanding, sharing...

But would he be confused by Ireland?

He'd want to meet her family! Would they all shout at him and talk at the same time, drowning him totally? Would it look foreign and strange to him with its churches and accents and monuments? Would he understand the jokes? Would he think that people sang too much? Or that it was such a different culture he would just give up on it?

Or, on the other hand, might it be too ordinary, too tame, too like a British provincial city? Not exotic enough—not nearly as different as he had hoped? Kate looked at her own city with critical eyes. The parts she loved so much, like the outlines and shapes along the Liffey, he might think they were just higgledy-piggledy. Would he like to look at people crossing the Ha'penny Bridge like Kate did—watching their faces against a Dublin evening sky?

Would he enjoy going out to Killiney on the little train? Everyone in Dublin was so proud of the DART. Did it get diminished when you called it the Dublin Area Rapid Transit? Kate thought it sounded a bit pretentious, but you'd have to tell him that's what it meant. Paul wasn't a man who just assumed things were called the DART for no reason. Would her mother start showing him wedding pictures?

Kate wished that she had been the one to make the journey. But then that would have been stupid, she knew London. And he'd have to come to Ireland one day, wouldn't he? She did love him, which was so inconvenient. Kate knew that the only way the visit could be a success was to plan it down to the last detail. She knew that he must meet her parents only at a time when there was no family gathering where he would be suffocated. He must meet her brother-in-law Gerry not at all. Gerry had a line of bad jokes that would put off any potential suitor, even if he were not a quiet Englishman. She would take him to pubs where there was no danger of an impromptu sing-song. She would book the theater and a couple of nice restaurants.

They would go to Dalkey and on a drive to Kildare where she would make sure he saw wealthy properties and realized that the Irish were successful, smart people in their own right.

She met him at the airport and they kissed and she almost forgot the carefully structured plan. She drove him home, pointing out sights. He was admiring and eager, but mainly he admired the way her hair curled over her cheek or how her eyes sparkled.

"It's lovely to have a capital city on the sea," he said, and Kate was pleased. She hadn't thought of that. It was indeed.

"Everyone's very young," he said approvingly.

Again, she thought this might be a disadvantage. It was a young country, certainly, but she had been afraid he wouldn't like too many hordes of kids.

By the time they got to her flat, Kate

was so relaxed she had forgotten entirely about the roadworks that had been under way for some time. She fell straight into a trench and broke her leg. Paul found her house keys, phoned the ambulance, and got her to hospital.

"I'll look after you," he promised into her ear as they carried the stretcher along.

"But who'll look after **you**?" she wept, her careful plans wrecked around her.

He telephoned her mother.

"Are you the intended from England? You're very welcome to these shores," her mother said. Kate said she was never going to be better now; her leg would never heal. Why had her mother said that? But Paul just laughed.

Then she heard that her brother-in-law Gerry had a few days off work and was going to take Paul under his wing.

"I've lost him," Kate wept to the nurse. "I finally fell in love and I've lost him before it even got to start properly."

"He seems very attentive," the nurse said soothingly, touching the big bunch of flowers with the loving message.

"That's now. Wait until Gerry's had his hands on him." Kate was now without hope.

Through the blur of the days that followed she heard that Gerry had taken Paul on a pub crawl, ever looking for the perfectly poured pint and having to try four establishments before they found it. She heard that her father had taken him to Croke Park and explained the finer points of hurling to him; that her brother, who was a soccer fan, had taken him to Dalymount Park and shown him two hours of videos of the glorious summer of the World Cup. He had eaten most of his meals at her mother's kitchen table.

She remembered him sitting by the bed holding her hand saying that he only wished she was better so that she could come out and enjoy this fantastic city with him.

"Shouldn't you have gone home?" she asked groggily.

"I got compassionate leave," he said and kissed her hot, fevered forehead.

As she got better, the picture of Paul's

holiday seemed to become alarmingly clear. Kate's twelve-year-old niece had taken him on a tour of the places where **The Commitments** had been filmed, and out to South Dublin, not to see the fishing harbors and eat in the smart restaurants but to take his camera and photograph where Bono lived, and Chris de Burgh and Def Leppard. Paul said his sister would die when she knew he had seen the places, she would probably be over on the next plane.

He had been to markets, to church bazaars, he had been taken to the big cemetery to put flowers on the grave of Kate's grandmother, whose anniversary it was; he had been encouraged to go out on his own and explore and told always to ask people's advice, saying that he was a stranger. Soon he stopped doing this because people gave him so much advice it wore him out, and also because he didn't feel like a stranger anymore.

The day Kate came out of hospital they had a big family get-together, the kind she had dreaded Paul having to witness. But now he was part of it all.

"How did you get so much compassionate leave?" she asked, hoping to ease him
out of Dublin before he saw them at their
worst.

"My fiancée broke her leg before we
could even tell the family our plans," he
said simply. "What's more compassionate
than that?"

By the time she got to her mother's home,
they had planned the wedding. Without
her. They had talked of the numbers, the
food, the time of year, the priest who would
be nice and ordinary and not frighten the
wits out of what used to be called Our
Separated Brethren. They were on to the
honeymoon before Kate got a word in.

"Are you all going to come with us?" she
asked.

Gerry, her brother-in-law, wondered where
they were going. It would all depend.

"I want the honeymoon in Dublin," Paul
said.

Paul! In front of this mob he was giving a
dissenting opinion.

There was a chorus of other counties. It
was like a geography lesson. Every sister

and brother and spouse had a view.

The compassionate leave would soon be over. Kate's leg would be better. The roadworks would be completed. And it would be easier to have the wedding the way her mother wanted it. That's what her sisters had done. And they had been fine weddings. And the tourist-as-husband had chosen the honeymoon.

Kate sighed.

Her mother said that Kate was tired. Her father said that Kate needed another drink.

Only Paul knew she sighed because it had all turned out so well.

Forgiving

At the beginning of December, Mary decided to forgive them and go home for Christmas. She saw this documentary on television about people who held grudges and people who took stands and did things for a principle, but still the principle only made everyone else unhappy and meant nothing to anyone. It was as clear as daylight to her: she would forgive them and go home. She looked up the plane times, and decided to go on the Wednesday. That would give her a day in Dublin and she would travel home by train on Thursday night.

She felt years younger, once she had decided to forgive them. She wondered whether anyone else who saw the television program had got such a clear insight. She might write to them afterwards and tell them about it. People said that television folk loved to hear from people that programs were good. She walked around her little room hugging herself. She hadn't felt so lighthearted for years.

She must tell them in plenty of time too — no point in all this surprise business, arriving, long-lost prodigal on the doorstep, on Christmas Eve. It was fine in the parable, but she'd always felt sorry for the Prodigal's brother, the one that had been there all the time and nobody called him a scrawny chicken, let alone a fatted calf. No, they must have time to think about it. Because obviously they would need to adjust to the relief of it all, just as she would. She would write to her mother tonight.

Her mother would be so happy; Mary could almost see the way she would hold the letter to her chest as she did whenever she got good news. In the old days, she had suspected that a letter meant bad news and it was always opened in fear. It would be funny to see her mother as an old woman—she would be seventy-five on Stephen's Day. Imagine her mother being like one of the old women she saw in the supermarkets here. Imagine, her mother probably had a stick and glasses, her mother, who used to be so tall and strong. And so convinced that she knew everything. So sure of herself, and her notions.

There had been none of that sureness and accusation in the letters she had written begging Mary to come back. Oh, no. There had been different rules. "Life is very short," "families shouldn't fall out," "it's very hard to have you turn your heart against us."

Mary remembered the letters; she had filed them neatly in a box that had once contained a rotary whisk. She had written on each envelope the date it had arrived. She had read them once and placed them in neat rows. She had answered none of them—there was nothing to say. She didn't mind that they were saying an extra decade of the Rosary for her; she didn't get any satisfaction out of the grudging admission that her father might have let himself go a bit far. She knew that there was no way she would forgive them because they didn't want to have anything to do with Louis.

Louis had said that she should be patient, that she should be sensible; they would see things differently in time. But Mary didn't think there was enough time. Louis had said that her mother and father were kind to worry so much; he wished that he had someone to worry about him because he had no one, but if he ever had a daughter he'd be careful who she went off with. Mary told her mother this one night, with tears running down her face.

"He's all for us to wait, Ma, he says we'll wait two years if you like, just if we can get engaged. See how sensible he is. Ma, how can you call him a fly-by-night?"

To Mother and Father this was further evidence of Louis's cunning. It proved that he must be after her money. But what money? Mary used to throw her eyes wildly up to the heavens; Lord God, they were talking about a few hundred pounds. Twelve hundred pounds. How could they be so stupid and so cruel as to think that

Louis wanted to marry her so that he could get his hands on twelve hundred pounds?

Ah, but her father had said, does he want to marry our Mary? That's the point. Doesn't he just want to go off and live with her until the money is spent? What was all this nonsense about not wanting a big wedding, because he had nobody to ask? What kind of trickery was that? What kind of a man had nobody to ask for a wedding, had appeared from nowhere in the town with no background, no recommendation? Wasn't it funny that he had picked a girl that nobody else had seemed to make much of a run for? Answer him that. How was it that none of the other fellows in the town had seen fit to run and propose to Mary when it was time for them to pick a wife? No, only a fellow from God knows where, running from God knows what, picking the town's settled spinster because she had a few pounds in the post office.

Mary Brennan had been twenty-nine the year she met Louis; he had come to work in Lynch's grocery for the summer. He had cut ice creams and the children liked him because he made the fourpenny ones big and put a little extra in the threepenny cones. The Lynches liked him because he was always smiling and didn't mind staying open late after the cinema crowds, or even until they came out from the dance, when he'd sell crisps, and he always knew how to move on anyone who was a bit noisy. They made more money that summer than ever before. He used to tell them to go in and listen to the wireless; he didn't mind sitting in the shop.

Mary had been dreading the end of the summer, but no, the Lynches had kept him on. Then, when all the tourists had gone, Mary used to have him to herself. They walked the cliffs in autumn, and when the winds got cold in October he put his coat around her shoulders and told her that she was lovely. Nobody had ever kissed her, except two lunks at the dance, and she thought it was great to have waited so long for it because it was even better than she had ever hoped. Then people started to tell her that he was making a fool of her.

Her father had been the worst—even her mother and Nessa and Seamus had tried to stop her father when he got into one of his attacks. Nessa had turned away when her father had said to Mary that she should look in the mirror and have some sense. How would a young ne'er-do-well like Louis, six years younger than she—how could he want a woman like her?

The winter days had melted into each other and Mary could only remember a blur. She used to go to work in the post office every day, she supposed. She must have come home for her tea, but did she have it on her own or were there rows every single night with them all? She remembered that Louis was always shivering because they used to talk on the street. They couldn't come home: her father wouldn't let him into the house and he couldn't ask her into the Lynches' house—it would be setting them up as enemies of her parents. Sometimes they talked in whispers in the back of the church, where it was warm, until once Father O'Connor had said it wasn't very respectful to the Lord to come into his house and talk and skitter in it like a couple of bold children.

The night that Louis had said maybe he was only being a cross for her to bear, she made up her mind. Louis had said maybe he was bringing her more bad luck than happiness and that he should go off and she would forget him. Mary was very calm. It was three days before Christmas, and she filled in all the forms about transferring the money from her post office account. She tidied up her little section of the counter and told the postmistress that she should look for someone else in the new year, and then she walked home and told her mother and father and Nessa and Seamus that she was leaving on the bus, and they would catch the train and they would go to England.

She left the house in uproar and went to Lynch's and told Louis. He said they couldn't go now.

She said simply, "You have to come with me, for I'm cleaving to you like it says in the Old Testament—you know, about a man cleaving unto a wife and leaving father and mother and all. That's what I'm doing. Don't leave me to cleave all by myself."

Louis had laughed and said of course he couldn't do that; he packed his case, told the Lynches that they needn't pay him the Christmas bonus because it wouldn't be fair. He came and stood outside the Brennans' house with his suitcase in his hand, a bit like he had looked when he arrived at the beginning of the summer but colder, and waited until the door opened and all the crying and the noise came out into the street and Mary came down the steps slowly, but without any tears.

They had never cried on that journey; they laughed and thought what great times they would have and they found a room near Paddington Station, and though they pretended to be married, they slept in separate beds until they were married by an Italian priest three weeks later, with two Italians as witnesses.

She wrote one letter home. Early in that next year, in the spring of 1963. She said that they had been married in a Catholic church and that they had used her twelve hundred pounds to buy a share of a small corner shop. They thought the business should be very good.

They were both prepared to work long hours, and this was how you built up good trade in a neighborhood like this. She said she had nothing more to say, and she didn't really expect to hear from them—she thought they had said all they ever wanted to say that last day. But still, Louis had been very keen that she should let them know where she was. Louis sent them cordial wishes. She was merely pleasing him by writing this once.

They wrote, they tried to write letters explaining what had been done was done with the best motives. Nessa wrote and told her about the visit of President Kennedy and how they had all gone on the excursion to see him. Seamus wrote and said it was a bit dead at home now, and you'd sort of feel sorry for the old fella. But Mary never wrote back.

Once, when she was combing her hair, Louis said she should look in the mirror. "Look at yourself in the mirror, there's a bit sticking up there," he said good-naturedly. Mary had burst into tears. She never looked in the mirror. She was afraid she might see a mare like her father had seen.

When he knew the result of his exploratory operation, Louis wrote to Mary's parents.

"She is very proud and she feels always that to open up her heart to you is to let me down somehow. She thinks that it's further loyalty to me if she cuts you out. But when it's all over I'm sure she'll need you. Please let her know that this is what I wanted. I'll leave her a letter myself."

They had tried to contact him at the hospital, but it was too late. Mary had sent them a black-edged printed card, thanking them for their condolences.

As she had worked for ten years in the little shop as a wife, so she worked ten years as a widow. Other little shops were bought by new immigrants, Pakistanis who were prepared to work equally hard hours, and once or twice an elderly Pakistani had made her a good offer for her little corner business, saying he wanted to set his nephews up in a good trade. That day she remembered that she too had nephews. Nessa had three sons, and Seamus had two. She wondered what they heard of their aunt Mary in London.

The night she forgave her family Mary looked at herself in the mirror. Nearly fifty and she didn't feel it; perhaps she looked it. She didn't really know how she looked nowadays. No Louis for many years to admire her, or tell her she was frowning too much, or that she had beautiful big gray eyes. Her father was nearly blind now, and her mother's yearly letter seemed to imply that he was no longer able to leave the house. Her mother seemed to go to the church even more than she had done all those years ago.

There was a lot of mention of Nessa's family; she had married the son of the pub owner, which was a good thing to have done. They had three boys and three girls. Nessa had her own car. Not much mention of Seamus. His wife was hardly mentioned at all. Perhaps she had been another Louis in their eyes, a no-good, mad for the Brennan money. The poor Brennan money. It was laughable. Within two years, she and Louis had gathered more than her father had got in his lifetime. But she mustn't speak like that when she got home.

No, no triumphant tales of how well it had all gone, what a good man Louis had turned out to be, how wrong, how very wrong they had been to say that he was anything less. No, if you forgive, you must forget a lot too.

They had obviously been able to forget too, no words of apology these days. Not since Louis had died, and they had sent her his letter and asked her to come back. Begged her.

Excitedly, she wondered what it would be like. She would stay for a week; young Mr. Patel, who was her assistant in the shop, could easily run the place. His family didn't celebrate Christmas anyway. She could even stay for two weeks. She wondered where she would sleep. In her old room? She supposed that Nessa would want her to stay in her house too, and she'd make a great effort to go and stay with Seamus and the wife and make a fuss of them. She would be like Santa Claus for all the children—she must look through the letters again to see how old they were. It would be desperate to bring them all the wrong things. Lord, Nessa's eldest would be seventeen now. A grown man, nearly.

What would he have to say to his aunt, his new aunt—or rather, his old aunt? Her gaiety left her for a moment. What would any of them have to say?

There was a nagging voice that wondered would they like to be forgiven or might it all be a bit too much trouble now? Perhaps they all had their own Christmases planned. Perhaps the priest was coming to lunch on Christmas Day, and old Mrs. Lynch from the shop where Louis had worked. Perhaps Nessa and her fellow had to go to the publican's people for Christmas. Who knew what Seamus was like now?

She touched her gray hair as she looked in the mirror. She was a stranger to them all. It didn't really matter whose fault it had been, or who'd said what: the main thing was that they didn't know her. They didn't know what her life had been like with Louis; they'd never heard that she and Louis took a train to Rome one year and had picnics with Italians all the time. They didn't know what her little flat was like here, and how she had made a patchwork quilt and how she had gone on a holiday to an old hotel with a lot of other people who wanted to learn about antiques.

Her mother and father didn't know that she'd had her gallbladder out three years ago, and that she had given up smoking three times and the last time it seemed to be working. They didn't know she could make pickles and that she had a friend, Phyllis, whom she went to a show with every week. They would look up the papers and choose what seemed suitable.

They both had the same taste. Phyllis had been going to book them a Christmas lunch in a hotel—she had probably made the booking by now. She would understand, of course. But still...

No, perhaps it would be foolish to rush into it. She might do more harm than good. Perhaps this year she should just pave the way. Send them a card. Let them know that she was holding no more grudges. Yes, that would be the way, and when they wrote and thanked her...then, little by little. And next Christmas...**That** was it. Not immediately, people don't like to be forgiven too quickly.

She found a card and put a second-class mail stamp on it. There was still plenty of time—no point in wasting first-class postage. She thought for a while. People mustn't be rushed.

After a lot of thought she wrote: **Seasonal Wishes to one and all. Mary.**

She put it on the little table to post early next morning, on her way to the shop. She thought that it would give them all a nice warm glow to know that she had forgiven them, and she was glad that it had happened at Christmastime.

New Year's Eve and the Garden

They used to have a big New Year's Eve party every year—sometimes as many people as forty turned up. It was a tradition: "Are you going to the Whites' on New Year's Eve?" Well yes, people said, they'd try to drop in or they'd see if they could put in an appearance. There was always the suggestion that something better and more glittering might turn up, but it rarely did. So Mr. and Mrs. White would stand there in the hall, which was covered with holly and Christmas cards, welcoming people every year.

That's why it was going to be so terrible for her this New Year's Eve, people said. Imagine that he had gone so quickly, in the whole of his health and never a day sick.

The shock alone would be enough to upset her nerves, not to mention the loneliness and trying to get used to life without him.

She had been very calm, Mrs. White, very calm indeed. She said that she was glad he had no long illness, no pain; she said that it did seem sad he wouldn't live to see his retirement, but she reassured those who sympathized that he was not a man who could bear any kind of discomfort. Perhaps the Lord had been wise to take him before pains and aches set into his joints, before he noticed that his body wasn't firing on all cylinders.

What should they do about her on New Year's Eve? friends wondered. It was too soon to consider gaiety and a big noisy party. No, no, something much more restrained. Supper at home around the fire somewhere. But as the day came nearer, nobody had planned anything. After all, for years and years they had never had to think of what to do on New Year's Eve. There had always been the Whites. The Whites had the streamers, and the bottles of red wine on one table and white wine on another; the Whites had a big buffet and

"Auld Lang Syne" at midnight. Nothing had come up yet to replace it.

The Whites had no children, so there wasn't a nice convenient family where she might have been expected to go. She had cousins in the country where she went for Christmas, but she was due back a day or two afterwards. She would be all alone in that house, unless someone did something.

Freda wondered if they should all go to a hotel, about ten of them, but Freda's husband said that was madness; it would be artificial and phony, it would cost a fortune, and Mrs. White would still be left at the table without a partner. It would only highlight the fact that she was on her own.

Grace said that maybe they should try to have a New Year's party instead, but Grace's husband pointed out that they were no good at entertaining and they didn't do it often enough to feel relaxed and who would they ask, and should they have people from the office and neighbors, and Grace said she was sorry she had even mentioned it.

Michael, who had been a friend of

Mr. White at work, was a bachelor. He wondered if he should ask his friend's widow out on New Year's Eve—or would this be tasteless? Perhaps she might think he was trying to step into the shoes, or something. It was so difficult to know the right thing to do. Better say nothing.

But as the day got nearer, people began to feel that **something** must be done. Year after year, they had arrived at that house slightly merry already. Year after year, they had picked up a plate at one end of the table and oohed and aahed over slices of cold turkey and salads and four different desserts. It wasn't fair that she should sit alone there after all those years of opening up her home to them all. And following on the worry about what Mrs. White would do for New Year's Eve came their own worry. What would **they** do?

When the tentative inquiries began, when people asked in hushed tones what she planned to do, Mrs. White knew they wanted to hear that she was going somewhere, that she was going to spend the most emotionally charged night of the year with some friend. But no. She told them simply that she would have a quiet evening on her own. No, she brushed aside their protests, it wasn't morbid, it wouldn't be sad—it would be peaceful. Really, thank you. Thank you again, but it was what she wanted to do. They didn't like it, but she was unyielding, polite but firm.

Freda got highlights in her hair so that she would look well at the posh hotel they were going to, but something went wrong with the bleach, and she looked as if she had gone prematurely white after seeing some supernatural happening. She cried and cried and had almost recovered when her son said she looked fine, she looked a bit like Santa Claus, and then she started all over again. Only the thought of poor Mrs. White sitting alone in that house made her pull herself together and count her blessings. "At least it's not nearly as bad as that," she said, trying to cover her white, straw-like hair with a festive scarf.

Mrs. White was building up a nice fire; she prepared a supper on a tray and drew in a small table beside her.

Grace had been stung to the very core of her heart about the aspersions that had been cast on her as a hostess. She had invited three couples to dinner and had been cooking all week. Even on Christmas Day she had not been able to relax properly, thinking of it all. An hour before they were expected, she had spilled a bottle of claret over the beautifully set table. Oh, God, why couldn't it be like other New Year's Eves where they all went over to the Whites'? A pang of guilt nearly knocked her down. She threw salt on the red wine in a fury and hoped that it would not be too lonely for that poor woman all on her own.

Mrs. White took the books, fourteen of them with their faded blue covers, and rearranged them in the right order. She was going to read them very slowly.

Michael, Mr. White's friend, went to his sister. The house was very warm, the television was on, and his sister's husband had laid in enough drink for twenty people.

Michael looked into the fire while his sister ironed, the television roared, and his brother-in-law opened bottles with a new gadget he got for Christmas. It was very festive, he supposed; at least it was family. Think of the widow on her own...

She read only the bits about New Year. In his careful, neat, slanty writing, he had kept a diary every day of his life. "What on earth do you find to write?" she had asked him, mystified, early on. Nothing much happened to them; they were always living days that seemed like other days.

He said he wrote about his thoughts and what he felt. He said she was to have a great time reading them when he was gone—she'd discover then what a complicated old devil he had been.

She had discovered how happy he had been; he had been happy almost all the time. This had given her great strength. He had loved coming home from work. He had written about how it felt on a summer's evening, coming in and having tea in the kitchen before he went out to the garden.

He had written about the peace of home,

about how well she had looked in the green dress, how funny she had been when the Yorkshire pudding had burned and she had thrown it out the window and hit the postman, who was coming up the steps. Little things she had forgotten, little things she had never noticed, realized. It was like seeing a film of their life made by a loving director.

No mention of rows or fights...the worst that ever got written down was a "silly disagreement" and how strange it was that people who were so fond of each other should grope for and find the new words in the language that would hurt. He blamed himself for that silly disagreement, even though Mrs. White knew it had all been her fault.

But tonight she wanted to read the entries about the New Year's Eve parties. For fourteen years they had been having these gatherings. She thought it was nice for him to see all his friends together—it made up for the fact that they didn't go around visiting much during the year; it made things a bit lively for him after their quiet Christmas, she had always thought.

She had been wrong; he hated them. She read a catalog of effort and duty and concern. He had gone along only because he thought that they cheered her up. She read one after another, gentle accounts of the getting ready in 1968, of the bad weather, of the year that the roads were icy, of the time when they had made a punch and it had been far too sweet. She read of the fight that Grace had had the year she went home in tears, the time when Michael had cut his hand on a broken glass.

Every New Year's Day began with the hope that she had enjoyed the party, the belief that she looked more cheerful, and the resolution to give her more fun and let her meet more people. There was relief that it was over for another year; there was delight to be back out in the garden.

Year after year, he spent New Year's Day in the garden, oiling the handles of the rakes and hoes with linseed oil, ferreting out the little bits of moss from the plant pots, trimming the edge of the grass. It was only a very small garden, but he said, "It's enough to handle...enough for any one person."

She hadn't ever been interested; oh yes, she liked the flowers and the tomatoes, and she admired his work, but she had never even learned the names. She read on about the New Year's Days when he had shown her the seed catalogs and wondered what they would choose. She had always looked at them briefly and said that he was better at knowing.

There was no blame in the diaries, no sadness. He had accepted that she would never share that. It hadn't made him love her less. Mrs. White looked around the sitting room, quiet on New Year's Eve for the first time in fourteen years. She had no regrets: his diaries told a story of a happy man. But she did have a resolution that she would build up his garden; she had a manual better than any gardening book...All she had to do was to read his own records, year after year, patient and uncomplaining. She would do what he had done and learn from his mistakes.

Oh yes, he had made mistakes. Way back in the early diaries he had done some forking and digging one day when there was snow on the ground…He learned later that this had been a mistake; he was only forcing the frost down to the roots still further.

She took this year's diary—which had ended so abruptly in mid-October. She turned to December 31 and began to fill it in. Her writing was bigger; perhaps she should get a larger kind of diary for herself when the shops opened?

The Sensible Celebration

As soon as she had planned the little gathering Lorna felt better. She had written to them all, four couples, their best friends. Nothing tacky like a printed invitation, but a warm handwritten note, saying that they would have a sensible celebration to mark the passing of the last ten years. With all the nonsense and the ballyhoo there was bound to be, Lorna thought that her little celebration would be the one they would all talk about, look back on—and remember.

How like Lorna and George they would say, to have a **sensible** celebration. Nothing over the top like poor Anne and Kevin did with their theme party, which nobody understood. Nothing vulgar like

Doris and Jim had done, with all that game which nobody could eat properly and the dessert with all the liqueur in it that had made everyone feel ever so slightly ill. And then Brian and Hilda had done that frightfully worthy party where they asked everyone to give money for starving children, which had been a teeny bit of a downer since it had made them a bit uneasy about approaching the buffet supper that Hilda had been slaving over all week. And then, of course, there had been that awful time—you couldn't call it a party, really—that evening when Teddy and Lola said let's play the Truth game and almost everyone had been lured into the most unwise revelations, and almost everyone had ended up very hurt. That had been **such** a foolish thing to do. Lorna remembered Anne's face when Kevin had said that she was no fun anymore. And she would never forget Lola's face when Teddy listed how many ladies he had... er...well, **known** in his life.

She remembered how Jim had gone a dull shade of red when Doris had said that, truthfully, she had always expected him to be a success in life and might not have married him had she known how often he was going to be passed over at work. And there had been that moment when Hilda had said in answer to one of those silly questions that kept going around, that Brian loved the poor and the needy in the world much more than he loved his own family, whose names and birthdays he often had difficulty in remembering.

Lorna and George had been very quiet after that party, a year ago. They had driven home in near silence. She had managed to turn all the questions into little jokes and answer them with a loving pat on the knee to her husband. George had done the same. But in the car there had been nothing to say. The emptiness seemed to hang between them like a curtain. All those questions that the other eight had battled with, trying to find honest answers and ending up red-eyed and angry, Lorna and George had managed to ignore. But the questions themselves could not be taken back. What sense of disappointment did they feel? Had there been any great letdowns? Did they still feel excited to see each other? Did they ever look lingeringly at any others?

Lorna had always told herself that she and George had escaped unscathed from that silly, **silly** party that Lola and Teddy had been mad enough to dream up. The others had all endured a public humiliation—George and Lorna may have been a little more silent and withdrawn at home than they were already, but at least in the view of their friends they were still what they had always been, a very well-suited couple. In fact, they had weathered the decade very well, Lorna thought, no terrible high-flying brought down by the whims of a stock exchange as had been the case with Kevin and Anne. Well might Kevin complain that Anne was no fun these days—it can't have been fun to have had so many lovely things repossessed, such a change in lifestyle. And then of course they had been luckier by far than Doris and Jim. Doris should never have said it of course, but Jim **was** a bit of a plodder, always satisfied with the very lowest position in the office, the cheapest

car, the really awful furniture and decor.
Jim never seemed to notice that all the
others had gone far ahead of him. It would
have been somehow more acceptable,
Lorna thought, if he had been just a little
bit apologetic about things, acknowledged somehow that he hadn't climbed
as far up the tree as the others.

And Lorna often told herself that even
though her George was very silent, no one
could deny that it was better by far than
all the prattle that Teddy and Lola went
on with, especially since it had led to all
that business at the party, counting the
number of ladies there had been, listing
their names. Oh, dear me, Lorna would
much, **much** prefer a little silence than that
sort of thing!

It wasn't even as if George's silences
were moody like Brian's and Hilda's were,
he wasn't always worrying about Society
like they were, or about the Third World,
things you could do nothing about. No,
indeed. If George and Lorna were silent,
perhaps it was because they had everything said by now and it was normal for
people who were in their early forties in the

late eighties to keep their views to themselves. It wasn't like the silly sixties when people had been talking about Love and Flowers and Hippies, nor the seventies when they had all been working so hard, long, **long** hours at the office in order to get noticed and get on, and then when they **did** relax they had all drunk far too much.

In those days too, of course, they had eaten the wrong things, all the time! No wonder there was so much cholesterol and stress and obesity even in their little group of friends. The eighties had meant that they had taken care of themselves at least. Now no long happy chats with George across a dinner table, of course, no snuggling up with a snack to watch television together.

To be strictly honest, and even to be a teeny bit selfish, Lorna did rather miss those times when they had so much to talk about. In those times, the days were just not long enough to say all that had to be said. They tumbled over the words, and they had never known a silence. Still, Lorna would always give herself a shake when her thoughts went down that kind of road.

It was deeply silly to get worried about little things like long silences. After all, look at what all the others had to put up with! And really and truly, one could only measure one's life by comparing it with everyone else's.

Lorna had been very good at the measurement game. Even from the start. They had always been richer than Doris and Jim, they had been more practical than Brian and Hilda, more cautious in business than Kevin and Anne, more circumspect in talking about their past than poor Teddy and Lola. How else did you know how you were doing unless you had some yardstick? There had been a time when she used to discuss this with George. Not very satisfactorily, though. George had always missed the point slightly, he kept bleating like a sheep, "But they're our **friends,** Lorna!" as if she didn't know that for heaven's sake. He always made it seem as if it was some kind of sacrilege to say anything that showed their friends to be less than perfect.

Lorna had asked George what he thought about a party. "Yes, fine, if you like" was what he had said.

"Just our friends?" she had said.

"Well, yes." George had seemed surprised that there might have been anyone else. It had irritated Lorna slightly. It seemed to imply that they only knew eight other people, which was ridiculous—they could have fielded a huge team if they had wanted to.

"And I think we'll call it a Sensible Celebration?" she had said, waiting for his nod of approval.

"Why?" he had asked.

"To let them know what it's going to be like," Lorna had said, surprised.

"Oh," George had said.

The evening seemed very long. She made list after list of what they would eat, crossing things out as reasons presented themselves why shellfish wouldn't be a good starter—too many nervous tums these days; no hot puff pastry—too fatty, too much waist-watching. Nothing eggy in case cholesterol watchers had had their quota of eggs for the week. Soup was rather ordinary and it did encourage the feeble of spirit to overdose on crunchy

French bread. Avocados were so predictable, and simply chockablock with calories for those who counted such things—which was anyone with a brain these days.

Lorna patted her neat little rump and wondered how so many of their friends had let themselves go. I mean, did one really wonder that Teddy had looked elsewhere so often—Lola wasn't exactly an oil painting. And after they lost all that money Anne had looked positively geriatric for a long time. It was so **easy** to keep oneself trim, Lorna thought, pausing in front of the mirror to admire herself. All one needed was a little discipline and some practical good sense.

Lorna had always prided herself on being sensible. Every single year she went down to the big store and had a makeup lesson from one of the girls demonstrating cosmetics. That way you kept up with the trends and didn't look silly drawing big heavy black lines around your eyes like they did in the fifties as poor silly Doris still did.

Lorna always said that one owed it to

oneself to keep oneself looking well. She glanced once more to reassure herself about the success of her efforts. In the mirror she saw the troubled face of her husband no longer buried in his newspaper, but looking at her. Not admiringly, as she looked at herself. The only word to describe the expression on George's face was **sad.** He looked as if something very, **very** sad had happened. The years of self-control had taught Lorna a lot, she believed. She certainly knew not to rush into questions she might regret later. She pretended she hadn't seen the look on George's face: the look of an unhappy man.

She must get him more involved, Lorna decided. **That** was what the look showed her, he wasn't **sad,** he was just a little left out. How could George be sad? He had everything he could possibly want. A happy marriage, a beautiful home, two successful children, a wife who looked after herself.

Perhaps poor George had just begun to feel a **little** bit redundant in this life that went on around him like clockwork. He must thank his lucky stars every day that he didn't have to help constantly with chores as did his friends. Kevin, Jim, Brian, and Teddy didn't return home in the evening to perfectly run homes. They spent time chopping logs and carrying in coal, even cleaning grates. George never had known the need to do that; Lorna had seen that all fireplaces were walled up immediately and tasteful arrangements of dried flowers placed in front of where they used to be. When Jim, Brian, Teddy, and Kevin finished a day's work there had been endless problems with children. As toddlers, as schoolchildren, and as rebellious teenagers. All this Lorna had been able to circumnavigate as well. From the start she had insisted on boarding school because it made the children independent, and there were always plenty of courses and camps and projects during the holidays. Now they were away again, one doing nursing in a far-off city, one learning word-processing skills even farther away.

Lorna had never listened to the concerned questions of her friends, Doris and Anne, Hilda and Lola, when they had wondered was it wise to let the children go so early and so far.

Lorna would smile to herself and reflect that in her home at least there was calm, there was tranquillity—and an absence of family dramas, something that could not be said for the homes of Lola and Hilda and Doris and Anne.

So Lorna didn't meet George's eye in the mirror; instead she walked purposefully back to the sofa where George sat. Lorna had read in a magazine once that loving couples didn't have chairs, they always had small sofas instead. More cuddly, the article had said.

For years now they had been sitting on separate sofas, George with his newspapers, Lorna with her books on entertaining, etiquette, and lifestyles of the rich and famous. This time she squeezed in beside him.

"We **have** been lucky, George, haven't we?" she said.

Slightly startled, George moved to make room for her and said, "Yes...oh yes."

"No, I mean it, we've had everything, and so many of our friends—well really, **most** of our friends—have had nothing. It's only right we should try to share what we have with them by having a party like this, but I want **you** to help me, help me to do it right, make it sensitive as well as sensible."

He had that look again, the one she had seen in the mirror.

"Lorna, dear," he said, as if speaking to a very slow learner, "dear, dear Lorna, you're talking about our **friends,** you're not talking about four couples in some kind of case study called Tragedy of the Eighties. They'll love to come and sit down and eat and drink anything with us and talk. Like friends do. You don't have to talk about being sensitive and sensible as if they were all some kind of victims."

His voice was affectionate, and Lorna noticed, with a rising sense of annoyance, also rather patronizing, as if he were patting her down.

"Well, it comes to the same thing, darling, doesn't it?" she said in a silky voice.

"**That's** how you see our friends? Over twenty years and longer, **that's** how you've always thought of them?"

"Not all the time, George. Oh, come on, you know as well as I do that life hasn't treated all of them very well. They didn't

exactly come through the last decade...
well, **unscathed,** did they?"

George had stood up and moved away
from the sofa that the magazine article had
said would show they were a family that
was into cuddles. He stood at the
mantelpiece that had never known a fire.
He looked across at his wife, who was
dressed immaculately even though they
were not going out.

Lorna looked up at him, that upwards
glance she had practiced so long and so
often. She saw something in his face that
she didn't want to read. Something that
said that **she,** Lorna, was the one who had
fallen victim to the eighties. For a long time
he said nothing. When she could stand it
no longer she asked, "What are you thinking
about?" It was a question she didn't
normally ask. Lorna knew from experience
that men were rarely thinking of anything.
But at least it put the ball in his court; he
would have to say something.

"I was thinking about the farmyard years
ago, when I was a boy, and how the cock
would come out and crow, and he always
managed to find something high to stand

on where people could see him crowing and know what he was doing. I was wondering what part of the house we could use for it."

He didn't look at her; he went and got his hat and coat. She knew he would come back again, later in the evening. He wasn't a man for grand gestures. And she knew he wouldn't mention it again, and that she would be big-hearted enough to forgive him, unlike the other wives, who would have made unmerciful scenes over it all. But she also knew, which was most important of all, that he wouldn't go and cry on the shoulders of Kevin or Teddy or Jim or Brian. So that when the day of the party came there would be no chink in the armor, and no one would ever know about this silly little nonsense that, in less wise hands, could have become an Incident.

The Mirror

It would have been all right if on the day of
the viewing she hadn't overheard the
couple talk about how valuable the mirror
was. Geri would never have even considered taking it otherwise. It was enormous
for a start, very old-fashioned, and rather
overfancy. They were each to choose one
piece of furniture from their aunt Nora's
possessions before the auction took place.

Geri's sister had taken the piano, her
brother had taken the rocking chair, and
she had been about to select a little
octagonal sewing table when she heard
that the mirror was worth a lot of money.
Geri loved a bargain; the others used to
tease her about it, but she said that she
got such genuine pleasure from knowing

she had bought something valuable, they surely couldn't begrudge it to her.

So she told nobody about the overheard remark and said that the mirror was what she would choose.

"We don't **want** a huge mirror," her husband, Seán, said.

"Why don't you take the bath with the funny legs?" asked her son, Shay, who was eighteen and into weird ideas.

"It would fall on someone and kill them," said her sixteen-year-old daughter, Marian, who would disagree with anything on earth that her mother suggested.

But it was Geri's aunt who had gone to the retirement home, and Geri's choice when it came down to it, so the huge mirror was taken down from the hall and delivered to their house.

Aunt Nora had been surprised. "You don't have a hall big enough for it, dear," she had said.

This was, of course, true, but Geri hadn't wanted it for a hall: she wanted it as a big showpiece in her dining room. She knew just the place, and there would be candlesticks beside it. It would knock everyone's eyes out, and gradually she would let slip how valuable the ormolu mirror was and how rare a piece, how lucky she was to get it.

She wouldn't need to say that to their neighbors Frances and James—they would know at a glance. And what a wonderful glance that would be. Even though Geri didn't like to admit it to herself, she was very anxious indeed to impress this couple. They seemed to have effortless style and confidence.

Geri would enjoy their reaction when they saw the mirror at the dinner party.

"Where **are** you going to put the mirror, dear?" Aunt Nora wanted to know.

Sometimes her aunt irritated Geri: she seemed to know everything and be right about all subjects.

"In the dining room," she said, and waited for the objection. She hadn't expected it to be so forthright.

"You can't be serious!" said the old woman, who had settled herself into the nursing home with a small selection of perfectly chosen pieces around her. Aunt Nora did have good taste, that couldn't be denied, but she was also very, very dogmatic.

"That's where I'd like it, Aunt," Geri said, with more confidence than she felt.

She wondered why she felt so defensive, so apologetic.

Geri often asked herself this. She was a perfectly acceptable-looking woman of thirty-eight, she worked in an office five mornings a week, she went to the gym two afternoons a week. She was married to Seán, a civil servant, a man who loved her inasmuch as we ever know if anyone loves us. She had a handsome son, Shay, who would eventually get his act together and realize he had to work for a living, she had a discontented daughter, Marian —but all girls of that age hated their mothers. She had a nice house, and she worked hard to keep it looking well.

Geri would go miles to get an inexpensive rug that people would think was much more classy than it actually was. But when you thought about it, was this a crime? Was this something that should make her feel guilty and humble? And in front of an elderly aunt?

"Why is that a bad idea, Aunt Nora?" she asked, keeping her temper.

"My dear girl, **nobody** has a mirror in a dining room, you must know that."

Geri hadn't known it and doubted if it was true. She listened patiently while her aunt, speaking from the point of view of another generation, told her it was unwise to let people see their own reflections. They spent ages titivating and making faces at themselves in a mirror and totally lost interest in the art of conversation, which was what a dinner party should be all about.

"Everyone knows that, Geri," Aunt Nora said disapprovingly.

Geri decided to be very understanding —this was an elderly woman who had just been forced to leave her own home. Allow her to have the last word. Pretend to agree.

"I'm sure you're right, Aunt Nora. I'll have to think of somewhere else to put it," she lied soothingly.

Aunt Nora snorted. She had been around a long time and she knew Geri hadn't a notion of changing her plans.

By chance, that evening on a television

program about interior decorating someone made the remark that you'd never put
a mirror in the dining room. It unsettled
Geri for a moment, but she rationalized it.
It was one of these old superstitions, like
not walking under ladders, some fuddy-
duddy thing about having to have anti-
macassars on your sofa.

The mirror arrived in Geri and Seán's
house and was hung over the dining room
mantelpiece.

"It sort of dwarfs the room a bit, doesn't
it?" Seán said tentatively.

"You have no idea how valuable this is,"
Geri implored.

"Oh well, all right then." Seán was all for
an easy life.

"I'd have loved the bath. It was like
something from a horror film," said Shay
wistfully.

"It'll fall down in the middle of their dinner
party, mark my words," said Marian
confidently.

But Geri took no notice. She planned the
party relentlessly. Seán had met some
fellow who was in the running to be an
ambassador, and Geri insisted that he and

his wife would be invited. She planned for happy hours how she would drop this piece of information in front of Frances and James.

She had also invited an old and rather tedious woman who was leasing her castle to Americans and a man who was involved with the development of film. It would be a guest list that would impress anybody; all that and the new mirror—Frances and James would be stunned.

The children were being well paid to serve the meal, money to be handed over discreetly when the coffee was on the table and Shay and Marian had said a courteous good night to the company.

To Geri's great disappointment, nobody mentioned the mirror when they filed into the dining room. She just couldn't believe it. Frances and James had been in this house before: they **must** have noticed it. Perhaps they didn't comment on it out of sheer jealousy. The young wannabe diplomats must surely have been in smart places with heirlooms and antiques before, maybe they just expected such elegance.

The elderly castle owner and the future

filmmaker said nothing.

And so the meal was served. Geri noticed that Frances was constantly moving her hair from behind her ears to in front; twice she took out her lipstick and once even a powder compact. Her eyes never left her own reflection. She heard nothing of what was being said.

The film man frowned at himself darkly, held up his chin with his hand, sucked in his cheeks, and kept bringing the conversation around to liposuction, laser therapy, and the unfairness that it should only be women who had a little nip and tuck under the eyes.

The old castle owner sank into an ever-deeper despair and asked for neat whiskey.

"I had absolutely no idea I looked like this," she told Geri four times. "I'm a perfect fright. I shouldn't be allowed out. What a depressing, depressing discovery."

The young diplomat couldn't see himself, but he was so alarmed by the way everyone opposite him was looking over his shoulder that he kept turning around to see what was behind him. His wife said to him that he'd better stop acting so nervy if they were ever to land that plum post.

Seán just talked on good-naturedly, smiling at her proudly from time to time, and noticing nothing of the disarray. Geri had never known such failure and letdown.

Perhaps it was just too dark, the whole thing; she must light more candles. As she stood to do so, she saw her son, Shay, reflected in the mirror. He had worn a collar and tie, part of the exorbitant price she was paying him for his good behavior. She noticed that for every glass of wine he poured he was drinking one himself.

Her eyes hardened as she sat down.

"Perhaps you could just leave the decanters on the table," she said in a voice of steel. One of the candles was dripping wax, so Geri went to sort it out. Again she looked in the mirror to see how what she had fondly believed to be the most elegant dinner party in Ireland was progressing.

This time she saw Marian, who had worn a rather shorter black skirt than Geri would have liked, being fondled by the lecherous filmmaker. And Marian was not running away from him. She was smiling in a very upsettingly knowing way. Geri sat down abruptly. Nothing was going right.

Her aunt had known. Nobody should have a mirror in their dining room, it was a disaster. Why had she not understood?

Frances had momentarily stopped pouting at herself in the mirror. She was smiling at Seán: a very fetching smile.

"Seán, will you please come and pour my wine for me, now that Shay has stopped being wine waiter?" she said. Seán stood up obligingly.

This was the moment that the silk flowers on the mantelpiece caught fire and Geri leaped to her feet. Everyone's eyes and attention were on the activity.

Tears of rage and humiliation were in her eyes. And as she doused the candles and rescued the charred silk stems, she saw Frances smiling at Seán and reaching out her hand for his. Geri had thought there was nothing else that could go wrong; she believed that she had seen as much upset as was possible for one human to see in this terrible mirror.

Geri looked down at her square, practical hands. She wished they were long and narrow and white, and had long pink nails.

She wished her watch looked too heavy for the fragile wrist, as Frances's did. But Seán had managed to move away from the perfectly groomed long white fingers and he was sitting back in his place.

"Well done, Geri, firefighter," he said. It wasn't exactly the role she had wanted to play, nor the words she had wanted to hear, even though he spoke them with praise and love.

"And the mirror didn't get burned at all?" He was cheering her up.

Please may he not mention the awful mirror and that it was valuable. Please let him understand that she had totally changed her view. There was so much she had to sort out, like Shay's drinking, Marian's sexual awareness, the fact that her admired neighbor Frances was coming on strong to Seán, that the two other guests were still staring at themselves gloomily in the damn mirror, and that the would-be diplomats were in the middle of a major row.

"Geri took this mirror from her aunt's estate," Seán said proudly.

Geri closed her eyes.

"How very kind of you," Frances said patronizingly.

"Geri is the kindest person in the world," Seán said.

Geri opened her eyes. She stood up slowly and walked to her aunt's mirror, which she was going to sell tomorrow. She looked deep into it and she saw the wreckage of what had seemed an important dinner party. She was a better-informed person, a better-armed person.

She knew much more than she had known four hours ago. She knew that whatever old fool had said you shouldn't have a mirror in a dining room was right. She knew that you could never impress James and Frances, no matter how you tried. She knew the old trout with the castle was self-obsessed and would be of interest to no one. She knew that the filmmaker was a pathetic old lech, driven to groping teenagers to prove he wasn't over the hill. She knew that the future diplomats wouldn't get to first base with the Foreign Service or with each other.

She knew that Frances, elegant Frances, fancied Seán, her Seán, and that she couldn't have him.

Because Seán loved Geri.

Geri hated to make a bad investment, and maybe the mirror had been a poor choice. If the sewing table hadn't made its reserve at Aunt Nora's auction, she would take that.

Seán was helping the guests into their coats and waving them good-bye. He came back in and stood behind her as she looked in the mirror. He put his arms around her shoulders.

"The mirror was a mistake, Seán," she admitted in a small voice.

He smiled into her hair.

"Maybe, but it wasn't a **total** mistake," he said to her, and held her tighter.

"I don't know." She wasn't convinced.

"Well, don't the pair of us look fine in it," he said. "Doesn't that make it the bargain of the century?"

Mr. Mangan

They had this teacher at their boys' boarding school, and he was called Mr. Mangan. Apparently he'd been there for years and years and all you ever had to do was to mention his name and they would all talk about him for hours.

He had very pale blue eyes and nobody knew anything about his background. It was thought that he had once been a priest but that was never confirmed. There was no Mrs. Mangan, and he had lived in a boardinghouse one mile from the school. He walked there and back every day, sunshine, rain, or snow.

As boys, they had been very incurious about what kind of life he led. Only later, when the women wanted to know about

him, did they ask each other and themselves what Mr. Mangan did to sustain his
life in that remote part of the country.

He could hardly have been propping up
the local bars, of which there were many in
the small town. Word would have reached
the religious community; it would not have
been viewed favorably.

He certainly had no romantic interest
that had ever reached their ears. That too
would surely have been frowned on.

There was no theater, no real library;
the cinema changed its film every Sunday
night in those days twenty years ago. It
was hard to imagine Mr. Mangan going
out to play bridge with the local ladies. He
didn't have a car or a bicycle to take him
further afield. He was known to be against
blood sports, so he would not have gone
hunting or shooting with the local farmers.
He would shake his head and say that
sadly he was not a gladiator when they
asked him about sport.

So what **did** he do?

He must have read a lot, thought his
pupils, who last saw him when they left
their school in 1975. Read a lot and thought

a lot—this was all they could produce when pressed hard to come up with some explanation of his lifestyle. He seemed to know everything and be interested in everything.

In theory, he taught them geography. In fact, he taught them everything: how to do crosswords, to interpret political dynasties, to translate road signs, to read palms, to make real mayonnaise, to explain proportional representation, to identify trees by their leaves, to avoid congeners in alcohol as the source of hangovers, to look at buildings, and to think about what words meant.

In two decades they must all have remembered and repeated the things he had said over and over. And whenever they got together it was intensified. It was as if they were back in his classroom again.

The wives and girlfriends sighed a lot whenever he was quoted—everything he had said seemed very banal, very obvious. Perhaps he was one of these people who was better to meet than to hear about, they decided.

Renata, their beautiful friend who was

single and glamorous and much feared by all the wives and girlfriends, was highly dismissive of him. "Sounds like a daft old queen to me," she would say. But she could say that because she wasn't involved with any of them.

Officially, Renata was the one who had got away. She was her own woman— stylish, confident, and much lusted after. All the wives pretended a greater warmth towards Renata than they actually felt.

Mr. Mangan was still there in the school, they heard from younger brothers and cousins. He was still hugely admired and widely quoted.

"He must be a great age now," said Hugh, who was going to be forty just before New Year and didn't like the notion at all.

Hugh's wife, Kate, was already weary from the possible midlife crisis that lay ahead. First Hugh was going to have no party, then he was going to have a huge party, then just a gathering of old friends, then he decided to add new clients to the guest list and make it more of a business do.

Renata would be there, of course. The Queen Bee.

"He can't be **that** old surely. He is still teaching after all. Why don't you invite your famous Mr. Mangan to your party?" Kate suggested.

It was an amazing suggestion—imagine seeing him again.

They tried to work out how old he would be. Seventy? No, they retired at sixty, didn't they? Still, he'd be able to walk and everything. Eat probably, and drink. Then all the men went back into an orgy of remembering all the subtle and enlightening things that Mr. Mangan used to say. Each one sounded more like a blinding glimpse into the obvious than the one before. Kate and the other wives looked at each other as mystified as ever. "Be good at some one thing, at one thing, find one area of excellence and revel in it. An old man once told me that we should all be brilliant at just one thing." That was one of Mr. Mangan's major pronouncements, apparently. It had seemed like something mint new to them when they heard it, and they all honestly believed that by following it they had changed their lives.

Look at the way it had all turned out!

Kevin was doing well in antiques, Martin was a barrister, Brian a dentist, Hugh had concentrated on cars. He had taken Mr. Mangan's advice, and now he had the agency for the car that everyone would die for.

What would they have done without this brilliant man?

Privately, Kate thought that the man had the brains of a motto in a fortune cookie. A geography teacher mouthing platitudes to generations of impressionable school-boys, and they all thought of him as one of the world's great thinkers. What was so unusual about boys from an expensive boarding school ending up as dentists, doctors, lawyers, antique dealers, and souped-up car salesmen? That's what the middle classes **did.**

"What was his own area of excellence?" Kate had wondered.

None of them knew.

Boys, and indeed men, could be amazingly uninquisitive, and even uninterested in other people's lives, Kate thought.

Not for the first time. Hugh's obsessions with being forty and flattening his stomach and halting the retreat of his hairline were becoming increasingly tedious. His hopes that he might be taken for the elder brother of their teenage daughter were embarrassing. The male bonding with Kevin, Martin, and Brian about the wonders of Mr. Mangan seemed more and more surreal.

She sighed heavily and arranged the party. She gave him a present of a hand-tailored jacket that accentuated the positive. The cunning tailor pretended that he thought it was a thirtieth birthday and threw his hands up in the air at the thought of such a young man being forty.

The house looked festive and Christmasy when the guests began to arrive. Kate was busy coping with a recently separated man, and trying to lower the volume of his complaints about the ex-wife who was demanding monstrous sums.

She knew everyone except Mr. Mangan, and he didn't seem to have turned up. Hugh and the fellows would be so disappointed, and she wished she had never suggested it. He had let them down by not appearing, even though he had sent a pleasant letter saying he would be delighted to attend.

Renata was there, beautiful, cool, and never fussing like the wives fussed. Well, she had nothing to do except lavish attention on herself. No children, no in-laws, company entertaining, no patting down a forty-year-old husband. No wonder she looked well. She was the same age as all of them, very late thirties, but she looked twenty-five. And she had brought a man with her. That would annoy the fellows. They regarded her as their property.

They were still buzzing around her as always. Kate narrowed her eyes and studied the scene. Renata had her hand lightly laid on the arm of a handsome man, mature, graying, maybe fiftyish. Confident but not arrogant, casually dressed but not sloppy. Trust Renata to find someone like that.

And wasn't it odd? The fellows, including the newly forty-year-old Hugh, seemed to be delighted with Renata's new flame—they circled him as they had always circled the Queen Bee.

Kate went to investigate. It was not a

new flame, it was the old teacher. It was
Mr. Mangan. There he stood, ten or
twelve years older than the boys who had
idolized him, a man without pretensions,
and also, Kate realized instantly, a man
without any real insights either.

They introduced her rapturously and she
was courteous and cool in her welcome.
What did this pied piper have that excited
these men? Some strange quality that
brought a sparkle to them which no well-
dressed trophy wife seemed able to do.

"You are a magnificent wife for Hugh,"
he said to her admiringly when they were
alone.

"Why do you say that?"

"Because you make him very happy and
confident and you have given him two
wonderful children. Who could ask more
from a partner?"

Kate was pleased but she would not let it
show.

"And you taught geography, Mr. Mangan.
Why is it that they think you were a
psychologist?" She tried to keep the
irritation, the impatience—and indeed, the
sheer jealousy—out of her tone. A man

who had never been in this house until ten minutes ago, already knew and remembered that she had two children, and already had the lovely Renata laying claim to him, marking him out as her territory. Where did he find all this homespun philosophy?

If Mr. Mangan noticed an edge in her question, he gave no sign of it.

"Oh, I don't think they saw me as anything but a pathetic old teacher, Kate, and I gather I wouldn't have been invited here if you hadn't suggested it. Schoolboys are very fickle, you know, they forget."

"They never forgot you. They go on and on about you."

"No, that can't be so."

"Believe me, it is. All kinds of things you told them, like sunsets are good and killing small birds is bad."

"Oh, please, may I have said something less banal. Please!" He held his hands up in despair.

"Nothing they remember."

He looked at her quizzically. Now Kate realized that her tone had been a little too sharp.

"You talked about areas of excellence. What was your area of excellence, Mr. Mangan?"

"Why do you want to know?"

"Well, it seems to me that anything you said to them about being good at one thing just reinforced what they already thought and hoped already."

"And if that were true, would it be so bad?"

"You haven't answered my question," she said.

"Which was?"

"What were you good at?"

"I wasn't particularly good at anything." He had a very warm smile.

"And what do you **do** all the time buried in that remote part of the country? What kind of a life do you live that makes us all think you have some secret? Some inner track?"

"Oh, I never claim to have that."

"Not in words, you don't." She knew she was going too far, that her face was flushed; she was weary from organizing this party, assuring Hugh that he was a young man, fearing that he was having an affair with Renata. It irritated her beyond measure that this smug man could hold her husband's attention and admiration so easily.

"What were you good at? You told them an old man told you that everyone should be really good at some one thing. Did you just make that up?"

"No, indeed I did not."

"So?"

"So I became very, very good at stain removal," Mr. Mangan said.

Kate took a deep breath.

"I realize I may sound hectoring and overintrusive, but please do not make a fool of me," she said.

"You asked me my area of excellence, that is it." He spoke simply and pleasantly.

All around them others were dying to join in their conversation—Kevin the antiques dealer, Brian the dentist, Martin the barrister, and her own husband, Hugh, who could not have been more pleased if he had Frank Sinatra as a guest.

But by his body language alone, Mr. Mangan managed to exclude them all, even the lovely Renata.

"Stains?" she said.

"Stains," Mr. Mangan repeated. "You have no idea how pleased people are to know that you make a hardened stain soft and much easier to remove by applying glycerin, and where to use alcohol and where to use white vinegar. You can make a paste of vinegar, salt, and flour and your brasses will just gleam. My landlady was very grateful for this piece of information. Very grateful indeed," he said, with a look in his eye that seemed to speak of hours and hours of enthusiastic gratitude shown by the landlady in a narrow bed.

"And you think this is the secret of the universe?"

"Why are you so angry with me, Kate?"

"Life isn't as simple and blokish as you think it is," she said in spite of herself.

"For blokes it often is," he said simply. "They don't think the whole thing out in the convoluted ways that women do. That's why you often think we are insensitive. There's no need to worry so much and be manipulative; men are basically school-boys, and all they want is a bit of hope and enthusiasm and information."

Kate's face must have shown how little she believed him, and how great a manipulation and game plan she felt was needed to cope with the male psyche and the dangers that lurked everywhere.

"Why did you stay teaching in an elitist school in a one-horse town for so long if you know so much?"

"I liked them; I still like them. Just because their parents have money to send them to a boarding school doesn't mean that they have to be monsters. They're as decent as anyone else."

Perhaps he was right, Mr. Mangan. Perhaps men were basically simple. But he didn't know how much you had to worry about these days, when marriages weren't written in stone, and when fellows of forty needed outside reassurance.

Mr. Mangan seemed to realize that it was time to join the general conversation again. But before he did, he said what a nice party it was and what a delightful lady Renata was, he would be taking her home and seeing her again.

"And telling her how to polish her brasses, no doubt?" Kate said, almost giddy with a huge sense of relief.

"No, but she does have nice jewelry and I could tell her that porous stones should not be immersed in water, just polished with a chamois, but that others should be cleaned in a mild washing-up liquid. She might like to know that."

Renata would love that, Kate realized, just as the landlady and many others had loved this strange man who was no saint and no guru but who liked people for what they were.

A Tactful Conversation

When Beth met Larry he had a picture of his wife and toddlers in his office. A very posed picture: toothy smile from the blond wife, lots of smocking on the children's dresses.

A real trophy picture, she thought, as she glanced at it from time to time.

And then, as the years went on and Beth ceased to be Larry's secretary, but became his personal assistant, the photograph changed. The children were now seven and eightish, well-cut straight hair, expensive casual clothes, arms draped around Mummy, who looked as toothy and lineless as before.

Interesting that the smile was exactly the same.

Heigh-ho, little to worry about except spend the money that Larry was bringing home in ever-increasing amounts.

By the time Beth and her longtime love, Martin, had said good-bye, the picture had changed again.

Just the girls this time.

No wife.

No one commented. Beth ran her own department in the travel company now; she was nobody's assistant. She didn't have coffee with the girls who might have giggled about the disappearance of Larry's wife.

It was interesting, really, that she didn't feel free to ask him herself.

After all, they had a drink together almost every evening.

But then she had never told him about Martin, about all the false stops and starts, about the endless discussions on parenthood, the rows about commitment, the dizzy mornings in bed on Sundays, about the maddening way he had of stepping out of his clothes and leaving them on the floor and leaving ashtrays all over the place.

Beth and Larry talked about the business

and how to improve it, about their rivals, about new destinations and dodgy carriers, and ticket prices and the opera, and football and hanging baskets. The company had competitions each month to see who could provide the best display. It had often been written up in the papers—a travel company that really looked festive.

They never talked about her Martin who had gone, and his Jane who had disappeared from the photo frame.

People always said that Beth and Larry had been an item for years; that it had been going on since she arrived in the office.

She had always carried a torch for him, they said, and funny how she managed to get such rapid promotion. Well, it all figured, didn't it?

But it wasn't true. Beth never thought about him in that way until shortly after she heard about Jane.

So in fact she was utterly blameless, had no part in the breakup and certainly had nothing to hide.

But only Beth and Larry knew that.

Jane told Larry one weekend that she

was tired of his office flings, his cheap behavior, and the way he ignored her.

She said she was going to get a divorce and make sure he saw as little of the girls as possible.

Larry said, hand on heart, he had been in a few foolish situations while on conferences or press trips abroad, but there was nothing ongoing, and nothing that was worth talking about. Jane said she was not easy to fool, that he was hardly ever home before nine o'clock at night. Larry said that was because Jane had insisted on living in deepest Sussex and you couldn't **get** home any earlier. But somehow they knew it was over.

And later Larry learned that Jane had a new friend, a man who ran a country club, a man who played tennis and was sociable.

They would marry when Jane was free.

Beth knew none of this.

Not for a long time.

She did know that Larry was suggesting that they have two drinks each evening and sometimes suggested supper as well. But it was always so businesslike and connected with work or whatever they had been talking about. She didn't make any deductions.

After three weeks of this patter she asked, without guile: "Is Jane away at the moment?"

"No, I'm away at the moment, as it happens."

"Oh."

They looked at each other with the same solidarity that had always been there. Like the time the brochures had all been printed with last year's prices, or the day the dignitary came to open their building and had been refused admittance by security.

"Yes," said Larry.

"Will it be for a bit or forever?" Beth asked.

"Forever, I think."

"We'll survive, we always do." She spoke as if it was the company that would survive, but it had a different meaning.

"You and I will always survive as friends," he said.

"I know." There was a lump in her throat, and, looking at him, Beth knew that it was very important that they did. He was such a dear friend and such a good man. She asked him no more about Jane; they talked football teams and whether to get more impatiens for the basket near the door. If you had them in huge clusters they were hard to beat. They talked of their autumn campaign and they said good-bye outside the restaurant.

Beth hadn't asked him where he stayed.

Larry hadn't told her.

Six weeks later Larry and Beth went back to the apartment he had rented near work and he cooked her supper.

Then he said it was a pity to go all the way home since they would be so near work in the morning and Beth said she had brought a change of clothes just in case.

And then everything moved very quickly and they couldn't understand why it all hadn't happened before.

And he told her about the two great loves of his life: his daughters, Lara and Anna. They were fourteen and fifteen.

"They will adore you," Larry said.

"They will hate me," Beth said.

He was mystified; why would they hate Beth? She had nothing to do with his breakup with their mother. After all, their mother had a new friend. It didn't stop anyone loving them.

But Beth hadn't got to be so senior in the travel business without understanding a little of the world.

"Let's not worry about Lara's and Anna's feelings about me now," she said. "You must build up your own relationship with them and never let them think they are forgotten. That has to be the most important thing."

And in the months that followed Beth made huge efforts to keep Larry in touch with his girls.

She kept dreaming up new things for them to do, places to go, and even suggested that he take them to his flat and let them cook him a meal.

She would install all the ingredients for something simple and teach Larry how to make it, then he would let the girls make it for him.

They loved it, he told her, cooking for their dad.

She encouraged him to get them to choose a shirt for him, or to take him to get his hair cut. They would be involved still in his life if they did this.

It all worked very well, and, as she knew they would search his flat for evidence of another woman, she made sure that they found none. The time wasn't right yet. Larry told her that truly he had never got on so well with his daughters. They were even going to go on holiday with him.

He would take them to Greece.

"Why can't you come?" he begged her.

"It's too soon, Larry; please believe me."

"But they'll have to know sometime. We are going to get married, aren't we?"

"Of course, but later. Let them know they have you. Then they won't resent sharing you."

He grumbled, but agreed. The week was very long without him. Beth worked all the hours that she was awake. She was determined that she would feel no self-pity.

He returned suntanned and happy.

The girls had told him that they had never had a better holiday.

They had stopped attacking him for leaving home and ruining their lives. They told him secrets and stories of their own lives.

They told him that their mother and the man from the club drank lots of gin and laughed a lot and they argued a lot.

Lara had even asked him, "Why don't you get a sort of aging girlfriend, Daddy?" and Larry said that he might.

Anna had said, "Don't have any children, though, we'd hate that," so Larry said he would take that on board.

Beth wanted to crush them both under a large machine, but she knew that Larry loved them.

"Aren't they marvelous?" she said insincerely, and was rewarded with a look of such devotion that it nearly broke her heart.

"I don't deserve to be so happy," said Larry, who was regarded in the trade as a businessman with a highly developed killer instinct.

After the divorce Jane married the man from the club. His name was hardly ever mentioned by Larry—not because he couldn't bear to, but because he didn't think of him as a person, only someone connected to a place with tennis courts, swimming pools, and miniature golf.

The girls seemed less than overjoyed with their new life.

"He's very boring, Daddy," Lara confessed.

"And he's not really interested in us," Anna added.

Perhaps, Larry said, it was now time to tell the girls the good news that their father had found a wonderful person who really would be interested in them.

Again Beth urged caution.

"Introduce me as a friend first," she begged.

They agreed that Beth should join them by accident as it were, in a bookshop, and they should all go and have a pizza.

It seemed pretty forced, but it was better than what Larry wanted, which was a huge announcement of love and happiness and devotion.

Beth went to the assignation with no great hopes.

It didn't matter what she wore; the girls would hate her.

There was no point in being interested in

them, they wouldn't like that; it would be called prying or interfering. Just as objectionable as the man from the club.

She went along, hands in pockets, slouched and prepared for the worst.

She knew them well from their pictures, not just the pretty, pretty ones, but the dozens of snaps that Larry took on his outings with them.

She could recognize the more outgoing Lara and the more mutinous Anna. Teenagers who had thought that their life was secure until this year.

Taking a deep breath, she said, "Hello, Larry, fancy seeing you here of all places."

She said the words like a very poor actress in a school play.

Anna's eyes narrowed.

"Girls," said Larry, "you won't believe this, but do you know who has just walked in?"

"Your ex-secretary," Lara said. Larry and Beth looked at her, mouths open, faces riddled with guilt.

"How did you know?" Larry asked eventually.

"Mum said you'd been having an affair

with her for years, but that it was probably over by now," Lara said.

"Run its course was what she said," Anna corrected.

Larry fought for words. "We weren't having an affair...not then," he added lamely.

Lara shrugged, Anna went back to the book she had been leafing through.

"And anyway, Beth isn't a secretary, she is a senior manager."

"That must have been difficult...to become a manager," Anna said.

Beth looked at Larry, the man she loved more than anyone else in the world, and his poor anguished face.

There was a big, tall pile of books placed precariously on a high shelf. She wondered if she could knock it so that it would hit both girls instantly. Or would she risk just injuring them and spending a lifetime visiting them in hospital?

If she walked out, it meant walking out on Larry.

If she stayed it would mean a lifetime of this.

This was a problem of greater magnitude

than any she and Larry had faced and solved over the years.

And she couldn't enlist his help because he was blinded by love for all of them. This was where she was all on her own.

She began to speak very slowly and quietly, as if she were talking to foreigners in a reading room.

"Your father and I have only become close since he and your mother separated, but I know that doesn't make much difference to you—"

"Too true," said Lara.

"She would say that, wouldn't she?" Anna said.

"But your father loves you both so much," Beth hissed through clenched teeth. She so much wanted to say that the Lord knew why, and it was a grave fault in an otherwise sane man.

"He loved us so much he ran off with you!" Anna said.

Larry began to splutter.

Beth interrupted. "Larry, leave it. Dates, times, details have nothing to do with it. They couldn't care less."

"But it's so unfair, unfair to you…"

He was making it worse.

Without realizing it, her voice raised a notch.

"Anna, Lara, I'm just going to say this once. I know how you feel. Yes, I do. My father left when I was eleven. He used to write twice a year, birthday and Christmas, and after I was seventeen, only at Christmas. I think he forgot when my birthday was. I hated the woman he went off with—I never wanted to hear her name mentioned. I didn't know until years later that he had gone off with someone totally different. He just met her later on. Now, this is the point. When he telephoned me he used to say, 'Barbara sends you her love,' and I used to say, 'I don't want Barbara's love...'"

They were looking at her now, the two monsters.

"I don't think he loved me very much, my father. I mean, he can't have if he only got in touch twice a year. It's different for you. But whatever bit of love my father did have for me I sure managed to drive it away by all this grousing about Barbara."

Beth was serving aces; there was no

response from the other side.

"And so know this: I will love your father always, and when you are grown up and busy and have lives of your own, and don't want to give up Saturdays for him, you'll be damn glad that he has some aging bit on the side as you'll still call me, to look after him...And I won't ask him to choose between us. I wouldn't dare. I think there's enough room there for all of us. In different places and at different times.

"If we get married, I will not want to be part of your awful, boring teenage lives. I hated it myself and I am not going through it again for anyone, least of all for two youngsters who dislike me—and I may or may not have my own children. That is my business and your father's business and it has nothing to do with you.

"So I think we all know where we stand now. It's up to you if you want to make it an issue; you or me. It's too big a gamble, girls—you might lose. Who would you have then? Only one parent when you could have two. And suppose you win? Could you take on the responsibility of him looking miserable and wretched and lonely? How could you make it up to him?

"Think, that is all I say. Think before you go on with this pathetic charade of sulks and grunts and insults. Who needs it?

"Your father doesn't, and I certainly don't."

Larry, Beth, Lara, and Anna left a bookshop they would be unlikely to visit again. They stood in silence on the pavement for a moment.

"Did you say something about a pizza earlier, Dad?" Anna said.

And, as a dangerously normal family, the four of them walked towards the restaurant.

Beth's only fear now was that they would want to come and live with her.

Your Cheating Heart

The Afterthought

She said that she'd come away with him when the children were old enough. How old is old enough? he had wanted to know. Old enough to understand, she had thought, but he was very sad about this and thought they would never be old enough to understand, not even if they were as old as anything. You never understand your mother going off with the great family friend. It's not the kind of thing anyone could understand. So things went on the way they were for a long time.

The way things were was extraordinary. He went to lunch with the family every Sunday, summer and winter, except the three Sundays they were away in the west for the summer holidays. And they saw him at least once a week, either at one of his suppers, as he called them, or else they went to the theater or the National Concert Hall. And in the summer he saw even more of them because they had a garden and he only lived in a flat so it made sense to drop in to have a drink and admire what Rita had done with the flowers that day. He hadn't been very interested in gardening before but he had bought himself a beginner's book and asked her lovely intelligent questions, which made her very happy. Mostly he was there before Alec got back from the office. Alec would park the car, see him, and be very pleased. Sometimes that gave Frank's chest a small, tight feeling of guilt, but he was able to stifle it. There was no point in loving someone, offering them a new life, and being loved in return if you were going to cloud the whole thing up with guilt and destroy it for everyone. No, it was all luck and chance. Alec had the luck and had met Rita by chance before Frank had, otherwise everything would have been different and he would have married Rita. Think of it as chance, not betrayal. It was more positive.

Of course he also met Rita on Tuesday lunchtimes and Thursday nights. Tuesday was when she did her little ramble, as it was called, around the shops. Mummy was always being asked to buy this or that when she went on her little ramble. The ramble had been in existence before Frank came to redirect it towards his flat. It was so lovely and vague and a perfect alibi because if ever they were seen what could be more natural than their having met accidentally and going back to the flat to look at some new purchase? Same with the Thursday night bridge lessons. Frank had taught her to play bridge quite adequately and there were so many at the bridge classes, which were extremely badly organized, all she had to do was go in, say hello to a few people she knew, and leave almost at once. They were all too busy frowning and puckering over their cards to notice which table, if any table, Rita had been given. The whole thing was foolproof and frustrating and it had been going on for three years.

Sometimes in his office Frank had a little

daydream. It went like this. Alec would call around, white-faced, to his flat and tell him that the most dreadful thing had happened. He, Alec, had fallen hopelessly in love with this woman from Brazil and he was going to leave with her the following week and become a partner in a solicitor's office in downtown Rio de Janeiro. Oh yes, he spoke quite good Portuguese, actually. The thing was that this woman didn't want him to have anything more to do with the children and he wondered if he could ask Frank to keep an eye on the family for him; move in, maybe, to look after them better. Then, as a parting shot, Alec would say that he had just realized that he and Rita had never been properly married because there had been an Impediment at the time. Frank saw himself in a very supportive role over the whole business: manly handshakes, assurances of solidarity, a quiet unobtrusive marriage to Rita.

And always with a strong, supportive role towards the children. These things happen; you must not feel too harshly about your father; you must write him a cheery letter every month telling him how you are getting along. I know I can never replace him but at least I'm a friend. I've always been that. Gradually everything becomes natural and accepted and those early Tuesdays and Thursdays are long forgotten, part of a childish past, silly and never coming to mind again. Little by little changes would be made. The kinds of pictures that he and Rita liked would hang on the walls, a man would be paid to come and do the rough work in the garden twice a week to save Rita's hands. They would put their car on the ferry and drive to France not to Galway. They would have garlic bread and vinaigrette dressing, not mayonnaise. Maybe if a good house that suited them came on his books in the estate agency then he might buy it and start a new phase in their lives. But the house wasn't really important, not the food, not the holidays abroad. The children were what mattered—or really, the youngest child, Eoin.

Eoin had always been a solemn little boy with big eyes. He looked like those Italian children who broke hearts and box office records in the fifties in those subtitled films.

He was nine now and very lonely. The others were a great hulking seventeen and sixteen. They had no time for Eoin and he spent a lot of his time this summer sitting in the garden with his mother, and especially from the late afternoon with Frank as well. He had said that he'd like to drop the word **Uncle,** all on his own. His big brother, Jim, and his big sister, Orla, had said he was being a show-off, but Frank said he thought it was a great idea because **Uncle** made him feel a bit ho-ho-ho-ish, like Santa Claus, but to be called Frank by young people made him feel a dashing young man again.

They had rolled around with what he thought was unnecessary mirth at the thought of him being a dashing young man, but still he was Frank now and that was better. If you are going to run away with someone's mother it's better that the someone doesn't call you Uncle.

Eoin always seemed glad to see him arrive at the house, Frank thought. He would ask him long, searching questions about his work at the auctioneer's. You mean that one person wants to sell a house and another person wants to buy a house and they pay **you**? That's brilliant, Frank. Frank felt somehow that he hadn't totally explained the world of the estate agent to Eoin. But, it was the same apparently with his father. Alec confessed that Eoin's grasp of the law would make the Incorporated Law Society shudder. Rita laughed at both of them and said they should listen to Eoin talking to her. He thought she had been very clever to marry Daddy so that she need never work again.

Yet despite all this they loved him, the three of them, and Frank and Rita were always happy to have him sitting there when they met in the summer after-noons. They never whispered or plotted; they talked the talk of close friendship and laughed as companions. Sometimes Eoin looked up from his book and laughed too.

Eoin didn't talk much about himself. He seemed to be happy enough at school and he had a few friends who came round to the house but not many. Not enough to console him, Frank thought; not enough to lean on when his mummy was gone. He liked reading and said that he was going to have two jobs when he grew up—one would be writing books about children where the children were real, not eejits like they were in so many books, and his other would be teaching hardened criminals to read. Probably in California.

Once, he said they called him E.T. at school. He said it sadly.

"That's because of your initials, Eoin Treacy."

"No, I think it's because of my eyes," he said matter-of-factly. "They're a bit too big as eyes, you see," he explained.

The three grown-ups, sitting sipping their summer drink, all leaned towards him with words and gestures of protest. He smiled back and accepted their assurances that his eyes were magnificent.

"You could be a film star with those eyes, a real Valentino."

"Yes, but is it a real job?" Eoin wanted to know.

Sometimes he asked dangerous questions. Why did Mummy have to go on rambles on hot Tuesdays when they did all the shopping in the supermarket on Fridays anyway? Why did Frank not get married and have a garden of his own now that he knew all about gardens? Why did Mummy learn bridge with those awful people in that hall she didn't like if she never played bridge? He seemed satisfied with all the answers. And full of innocent chat. Frank often felt he could talk to him for hours even if he wasn't Rita's son. In fact, he often forgot totally about the relationships as the boy chattered on.

Eoin told Frank that it was hard on him having nobody his own age but really he was lucky he was here at all. He was an Afterthought. Frank had laughed, delighted at the grown-up language, thinking that Eoin had no idea what the term meant. But he was wrong. "Daddy and Mummy were having rows, you see, when Orla and Jim were about six and seven, and it was either go their own ways or have me."

"Nonsense!" Frank was shocked to the core. How could a child of nine know or think he knew such things? And anyway, Rita and Alec had no rows. There had not been a great deal of love or gaiety in their married life—Rita had told him this—but there had been no rows. That was why she found it so hard to leave Alec.

"Oh yes, honestly." Eoin's huge eyes were full of sincerity.

"But how would you know, even if it were true, who would have told you?"

"Nobody **told** me, but people sort of forget I'm there. They say things in front of me." He looked at Frank levelly. Yes, that was true. They did, Frank remembered only too well.

"So that's how I heard of Mummy's friend then. He was in Daddy's office. But he went away when they decided to have me as an Afterthought." Eoin felt he had explained enough and decided to talk about cycling instead and whether you'd have to be very good very young like swimming or if it was something you could take up in later life, like at about nine. "You shouldn't think of yourself as an Afterthought," Frank said. "All that business about your mummy's friend— who was he anyway? It's all nonsense."

"He was called Stephen something, I don't know. I wasn't here, but that's what I heard when people were talking, you

know. Ask Mummy?" he said innocently
but as a sort of question, knowing it
was far from likely that Frank would ask
Mummy.

"Who was Stephen?" he asked her the
next Tuesday.

She sighed. "I knew Alec would mention
Stephen sooner or later. He must suspect."

"Alec suspects nothing. He never said a
word."

"Then how…?"

"Eoin told me."

"Don't be ridiculous." She threw her head
back and laughed. "Eoin wasn't even born
when I knew Stephen."

Frank was silent.

"Not that there was anything in it," she
added.

"No," said Frank.

"But who was gossiping, who really tried
to stir things up?"

"I told you, it was Eoin, but he wasn't
stirring things up. I think he was trying to
dampen things down."

She looked at him slightly amused. "And
has he?"

"I think he has, for a while. A lot of the

color seems to have gone, the freshness. I don't know, the romance."

"Ah yes, my love, the Romance is all," she was mocking him gently.

"So," he said. "Did you have little rambles and bridge lessons to meet Stephen?"

"No. No, different things entirely."

"Good," he said.

"You'll still come round to the house?" she asked.

"For a little while anyway," he said.

He told Eoin later that he thought he might be going to the firm's office in Cork and leaving Dublin altogether. Eoin was interested. "Do you think Mummy'll have another baby? She's forty, you know. Would that be too old for another Afterthought?"

Bella and the Marriage Guidance Counselor

Bella discovered that her husband was unfaithful to her by the purest chance. She wondered often what would have happened if she had never discovered, if she had never gone to the off-license that day for a bottle of sherry. Everything would have been different, or, more accurately, everything would have been the same, and gone on in the same old way, which was what she liked. None of the dramatic happenings would have happened. Life would have been as it always was.

She needed sherry because she was going to make a real, old-fashioned trifle; there was nothing she could use instead.

To have put in two glasses of brandy would have been ridiculously wasteful, and gin, she thought, wouldn't have worked. Beer was out, so she had to go to the off-license, and since it was a nice day she decided to take the dog and have a proper little walk. She had been sitting down too much anyway; it would be good for her to have some exercise.

She knew Mr. Elton in the off-license slightly. She and Jim usually called in there on Saturday mornings after they had been to the supermarket. They were very organized as a couple: she would provide the shopping list in two sections and Jim got the heavier, bulky items each week-end, she got the smaller ones; then, after stocking up on a couple of bottles, they would go to the pub, where Jim had a pint and she had a gin and tonic.

Jim would read the morning paper and she would read a magazine, then they went home to lunch. She could never understand couples who found shopping a chore—all you had to do was be organized.

"Lovely morning, madam," said Mr. Elton,

rubbing his hands happily behind the counter. Mr. Elton was a little too hearty for Bella, but then you can't go around condemning everyone for their irritating little habits, she told herself firmly. She greeted him pleasantly and let her eyes roam around to find a cheap sherry, one which would be good enough to drink, yet not too good to waste by putting in a trifle.

"Did you enjoy that bottle of bubbly last night, then?" asked Mr. Elton, all cheer and grins and winks.

"Last night? Bubbly? No, we didn't have any sparkling wine last night," said Bella.

"Aha, yes you did! Mr. B. was in here around seven looking for something nice, white and dry and sparkling. I asked him was it an anniversary or something; and he said no, just a little treat."

Bella looked at him in amazement. Jim wasn't at home last night for dinner. He brought no bottle of anything sparkling when he did come home at midnight. He was exhausted from going over the papers with Martin at Martin's house. Martin's wife had fixed them a nice supper he said;

nothing special—more a glorified snack. He had mentioned nothing about bubbly. Bella's brow cleared. He had probably decided to buy something to take along to Martin's house. He hadn't implied it was a meal that went well with bubbly, but then men never tell you the things that are important.

She thanked Mr. Elton as distantly as she could without actual coldness and left him with the cheapest sherry that might actually be drunk by human beings. The incident went from her mind and remained gone until Jim came home at six o'clock.

"Well, you know," were his first words, "I was going to tell you anyway, so I'll tell you now."

Know what? Bella's first thought was that he had been sacked. Made redundant. Nothing else could account for the look of seriousness on his face.

"Tell me what?" she said, saucepan in one hand, tea towel in the other.

"Elton told me he had mentioned the bottle of champagne and said he hoped he hadn't let any cats out of any bags. I told him he had but it didn't matter. He's full of excitement up in the wine shop there, he thinks he's in the center of some drama. Silly fool."

Jim had never spoken like that of Elton or of anyone. What cat had been let out of what bag? Bella was very confused.

Jim sat down on a kitchen chair, took the phone off its hook, turned off the bubbling saucepan on the gas cooker, and explained to Bella that he was having an affair with a girl in the class he lectured in the polytechnic, and that he loved her. He was going to ask Bella for a divorce.

It had been going on for over six months. Martin knew and covered up for him; so did his secretary. Nobody else knew apart from Martin's wife possibly, and now that jovial fool Elton in the off-license. The girl's flatmate knew, of course, but she didn't count, she was from another life, another world.

Bella still had the tea towel in her hand; she began to twist it around and around.

"What's wrong with **me**?" she said in a little whimper. "Why don't you want to live with me anymore? You promised to live with me when we got married, not someone else."

"I know," said Jim. "I **know** I did, but I didn't know it was going to be like this. Everything's changed. Don't say you haven't noticed how dull we've got together. You must have been feeling that everything we'd ever hoped for and promised ourselves has all got in this dreary sort of routine of catching up with things, forever. Once the sitting room's been done up it's time to do up the hall, when the car is washed it's time to clean the garage, when the roses are pruned it's time to do the beds by the wall, when the shopping's done it's time to label things in the deep freeze...People weren't meant to live like this—they were meant to spark away and react to each other. We've stopped doing that, haven't we?"

"I'll try and spark and react a bit," said Bella weakly.

"It's too late now," said Jim, and he put on his coat again. "I'm just going for a drink, by myself, not with Emma. I'll be back in an hour—I want to think out what we are going to do."

"**We** are going to do nothing," screamed

Bella in pain. "No, I tell you **we** are making no plans! **You** are making all the decisions and plans. I have no part in it. I'm quite happy to go on the way we are. If there are any changes to be made they are yours, not ours. Just present me with the list of how you are going to go back on all your promises. That's all."

"Let me go and think things out. I know it will be simpler if I've time to think. I'll write it all down and then we can discuss it as calmly as possible," he said, not even fooling himself that it would be possible.

Bella put her back to the hall door.

"I want no lists of options, or alternatives. You are going to go on living with me, that was the bargain, that's what we said we'd do. What kind of a life would I have if you went away? What would I do?" She burst into very noisy tears and Jim looked at her with pity from a distance.

By midnight it was clear that he was going; he sounded very weary and anxious to be gone. Nothing she said would sway him. He used very few phrases about how much they had shared together and she did not say at all that she would miss **him,** only that she couldn't cope with a life without him. There were thousands of words, most of them useless. Everything that had to be said was said in the first five minutes. Jim slept on the sofa, and Bella slept not at all.

She tried to preserve some air of normality at breakfast and made him a nice fry. He only wanted coffee. She begged him to give the marriage another chance; she said she'd never ask him to help with the housework if that was the problem. He shook his head and said nothing. As he left the house he said he would be home late and would take tomorrow off work so that they could sit down and draw up a proper financial settlement.

"You're never getting a divorce!" Bella shouted. "Never, never!"

"Well, I'll just go then," said Jim simply. "And in a couple of years Emma and I will be able to get married anyway. I'd prefer if we could talk about things, because you might like a smaller house, or you might want rent paid on a flat for you. It would be much calmer if you accepted that I literally won't be here again, and that

I'm willing to make things as simple for you as possible."

He was gone.

The morning was interminable. On a writing pad that she usually used for shopping lists, Bella wrote down all the possible courses of action she could take. None of them seemed any use at all when faced with the unchanging fact that Jim was going to go anyway.

What did people do when their husbands walked out? Often enough she had gossiped and tut-tutted about other families where this had happened. But what did a wife actually **do**?

By midafternoon, no housework done, endless tea and biscuits consumed, Bella had stopped blaming Jim and decided that it must be something in herself that was wrong. She took out the old photograph album she and Jim had kept meticulously during the fifteen years of marriage. It went back even further to the year that they had been engaged.

The summers really did seem to have been hotter then, sleeveless floral dresses, funny bouffant hairdos, how thin she was.

And how slim in the very formal wedding pictures. She had a real waist then, and her jaw looked very frail instead of padded as it did now. All Bella could see was more flesh and fewer smiles in the progression of snaps. The most recent were the most distressing. They had been taken at Christmas, when Jim's sister and her husband had come for Christmas dinner.

The curiously formal pictures of everyone holding up glasses at whoever was taking the snap seemed to explain everything to Bella. Look at her, for heaven's sake, she had a roll of fat around her waist. Whatever had made her wear a silly tight dress, and how had she let herself become so fat anyway?

In every magazine that Bella had read, the dangers of Letting Yourself Go were written large and menacing. Agony columns used to suggest that you had a facial or lost weight to revive an ailing marriage; girls who had no boyfriends were urged to slim down and they would be rewarded. Anyone who felt depressed or low would feel cheered and high if they were a few inches less around the middle.

Bella must have been too complacent; that's what it was. Jim had never said anything, but he was a man, and, as a man, he must have been put off by her flesh. What Bella must do now was to lose a lot of weight, dramatically, then he would come back again, and the whole horror of last night would be forgotten. In fact, there would come a time when they could laugh over it together.

The biscuit tin was firmly closed. Then firmly opened again and its contents shaken into the rubbish bin. The remaining bread was put out in the garden for the birds. This was going to be a dramatic diet, not one of those where you started and stopped. This one had to work. But Bella knew that weight fell slowly, whereas people who were hungry fell quickly. Perhaps she would go to the doctor about it. Some people got marvelous tablets from doctors, which meant that you were never hungry again. She didn't know why she hadn't thought of this before.

The doctor had surgery from four to six, and Bella sat in the waiting room, full of determination. Dr. Cecil, who was a kind young man, would help her. She had only visited him a couple of times, but he had been very pleasant on both occasions.

"Well, a woman who wants to lose weight is a cheering thing for a medical man," he said briskly. "Step up here and we'll have a look, you don't seem very overweight to me. Now let's see...yes, a stone less and you'll be in perfect health. Are you feeling short of breath or anything, is that why you want to lose weight?"

"No, it's because I've got so fat," said Bella, amazed that he couldn't see this for himself.

He listened to her chest, took her blood pressure, and told her that she was a very healthy woman, but she looked a bit strained. Had she any other worries apart from her weight?

"No," lied Bella. She was going to fight this one on her own.

Dr. Cecil could give her no tablets; she didn't need them, he said, just more exercise, fewer fatty foods, plenty of protein, less carbohydrate. The usual advice.

Could she have some sleeping pills perhaps? Not unless she told him why. He didn't just hand out sleeping pills like candy.

Bella was vague. Dr. Cecil was firm. She left with no prescription of any sort, and a cheery wave from Dr. Cecil, who decided that she was going through an early change of life and asked her to keep in touch, to drop in now and then just for a chat about her health.

So it would have to be a health farm. That might get a stone off dramatically. Bella had plenty of housekeeping money. Three months ago Jim had opened a special account for her and put in a generous sum each month. With a sudden start she realized that he must have done this when he had decided to leave her anyway: a method of giving her money of her own in advance of the departure date. She had enough to pay for a week in one of those expensive places if she needed to, but might that be playing into Jim's hand if she just cleared off at once? She would wait and see. Meanwhile, eating nothing.

Bella was very hungry when Jim came in at midnight. She was wide awake and dying for a bowl of soup, but she would have nothing. Didn't those magazines tell you that slimming should begin with a shock to the system? Jim looked tired and not anxious to talk. He got a throw ready to sleep on the sofa and said they'd have a proper conversation in the morning.

Bella said that there was nothing to stop him sleeping in his own bed, where he had slept for fifteen years. He looked startled, as if she had said something in bad taste. No, he'd prefer to be in the sitting room, please.

"You were able to sleep in our bed all the time this affair was going on, and it didn't revolt you," said Bella.

"I know," he said, ashamed of himself.

That night was almost entirely sleepless for Bella, but she dozed a little.

In the morning, she put on her long navy caftan, the most slimming thing she owned; she made up her tired face carefully and brushed her hair. She came down as Jim was making the coffee.

"Let's decide on a temporary parting," she said before he could say anything. "Let's just say a period like two months, and then we meet again and see how we are getting on without each other. If we are miserable then we'll come back together and there's no harm done. If we still want to stay apart then we can make all the arrangements then. How about that?"

"No," said Jim. "That wouldn't do at all. You see, I'm not going to be miserable. It has nothing to do with trial separations. I want to marry Emma, and I don't want some more hypocrisy—I'm responsible for enough of it already. So what I want to discuss today is what you are going to do, how much money you'll need, what way you'll need it."

This wasn't going as Bella had planned.

She listened and watched as the sums were done on her shopping list pad. So much going in here, so much there, insurance policies to be kept up. Bella was to let him know if she would like him to sell the house—it might be better all round, new starts, and money in the bank.

"Where are you going to live?" she asked dully.

"I don't know yet, it depends on whether we sell this place or not..."

The calculations went on. She felt very

low. She walked away from the kitchen table in the middle of it.

"I'm going out," she said suddenly. "We'll talk about it again."

"I won't be here again," said Jim despairingly. "This is our day for talking about it."

"No, you can write to me about it," she said.

A shadow of relief came over Jim's face.

"So, I'll take some of my things—well, most of my things—today then. I mean, I won't take anything joint, we can discuss that again."

"Yes," said Bella.

She walked down to the shopping center and in the coffee shop looked up the National Marriage Guidance Council in the phone book, asking them for their nearest branch. It wasn't far away. She rang the branch and they said to call in that afternoon and make an appointment. She filled in the time wandering around the shops. Perhaps they could cure her marriage? Why else would they have been set up if they couldn't mend marriages that had gone bad?

The woman said that Bella could make

an appointment for counseling next week.

"Why not now?" said Bella in distress.

That wasn't the system, apparently. It might have been based on the fact that people had run in for counseling after a row, and that they didn't really need it at all. Bella didn't know. Anyway, she had to accept next Thursday or nothing, so she took next Thursday.

She went to a bad movie and went home. Jim had gone, leaving a note saying that he had put another hundred pounds into her bank account for emergencies and would write to her next week. His clothes, suitcases, and a few of his books had gone. Nothing else.

It's a hard life if you keep up pretenses, but you can keep going on some kinds of hopes, and Bella had two lifelines, the diet and the marriage counseling. She parried questions about where Jim was, she refused one invitation, and canceled the people she was going to have for drinks. She accepted another invitation to a neighbor's house, saying that Jim was away, but she felt dizzy from lack of food, and she wouldn't eat anything there so the evening was not a success.

Finally Thursday came and she found herself in front of a clergyman of all things. Bella hadn't much time for clergymen, but this one seemed very nice and relaxed, and he never suggested that religion might be the answer for anything, which eased her mind.

In fact, she thought, it must be very easy to be a counselor, you only have to listen and nod. He gave her no advice; he gave her no suggestions. She told him the whole story about Jim and how it was a middle-aged madness, and about Emma, who must be twenty-five years younger than him, and about the nice home that Bella and Jim had built up for years. But the counselor didn't have any ideas about how to get Jim back. No helpful hints or schemes, no plans of campaign.

"Well, naturally I've gone on a diet," said Bella in a businesslike way. "That was probably half, if not two-thirds, of the whole problem. I've eaten practically nothing for six days now, and I've lost five pounds, so

that side of it is under control at any
rate. It's just that I don't know what to
do in terms of making him come back,
when I should expect him back, and how
to work on it."

The gray eyes of the counselor were
friendly and reassuring, as was his gray,
shabby cardigan. But they didn't seem
to flicker with any recognition or pleasure
when she mentioned her diet, he didn't
seem to see that this was the best thing
she could have done.

"It is a good idea to lose weight, don't
you think?" she asked anxiously.

"Has your weight made you feel
unhappy?"

"Well, obviously since I'm much too
fat, and this girl is probably a skinny little
thing, it must have a lot to do with that. I
know I have the willpower to lose the
weight. What I was hoping you would tell
me is what to do then?"

He was a good listener; he had said
nothing when she had gone into little
bouts of self-pity about who was going to
help her dig the garden, and why should
she be turned out of her own house at

the age of forty-five, and when was this country going to have laws that protected marriages?

He had prompted her with a few little grunting remarks about why she and Jim had drifted apart, and whether she and he had been able to talk to each other about things that mattered. He said that it was usually better if both parties came to counseling, but she had said vacantly that Jim wouldn't consider it. He seemed to have a debt of honor to this little tramp at the moment. When they got back together, perhaps he might come then. But she said it doubtfully.

"You really think that the relationship was so alive that it will be saved," the kind gray man said, not as if it was a question, more as if he was just saying a statement, expecting her to agree or disagree.

"Well it must, if I get my figure back, and have as much to offer him as this teenager."

The counselor said nothing. So Bella went on, "I've decided I'm going to get as much money as I can from him, and the first thing I'm going to do is go to a health farm. I'll stay for three weeks, and then I'll be in such good shape that I'll be able for anything. I'm not going to take this sitting down. Some women would let themselves go completely, but I've learned my lesson. Once I'm two stone lighter, and can fit into size ten dresses again, there'll be no problem."

She felt a bit worried in case she had got the whole idea of counseling wrong, because he didn't seem to have much cheer for her, just a friendly handshake as she was leaving him, assuring him that once she was slim, everything would be as it always had been, a wonderful, close, good relationship, which was, after all, what Jim had promised when they were married in a church all those years ago.

Premonitions

Sara had always been what they called anxious. She jumped at the slightest sound. She hated having to read aloud in class, and she was always afraid that something awful would happen.

Mainly it didn't. But you couldn't explain that to Sara.

They could have been in the caravan that was blown off the cliff—all right, so they were not, but they could have been. So it was the same principle.

She worried about Nesbit, their dog, in case he might have rabies.

"Darling, he's just running around in circles. It's what puppies do," her mother said. But Sara was afraid that it was a mad thing to do and that Nesbit might have to be put down.

When Sara went to work in the bank she was always afraid there would be a raid and that men with machine guns would come in and ask them to lie on the floor. The others shrugged. So they would lie on the floor. There was a procedure for this, no one was to be heroic. But still she scanned the faces of perfectly innocent customers.

When she met Richard, who worked in an estate agency, he thought it was sweet that she was frightened of the world. "I'll always protect you, Sara," he would say, stroking her head.

The day they married, Sara was afraid that the wedding car would not turn up, that the vicar, who was somewhat red-faced, would have a seizure at the altar, that Richard's mother would get drunk, and that the guests would get food poisoning. None of these things happened, but the bridesmaid did twist her ankle by dancing too violently, so, as Sara said many, many times, you knew there would always be something.

In their new house she would start to

panic in case the deeds had not been properly drawn up, the roof adequately supported, the neighbors might be people on a witness protection scheme, and the whole area liable to be flooded at high tide. None of these fears was realized, but a car did crash on the corner and the learner driver was taken to hospital with whiplash, so, as Sara said over and over, you never know the day or the hour; there was always something.

And Richard was very eager to have a family immediately but Sara was worried about it. They were so young still and there was so much to be planned and thought out and got right before they thought of children. She also said that it was an increasingly violent world to bring children into.

Richard stroked her hair and said that it wasn't right to be so upset about things. Perhaps they might go to the doctor who could give her some medicine that would make her less anxious, or get her to see a counselor. He wasn't saying that he would protect her and keep her safe anymore—he was saying he had heard of this wonderful man or that wonderful woman.

Sara was very upset by it all. Richard thought she was mad. She was far from mad. She was sensitive, that was all. She could see things before they happened. What was the word?

Forebodings, was that it?

Richard didn't think so. Was it **present-iment**? he wondered. No, that wasn't exactly it either. They looked it up together in the dictionary and found **premonition.** Yes, that was the word. It meant when someone got a kind of warning ahead of time. Like a soothsayer maybe, or a fortune-teller, or someone very sensitive to the vibes around them.

Sara laughed, delighted with the word. And Richard suggested they go upstairs to bed.

But Sara said there was far too much to do.

What sorts of things?

Oh, like unplugging all the appliances in case of an electrical fire, checking the smoke alarms, patrolling the garden with Nesbit because there might be people watching the house and it was good to let them see that there was a big guard dog on the premises.

Richard said that Nesbit was such a fool of a dog he would welcome burglars in and lie down waiting for his tummy to be rubbed. Sara took no notice of this whatsoever. Instead, she reminded him that she had to check the house alarm in the kitchen: eighty percent of burglars came in the back door; you had to be prepared. So Richard went upstairs alone and was asleep when Sara came to bed. Something that happened more and more as the months went on.

And then Sara began to get premonitions about accidents that were going to happen to Richard on his way to work. One was very strong indeed. She could literally see the truck that mounted the pavement and killed Richard. She could hear the screams. So she telephoned him immediately. He was walking along the street near work with a colleague and had to go into a shop doorway to cope with her hysterical voice.

"Darling, you can't have these fantasies,

it's just not normal."

"Are you near the zebra crossing?" Sara cried.

"Yes, I'm looking at it, I'm about to cross it. Sara, this won't do. You can't go on like this…"

"Please don't cross it, Richard!" He hung up.

She rang his office ten minutes later, expecting to hear there had been a terrible accident. Instead they said they would put her through to Richard straightaway.

"No, Sara. Not now. We'll discuss it tonight. I am not going to live like this."

Sara staggered through her day at the bank. She called her mother and asked if she could meet her for lunch.

"Was there ever any madness in our family?" she asked.

"Not on my side," her mother said. "Though your father has a couple of dotty aunts. Why?"

"Richard thinks I'm going mad." Poor Sara told the whole story of the premonitions and how, in all honesty, she just could not let him walk to his doom.

"But it **wasn't** his doom," her mother

said.

"Well, that's because I altered what was about to happen. When I called, he had to stop and talk to me about it, you see."

"Yes," said Sara's mother doubtfully.

"So what should I say to him tonight?"

"Tell him that you are very sorry but it was only because you love him so much, then take him to bed and love him to bits. That usually sorts most things out."

So Sara did just that and the great row never occurred, and Richard seemed very pleased that marital relations had been restored again. Unfortunately he didn't realize that it was a one-off, and the next night he began to make signs that suggested he thought it was going to be a regular occurrence—but of course Sara had to check so many alarms, unplug so many appliances, and parade Nesbit that Richard was asleep when she got to bed.

She had two more premonitions, but instead of ringing Richard she telephoned her mother. One was that the ceiling was going to fall in the foyer of the estate agency; one was that he would get food poisoning from a salad. Neither of these things happened and her mother talked her down on both occasions.

Sara's mother had begun mentioning seeing a counselor who specialized in unreasonable fears. Sara pretended she hadn't heard. There was nothing wrong with her. She was just lucky that she had such sensitivity she got premonitions, that's all. And, all right, she wouldn't call Richard at work again. But everyone must back off trying to drag her to a shrink and make her take happy pills. She was fine.

And time passed. She had fortunately very few premonitions about the bank, which meant a fairly easy, uninterrupted working life; and only one or two about home, where she thought Nesbit might be nervous sleeping downstairs and brought him up to their bedroom, where he slept at the end of the bed and virtually put paid to any of the minimalist marital activity that had survived into the fourth year of their marriage.

Richard had stopped asking about starting a family. He was staying later at work, and they had very few friends and did little or no entertaining. Sara was usually too tired to go out anywhere, what with the ceaseless round of security duties and the statistics that most homes were robbed in the evening, when the owners had just gone down the road to the pub.

Most of Sara's friends had small babies now, and they would urge Sara and Richard to go the same route. Richard didn't bring anyone home from work anymore—Sara was too strange and uneasy. He sometimes talked about Ted and someone called Nell—when he was late home he had often had a pint with them, but there was no suggestion that they come back to Richard and Sara's for a meal.

And then one morning, right out of the blue, Sara got a premonition that Richard was going to go out and see a house with a client and the floor would collapse. She could see Richard falling and struggling to hold on and then the rest of the bricks and mortar collapsed on top of him, killing him.

Well, as Sara often said to people, what would you have done? It wasn't just that she thought such a thing could happen, she could actually **see** it.

Sara sat there in her bank, shaking all over. For the rest of her life she would live with the guilt that Richard went to his doom because she was too scared to speak up. Yet she knew that both Richard and her mother would have her in a funny farm if she dared to warn him. What a decision to make!

She sat for what seemed ages but was about half an hour, deciding between the two evils. If only she had a friend in Richard's office, someone she could confide in, someone who could help her. But he would just hate Sara to call Ted or Nell with what he said was one of her cracked ideas. So that wasn't on.

Unless.

Unless, of course, she called for some other reason—not the premonition. What would bring Richard running home? Suppose she was to tell him she might be pregnant? Later, of course, when the danger of the collapsing house was over, she could say it was a false alarm. But he had begged her not to ring him at work on any pretext. It always somehow turned into some alarmist issue.

So she had to ring one of his friends. She rang the estate agency and asked to be put through to Nell. It rang for a while and then she heard a voice saying, "Hold on, darling, I'll get rid of this. Yes? Hello, Nell speaking. Can I help you?"

Immediately Sara thought that this was very unprofessional. Imagine letting a client hear you say you were going to get rid of a call rather than dealing with it. Still, that wasn't important now.

"Oh, Nell, I'm Richard's wife, Sara. I wonder, can I have a word with you?"

Nell sounded very wary. "Um, about what?"

"Well, it's a bit complicated but you would be doing me and Richard a great favor if you were to ask him to come home straightaway. I'll meet him there."

"Oh, are you ill or something?" Sara thought that Nell sounded awkward, not friendly or helpful or anything.

"No, not ill, but I have some news for him."

"Couldn't it wait until this evening when

he'll be going home anyway?"

"No, it couldn't, actually."

"Oh."

"So will you ask him to do that then, Nell?"

"Why don't you call him and ask him yourself?"

"He doesn't like being telephoned at work."

"But if it's important…"

"Listen, Nell, I'm going to level with you. I think I'm pregnant. He will be so pleased and I just want to share the news with him immediately. Now!"

She ended in a bark of urgency.

"You think you are **what**?" Nell asked.

"Well, I can't be certain, but it looks very like it," Sara trilled.

And then Nell hung up. Or they were cut off. Hard to know which.

Sara telephoned the estate agency again and said that her call had been cut off. She was reconnected.

The phone was snatched up and thrown on a desk. Sara could hear Nell's voice saying that the damn phone was always ringing when you didn't need it. She was both crying and sniffing as she talked to some man. She had abandoned the phone completely.

Sara shouted "Hello? Hello?" but to no avail.

Nell was sobbing. "You told me that you haven't slept with her for over a year..."

"And it's true, darling Nell, it's true."

By the time that Nell said the name Richard, Sara already knew. Nell and Richard were having an affair. Those nights that he was late home had a reason. But as she always said later, let nobody tell her that she was wrong about premonitions. She knew something was going to happen that morning.

And, boy, wasn't she right.

Big Decisions in Brussels

She looked around happily and decided that the flight to Brussels was now becoming as routine a journey as the train in from Bray used to be. There were men reading files, men working with little calculators over columns of figures, men smiling and laughing with other men. The Common Market had taken away a lot of the excitement of travel. These men wouldn't become enthusiastic about foreign smells of good coffee and fresh-baked rolls, they wouldn't marvel any-more at the traffic being on the wrong side of the road, they wouldn't translate the signs triumphantly for each other. They all had opposite numbers who spoke perfect English, and secretaries who booked their rooms routinely, reminding them to keep the receipts for expenses.

They all seemed much more mature these days, Maura thought. She remembered that about ten years ago Irish businessmen would have laid into the gin and tonics on an early flight, delighted to have it offered to them, unwilling, almost unable, to pass up the chance of an airborne party. But this morning anyone she could see was having coffee. There would be a day's work ahead. And for her there was a difficult day ahead too. She had to be more watchful than ever before in her life. One slip could ruin everything. One little thoughtless reaction and everything Auntie Nell had taught her would be useless. She would never be able to look Nell in the eye unless everything went according to the master plan. Nell didn't accept that people forgot, or were tired, or didn't think. Nell thought that losers deserved to lose. She was very absolute about that.

Aunt Nell had insisted she go to Brussels with him. She had said that there was no other course. To refuse would be childish and petty; it would be playing into the hands of the enemy. Maura must be very enthusiastic about the trip, get herself a new outfit and tell all her friends that she was going. She must keep questioning Dan about the places that they would see. Above all, she must appear to suspect nothing.

It was hard to feign enthusiasm for a trip that she knew was a journey to say good-bye. It was very hard to pretend an eagerness to see a city that she knew would be the one where her husband would tell her he was leaving her. It was almost impossible to sit beside Dan now, after eighteen years of marriage, and watch him read **The Irish Times** with a calm, untroubled face when she knew that he was going to tell her that he wanted to leave her. She knew that he would take the job in America and she knew that he would take that Deirdre with him.

Nell had always advised her to read his letters and to go through his pockets.

"He's too good-looking for you, that Dan. If you must have him, and it appears you must, then be prepared, be a jump ahead.

Know your problems before they become too hard to solve." It had always seemed shabby and dishonest to Maura to spy on someone you loved, but she had to agree that, forearmed, she was able to make a much better fist of things than she would have done with no warning. She had been able to head off some mild flirtations in the past by arranging for the family to be doing something else when a little adventure was looming. The little adventures had fizzled out. Nell was invaluable on such occasions. Nell was wealthy and Dan liked to go and stay in her big country house. Whenever Maura needed help to distract him from a dalliance, Nell obliged by providing people who would be useful in his career. She had always been a prop like this for Maura, and it was agreed that it would be their secret till death. No letters were ever written between them.

"Why do I ask your advice like a silly schoolgirl?" Maura had wondered last week as she strolled with Nell around the orchard, picking windfalls.

"Why do I want to play God with you?" asked Nell.

"You're always right, that's what's so hard to understand. You don't make any of the mistakes that I do," grumbled Maura.

"I made them twenty years ago. That's why I like to steer you through the minefield." Nell had ended the conversation abruptly. Nothing of her own mysterious and rather scandalous liaison way back in the 1940s was ever discussed. She had married dull, wealthy Edward, who adored her. She was over fifty but she could be any age; she had charm and confidence. Everyone except Maura presumed that she was extremely happy.

Nell said that the trip to Brussels was Maura's last chance. If she played it properly she would win. Nell knew Brussels as well as she knew everywhere else. Every little street off the Boulevard Adolphe Max she seemed to have toured in her time. Romantic restaurants, big markets, quaint chiming clocks…anything that two people in love could need, Nell knew it.

"But we aren't two people in love," complained Maura with the hint of tears. "We're one person in love and the other gritting his teeth and girding himself and getting ready to tell me he's off."

Nell was impatient. "I'm surprised he hasn't gone already if that's your attitude," she said sternly. "You must make this trip what he has lyingly said he wants it to be, a chance to talk. Remember Scheherazade."

"What did she do? I forget," Maura said wretchedly.

"She talked," said Nell. "And by talking she put off the evil hour."

The plan was that Maura would talk. As they strolled around the lakes of Ixelles, Maura was to speak gently and happily about the future. She was to say that he should take the job in America. She was to say that she and the twins would not come out yet, not for six months anyway, and then only for a visit. This was so that he could concentrate on the job without the additional worries of settling in a family as well. He would be confused by this, because it was not in his plans. Thinking on his feet, he might seize the opportunity —in fact, the odds were that he would. After all, it offered him the best of both worlds. He could have his Deirdre and his

New York job with no confrontation, no accusations, heartbreaks, and recriminations. What man would be able to say no?

But then Deirdre would be outraged. After all, she had been urging him for months to tell his wife of their plans. Once Dan had postponed the great telling again, their relationship was bound to suffer. In New York she would feel shabby and second best, hidden and with no status—just as she was now. Their relationship would probably wither.

Maura wasn't so sure. It had been going on for ten months—that was about eight months longer than any previous flutter.

"Well," said Nell, "I did offer to kill her. Run her down accidentally with my car. I am getting shortsighted. No one could accuse me of doing it deliberately. I don't even know her." Maura's hand had flown to her throat in terror. Nell sounded so matter-of-fact. She actually meant it!

"But there is the danger that I might just wound her, and that might be worse than ever. She'd be a bloody martyr," Nell said, abandoning the scheme to Maura's great relief.

Dan knew quite a few people on the plane. "Nice to be able to bring the spouse, if it is the spouse," said a man jovially. "Of course it's the spouse," said Dan, annoyed. "I'm very flattered at being thought a bit more exciting," Maura said, laughing, and the moment passed.

They went in on the train, a journey so quick that Maura could barely believe they had arrived in the city. Nell had told her not to keep making provincial statements, so she bit back her comments on how long would it be before Dublin ever had such a system, and her views on a colleague of Dan's who always took a taxi, which was about ten times the cost and four times as lengthy. Instead she laughed like a girl and told Dan a funny story about the first time she had ever been on the Continent, when the school had taken them on a trip to Rome. It made him laugh, and she hoped that somewhere Nell would hear that laugh and congratulate her.

Dan's meeting included lunch and the afternoon. She had a million things to see, she said, and a guidebook and flat shoes. She would tour and sightsee, and when he came back they would have a bath and a drink and go out to dinner. She kissed him good-bye lightly and wondered why people didn't nominate her for an Oscar.

She didn't do any sightseeing. She went to the Church of St. Nicholas and tried to pray. Often God listened and understood. She didn't burden him with too many of the details since she presumed he knew them already. But today he didn't want to know. When she heard herself telling God that she needed his strength and help to preserve their marriage, a good Christian marriage, she realized she was being hypocritical.

"All right, God," she said. "All right. There's no point trying to fool you, any more than Nell. I want you to use every bit of pull to get him back for me. I can't see a life without Dan. Please can I have him back? Please? I never did much bad, except read his letters and tell a few lies."

She saw people lighting candles, and remembered that Nell had told her this was a church where young ballerinas, or would-be ballet stars, came to pray to St. Nicholas so that they would get a good part. It seemed utterly ridiculous of them, she thought impatiently, and smiled to herself when she realized what they would think of her.

That night they walked around the Grand Place, all lighting and fairy tale like the postcards he had sent home so regularly. He was tired; his meeting had been difficult. Everything was fine until the Italian had disagreed, then he had agreed, and just as it all settled the British viewpoint was reexamined. When that had been smoothed down the German had become apoplectic. Maura laughed at his descriptions: she knew what he was talking about. Since she discovered that Deirdre shared an interest in his work she had made herself very well up in all that happened. They had an unaccustomed after-dinner brandy and a stroll to the hotel. He seemed to think she expected him to make love to her. She took that decision away from him too. "Tomorrow," she said, and kissed him gently. She heard a

Brussels clock chime away the night.

Dan's meeting the next day was an all-day affair. They would finish in time for the suitable trains and planes back to the other countries in the Community. Everyone on this particular committee would go home to some kind of lifestyle. Dan would stay in Brussels and tell his wife he was leaving her. Maura looked at him and wondered how he could sleep.

Nell said she should go to see some of the war graves when she was in Belgium, it might put her own troubles into perspective, but Maura thought it might depress her too much. She went to Waterloo instead. She didn't know anyone whose grandfather had been killed there. It was easy to get there—she went on a local bus—and sat on the edge of the Lion's Mound and tried to reconstruct it all with maps and guidebooks, but suddenly it seemed too sad, and such a ridiculous waste for all those boys to come from different lands and homes to be cut to bits here that she cried, and cried, until the careful makeup which was meant to make her thirty-nine-year-old face look better than Deirdre's twenty-five-year-old one went into funny clown-like lines.

She didn't even bother to wipe them away as she sat on the bus back to Brussels, and she heard a father tell his sons that Waterloo wasn't the last battle in the world, that tomorrow they would go to see Ypres and Passchendaele and realize that battles went on forever. And very simply she realized that he was right, battles did. After she had won the American battle there would be another and another. Did anyone have that amount of energy? Certainly Nell didn't. Otherwise why had she married nice, dull, safe Edward?

Maura went back to the hotel and washed her face. She sat and waited peacefully in their hotel bedroom. That would make it easier, nobody to witness the scene.

And when Dan came in the door, she poured him a drink from their bottle of duty free and asked him had he anything special that he wanted to say to her.

The Custardy Case

Bernard knew there was something special about his seventh birthday, because they seemed to be talking about it all the time at home. Mother and Father were very busy, always rushing in and out shouting to each other about it. There hadn't been as much fuss since last Christmas with all the comings and goings and doors banging and not knowing where anyone was going to be.

His birthday appeared to be causing even more drama. Every time he came into a room people stopped talking. His grannie, or his auntie Helen, or Daddy's friend from the office, the very fat lady Katy, also came to see them sometimes. And Mother must be working very hard because Grannie and Auntie Helen kept telling her she was wonderful to be able to give a children's party in the middle of everything, and then at different times Katy would put her arm around him and say that he was a lucky boy because so many people loved him. Father didn't say much because he was very busy and not home a lot. Sometimes he had to sleep at the office, he worked so hard.

Bernard had asked Katy did she have to sleep at the office too. For some reason everyone went very silent when he said this. They had looked at each other as if trying to guess the answer. Mother had come to the rescue.

"Not anymore, no need for that anymore," Mother had said.

Father had got into a mood then, and had said that this was about as low as they had got, and that for everyone's sake he had to hope that there was no lower to go.

The birthday party tea was going to be at McDonald's, like everyone else at school did for their birthdays, so he didn't know why they kept talking about the menu. At Gerald's party his mother had taken down a list of what everyone wanted in advance and someone had driven ahead to order it. But that was all. In Bernard's home they kept talking about the food. He couldn't count the number of times he had heard them talking about the custardy case. It must be a new kind of pudding, and a huge secret. Because nobody mentioned the custardy case when he was there, it was only on the phone or when they didn't realize he was in earshot. It must be a difficult pudding because Auntie Helen was saying that there was no knowing which way it would go, and Grannie was saying that these things were usually cut and dried, which sounded awful, but Mother was saying that there was nothing cut and dried about it at all.

Nobody spoke about the custardy case in front of Father or Katy. Maybe it was a surprise for them too.

Bernard liked Katy, even if she waddled a lot. She had a lovely smile and she was interested in his school report and the sports he played. She said she loved the high jump herself. Bernard thought that she was probably far too fat to jump even three inches above the ground but didn't say anything of the sort. He nodded sagely as she told him about her school and how they had once put on a gymnastic display.

"Katy's good at the high jump," he told Mother and Auntie Helen.

"You can say that again," Auntie Helen said grimly.

"Shush," Mother said warningly.

He went out for walks with Father and Katy on Sundays; Mother never wanted to come, but Katy wasn't a bit insulted.

"Your mother has to work very hard, even on Sundays," she explained. Mother showed people houses for an estate agency. Sometimes couples wanted to see a place on weekends. It was the only time they had free. For as long as he could remember, Mother had to jump up suddenly when the phone rang.

"And don't you have to work anymore?"

Bernard couldn't quite understand: if Katy had been a friend of Father's in the office, why did she not go there anymore? It was no use asking Mother about it after all that strange fuss when he had wondered about Katy sleeping in the office. He thought it better to ask her directly.

Katy didn't seem a bit upset. They were walking together. Father had gone off to get ice cream.

"No, I'm having a baby, you see; it's in here." She held Bernard's hand to her stomach. "So I can't really go to work anymore. It wouldn't be fair."

"Why wouldn't it be fair?"

"On the baby, and on everyone else."

"When will it come out?" He looked at Katy fearfully.

"In about two weeks' time."

"After my birthday!" Bernard was pleased that none of this would interfere with the celebrations. He was going to ask Katy about this case of custard pudding that Mother, Grannie, and Auntie Helen were all so het up about. But he didn't. If it was meant to be a surprise then he had better let it be a surprise for him.

Father came back with the three cones.

"Katy's having a baby," Bernard told him, thinking, Father would be pleased and interested at this news.

"I know," Father said in a strange voice.

It sounded as if it was the most extraordinary thing in the world instead of something anyone could do. Harriet, the cat, had had four babies last month and the hamsters at school were always having them.

"Could we have a baby at home, do you think?" he asked Father. There was another of those silences. Bernard was beginning to find them very irritating. What could be wrong with people when you asked perfectly ordinary questions? Why did they suddenly get struck dumb?

At school the next day Bernard told Gerald that Katy was going to have a baby in two weeks. It was nearly ready, but not quite. "Will it be like a brother for you?" Gerald asked. Bernard was puzzled. How could it be like a brother when it was belonging to Katy from the office? He did what he did when he didn't understand things. He gave Gerald a punch in the arm and Gerald gave him a wallop back and soon they were rolling about on the playground.

Miss Hayes separated them. "What was

that about?" she asked. Bernard and Gerald looked at her blankly. They couldn't remember. Miss Hayes believed them. Children often belted each other for no reason. She would have forgotten it if Bernard's mother hadn't called in at lunchtime and asked was everything all right with her son. Miss Hayes mentioned the unexpected fight and almost immediately regretted it when she saw the woman's face.

Bernard was pleased to see his mother coming to collect him at home time.

"Can we bring Gerald for an ice cream?" he asked.

"I thought you and Gerald were fighting like tinkers?" Mother said. Bernard sighed; you couldn't do much without it getting home.

"That was nothing," he muttered.

"Why did he hit you?" Mother wouldn't have dreamed that Bernard was the aggressor. But Bernard had a very strong sense of justice.

"I sort of hit him first. He said I was having a brother—or something like that."

Mother looked very upset. She was biting

her lip. Bernard wanted to reassure her, let her know that he had sorted it out.

"It's all right. I told him it was Katy that was having the baby, not you." He expected her to be pleased at his grasp of events and his swift action in thumping anyone who got them wrong. To his horror, right there in full view of the school, Mother knelt and pulled him to her in a terrible bearlike hug.

"I love you so much, Bernard, don't ever forget that. You're the dearest, best boy in the whole world." He knew she was crying.

Bernard wriggled, trying to escape, because all kinds of people were looking at them. He beat on Mother's shoulders with his free fists, begging her to let him go.

When she loosened her arms from around him, he ran off as fast as he could.

He saw Mother standing looking after him but he didn't care. He had to be away from all the people who would laugh at a boy of nearly seven being hugged by a mother kneeling on the road. It was the worst thing that had ever happened to him in his whole life.

When he got home Father was there, which was nice. Father was hardly ever home at this time of the day. Bernard was pleased when he saw the car outside the door and ran in shouting for him.

Grannie and Auntie Helen were sitting in the kitchen, but Father was upstairs.

There were three suitcases open on the bed. Father was packing, suits and clothes.

Bernard's face lit up.

"Are we going on our holiday?" he cried out excitedly.

Father looked very annoyed to see him.

"Your mother **said** she was picking you up from school. She couldn't even bloody do that. She couldn't keep her word."

Bernard hated when Father and Mother said bad things about each other. He was going to explain that Mother had been there, but he was too interested in the suitcases.

"Where are we going? Where, Father? Please tell me!"

Father sat down on the bed. He looked old and sad suddenly. "Bernard, you weren't meant to be here, you were meant to be out for all of this."

This whole business about surprises was getting very hard to handle. There was the cake at McDonald's, there was this holiday...Bernard wished that people would let him in on things, let him look forward to it, tell people at school about what was happening.

He looked at the cases on the bed. These were the big ones; the ones they had taken to Spain and down to Kerry, and they only came out of the attic when it was time to go on a holiday.

"Will I go and pack too, Father?" he asked, hoping that this was the right thing to suggest. Father's face looked a bit gray. Maybe he just needed to be left on his own for a bit. To Bernard's utter horror, Father suddenly grabbed him in exactly the same awful hug that Mother had.

"Oh, Bernard, I wouldn't have had this happen for the world," he said into Bernard's hair. And Bernard tried to fight the thought but he really believed that Father was crying too. He escaped just as he had done from Mother and got to his own room.

Bernard had got an early birthday present

from Katy. It was a Super Walkman, and a little plastic rack for holding story tapes. Katy had said that it could be nailed up on a wall wherever he was and that he would always have his tapes near him and he could listen to them whenever he wanted to. Bernard had explained that Mother had said things shouldn't be nailed on the wall but he'd put it beside the bed and it kept falling over. He wished Mother hadn't said that about not nailing it to the wall, as Katy had said, what were old walls for anyway except to put things on?

He listened to his tapes, and wondered about the holiday and where it would be, and whether Katy would come too, and would the baby be ready while they were on holiday, and would Miss Hayes mind, and would they come back in time for the birthday?

He lay on his bed with his eyes closed and he thought he heard Grannie and Auntie Helen come in and go out, and he heard Mother's voice, but it was arguing with Father's, so he turned up the volume, and since it was only in his own ears, nobody else could get annoyed by it and come and tell him to turn it down. Sometimes, when he was changing the tapes, he heard Mother crying and Father shouting, and though he could hardly believe it, they were all still talking about the party and the pudding and who was going to order it or collect it or get it.

Mother was saying that a man never got custardy, never in the history of the whole thing. Father was saying it wasn't a man; it was a ready-made family; it was people who would stay at home all day and mind children, not gallivanting off with every Tom, Dick, and Harry who waltzed into an estate agency for an outing.

Mother was saying that some of the judges were women nowadays; they weren't medieval anymore, they knew a woman could work and mind a child.

Father said judges were judges whatever sex they were. They could see where the advantage lay. They weren't fools. Bernard now saw that there was going to be some kind of competition, a cookery competition involved about the custard puddings. Everything pointed to it, there could be no other explanation.

He went into the room, where the suitcases were on the floor and where Mother and Father were both crosser than he had ever seen them in their lives.

"I don't mind about the pudding," Bernard said with the air of a man who had solved it all. "Let's have no pudding, no custardy case at all."

They stood looking at him, and it was like a freeze-frame on the video when you pressed the pause button.

He knew that none of them would ever forget this minute but he had no idea why.

It kept coming back to him in the days that followed, the days when everyone seemed to have stopped talking like they used to talk. There had been no holiday; of course that was a false alarm. And there had been no custardy pudding on his birthday at McDonald's, but nobody thanked him for his solution to that one. And Katy's baby got ready and came out and was a girl, and Father was very pleased, and said he'd better stay with Katy a lot more to look after things because he wasn't able to stay in the old place anymore. He never called it home; he always called it the old place.

And there were all the conversations with other people who were called lawyers and Mother got more and more tired because she had to work so hard and Auntie Helen and Grannie got very cross and snapped the nose off everyone.

And Bernard still remembered the freeze-frame feeling on the day that he went to court and the judge said he wanted to see him in his chambers. Bernard knew that chambers didn't mean what you thought it would mean, but he didn't know it was going to be an ordinary room.

And the judge was nice. Bernard told him all about Mother having to work so hard and never being at home, and how hard it was to talk to Mother because of Grannie and Auntie Helen being there and being so cross. The judge seemed to know that kind of thing, and he was very interested when Bernard explained about not being able to nail things on the wall, and Mother kneeling down and crying outside the school. The judge asked about Katy, and Bernard said that it was amazing how thin she had got when the baby was ready and came out, and Katy often said that he, Bernard, was a lucky boy because so many people in the world loved him.

And no, Katy had never said a word against Mother. She had said that Mother was terrific but worked too hard, and was never there when you were looking for her, which Bernard, struggling to be fair, said was true.

And afterwards there was a lot of noise outside, and Grannie and Auntie Helen were saying terrible things to Katy and Father. Mother was very quiet and said nothing. Katy said that she had invited Bernard's friend, Gerald, to come and stay for a few days, and she had put up lots of shelves and racks for them on the wall.

Bernard couldn't understand why they seemed to think he wasn't going home. He must be going to stay with Katy and Father and the new baby girl. He didn't know when that had been arranged but it all seemed settled. He didn't know how long the visit would be for, but he thought it better not to ask.

Then Mother said she'd come to see

Bernard on Saturday. About eleven o'clock, and they'd go somewhere nice. Mother's eyes looked very strange, as if there was no light in them anymore.

She hardly waved when he got into the car with Father and Katy. She just kept looking in front of her as if she didn't see anything at all.

Relatives and Other Strangers

Be Prepared

It was to be their last Christmas as a family, all of them together. Next year, Sean would be married, Kitty would be in Australia, and it would only be the two of them, and Martin. So Nora decided that it would be something really special, something they would remember when Kitty was drinking beer from a can on Bondi Beach and Sean was dealing with his prissy in-laws. There was even an unworthy part of Nora that made her want this Christmas to be so good that they would remember it with longing for the rest of their lives and regret ever leaving the nest.

Everything she read in the papers said it was all about being prepared—buying the cooking foil in September, writing the

Christmas cards in October, testing the lights for the tree, measuring the oven, cleaning out the freezer in November—all of it very admirable, and particularly for a couple as busy as Nora and Frank. She was very pleased with her progress; she had even booked the window cleaners and arranged for a neighbor's child to bring her a ton of holly and ivy. And then she got the news that Girlie was coming for Christmas.

Girlie was Frank's aunt. **Eccentric** was the kindest word you could find for her. Somewhere in her late sixties, maybe older; always vague about details like that, always diamond-sharp at remembering the things you wanted forgotten.

Girlie was based, loosely speaking, in New York. She was mainly to be found traveling the world on the decks of expensive oceangoing liners. She would send irascible postcards from Fiji or Bali, complaining that the food on board was inedible or was so good that everyone had put on twenty pounds since embarkation. Nothing anywhere ever seemed to be right or good.

Yet Girlie, whose late husband had left her a staggering insurance policy, sometimes saved everyone's lives. She sent them money just when they needed it for Sean's and Kitty's school fees. She also sent a lecture about the appalling results of the Irish educational system that she saw all over the world, results that made her despair of the nation. She sent Sean a deposit for his house and Kitty a ticket to Australia that allowed her a few stop-offs so that she might see a bit of the world before she went to that god-awful place. Girlie disliked Australia as much as Ireland and the United States and, in fact, everywhere she had ever been.

Martin wondered if she had forgotten about him. Nothing seemed to be rolling his way from Girlie. But then he was only fourteen, the others told him; his needs had not become significant. Martin felt his needs were very significant indeed, and he certainly wouldn't waste his money on getting a horrible little box of a house and marrying some awful prissy girl like Lucy, as his brother, Sean, was doing, and he wouldn't go the whole way to Australia to be free, like Kitty was doing. You could be free anywhere if you had a good bicycle and a tent and were allowed to stay out all night in summer. But Girlie hadn't seemed to understand this, even though he had written it cunningly to her in many different ways.

Frank said it was preposterous; this woman always laid down the law and she shouldn't get away with it. How dare she impose on them, this, their last family Christmas? She was his father's totally loopy sister who had cut off all connection with the family years ago and just communicated in barking postcards and air letters ever since.

"And very generous checks," Nora reminded him.

Frank wasn't convinced. She only did what she wanted to do and people couldn't buy affection; he was very muttery and growly about it. But Nora was adamant. Girlie had never asked for anything before; this year, it would suit her to come to Ireland and be with family. It was the least they could do.

Frank said that not only could she afford

to stay in the Shelbourne, she could afford to **buy** the Shelbourne—but that didn't seem to be the point. She was going to come in the middle of November and leave before the new year.

The family met the news with characteristic rage. Kitty said that she was not going to give up her room; no way was she having that old bat living in there and poking around among her things. Her room was sacred; it had been hers for twenty years. Nora thought grimly about how eager Kitty was to abandon this room in order to go to uncharted lands in Australia but said nothing.

Sean said it wasn't fair for him to be asked to give up his room; he had so much to do, he was at a hugely important, stressful period of his life. He couldn't let this mad aunt come and take up his space.

Nora did not mention that it would be difficult for Sean to bring Lucy in for the night so often if he had to sleep in the box room on the camp bed. Lucy didn't stay for breakfast and there was a family fiction that she wasn't there at all—which covered everyone's honor and allowed Nora to meet Lucy's mother's eye with something like equanimity.

Martin said glumly: "I suppose it has got to be me."

"We'll get you the bicycle," said his father in gratitude.

"And can I sleep out in the Wicklow Mountains and by the side of a lake in Cavan, when it's summer?" he asked.

"We'll see," said his mother.

"That means no," said Martin, who was a realist. "What's she coming for anyway?" he grumbled. "Is she dying or something?"

The others, too caught up in their own lives, had never asked.

"God, I hope not," said Frank. "Not here anyway."

"Not before the wedding," said Sean.

"I couldn't put off going to Australia for her funeral; I don't even know her," said Kitty.

"We don't even know if there's anything at all wrong with her," said Nora, alarmed that the family had the woman buried before she arrived. But to herself she wondered long and without any resolution what made this aficionado of all the cruise ships of the world come to a suburban house in Dublin for Christmas—and not for a traditional four or five days but for four or five **weeks.**

Girlie did not want to be met at the airport; she had arranged her own limousine. Nora and Frank wouldn't have known where you found a limousine, but Girlie in America had no such problems.

She had discussed the upcoming referendum on divorce with the driver and arrived at the house well versed in the arguments for each side. Barely were the greetings over when she asked if she might be told whether she was staying in a Yes or a No household. They looked at her, a small, plump, overmade-up woman who could be any age between fifty and eighty. They raked her face, with its lines and its heavy-duty eyeliner. Which way would she swing? It was impossible to tell. So, reluctantly they told her the truth, which was that she had hit a family of two Yeses and two Nos. Nora was a Yes because of all the women she met at work who should have had a second chance; Frank was a No because he felt that society followed the law and that the place would be like California in a matter of months. Sean was a No because he and Lucy were taking vows for life and not just until they had a falling-out; Kitty was a Yes because she wanted freedom. Martin wouldn't have a vote for another four years.

Girlie asked Martin which way he would vote if he had one. Her small eyes had got piggy: he sensed a fight coming, whatever he said.

Martin was depressed by the whole thing: his poky bedroom, his clothes hanging on a rail borrowed from a shop, the roster of duties his mother had put up in the kitchen as part of Being Prepared.

"If I'm not old enough to have a vote and to stay out on a summer night in a tent, then I'm not old enough to have any kind of an opinion at all," he said. And he imagined that she looked at him with some sort of respect, which was very different from the glares he was getting from the rest of the family, who had recognized the mutinous rudeness in his tone.

She was, at the same time, much easier and much more difficult as a guest than they had thought. For one thing, she asked for an electric kettle and toaster in her bedroom and did not appear before lunch. This was a huge relief. She had retained the services of the limousine and went on outings on which she disapproved of everything that she saw. St. Kevin was barking mad, a basket case, she said when she came back from Glendalough— but then, if you thought that it might be safe to criticize the Church on anything religious, you would be wrong. There was a conspiracy against all these unfortunate priests; none of them had ever done anything untoward; it was a plot to discredit them, that was all.

One day Ireland was a pathetic backwater, the next day it was a society based on worshiping money and more affluent than most of the EU, from which it was demanding hardship money. One shopping day the place was gross with its conspicuous spending, the next day it was like a Soviet supply hall in the worst years of the Cold War.

"She's not very sane, is she?" Frank whispered apologetically to Nora in bed.

"She's not consistent, certainly," Nora agreed.

Frank had always been kind to her relatives; she would put up with this disagreeable and unpredictable woman for a few short weeks. It was, however, making her plans to Be Prepared much more difficult. Who could Be Prepared when you had Girlie in the house? She had brought the limousine driver in last night and they had eaten all the brandy snaps that Nora had stored lovingly in a tin.

Girlie would, of course, buy something unexpected and generous herself in turn. A fleet of Chinese waiters came up and set out an elaborate banquet for them on a night that Nora had been going to serve an Irish stew. Nora and Frank didn't know you could do this sort of thing in Dublin. Girlie knew everything and enjoyed remarkably little.

Martin saw more of her than the others. Sean was out with Lucy's family discussing the calligraphy on the wedding invitations; Kitty was with her friends arranging to meet them in Manly, or Randwick, or Kings Cross and all talking as if they knew Sydney intimately.

Nora and Frank were at their work until late in the evening.

"What are all these lists?" Girlie asked Martin once, looking at a roster in the kitchen.

"It's the nights we each do the washing-up," Martin explained.

Girlie took a ruler and made a few measurements. In minutes she had the right man in the right electrical store. It was never clear what she promised or gave, but he sent carpenters up to the house and the dishwasher was operational that evening.

Everyone said they were delighted. But in fact Sean felt inadequate now because Lucy admired it so inordinately and he would never be able to afford one. Kitty thought they were all mad to be tied to possessions when everyone should be free. Frank was sad because that had been his Christmas surprise; he had ordered a much cheaper version and now he had to cancel it. And Nora was sorry because she knew all about the secret and wanted Frank to have the pleasure of giving it to the family.

But they were all grateful for the thought and the speed and the gesture and they warmed towards Girlie until she said that it was a relief to have one in the house because this way you really **knew** that the cups and glasses were clean.

And the referendum came and went, and when she was with Frank and Sean, Girlie said that they were typical men trying to hold back society and ride roughshod over women. And when she was with Nora and Kitty she said that they were selfish women advancing a world where no one would care about the young.

To those who thought that the visit of President Clinton was overhyped, she said they should be goddamn grateful that the good old U.S. of A. was going to rescue them from their silly bickerings; to those who praised the trip, she said they were easily swayed by a vote-catching exercise. She took to reading the letters column in **The Irish Times** and would praise the side that appeared to have less support.

About herself and her lifestyle, she

revealed little. No amount of polite questioning about her late and extremely provident husband yielded anything.

"He was a man," she would say, and the family, feeling they sensed a less-than-joyful marriage, tactfully asked no more. Girlie, however, had no such tact and reserve. She would ask the very questions that everyone had been skirting around. Like asking Sean: "Are your in-laws putting too much pressure on you over this wedding? Why are you going along with it? Are you afraid of Lucy?"

Or Kitty: "Aren't you only going to Australia on this open ticket because everyone else is? You really want to go for three months and then come back and settle down."

Or to Nora: "Your job sounds terrible. Don't tell me you're getting any satisfaction out of it. You're only doing it to keep up the mortgage on this place, aren't you?"

And to Frank: "You're your father's son, Frank, that's for certain. He could never make a decision to save his life. You'd love a smaller place entirely but you have some notion that everyone wants this pile of red brick and that you owe it to them, and so you frown and wince over bills and estimates. I see you; you can't hide anything from Girlie."

By the Friday before Christmas, Girlie had the household near a collective nervous breakdown. Only Martin remained outside her influence.

"Why aren't you sulking and flouncing with me the way everyone else is?" Girlie said to him as she left the house to get into her limousine as usual.

"You haven't annoyed me like you've annoyed all of them," he said simply.

"Do you want to come out for a drive with me?"

"No thank you."

"Please?"

"No thank you, Girlie. I don't like shopping, I don't have any money left, I don't want you to give me money, and I won't tell you things about myself that will make you know what's wrong and then torture me like you do the others."

"I don't go shopping," she said. "Come on."

Martin got into the car and they drove

out to Wicklow Gap. As soon as they were miles from anywhere, the car stopped and the driver brought them white linen napkins, a box of smoked salmon sandwiches, and a bottle of wine.

"I don't drink," he said.

"You do today," said Girlie.

"Why did they call you Girlie?"

"I was the only girl in a family of six: they weren't very bright," she said.

"Why are you so awful to them all? They're doing their best to give you a happy Christmas."

"What I'm saying is true. **You** know that, don't you?"

"It might be," he agreed.

"Well, don't you hate poisonous little Lucy? Sean's much too good for her, and Kitty is as nervous as a cat about seeing the world, and your mother hates that damn job, and your father's in a state of panic about the new roof he thinks the place needs."

"Well, why don't you give them money then? You've got lots of it."

"Money wouldn't solve their problems, it has never solved a problem." Girlie spoke very definitely.

"That's easy to say when you have it." Martin was brave.

"No, it's true: if I gave Sean money he'd buy that horrible prissy little thing an even bigger ring, and Kitty would have to see the Kalahari Desert as well as the Outback when all she wants to do is to have a laugh with her friends in the sun. Your father would get the roof done and worry about something else; your mother would give up work and feel guilty and beholden to me. Much better make them see what's wrong. What do you worry about, Martin?"

"I won't tell you."

"Why not? I have been utterly honest with you."

"Okay, but you've got to answer a few questions first."

"Shoot."

He paused. Should he ask her about her husband? The one who left her all the money? Should he ask about how much she had left? Why she had come to visit them?

"Are you dying of something?" he asked

suddenly, surprising himself.

"Yes," she said.

Wicklow Gap looked beautiful as it always did. But, of course, he had never seen it from a heated limousine eating smoked salmon sandwiches and drinking white wine, and he never would again.

"I'm sorry," he said.

"Sure," said Girlie. "Now tell me what's worrying you."

He told her that next summer he would be fifteen and they wouldn't let him have a tent and come out to places like this and spend the night under the stars. They were afraid he'd get murdered or rheumatism or something. She listened with interest and without comment. Then she gave back the glasses and the box of crumbs to the chauffeur and they drove to the shop in Dublin that sold the most expensive kind of tent in the world.

"They'll kill me for getting you on my side," he said.

"I was always on your side," said Girlie. She didn't need to tell him not to talk about their conversation. Some things never need to be said.

It was a very strange Christmas. Nora said to Frank that a lot of this stuff about Being Prepared was for the birds. Look at all the great things that had turned out this year when they couldn't have prepared for any of them.

They had decided to put the house on the market. Sean and Lucy had postponed their wedding indefinitely. Kitty said she'd be back from Australia at Easter.

And Martin, he had been a positive saint with that dreadful old Girlie, who had bought him an entirely inappropriate tent and said what did it matter if he got pneumonia from sleeping out-of-doors, weren't there antibiotics for it nowadays? Which was actually true when you came to think of it.

"Do you think she liked it here? She's as odd as two left shoes," Frank said.

"I think she liked it too much. We should be prepared—she may well come again next year," Nora said.

And Martin just looked out the window into the garden and said nothing at all.

A Result

I knew that I could never marry George the day I found out he took little packets of sugar and sauce from restaurants to put in the store cupboard at home. He said they were ideal for picnics. I said, We don't go on picnics. He said that small economies like this amounted to huge profit in the years to come. Then he folded four paper napkins and put them into his briefcase and I knew I could not spend any time married to this man.

Sadly, it was the day before our wedding.

And also I was, though nobody else knew this, two months pregnant.

So this was a bit of a problem, but not as much a problem as marrying someone who was already building up a serious collection of marmalade portions. It was a nightmare, of course. My parents were very insistent that I should know all about the nonrefundable deposits on the hotel, the number of wedding outfits that had been bought, the people who had traveled long distances. They reminded me, as if I needed to be reminded, that I was their only child. And that the gifts would have to be returned, and a huge amount of gossip would result from it.

George tried to tell me I was having a nervous breakdown, common before weddings, he believed, and that it would all look very poorly in his office, where his chances of promotion might be adversely affected.

At no stage did he say he loved me and couldn't live without me.

At no time did my parents say they wanted me to do whatever would make me happy.

It was forty-eight hours I would never want to live through again, and relationships with everyone were severely damaged. Except, of course, with Eve, my unborn daughter, who did not know what was going on.

By the time she was born I had moved to another town far away. I returned all the gifts, wrote twenty-seven letters of apology, and tried to tell my speechless parents that we had all done the right thing. Then I left home two days after the canceled wedding. I told nobody that I was pregnant. I got one job as a hotel receptionist from eight to four every day, another teaching Internet for Beginners from five to seven, and I minded people's babies from seven thirty to midnight. I wrote a letter to my mother each week, giving her very little real information but keeping channels open. After all, they would be grandparents and I didn't want to spring that completely out of the blue. But they must never know the truth.

And George must never know that the child was his. That would never do: he would be back in my life with free samples of baby biscuits or disposable nappies.

So I wrote to my parents saying that I had been in a relationship which was now over and that I was delighted that I was going to have a child. They wrote back, totally bewildered, and said that if they lived to be one hundred years old they would never understand me.

My mother said that if I wanted her there for the birth she would come. I did want her, badly, but then she would know how old Eve was and that George was the father, and they must never suspect this.

I knew that the moment they held Eve in their arms it would be all right, so I waited until she was four months old, then I turned up on their doorstep and put her straight into their arms. And of course they loved her at once and they stopped trying to understand me and tried to understand her instead.

They were absolutely wonderful grand-parents, and we moved nearer to their home so that they could see more of little Eve. I had got into the habit of working very hard, so I sort of thought three jobs were the norm, and every year I took my mother and father and Eve on a holiday abroad. Our albums show us all in Italy, Spain, and Greece.

Perfect family, happy little girl, secure and loved. Eve was great at school too.

Glowing school reports, in the top of her class, enthusiastic, lots of friends. Sometimes, not very often but sometimes, I felt guilty about George. He was the child's father, after all.

He had never known her little arms around his neck; he couldn't swell with pride when she got a gold medal in front of the whole school. But then, if he were allowed to be her dad, he would be filling her up with nonsensical ideas about saving money and the importance of possessions.

No, better the way things were.

George had married, so I heard, someone who obviously didn't care about the way he collected jams and little packets of vinegar, maybe even helped him do it. He was going steadily upwards, he didn't need Eve in his life.

Of course, now that she was eleven, she did ask a bit about her father. But she seemed perfectly satisfied that I had once loved a young man but we had turned out not to be suited. He had gone away before I knew I was pregnant.

"Why could nobody find him?" Eve

asked.

"Very difficult, back then."

And that seemed to be enough.

Everything was just fine until that girl Hilda came to Eve's school. They were best friends from day one, which was Eve's twelfth birthday. And Hilda was a very unsuitable friend for my beautiful daughter.

For one thing she didn't have a brain in her little dyed head. For another, she was unable to dress winter or summer in a way that didn't expose most of her stomach. She had nose piercing and belly-button piercing and toenails painted scarlet. She had a way of shrugging and saying "whatever" that drove me mad. Particularly since the little shoulders of my Eve had started to shrug in a deeply irritating way.

There was a lot of talk about Hilda's mum and what fun she was and what a terrific house they had and how Hilda's dad, who was divorced from her mum, came to visit Hilda every weekend and took her to fantastic places.

And suddenly Eve wondered why her dad did not come and provide treats like a theme park or an indoor swimming pool. Eve wanted to know why didn't I join the golf club or the tennis club or play bridge with people or go to fashion shows like Hilda's mum did. Honestly, I could have done without all that.

Yes, I would love to have joined the tennis club. Loved it. But it would have meant big fees and a posh racquet, nice shoes, and buying rounds of drinks and maybe entertaining people I met there. Despite my three jobs there just wasn't the money for all that.

I needed to get endless amounts of school uniforms for Eve, and a laptop and an iPod and leisure clothes. And there was the holiday with my parents and Eve, and there were fares and dental work and expensive haircuts every six weeks for Eve. But of course I didn't say any of this because it would sound so whining and self-pitying. Instead I smiled brightly and said that heavens, no, I was much too busy to play tennis.

"Hilda's mum thinks some women work so hard they don't see the woods for the trees. Or the trees for the wood...or something," Eve said.

I wanted to hug her—she was only a little parrot, repeating the phrases of her empty-headed but exciting little friend. Surely I, who had coped with so much, could cope with this? Of course I could. It was harmless; it was called growing up. It was only when Eve said she wanted to go shopping with Hilda in the mall on a Friday afternoon that an alarm bell went off in my head.

Of course I let her go, but when I began to think about it, I remembered that Eve didn't even like shopping, and I hadn't given her any money to buy things. Maybe I could slip down there and give her something. I could go around five, between my job as a doctor's receptionist and my job at the cash desk in an Italian restaurant. I would have an hour to myself then.

I saw them before they saw me.

Eve's blouse was tied up under her bra, leaving her stomach bare; her jeans were low over her hips and she was wearing not her nice school knickers but a thong. I could see it only too well. Her eyes were black with some kind of heavy makeup;

her lips were scarlet.

She was standing with a lager can in her hand talking to a group of admiring young male gangsters and criminals.

She was smoking.

I felt faint.

I wished for the first time in over twelve years that I had let George play some part in Eve's upbringing. Collecting little individual milk portions or not, he could scarcely have made a worse job of it than I had. What was I to do?

I staggered away without them spotting me and managed to put in my hours at the restaurant.

Eve was sitting at the kitchen table when I got back. She looked pink and white and normal.

"You look very tired," she said sympathetically. "You work too hard, I'm always telling you."

"Yes, you are." I sat down.

"I'll get us some tea. Was it a bad day?"

"So-so. Did you do a wash?"

"Sure, there were a few things I needed, so I put in tea towels and table napkins to make up the load."

Yesterday I would have thought this was sweet-natured. Today I realized it was just concealing the evidence: the rolled-up shirt, the numbers of face flannels it must have taken to remove that makeup.

"Did you buy anything?" I asked faintly.

"Only a thong. It's not very comfortable but I'll be able to wear it on the beach when the weather gets hotter."

"Yes, of course," I said.

Eve looked at me, startled.

"I think I'll take my tea to bed," I said. I lay there for hours with my eyes open. Who did you consult over something like this? I thought about my mother. No, she would eventually say the unforgivable something about my bringing this on myself since I had decided to bring up Eve alone as a single parent. I couldn't tell my mother about it.

I didn't have to, as it happened. The very next day, a Saturday, just before lunch, I was doing the ironing when my mother called in on a pretext to give me a recipe which I didn't need and she didn't need to deliver. I sat and waited to know what it would be about.

It was about Eve, my mother said eventually.

"Ah," I said. It's a useful little word; it means everything and nothing.

"And her new friend, Hilda."

"Ah, indeed."

My mother came out straight and said she thought that Hilda, whom she had only seen twice, was rather a flashy little girl, not the right friend for our Eve.

It was such a marvelously old-fashioned word, **flashy.** I don't know what I would have said. **Tarty**? **Trampish**? **Vulgar**? Were these too destructive descriptions of Hilda—who was, after all, only a child?

Maybe **flashy** was more accurate.

I unplugged the iron and opened the sherry bottle. If my mother thought it was a trifle early in the day she said nothing.

"What do I do?" I asked humbly.

"Well, it needs to be planned carefully," Mother ventured.

"Whatever I do will be wrong: if I say she can't see Hilda then Hilda becomes a martyr and Eve wants to meet her more than ever. It's just that Eve is just twelve, **twelve years old,** and she was dressed like a young prostitute yesterday in the mall!" I'm afraid I cried a bit then and my mother poured a refill.

"Do you remember your friend Rosemary Roberts when you were about fourteen?" she said unexpectedly.

"She was never a friend," I explained. "She was in our class at school. I used to hang around a lot with her but I got bored by her in the end and used to avoid her."

"Ah," said my mother.

"Why do you ask about her?" I wanted to know.

"When you were fourteen she was **your** unsuitable friend and there was no one to turn to so I wrote to an agony aunt in this magazine..." My mother's face looked somewhere between proud and slightly guilty.

But it wasn't a similar case. I was **never** a friend of that Rosemary Roberts. My mother had got it wrong.

But she went on calmly, "You see, Rosemary always wanted you to go on these 'dares,' that's what **she** called them. **We** called it shoplifting. So in order not to have you going out on dares, we kept inviting her to our house. Lord, she was there morning, noon, and night for a while; we even invited her on holiday to Brittany with us when we went camping. Don't you remember?"

"Yes, she did come, I remember, and I was so sick of her then I didn't know why she was there really."

"She was there because I **wanted** you to get sick of her and, amazingly, it worked. When we came back you didn't want to go on dares anymore, you had different and nicer friends."

"You old fox," I said, astounded. Imagine, it had all happened without my knowing! I would never have known, if it had not been for the fact that we needed to use the tactic again.

We began planning in earnest.

"Where is Eve now?" my mother whispered like a conspirator.

"Still in bed. That's what girls do nowadays, they sleep till lunch every Saturday morning."

"Wake her and ask her to invite Hilda to lunch today. Ask what Hilda particularly likes to eat."

"Are you sure, Mother?"

"Absolutely sure." There was a flash of steel in my mother's eye.

I shook Eve awake—she looked like a baby rubbing her eyes. I felt very devious but we were talking about a Greater Good here. It had to be done.

Apparently, Hilda really liked sausages, but her mother never had them at home because they weren't posh enough. So my mother and I looked up a dish called saucisses de Toulouse, which was just sausages in a fancy sauce. And Hilda came and said it was terrific, and was very interested that Eve's gran had eaten it in a posh hotel, and then we played Monopoly on a French set that had all the posh streets in Paris. My mother admired the braids in Hilda's hair and asked was it difficult keeping the color right all the time.

Although Hilda yawned a bit and put her feet up on the furniture, I kept a smile on my face. I refused to think that the sofa had cost fifty-two long, tiring evenings working in the Italian restaurant and this girl had her boots on it. **Boots.** No. There must be calm. Great calm. Even enthusiasm when my mother was asking Hilda where she was going on her holidays and Hilda yawned and said that she wasn't sure. Her mother was going with some ladies on a bridge holiday and her father and his girlfriend were going on a cruise. I saw my mother nodding at me like a madwoman. This was my cue.

"Well, Hilda, I'm taking Eve and my mum and dad to Brittany for ten days this year. We know a lovely place and we'd just love if you came with us."

Eve's little face lit up like a candle. "Oh **do,** Hilda, **do** come!"

And so she came. Horrible, **horrible** Hilda, sulking, lying around expecting to be waited on all the time, complaining that the place didn't have any celebs in it and that we weren't members of the yacht club.

"This is the worst, but," my mother whispered to me, "but it's working. Believe me."

I wished I could believe her. An entire holiday wasted as we pandered to this selfish girl.

As the days went by I saw that Hilda was a lonely child. She had little real attention from either parent: her father's only solution to a problem was to throw money at it and her mother's was to find a pecking order and try to rise to the top. Possessions were good, membership of clubs was good, but talking and listening and understanding weren't very high on anyone's agenda, neither were they fun.

I found myself genuinely trying to entertain the terrible Hilda, to give her a holiday she would remember. I suggested she might try tasting an oyster.

"I don't want to," she said. "But it will be good to talk about afterwards."

"That's really no reason to do anything," I said. "No one is very interested."

Hilda thought about it for a while. "I think you're right," she said suddenly.

"Oh, I think so. I've been around forever, you get to know things," I said, not wanting to take too much credit for anything.

"You're not bad at all," she said, patting me unexpectedly on the arm. I told my mother secretly that it wasn't working at all. The monster Hilda was beginning to like me, and little Eve loved to see us all as a big happy family.

"There were two ways it could have worked with Rosemary Roberts," my mother said. "Either she began to bore everyone in Western Europe, which is what happened in our case, or else we reformed her and made her a nicer person, which could well be what's happening with you and Hilda."

I didn't want it that way. I wanted her out of here, miles away. She asked quite normal questions like why wasn't Eve's dad involved in her life, and I answered the same vaguely dishonest way as I had done before, saying he was long out of our lives before Eve was born and that he knew nothing of her.

"He should pay something though, shouldn't he?" Hilda said.

I told her I didn't think so at all. I had made all the decisions so the responsibilities were all mine. She gave me a sort of a hug.

"You're really all right, you are," she said.

I was furious, of course, but a little bit

pleased. Like we all like to be all right. When the holiday was over, I told her that I was going to give up the Italian restaurant one day a week and that Eve and I were going to learn how to cook some terrific dish, on a Friday afternoon. Did she want to join?

Did she want to join? Of course she did. And she chose things like apple tarts and chopped herrings because she liked the taste, not because they sounded posh or looked well.

So that was a bit of reform along the way. And she was only a child, a child that nobody had been nice to. I got to like her. A lot. Never quite as much as on the day I told her that I was going to look for a husband next year and maybe she might give me some fashion advice and maybe she could come shopping for an outfit. Hilda looked at me thoughtfully and said that, honestly, she didn't think it was all a matter of expensive outfits, that fellows probably just liked you as a person. You know, with views and ideas and jokes and things.

I could barely find the usual lighthearted

tone that I used with her. So I gave her an awkward sort of a bear hug and when it was over she said that I wasn't to go and marry someone awful, that Eve and she were to be consulted all along the way. When I told my mother about it I had to do a lot of heavy blowing of my nose.

My mother, who is much less senti-mental than I am when all is said and done, said that we should regard that as a result.

A result?

Where does she find these phrases?

Broken China

It was as bad as a bereavement when Kay's engagement was broken off. Nobody quite knew what to say. They were afraid to say that she was better off without Larry even though a lot of them might have thought so. They didn't want to say it was just a lovers' tiff, because it was obviously much, much more than that. It would have been heartless to shrug and say that, like a bus, there was a new man around every corner.

So, with the best of motives, Kay's friends decided not to mention it at all. Sooner or later, they reasoned, Kay would give them an indication of how she wanted it discussed.

Kay felt unbearably lonely. It was as if a

hand had reached in and taken Larry out of her life: his name never came up in conversation and the subject of weddings was hastily dropped if, by accident, it was ever mentioned. For a group of young women who used to talk regularly about marriage and babies and engagement rings and wedding dresses, a huge and tactful lack of interest in the subject seemed to have descended on them.

Kay was puzzled. These were her friends; they all worked together in the big deli-catessen, making salads and pâtés and dips. They did outside catering as well and served food at business functions. This is where Kay had met Larry eighteen months ago.

If not love, it had been huge interest at first sight, for both of them. She kept circling him with the best canapés, he kept following her and asking serious questions about what filling was in the tiny vol-au-vents and whether she was going anywhere after the reception.

They had been so happy, so sure of each other. They had saved the deposit for their house together. Their wedding was planned for summer.

Larry was getting four weeks' holidays from his firm; Kay's colleagues were giving them the wedding reception as a present; they had booked a honeymoon in Italy.

And then he met another.

The Other was a tall, noisy girl called Zappie, who seemed to be a combination of everything that Larry hated. Or said he hated. She was very showy and calling attention to herself; she knew nothing about cookery, she said life was too short to own a kitchen oven; a tiny microwave and a nearby Chinese restaurant were all any couple needed.

When Larry started to tell her about Zappie, Kay thought it was a joke; she wondered was it April Fool, or **Candid Camera.** He couldn't mean these things he was saying. He was talking to her in that responsible tone he always used when speaking of money. He would work out exactly what her contribution had been to their building society and return it to her, together with the correct interest that had accrued.

She listened, horrified. He was talking

about their life! He was unpicking their plans neatly and meticulously, as he would have done a file at work. He was going to put all her records and tapes in a box— they would divide the ones they had bought jointly, with Kay having first choice.

Three times, and three times only in the middle of all this, did he tell her he was sorry and that he wished things had been different—it was just that when Zappie came into his life, there was no room for anyone else.

Kay didn't sleep these nights. She got up and paced her flat. She felt that some-one must be mad. Was it Zappie with her crazy clothes and her shouty voice? Was it Larry with his nit-picking division of goods and insistence that they were very lucky Zappie had come into his life before he and Kay had married rather than after? Because the end result would be the same, and there might have been more to divide, like children.

Or was it Kay herself who was going mad? Had she been insane to think that Larry loved her? There must have been signs all along the way that he was looking for someone much livelier than the dowdy little Kay who worked in the delicatessen.

She grew more and more silent and worked harder and harder. She knew they talked about her behind her back and worried about her. She knew that the dark circles under her eyes weren't covered by makeup and that the sparkle had gone out of her voice.

Years ago, in the olden times, women went into a decline after a Broken Romance, they had the Vapors and they were sent on a world cruise. Or the rich ones were. The ordinary ones just got on with it, Kay supposed. And in those days they had to marry the next man that turned up, because there was no other life for women.

She was not going to marry the next man, or indeed the only man who had turned up. He had been there for years, hesitant and hopeful and constantly saying the wrong thing. She would not take consolation from Eric. Not even if the world was going to end would she go to him. She had always told him that she felt nothing for him, and that was still true. He had been mute with disappointment

when she announced her engagement to
Larry and had sent an entirely inappropriate
flower-covered card saying he would be
waiting in the wings in case Anything
Happened.

How could he have known it would? Did
he dream up Zappie?

The date came when it should have
been her wedding and her honeymoon in
Italy. In order to avoid any silent sympathy,
Kay said she would take holidays anyway.
They seemed relieved, but didn't even
dare to ask her where she was going, which
was just as well.

Kay had no idea where she would go,
and she cared less. Her last job was to
deliver a birthday cake to an elderly woman
who lived in a cottage about ten miles
away from town. Kay would go on the bus,
cake on her lap.

It was like the kind of cottage you see on
the front of a calendar, beautiful thatching
and window boxes with flowers tumbling
out. In the garden tall hollyhocks were
waving and there was an air of peace
about the whole place, which was in great
contrast to the busy traffic and crowds she

had left behind.

Anna Whelan held back the door to let her in and Kay looked at the brasses, the jars of dried flowers, the rugs, and the walls covered with different kinds of plates. This was a happy place; people had lived a good life in this house.

The cake was examined and praised. The money was paid and the receipt given. Mrs. Whelan was highly impressed that an employee would travel all the way out on the bus. Kay explained that it was all good public relations and perhaps Mrs. Whelan would now recommend them to other people. She had a little card that she would leave, with their phone number. But she wasn't really thinking about work and getting further business, she was thinking about this lovely house. She looked around and sighed happily.

Anna Whelan was making tea and they sat together in the kitchen. They talked easily. The cake was for a neighbor. He would be seventy tomorrow. They had been friends for years. He came to tea once a week. Always had for years and years, ever since they had been young.

Sometimes the days went by so quickly she didn't realize it was time for him to come again. She worked, you see, mending broken china. It was deeply satisfying, she said. She wasn't up to museum standard or anything, but she could mend pieces that people valued. She had a little workshop out at the back, and she never noticed the hours passing as she worked with the broken cups and plates and cracked jugs that meant so much to the people who had brought them to her.

Kay found herself telling the whole story of Larry, and how they had met and that tomorrow should be their wedding day. She told Anna Whelan about the honeymoon they had planned, and how Larry had divided up the refund they got from the travel agency. She told her about Zappie and the hurt of it all, and even about Eric, who said he would always be there, and how that seemed to irritate her more than any other single thing in this unhappy story.

She was a wonderful listener, because she remembered everything and everyone in the tale. She asked if Larry were mean, and, thinking back, Kay decided that he was a little. Not dishonest or unfair but tight with money. She asked whether Zappie came from a rich family. Again, something Kay had not thought about, but it could well be so. Those clothes and that manner could well be the product of a rich, spoiled upbringing. She asked about Eric and if he were reliable and plodding and stable.

"I'm never going to marry Eric!" cried Kay.

"No indeed, my dear, that's the very last thing you should do. Come with me to my workshop and I'll show you some of my broken china."

Together they went down the path through the back garden. The table was covered with pieces of china and ceramic.

"Let's try a little blue bowl," said Anna Whelan.

She wiped the edges with acetone, then with a tiny toothpick she spread the glue over the edges to be joined.

Very, very little was all that was needed, she explained, and if a tiny bit oozed out at the sides you wiped it away with alcohol.

If it had been a plate she would have put it on its side in a biscuit tin of damp sand, but bowls and cups were best just turned over on their rims. It would be as good as new in no time.

It did look deeply satisfying, Kay thought.

"What a pity you can't do that to a heart," she said.

"But that's just why I took it up," said the old lady. "My heart was broken, not simply like this bowl, but cracked all over; I thought it would never mend. And I too had a man waiting in the wings."

"I expect you married him." Kay was gloomy.

"No, I most certainly did not. The wings are where he waited for fifty years. It's his birthday cake that you brought along today. He wasn't the type to mend a broken heart, nor is your friend Eric. There are men who should be invited to tea and men who are allowed into your life."

"And the man who broke your heart. Did he come back?" Kay asked. It seemed very important to her to know how Anna Whelan's story had ended. She seemed to live alone in this cottage and yet it had a look of a place that had known years of love and contentment.

"He tried to come back. But by that stage I knew that hearts could mend. And mine had. Perhaps it was all that china restoring. You see, I knew that you could mend things even if there was a piece missing; you got some kaolin at the chemist and mixed it with the glue, or powdered clay."

She smiled brightly at how simple it was once you understood.

"And did someone else..."

"Oh yes, someone else did come along, when I least expected it. And he wasn't like the man who broke my heart, or the man who waits in the wings. He was just like himself."

They went back to the house and Kay saw pictures of the man who had been just like himself. Who had been married to Anna for forty-five years, who was as alive now in her mind as he had been when he was on earth.

Anna Whelan said that she was behind on a lot of her simple work and that if Kay would like to spend a couple of weeks here helping, she would be very pleased.

She would see the man who had waited too long in the wings when he came for his tea and birthday cake, she would see also how fragile things could be put together again if you realized that this was possible. Rather than just putting them in the back of a cupboard and pretending that the break hadn't happened at all.

No Tears in the Tivoli

It was hard to know what to wear at the school reunion. Laura spent a great deal of time trying to choose. She was not at all like the women who wanted to look smart in front of school friends they had not seen for a decade. Laura's problem was different.

She was married to an extremely wealthy man and her aim was **not** to look too smart.

She went through her clothes. The gray outfit was simple looking but they would know it was a designer suit; the navy jacket had cost a fortune and yet she couldn't go out and deliberately buy an outfit in the High Street, something in Marks & Spencer that was within everyone's reach. They would talk even more about her.

And Laura knew that she was already an object of interest. Mousy little Laura having married Don Dixon, the tycoon. Laura with a house in London and in the country and a holiday home in France. Twenty-eight years old like all of them, pale as she had always been, and yet set aside from all her old schoolmates. She would never worry about paying the mortgage, the chance of a holiday abroad again this year, what it meant when the car wouldn't start.

She would have to be careful enough in her conversation with them so she must make sure not to anger them by her clothes. If only she had a good friend to ask—but that was another thing that being married to a very wealthy man had meant: she didn't have a real friend anymore. There were so many people to meet with Don, to entertain, so many Other Wives to go shopping with. Pleasant women, all of them, confident, and easy-going, but you had to be watchful, for they were the eyes and ears of their husbands. Laura couldn't say things that might be repeated back. Things like she was lonely, isolated, and wanted a family so badly that she ached when she passed by a baby in a stroller.

The day of the reunion lunch turned out to be very wet, which solved Laura's problem. She wore a smart scarlet raincoat over a simple black-and-white dress. They wouldn't know that the raincoat had cost in a New York boutique what would run their homes for three months. She could always shrug and say it was only a mackintosh if anyone praised it.

She decided to go by taxi, that way they wouldn't have to see her car.

Don was annoyed at the rain. He had planned a day's golfing with an important business contact. It had been arranged months ago. Don hated things that were out of his control, like the weather. His face was dark and angry.

It would have been useless to try and cheer him up, to suggest that he and his colleague play instead at an indoor range. He would have already considered this and other alternatives. Four years of marriage to a difficult and demanding man teaches you lessons if you're a good learner. Laura had been a very good learner and she was good at smiling sympathetically and saying nothing. Her support and quiet solidarity seemed to work.

Soon, the frown left his face and he continued to eat his wholemeal toast and fresh fruit that she served in their conservatory at whatever time it suited him.

His good humor had returned.

"Well, enjoy the ladies today! Ten whole years since you all left school. There'll be lots of crow's-feet and plastic surgery to examine, I'd say."

He laughed at her good-naturedly. Fifteen years older than she was, he often made jokes about how she was nearing thirty and therefore approaching middle age.

It never ceased to amaze Laura; she was nothing special and yet she had managed to marry one of the most eligible men in Britain **and** keep him interested in her.

He was so obviously proud of her and loved her to dress well and be admired.

Laura wouldn't tell him that the girls she was at school with wouldn't recognize the scarlet raincoat for what it was and later she would pretend that it had knocked their eyes out.

That would please Don Dixon much more than the fact that she had been thoughtful, considerate, and had not wanted to stress how much better her financial circumstances were than her schoolmates.

In Don's world, such sensitivities had no place. They would be considered devious and hypocritical if they were considered at all.

"Don't stay out drinking with your school chums all day and night, though, remember we're off to Copenhagen at the crack of dawn," he said.

He stroked her face tenderly.

The very notion of Laura carousing with a crowd of women was ludicrous; she drank so little anyway, and she was always at home long before him, making sure that whichever house they were in ran smoothly.

"Will you be late?" she asked.

"Probably. You know when this lot fly in they want a good time. It's discourteous not to stay until they think the party's over."

He looked weary at the very thought of it, yet Laura knew he loved to play host at a flamboyant evening.

"Yes, silly to spoil the ship for a ha'p'orth of tar," she said.

His face lit up as it often did when she came out with an old proverb or meaningless cliché.

It was easy to keep Don Dixon happy. Just as long as you lived by his rules. If you didn't ask any questions, or have any suspicions about other ladies in his life. Then it was very easy.

At the lunch the years rolled back. They laughed and talked as they had at seventeen, eighteen, they traced their lives and there were pictures of children, chubby toddlers, serious boys and girls in school uniform.

Shirley was as wild as ever, and having an affair with a well-known married actor.

Celia was as disapproving as ever: sensible shoes, and her mouth in a hard thin line.

They had all read about Laura's houses in magazines.

"Next time maybe we should have a

reunion in one of your properties?" Celia said in her clipped, jealous voice.

"Certainly, if anyone likes, but isn't it more fun to meet like this and let a hotel do the work?" Laura smiled broadly at them all. She had learned a lot over the years, how to diffuse a mood, how to say nothing while appearing to say everything.

"Does he take you with him on his business travels?" Shirley asked, eyes flashing suggestively.

"Yes, if I want to go."

"You go, Laura! Believe me, go everywhere, I could tell you what they get up to on these outings, believe me, I know."

Laura believed her. It was a side of life with Don that she had closed her eyes to. Her view was that nobody could have everything, and that she, Laura, had a great deal.

"I'm going to Copenhagen with him tomorrow morning," she said brightly.

"Very wise," Shirley said. "Very beautiful women, the Danes, smart **and** beautiful."

Don was in good humor as they set out for the airport. Laura had supervised the packing—there was never any last-minute fuss or confusion when they left for anywhere.

She had dressed with care, a very chic cream outfit and her scarlet raincoat over her arm. People looked admiringly as they walked through the airport.

"Shouldn't be too busy this visit," Don said. "Suits me. I'm tired—I wasn't in until after one o'clock last night. You were fast asleep, I didn't wake you."

"That was good of you, darling." Laura smiled her gratitude. She had not been asleep as it happened when he came back. She had been lying in the dark with her eyes open for a very long time. And it was nearly four when Don had finally come home to bed...

Monika met them at the airport. She was tall, blond, perfect skin, and spoke such fluent English that Laura thought she must be English herself, but no, she was from Bornholm, she said, an island out in the Baltic Sea; she showed it to them on a map, and laughed happily as she told them about the ferry that would take her home.

Laura noticed the appreciative glances that Don was giving to this handsome, lively woman, whose face lit up when she talked of the rocky cliffs of her homeland. A wave of the familiar jealousy flooded her but she hid it with a practiced smile.

Oddly, Monika seemed to understand what was happening. Suddenly she spoke of her son, Erik, and how he too loved the journey on the ferry with his grandparents waiting and waving a welcome. It was done in a very subtle way. But it definitely sent a message: it told the handsome, wealthy Englishman that Monika was a family woman, she wasn't a beautiful conference organizer who might be available for more than tourist and business advice.

She brought them to the hotel, handed a schedule of meetings to Don, and suggested that she show Laura some of the sights, until lunchtime.

"Amazing girl, that Monika," Don said as Laura swiftly unpacked for them and he glanced over his notes for the meeting. "Could win a beauty contest if she wanted to."

A lesser woman, a more obviously jealous wife, would have referred to the little boy Erik, hinting that she was already settled in her life. But not Laura. Laura agreed.

"Delightful, isn't she? I'm so glad she has time to take me on a little tour. I'll be the Copenhagen expert when I see you next."

It worked, as these things always worked if well thought out. Don kissed her and held her tight for a moment.

"Wasn't I clever to find you?" he said.

"Only what we'd expect, Don." She laughed lightly and went down to the hotel foyer to meet the amazing Monika. Shirley had been right. These Danish girls were a deadly combination...both beautiful and smart.

"We'll start in the Town Hall Square—it's not a very original idea, actually, that's where everyone starts." Monika laughed. "But I thought we could just stand there and see what was most appealing and head for it."

They chatted easily, two handsome women on a bright, cool morning, attracting many a glance as they strode along to the square.

Laura had been about to ask if she could tour Royal Copenhagen porcelain, or one of the museums, something she could talk about at lunch, make herself appear knowledgeable and make Don proud of her. But today she was restless. She didn't feel like doing her homework in order to make her handsome, successful husband look even better by demonstrating what a bright, supportive wife he had managed to find for himself. Today she wanted to be a tourist like other people who were on holiday.

"Can we go to the Tivoli Gardens?" Laura asked.

"Nothing upon earth I would enjoy more," said Monika, and they headed along the Hans Christian Andersens Boulevard like children released from school.

Monika told tales of how they had come on a school trip to Copenhagen from Bornholm, and a wonderful teacher had let them spend hours in this great amusement park among the flowers, the fountains, the little shows, the fireworks. None of them would ever forget it. It was a magic place then and now.

They sat on a park bench and talked as if they were old friends.

"Does your little son Erik like coming here?" Laura asked.

"He loves it, like any child. This place is made for them."

"I suppose he's at school today, a pity he could not have come with us," Laura said.

"That's very kind of you to think of including him. If it's not too personal a question, do you and Don intend to have children?"

"I do, I don't think he does." Laura had never spoken so directly before. There must be something about this place that made her drop her guard.

"Do you think that he would be delighted if a baby came along?"

Monika was sympathetic, interested; it was easy to talk to her.

"I don't think so. Don doesn't like surprises, or anything that is not planned. He hasn't planned for a child yet. I am twenty-eight and he thinks that's still very young, plenty of time, he says. After this merger, after that takeover, after this deal…"

"I know, I know." And it appeared from her face that Monika did know. She seemed to understand that Don Dixon was not a man to be crossed even in a matter of delivering him a son and heir before he was ready.

"Was your husband delighted when Erik came along?" Laura had to know.

Monika paused for a moment before she answered.

"I have no husband. I had for six years a man I loved very much, but we were not married; we did not even live together. It is a long and complicated story. He was a musician, he wanted to be free, wanted nothing domestic to tie him down. No home, no rent, and definitely no child."

Monika's eyes were misty as she spoke of the free spirit that had been the center of her life for six years.

"Many of my friends were in the same position, but they carefully forgot to take their pill and it had all worked out very well for them. And that's what I did too."

There was a silence; the two women sat

there in the morning sunlight as families went by to morning coffee in the little cafés dotted around the Tivoli Gardens.

"Tell me what happened." Laura's voice was a whisper.

"You have thought of this too possibly?" Monika asked. "Well, I will finish the story. For my friends, as I say, everything worked well, so why should it not be the same for me? Yet it was not the same. He was very angry when he heard I was pregnant. I came here to the Tivoli Gardens. I sat not far from here and thought about it for a long time. I hoped once he saw the baby he would change his mind. But I sat here and watched the children play and realized that it was a gamble. I faced the fact that he might not change."

Monika got up and threw a stick for a big, ambling dog that had come to visit them. She still smiled, but her eyes were troubled.

"For him, this freedom thing was more important than a son. He wanted to be able to go and play at festivals, stay out all night at a session—it didn't fit in with being a family. We said good-bye."

Laura was full of sympathy. "Was it very, very hard?" she asked.

"Yes, it was very lonely. I couldn't believe that we had shared so much and that he wouldn't stay around to share the greatest thing of all. But when you think about it, I should have known. I should have read the signs. It's so easy to do so in other people's lives."

"What about my life? Can you read my signs? Would Don change when he saw a baby?" Laura had never shown her hand so openly.

Monika spoke thoughtfully. "I think he values his kind of freedom with you there to help him on his career; as a mother you wouldn't be so available to him as a glamorous wife, traveling companion, hostess, all that."

"It's all a matter of timing." Laura sounded exasperated. "You see, one day he will **want** a family, someone to inherit all his great wealth."

"But at his time, not yours."

"And I can't wait much longer," Laura said.

"My musician too will one day want a

home and a family, and he will find one, make one, but not with me."

"Meanwhile, you have Erik."

"Meanwhile I have Erik. I don't have my musician, but nobody can have everything." Monika was philosophical.

They sat companionably, as if they were old friends rather than two women who had just met that morning.

"I can't imagine my life without Don now," Laura said almost to herself.

"You might not have to make the choice."

"No, I think you're right. I suppose I have known this for a long time, but I wouldn't think about it. I either have Don or a child. And if that were so, then I would not want Don's child, always with me to remind me of the man I had lost."

"No, that's not the way it is. Erik is a person, a real person in his own right, so would your child be just that."

Just then a man and a woman passed by, each holding the hand of a toddler, their faces lit up with pride for him as he took his faltering steps.

Laura looked down the months into the future. This was a picture where she and

Don would never play the roles of Mother and Father.

Suppose she did get pregnant? She would have to hide the child away, make sure that the baby did not disturb their life; there would be nurses and nannies and mother's helps. There would be business trips abroad where she would leave her child, accompany Don, closing her eyes as she already did to whatever little adventures he had, what knowing glances were exchanged. There would be more years of saying the right thing and never the thing that she felt or believed in her heart.

This was the price she would pay to be the wife of Don Dixon. And, in ten years' time, he just might think she should begin to provide him with a son. A decade from now, when she might not succeed in doing this, when she would be tired rather than young with her child, when so much would have changed.

When, indeed, he might prefer a younger partner like he always wanted a newer car.

The clear morning light seemed to reach into parts of her mind that had never been properly lit before.

"You look sad," Monika said and stretched out her hand to the other woman.

Laura took her hand and held it.

"No, it's not sadness actually. No tears in the Tivoli any more than there were for you. Just decisions."

They didn't need to say any more.

They had coffee at a little stall, they rescued a balloon from where it was stuck in a tree and let it fly again up in the sky.

Monika said that tomorrow they might go to the Little Mermaid down by the harbor. It was much smaller than tourists ever believed possible but very beautiful.

"Could we drive out to Elsinore and see Hamlet's castle, do you think?" Laura asked.

"Yes, of course, but I thought Don said that he didn't really like things connected with Shakespeare, it made him think of school?" Monika had brought up the subject on the drive in from the airport.

"That's true, and it's one more example of his shortsightedness," Laura said calmly. "But I would love to see it if it's not too long a drive. I may never be in Denmark again, it's something I always wanted to see."

"I hope you will come back," Monika said simply.

"Everything is possible," said Laura as they left the Tivoli Gardens and walked out along the streets where the greatest children's storyteller of all time had woven a magic future for children of every age and every land.

The Consultant Aunt

Mother had been the eldest of her family and Aunt Miriam the youngest. So Miriam was more like a cousin than an aunt. Miriam worked with management consultants. Sara had always been fascinated by the stories of how they got to the root of the problem here, spotted the trouble there, cut out the deadwood somewhere else. Miriam must have lived a very exciting life, Sara had always thought. Compared to everyone around her it was positively star quality. Mother always sighed when she spoke of Miriam.

"Thinks she knows everything, that's always been her problem," she said.

Sometimes she said it to Miriam's face. "You're too definite, dear, that's your weakness. Men don't like women with such very forthright views."

"Oh, I think they do," Miriam said.

"Well, you haven't shown any proof of it." Mother sniffed.

"Oh, by not being **married,** is that what you mean?"

"Don't get me wrong, dear, you're very attractive—much, much the best-looking in our family, but how was it that the rest of us were all well married by your age?"

"I don't know." Miriam pretended to consider it seriously. "It's a mystery."

Sara loved when Miriam came to supper and even more when she came for the weekend. Sara was doing A levels. Nobody else seemed to understand what it felt like. The feeling that you were too old for all this kind of study, that it was taking time from important things like the disco and Simon, who told Sara he liked her but he wouldn't wait forever.

Miriam would lie on Sara's bed as if she were seventeen also instead of being twenty-five. She never nagged Sara about getting on with her work, she talked about Simon as if he were a real person instead of throwing her eyes up to heaven about him as Mother did, or sighing heavily like Father.

"Why does he threaten, do you think?" Miriam asked about Simon. "Do you think it's because he's mad about you or could it mean there is a bullying streak in him?"

For ages they would discuss it, and then Sara always ended up, "What do **you** think, Miriam? What would you do?"

Each time Miriam was firm. "I'm hundreds of years older than you are, surely you don't want **my** advice?" But Sara always did, and it always worked like a dream.

She told Simon that year that she would be very happy to go out with him on Friday evenings but at no other time because she wanted to study. She would go out with no other boy and he could consider them going steady just as long as he realized that she literally would not leave her books.

Simon said he thought that was perfectly fair, and that he would concentrate on his work; he had a job in a big hi-fi and stereo store. When it came to July, Simon had been promoted within the chain, had saved enough for a small car, and Sara had done well in her A levels.

Simon was twenty. Two years older than she was. He said he'd like to get married when he was twenty-one. Sara lay on the bed this time and Miriam sat in the chair listening. Simon had been so good to her, had accepted all the restrictions she laid down. He had agreed not to discuss sleeping with her until the A levels were over. Now that they were over he was discussing it pretty regularly and talking about marriage at the same time.

"Well, would you **like** to make love with him?" Miriam made it sound as if it was a thing you could do or needn't do.

"I don't know."

"Well, you don't have to until you do know. I mean, it's not a thing you do because you think someone's been kind to you and might expect it. The postman's jolly kind here and I'm sure he thinks you're very attractive, but you don't have to make agonizing decisions about yes or no with him, do you?"

Things were always beautifully simple

with Miriam. You decided what you wanted and then you went ahead and did it. Miriam said it was all like management consultancy. The biggest thing was identifying the problem. Once you had done that, then it was quite easy to solve it.

Miriam was small and dark with lots of dark brown hair, which she wore in a thick, shiny bob. Miriam believed in consulting the best. She had gone once to a very expensive hairdresser and asked his advice. What hairstyle would be the most flattering? She took his advice and said she would go back to him every three years. He had laughed and said that his business would fall apart like a house of cards if everyone was as practical as Miriam.

Sara explained to Simon that she didn't want to get into a relationship yet. She wanted to think about her career. Simon had been very annoyed. He had called her a tease.

Miriam had curled up on the window seat and listened to the sad saga.

"I honestly don't know what he's complaining about. Because of you, he's saved his money, he's got a promotion, and he's had you as a date every Friday. It's not as if you took everything and gave nothing. No, he's got it so all wrong." With Miriam it was all so clear.

Sara gave an exact parrot version of her aunt's speech. To her surprise it worked. Simon said that was indeed true, he had been highly unreasonable. He agreed they should be friends, pals, mates, they would go out together when it suited them, they would have other friends or no other friends as they thought fit. Simon believed he had reached these dizzying heights of maturity on his own. By Christmas he told Sara that he had found another girl, and she **did** want to get married. So, if there were no hard feelings...There were no hard feelings; Sara even brought a Christmas present for his fiancée over to Simon's house.

The fiancée, a silly, giggling girl, said she would never be able to live up to Sara; she said that Simon's first love had been a star. "Do you think I'll be a spinster sort of star?" Sara asked Miriam in a troubled tone. "I mean, I don't want to have very high principles and be thought magnificent but live my life on my own watching enviously young lovers holding hands."

Miriam pealed with laughter. "A beautiful eighteen-year-old girl on the brink of life, and you talk like that! Look at me, I'm twenty-six, and I don't look like an old maid sitting primly on a shelf watching the lovers of the world go by two by two, now do I?"

Sara agreed. Even though Mother said it wasn't natural for Miriam to prowl the world in that expensive outfit and that glossy hairdo. She should have settled down like everyone else.

Christmas was always much more fun when Miriam came; she simply loved hearing about their problems and trying to solve them. She would take notes about Father's company, and ask him dozens of questions, and then triumphantly come up with the solution: they should give up their own transport, they didn't need a fleet of vans and lorries, which took up so much time and were not at all cost-effective, instead they should have a rental agreement. It worked and Father was the hero of the firm. It was the same with

Sara's brother, Jack, and the problems in the club. In their case, Miriam worked out, the difficulties arose from not having proper permanent premises of their own, which they could then let out and use to earn revenue. Jack was made president for his far-seeing views.

And Mother had groaned and complained about the kitchen. It really wasn't practical; it wasn't big enough to eat in, yet it was wearying carrying everything through to the other room.

It was Miriam who saw that if you had a long hatch between the two rooms it would give everyone more light, provide a place for books and the record player as well as a shelf for passing things through.

"There would be cooking smells," complained Mother.

"A fan," said Miriam.

"Suppose we wanted to keep the sitting room private for some reason?" Mother had protested.

"Why? Do you make love on the floor in there or something?"

When the alterations were finished Mother draped the shelves in houseplants and trailing ivy and received the compliments of all her friends with a lofty air.

For Sara, Miriam was her Consultant Aunt about everything: clothes, career, but mainly life and love.

The career was easy. Miriam recommended that Sara apply to a firm that took bright young management trainees. Soon she was on the ladder there, well in control of her work.

When Sara was twenty-one, Miriam pointed out the advantages of getting a mortgage and buying a small flat. Sara didn't want to live at home under the parental eye forever.

"I might as well, considering that I live like a nun," Sara had wailed.

Miriam was now an elegant twenty-nine, her hair was a mass of bubbly black curls, and she looked smarter than ever.

"It sounds to me as if you are ready to have a relationship," the Consultant Aunt said firmly.

"Find me someone, Miriam," Sara begged in mock helplessness.

"No, certainly not. But in the middle of negotiating loans and getting the flat, someone's bound to turn up. Wiser not to find anyone at work, I always think." Miriam's dark eyes twinkled with some memories possibly. Sara agreed.

Through Miriam she found the perfect flat, the right mortgage, the exact furniture, the out-of-work art student to paint the place for her, and Peter. Peter was the solicitor, thirtyish, blond, very handsome, and very unanxious to settle down. Sara fell hopelessly in love with him.

That was exactly what it was, she told Miriam on the first Christmas after she had left home. Hopeless. There was no hope that bachelor Peter would make a move; he was set in his independent ways.

They had gone to Sara's family home because Miriam had pointed out that Sara's mother would have nothing to think about all autumn if the prospect of a family Christmas was denied to her. They sat, as usual, in Sara's old bedroom, solving the problems of the world.

"This is one you can't solve," Sara said sadly. "You can't make him love me and want me forever."

"Like hell I can't!" Miriam cried, the light

of battle in her eyes. It was the most exciting campaign she had ever fought. Sara had to follow it exactly, every step. Otherwise it would fail.

The seduction was planned for New Year's Eve; Sara was to invite him to her friend's glittery party.

"What friend?" Sara asked innocently.

"Your friend Miriam, idiot," Miriam said.

The guest list was picked so that Peter would like the people there. Something happened so that his car wouldn't start. Miriam was very sound on mechanical things. So Peter and Sara had to stay the night, for who could get a garage or a taxi on New Year's Eve? Miriam's house was large; she would employ a waiter for the night so that when they woke next morning the place would not look like a pigsty.

She would disappear, leaving a note about orange juice and champagne in the fridge.

It worked like a dream, exactly as Miriam had predicted.

Peter had been very straight and said that he hoped he hadn't taken advantage of Sara and he didn't want any permanent commitment. She agreed utterly, it was the last thing on her mind.

They continued to visit each other's flats all that winter.

Miriam taught Sara how to make instant and gourmet meals for him without any of the mumsy, flour-covered scenarios that drove bachelors away.

Without appearing to take over his life, Sara, under Miriam's minutely detailed instructions, did so.

Peter found his laundry was always perfect these days, not because Sara did his washing, Miriam would have had a blue fit over such domesticity, but instead Sara arranged for a laundry service to pick it up and return it at convenient times and to send their account to Peter monthly.

When Sara wasn't around the service didn't arrive because Peter hadn't known how to organize it. He was always delighted to see Sara back from her business trips.

Miriam said that she should fix some social life for Peter, who, though highly successful in his office, was, like many men, utterly unable to get his act together at home.

Again, with meticulous instruction, Sara arranged little drinks parties, little theater outings, little picnics...

By autumn he couldn't live without her. And he told her so.

Miriam had advised playing a little hard to get, pretending that she didn't wish to be tied down.

"But I'll lose him!" Sara wailed.

"No, you won't, he'll want you more than ever. Believe me, I've studied the market, I know what's out there."

She was right.

Peter bought a ring at Christmas, he wanted to come and ask her father's approval. And this was the man that one year back had been busy explaining that he didn't want to get involved.

Somehow it seemed too easy to Sara.

At Christmastime, in her old bedroom, she and Miriam talked it through again.

Miriam was an elegant thirty. Again it was impossible to imagine her looking better.

She listened sympathetically.

"I think you've outgrown him," she said

eventually.

That was exactly what Sara had done. It had been too simple and somehow unsatisfactory to win a man by ploys.

It had nothing to do with love and trust and wanting to share a life.

Sara was very despondent.

"It might just mean he's not the right one—there are others," Miriam said.

Sara was thoughtful. "Is this what happened to you, Miriam? That you were so smart you didn't want them in the end because you had won them too easily?"

"No, I don't think so; if it was the right one it wouldn't matter how you won him," Miriam said.

Peter was astounded.

There was no way that Sara could explain it to him; each attempt was less satisfactory than the one before it.

They parted amicably.

"You're too ambitious, you think only of your work," he had said when they had their last dinner. It had been very civilized; she had brought him back his records and his books, two chunky sweaters and an alarm clock that played "Land of Hope and Glory." She had collected her own things without drama and they were already in the boot of her car.

She realized that he didn't even know how to work the dishwasher she had made him buy, but she hardened her heart. He would learn: there was a book of instructions.

"I don't think only of my work," she said and looked at his soft fair hair and kind face. He would have made a good father to their children. But she had got him too easily. She could have betrayed him as easily.

"But I will concentrate on work," she added as an afterthought. "I will spend two or three years thinking of little else."

Miriam hardly needed to help her rise and rise in the firm.

And she had learned about power dressing and how, under no circumstances must any woman at a meeting ever pour the coffee or clear up the cups.

When Sara was twenty-five she was a woman to be reckoned with.

Miriam, at thirty-three, looked dazzling. Her hair was now a wonderful red.

She was a full partner and director in the company. She had been written about in magazines and interviewed for the Sunday papers.

Sara met Miriam's partner Robert at the office Christmas party. Miriam's office parties were splendid: no paper cups, no silly groping over too much vodka, and, though it had all been planned months in advance, it seemed utterly casual.

Smoked salmon and scrambled eggs and lots of good brown bread were served. It turned out to be what everyone thought they needed.

"Isn't Miriam quite wonderful?" Sara said, turning to Robert, and as she spoke she felt something extraordinary happen inside her chest, possibly near her heart. She felt something slip out of place like a zip fastener opening or a strap breaking, and though she caught her breath the feeling would not go away.

As she looked into the dark blue eyes of Robert Gray, the senior partner and managing director of Miriam's company, she knew she had fallen ridiculously in love.

They talked about it at Christmas.

"His wife?" Sara asked tremulously.

"What about her?" Miriam asked.

"Is she…I mean, I don't want to…Perhaps she's quite awful and doesn't love him. Perhaps?"

She looked pleadingly at Miriam.

Miriam shook her head. "We've never won anything by refusing to face facts. Susie is quite lovely in every way; she is charming, good fun, great company, a devoted mother and wife, and she adores Robert."

"Well, that's it," Sara said, tears of shock and rage coming to her eyes.

"Not necessarily," said Miriam. And they sat and talked as they had so often sat and talked in this room while the sound of Christmas carols came up from the record player.

It was a busy three months. And Sara hated a lot of it. She hated the visit to Robert and Susie's home. She felt almost sick when Susie asked her to leave her coat in the bedroom and she saw the big bed with its patchwork quilt and lovely curtains. This room would be a different place at the end of the year. Would Susie Gray sit here and wonder where she had gone wrong and why it had to happen this way?

But Miriam had always said don't go into it unless you're going to go the distance.

Sara had hesitated, especially after visiting their home.

"Well, decide." Miriam was brisk. "If it's no, then we drop it now, we find you someone else. But if you want him, Sara, then let's go get him."

Three months after she had met Robert Gray at the Christmas office party, Sara was sitting in a small romantic restaurant with him. There had been a series of meetings in offices and business lunches before this, of course, on a series of excuses dreamed up by Miriam. Then they needed to talk longer and more privately about a company matter.

"I'd ask you home but there are children and wives running all over the place." He had smiled.

"I'd ask you home too but we might be misunderstood; let's keep it neutral in a restaurant," Sara had replied. And, with Miriam's help, had found the most impossibly attractive place with quiet tables, lots of flowers, and discreet music.

By summer they were lovers.

By autumn he said he couldn't live without her, but that he could not leave his wife. Under heavy coaching Sara said of course he mustn't dream of leaving Susie and the children. She forced herself to take business trips, to go on a holiday, to take a week at a health farm. It worked wonders. By winter he wanted her so desperately he said he would do anything.

Miriam said she should strike in the new year. Demand a Susie or Me situation.

"It's so hard to hurt someone good and trusting like that." Sara still felt guilty.

"What do we do in business every day except take advantage of people more trusting and simple than we are? If we paused every moment where would we be today?"

It was a fact.

At Christmas they sat in Sara's old room. Miriam seemed feverish with excitement.

"You were quite right to say no phone

calls, no letters, nothing at all. It will put him on his mettle. He will know he can't play fast and loose with you."

"Are you **sure,** Miriam? It seems so cold not to talk to him at all over Christmas, especially if we think he's making up his mind to leave her."

"But this is **precisely** the right way to firm up his decision," Miriam said. Her eyes were almost too bright. Sara wondered was it healthy for her aunt to take such an interest in manipulating people's lives.

She stuck it out, no calls, no letters. She went back to her own comfortable flat just before New Year. He would have left letters; he would have left flowers, surely? There would be anguished messages on her answering machine. There were no messages. Sara's heart gave several un-expected little jumps. She reached for the phone to call Miriam. There was no reply. But nobody was working today. **Where** could Miriam be? She would ring Robert's house, just to hear his voice; she would hang up then. Susie answered the phone; her voice sounded choked as if she had a cold, or as if she had been crying. Sara hung up.

She went round to Miriam's flat. It had an empty look about it. That was odd; Miriam had come back here yesterday, she should be there. She called on Miriam's neighbor, a kind old man who often took in parcels when Miriam was not at home.

"Went off to the sun, she did. Three weeks. Oh, she's a lucky woman is Miriam."

To the **sun.** It was beyond belief.

"And he was a nice man that came to fetch her. I've seen him with her, of course, but I thought he was just a business partner."

Sara phoned Susie again. It was not a cold, she had been crying. Sara went round to the house. It had been like a bolt from the blue, Susie said.

Sara went to her office. She let herself in with her master key. As she had expected, the notes were there.

Robert wrote that he could not believe how cold she had been, how unloving and dismissive when he had been prepared to dismantle his marriage for her, when he had, in fact, destroyed his marriage, and then to find this heartless and inexplicable staying out of touch. He would make a new life, but first he would have a holiday. He had got these tickets for the West Indies. He was sorry things had turned out as they had, he would always remember the good times.

The note from her aunt was shorter. It was the kind of note that could have been shown in a court of law without revealing anything. It said that in business you always had to take advantage of those more trusting and simple than you. It said that unless you were prepared to go the distance there was no point in starting the journey.

It wished Sara well for the new year.

Work and
No Play

Getting Grace to Be Reasonable

"Has nobody met Grace? I mean, is this what you are trying to tell me, that not one single person in the office has met her?" Mr. Street's eyebrows looked as if they were fired electrically from within, so violently did they agitate.

He was, as he always said, a very mild man. He was, as he also said fairly regularly, a man whom it was difficult to excite or annoy, but now the difficulty seemed to have been bypassed. Mr. Street was both excited and annoyed, and any element of mildness that remained was there by accident.

"For two years we have been having a correspondence with this woman," he said, waving a thick file of letters, "and now, on the eve of the publication, it turns out that not one person in the company has even met her. It mightn't even be a her; it could be a him, it could be a them, it may be an established syndicate, or an elaborate leg-pull. But only now, when I ask to see what the publicity arrangements are, only **now,** three weeks before all the publicity has to be ready, two months before the book that will make our fortunes appears, we discover that **nobody** has met Grace."

"I've spoken to her on the phone," said a man from the accounts section. "So have I," said the secretary to Mr. Evans.

"I've often telephoned her," said Mr. Evans. "Her letters sound as if they come from a real person," said Mr. Trader, foolishly. Mr. Street lowered his eyebrows; he looked with no confidence at the group around him. "I'm glad her letters do not have the stamp of a computer about them," he said to Mr. Trader. "I'm glad you have, over two years, been connected with somebody called Grace each time you telephoned her," he said to Mr. Evans. "I want her in this office tomorrow. I don't care who does it, or how, I don't care at what time or at what cost. She is to be **here**."

Mr. Street went back with his eyebrows to his office, and the babble of excitement began at once, with everyone blaming everyone else, and then a flood of mutual reassurance. Of course, there is a person called Grace Smith, naturally everyone laughs at the name Smith, but obviously Grace Smith wrote this book. Didn't she? After all, this book was the book that was going to make Streets reach the big time. This was the book they had sold as a film, as a television series, as a Book-of-the-Month choice, as a magazine serial, and organized the translation to over a dozen languages; this was the prepublication best seller. How had it happened that nobody had met Grace? They worked it out; everybody thought that somebody else had. Grace herself must have been quite devious about it because she had implied, if not exactly stated, that she was in close personal contact with almost half the Street company.

Together, a dozen frightened employees

went over what they knew of Grace Smith. She was in her thirties. How did they know? Well, she had sounded as if she were. The book, the great smoldering best-selling book, was about a woman in her thirties. That's why they thought that Grace might be...well...er. She was single. How on earth did they know that? Well, she had never mentioned a husband. That meant nothing these days, Mr. Trader said, wringing his hands sadly. Grace might have five husbands for all they knew. A woman who could deceive a good old family firm into believing that she had been in and out of it, while never darkening its door...there was no limit to the amount of undeclared husbands she might have.

Mr. Evans thought that Grace Smith sounded like a real lady. Any time he had telephoned her about contracts or rights, she had been very courteous, and intelligent too, he added as an afterthought. There was no fluffy handing over of all responsibility. He had congratulated her on her quick ability to grasp the finer points of publishing, especially since this was her first brush with it. "Oh, I knew nothing at all about it, Mr. Evans," Grace had said cheerfully. "I just bought myself a book about it so that I wouldn't be a complete fool."

Mr. Evans's secretary wondered whether Grace might be an invalid. "She always had a very pleasant way of talking on the phone, you know, the way people who have been housebound for years and years have. And she remembered my name, I think that's a sign she might have been an invalid." Since none of the so-called healthy members of staff could remember Mr. Evans's secretary's name, they were prepared to think that this could indeed be true.

Mr. Trader said he would undertake to ask Miss Smith to present herself the next day, and he went to his own office and had two cups of tea before he made the call.

"Ah, Miss Smith, Trader of Streets here," he said with a nightmarish bonhomie.

"Hello, Mr. Trader, isn't it a lovely day?" said Grace.

"Yes, I suppose it is," said Mr. Trader, doubtfully. He had no idea what kind of day it was, but he didn't want to alienate her. "Yes, it's a very good day really. Could you come in to our office tomorrow, please, Miss Smith, any time you like, any way you like, it doesn't matter how much it costs..." he said desperately.

"Well, how much should it cost?" asked Grace anxiously. "I mean, will the bus fares go up tonight or something? I suppose it will cost what it always costs."

"Ha!" roared Mr. Trader. "Ha! Miss Smith, you have no idea how much it costs, you have never been here."

He paused, thinking that he had her nicely with that one. Grace paused too, perplexed. "Well, I suppose it costs about twenty pence by bus, or if you took a taxi about a pound and, say, fifteen pence. No, of course I've never been there, but I know where it is. I've often seen it from buses when I've been going into town."

This was a bad turn of affairs, Mr. Trader thought. She seemed to be admitting quite frankly that she hadn't been in the place. "So, will you be here tomorrow at...at eleven o'clock?" he asked.

"Why?" asked Grace.

"Mr. Street insists on it," said Mr. Trader.

"He said he didn't care how, or how much it cost, but he wanted you there, here, tomorrow."

"You all seem very obsessed with the cost of getting there and I don't know why," said Grace, but she agreed to come in at eleven. Just as Mr. Trader was beginning to loosen his collar, and even to entertain a disrespectful thought or two about how Mr. Street had frightened them all, Grace said, "Oh, tomorrow's Tuesday. No, I'm sorry. I forgot altogether that it's Tuesday. I can't possibly come in on a Tuesday morning. I've got to go to the clinic each Tuesday morning at ten-thirty. No, not a chance, it usually takes the whole morning." Mr. Trader sweated a bit as he suggested Wednesday.

"But what does Mr. Street want to see me for? Really, Mr. Trader, you have always been so helpful about everything— and you know I'm a busy woman. Well, I've nearly finished the next book, and that takes four hours' work a day. I never mind doing anything for anybody, but I do like to know why. Listen, ask Mr. Street to ring me himself. I'm at home all day, and then we can sort out, Mr. Street and myself, what he wants. Perhaps there's no need to come in at all; it could be something that could be solved on the telephone, without anyone dragging in all this expensive bus journey that you keep going on about."

Grace hung up and Mr. Trader felt that he was a failure at almost everything in life, and he sadly asked his nice, worried-looking secretary if she would make him another cup of tea and buy him a sticky bun. It was twenty minutes before he heard from Mr. Street's office.

"Can't say you did a very good job on Miss Smith," said Mr. Street.

"It's very hard to pin the lady down, Mr. Street, if indeed lady she is," said Mr. Trader, with a hopeless attempt at a little joke.

"Well, I was very put out when I got your note saying that she wished me to call her, but since I appear to run a company that doesn't even bother to meet its most successful author in decades, I thought I should at least make some kind of gesture."

"Very good of you, Mr. Street, and when

is she coming in to see you?" asked
Mr. Trader.

"Well, she's not...at the moment, that
is. She's not coming in," said Mr. Street.
"Quite obviously things have reached
such a ridiculous level of nonsense here
that the woman thinks we are all mad.
Anyway, tomorrow's Tuesday." He
glowered at Mr. Trader.

"It's what?" said Mr. Trader.

"Tuesday, the day she goes to the
clinic," said Mr. Street impatiently, as if
everyone should have known this always.
"The clinic, from ten-thirty on, and it will
take the whole morning."

Mr. Trader wondered for the millionth
time about the nature of Power and
Authority. If he, the unfortunate and power-
less Terence Trader, had repeated
Grace's idiotic nonexplanations in that
tone, everyone would have said he was
burbling and rambling, but Mr. Street
could repeat them in a trusty way as if he
were saying something utterly self-evident,
and, because Mr. Street was who he
was, everyone nodded respectfully. Well,
damn it! Mr. Trader wasn't going to nod

respectfully. Just once, he was going to answer life back.

"So have you made any arrangement to meet Miss Smith, sir?" he asked courteously enough, but with a little hint of "let's see how you'll get out of this one, smarty-pants."

"I'm going to see **her,**" said Mr. Street.

Ah, that's what power was—it was changing the whole game. An hour ago it had been a matter of **Get that woman in here. I don't care how much it costs.** Now Mr. Street was going to see her.

"At her house?" probed Mr. Trader.

"At the clinic," snapped Mr. Street. "The obesity clinic."

Mr. Trader had another bun in order to get this piece of information programmed into his subconscious. He wanted it down in the subsection because he couldn't bear to consider it on an ordinary, conscious level.

Now Mr. Trader had never been really stretched in what they liked to call the "publicity" side of his work. There was never any great publicity about anything Streets did. It was a matter of writing to various educational correspondents in the newspapers by name when some sociologist was producing yet one more volume about trends or thinking or spending. It was a question of gently pointing the various Streets publications in the right direction. It had always been that way. A few months ago, when Grace Smith's extraordinary story about a bored woman who took on unlikely lovers to prevent herself from going mad suddenly looked like being a book which would get a great deal of publicity, Mr. Trader wasn't even challenged. Because at that stage, outside people, and salespeople, and almost everyone got involved and the amount of money that seemed to be going through the various books and files was enormous.

Mr. Trader wondered sadly as he thought of big, fat Grace waddling in and out of her obesity clinic on Tuesdays. Life was very peculiar. A woman so sensitive and, indeed, passionate…that she could write a book like that! A book that made it seem totally reasonable for a woman to have a voracious sexual appetite because otherwise her dreary social life, a half life imposed on her by a rich, selfish, narrow-minded husband, would have made her go technically mad. Imagine that it had been written by a poor woman between visits to an obesity clinic! Mr. Trader wasn't sure whether this was going to be an embarrassing fact that people would not like to mention, or whether the media would literally grab such a story with both hands and put it in every part of their papers. Mr. Trader was old-fashioned: he wouldn't like to see it widely publicized, but he knew that other people did not necessarily think as he did.

Mr. Trader's secretary was a nice, kind girl called Hope, who was always rushing out to buy him soothing buns or antacid pills in the little row of shops nearby. Hope worried about him, and even though she was possibly twenty years younger than he was, she mothered Mr. Trader in a way he found very pleasant.

Sometimes he deliberately went out without his coat or scarf so that Hope could run after him and fuss a little. Mr. Trader hadn't enough fussing about him in his private life. He rarely consulted

Hope about anything, treating her more like a favored domestic or an intelligent animal than another human being of his own kind, but today was different.

"Hope, my dear," he called.

"Another bun?" asked Hope, anxiously gnawing her lip. Dear, dear Mr. Trader must really cut his intake of sticky buns. She was getting quite worried about it.

"No, my dear, could you come in and talk to me?" he asked.

His eyes looked quite tired, Hope noticed sadly. She really wished he would take more care of himself, or even, in her more fanciful moments, that he would let **her** take care of him.

"Did you know that Grace Smith is grotesque and obese?" he began.

"Oh, but she isn't, Mr. Trader," gasped Hope. "Whatever makes you think that?"

"She's so bad, the poor thing, that she doesn't go out at all, never visits people. **That's** why none of us have seen her. She's having treatment, though, once a week, at an obesity clinic. It takes all morning."

Hope's eyes were round with disbelief.

Mr. Trader was encouraged by this great amount of mute interest to go on. "So you can see, my dear Hope, it's hardly a publicist's dream, is it? Instead of a beautiful, tormented-looking young author to introduce to the public, we have a huge woman, who eats compulsively, and whose book is only the wildest realms of fantasy and wish fulfillment. I just don't know what to say about her. I'm not one of these modern young men who can turn the whole thing to some kind of positive advantage. I don't approve of these gimmicks. Mr. Street is going to go to see her tomorrow and come back with the news that it's all on my desk now. As publicity manager, I'm going to have to present Grace Smith to the world, in a way that won't make us look indecent. I have to take a huge woman, a joke, a travesty, and tell the readers and buyers: 'You must buy her book, she really knows what she's talking about.'"

Hope looked at him. "How do you know she's so huge?"

"Oh, Hope. She **has** to be huge. Why else would she go to an obesity clinic, my child? Why else should she hide herself? It's just our luck, isn't it? We get a best seller and we get a damn giantess who has written it."

Hope was silent.

"Well, I thought I'd tell you about it, my dear. That's the kind of thing that's turning over in my mind today, and I need young ideas. You're a woman, and a young woman, Hope. You're the kind of person I'll be looking for when I'm writing this publicity material. Would you be put off the book entirely if you knew Grace Smith was obese?"

Hope looked back at him levelly. But she still said nothing.

Mr. Trader was stirred enough to look at her curiously, and he didn't like the look in her eye.

"Well, Hope?" he prompted. A cross between a kindly but impatient schoolmaster and a loving but testy uncle.

"Well, nothing," Hope said rudely, "there's nothing to say." She looked at him with two looks, one chasing the other around her pale face. One was bitter disappointment, and the other was scorn.

Hope would never feel a tender, warm affection for Mr. Trader anymore. She was disappointed that this emotion was dying there and then. But her scorn was because he couldn't see that he was talking to a very, very fat girl.

Hope was seriously overweight and had been attending an obesity clinic for six months, with slow and steady results but nothing dramatic. The clinic took place on Tuesday mornings, which was why Hope worked staggered hours, and came in on Saturday mornings to serve in the Streets bookshop. Hope had become very friendly with the kind Dr. Helston who ran the clinic. Dr. Helston was very dedicated to her job, she felt a lot of it was social as well as medical, so she invited many of the patients to her own house for evenings where they mixed with Dr. Helston's friends, and no mention of illness or fatness or unacceptability was ever introduced or allowed. It had done wonders for Hope's self-confidence. She would never have applied for a job without Dr. Helston.

It had been such a funny coincidence that one of the first letters she had had to type had been to Dr. Helston's address. She mentioned this on one of her visits, but Dr. Helston said that for professional reasons she was calling herself Grace Smith. She had asked Hope to keep quiet about it. In the unlikely event of the book being a best seller, she had said, then the clinic wouldn't have to worry. Getting people to deal with obesity was her main interest in life. Anyone could write a book, but not anyone could help fat people to see that it was quite all right to be fat. She had made them all believe that nobody thought less of fat people; that the world was not out there laughing at them.

She had succeeded with Hope, who was cheerful and had even joined a golf club—which proved how unself-conscious she was becoming. And now, suddenly, when she least expected it, dear, dear Mr. Trader, whom she loved in a sort of way, was proving that Dr. Helston was wrong. Or did it just prove that Mr. Trader was a silly old meddler and messer and bungler who had got everything wrong?

Decision Making at Christmas

There were five places she could go for Christmas. Now, according to statistics this must be a very good average. You didn't often find middle-aged spinsters with five invitations for Christmas Day. Janet knew that she was, by any standards, lucky. So many people felt beached and lonely with nothing to do for the season that everyone else had defined as festive. Which one would she accept?

Years of working in an office where decisions had to be made came to her assistance. Janet would look at the choices calmly and reasonably and make the best one.

She could go and stay with her mother. Mother was, in fact, seventy, dressed like thirty-five, and married to a man many years her junior. Mother would enjoy seeing her, but Janet would have to dress up spectacularly. She would have to pretend to be much less than her fifty years. It wasn't in Mother's scheme of things to acknowledge a daughter who was half a century old.

There would be cocktail parties and a great deal of socializing. Mother had never been one for the hearth and home.

Or she could go to her father. Father lived alone, surrounded by his books. Father, who always seemed to have difficulty in remembering who anyone, including his nearest family, might be. Father, absent-minded to such a degree that everyone assumed he was putting it on.

Father just didn't care for people. He never had. It was a mystery how he had ever married and had three children. Since the divorce Father had never contacted any of them, but always seemed mildly and politely interested to see them when they turned up.

Father always said courteously, "If you're stuck for anywhere to go at

Christmas you're always welcome to bring a few books over here."

It counted as an invitation.

There was Janet's sister, Kate. Kate had said firmly, "You can't possibly stay on your own at Christmas. You **must** join us. We have a rota and everyone contributes. Suppose we say that you do the washing-up Christmas Eve, make the mince pies, and prepare the vegetables on the day after Christmas?" It had been business-like, brisk, almost like booking in casual labor for the Feast. But it **was** an invitation to join them.

There was Janet's brother, Shane.

Shane was an alcoholic and so found Christmas a trial. Everything in the way of entertainment seemed to be connected with drink.

So Shane liked to get away from it all. He rented a cottage, miles from anywhere, and holed up there for four days. Some-times his friends from the support group came as well. Sometimes it was just Shane and his girlfriend—who was recovering from addiction to tranquilizers. They both talked long and earnestly about Getting

Sorted, and often raced to the telephone to call their therapists. It wouldn't be restful, it would be far from festive, but it **was** a place to go.

And of course there was Janet's friend Rose.

Rose, who had warned her against the faithless Edward. Rose, who had predicted the way Edward would leave her: at a time of maximum inconvenience and major heartbreak.

Rose had said grimly that if Edward had not left his wife for Janet when Janet was twenty-eight, he was becoming less likely to do so with every passing year. And now that Janet had actually reached the age of fifty the situation had become ludicrous. Rose had said to mark her words. Edward would bow out as soon as his long-term girlfriend, his faithful Janet, who had sacrificed everything for him, had reached fifty and could no longer be called a girl.

Rose had what she called a healthy disregard for men. Janet thought that it wasn't totally healthy to dismiss half the population of the globe, but Rose was firm in her convictions. She knew **all** about men, she said firmly. She had married one of them.

He had long gone and was not greatly regretted.

Rose, for many Christmases, had urged Janet to accompany her to the sun.

What could be nicer than a hotel where there would be anonymity, and a swimming pool with sunshine?

But year after year Janet had always refused politely.

Edward always called with Janet's Christmas present each Christmas Eve. She couldn't possibly be away.

But what about the day itself? Rose would snort. A day when people could feel low and vulnerable unless they were in a secure situation.

Did Edward call on Christmas Day? No, for over twenty years he never had.

Now that it was finally over, surely Janet could break the mold of her existence and come abroad with Rose.

Together they would walk through the Moroccan souks and buy jewelry, they would take trips into the mountains and photograph the local markets. They would have meals in Arab restaurants and listen to traditional musicians and admire the belly dancers.

It would be a different world, a different universe.

That was her fifth choice.

Poor Miss Mills, sad Janet Mills aged fifty, deserted now finally by the man she had loved so foolishly for almost half her life, had five places to go for Christmas.

So when anyone asked her what she was going to do, she told them, truthfully, that she still had to make up her mind.

Janet Mills had worked for a long time in the office. She had never got any serious promotion but she was considered very sound. People often said that if you wanted to know how something was done ask Janet. Young employees were told that Miss Mills knew everything.

She kept in the background because of Edward, of course.

How could he shine so brightly unless she had dimmed her own light? It was obvious to her and clear.

She couldn't understand why everyone

else seemed to think it so puzzling.

"That shark is using your brains to get where he wants to get," Rose had hissed through clenched teeth. Most men were sharks to Rose. Some of them were barracudas; it was hard to know what system she used to differentiate.

"Surprising that you haven't got a promotion if your **friend** is doing so well," Mother had hinted heavily.

"Do you **like**...doing this menial office work?" Father had asked mildly.

"If he's not going to make an honest woman out of you, the very least he can do is make you his deputy," Kate had snarled.

"Dependency is a kind of addiction," Shane, her brother, had confided. "Your dependence on Edward in many ways mirrors my own on alcohol. Perhaps as a family we are just very sick people."

Miss Janet Mills had a very simple way of making decisions. She worked in exactly the opposite way to everyone else.

Instead of deciding which would be the best, she would always go for which would be the worst, and then she would eliminate the alternatives one by one.

Usually the last one to be eliminated was the wisest decision.

So Janet took her spiral notebook and began to work out her priorities by starting at the place she would least like to go.

That was definitely to her brother, Shane.

For one thing, Shane would hardly notice whether she were there or not. So there would be no question of disappointing him or letting him down. He was the most unfestive of creatures. There would be no holly or ivy or mistletoe decorating the frugal cottage. There would be no news-papers or magazines in case they advertised alcohol, there would be a litany of woes against the world.

Janet had always decorated her apartment in seasonal berries and put up her Christmas cards. For twenty years and more Edward had said that it was like a parody of Christmas Eve when he would come to sip his drink and give her his gift, something she would have hinted at, suggested, and all but bought for him to give her.

But the place had never been joyless, and denying the season like Shane's surroundings would be.

She rejected her father next. He too would be barely aware of her presence. She would add nothing to his celebration by being there. His housekeeper would have prepared a meal and it would be eaten in agreeable and, from his point of view, companionable silence.

But there would be no music on the record player, no lovely old traditional carols like Janet would play. No midnight mass or service of nine carols and nine lessons on the television. Such noise would distract from reading.

So she struck his name from the list.

He was closely followed by Janet's sister, Kate. Kate had a marriage that worked. Or sort of worked. That is, if you thought of marriage as a military campaign.

They operated by some kind of schedule in that house. If Janet was ever invited to dinner it was a case of: "See you in your right mind at nineteen forty hours, we sit down to eat at twenty hours and let's say carriages at eleven."

Christmas there would be ordained and planned by a schedule typed out on a clipboard.

Janet's own little home had never needed any such severity. Edward always said it was a place where anyone could feel truly relaxed. There were no rules, no timetables. It would be hard to spend Christmas in a place where there was a Program of Activities and Duties. Kate was eliminated.

Would Mother be very disappointed if Janet were to refuse the invitation?

No, in truth she believed that Mother would be relieved. There was always so much to do, those hours on the exercise bicycle, those long sessions at the facial sauna, the careful painting of nails, lacquering of hair into position.

And Janet would have to do something similar if she were not to let Mother down, blow her cover, and reveal her as a woman with a middle-aged daughter. Such pretense would be wearying.

Here, in her own place, there was no need to impress or create an image. It would be hard to leave such a peaceful place and go to one of such frenetic activities as her mother's.

A line went through her mother's name.

Now it was a matter of Rose.

This was the option that made most sense. Rose had said so from the start.

"Why go to your dreary family, each one of them set in their own ways?" she had asked Janet in the tone of voice that brooked no disagreement.

"This is what you should have been doing for years rather than waiting for that lowlife to get in touch," she said. She would say it again and again.

Rose would be a good friend and a pleasant companion.

But it would be sun-filled days and moonlit evenings full of I-told-you-so, full of fury about the known faithlessness of men.

In order to have any peace she would have to deny Edward. She would have to say that he had been a waste of time. Admit that he had taken the best years of her life and given her nothing in return.

But this was too high a price to pay.

She would not betray Edward.

He had not taken the best years of her life; he had given her the best years.

She had been happy. Deliriously happy when he was there, happy in remembrance of his visit and happy in anticipating the next time she would see him.

She felt no sense of being passed over, or having sacrificed her own career for his.

His various promotions were a joy to her on each occasion, celebrated in her peaceful, cheerful flat with champagne and lovemaking.

He knew she wanted the best for him as he did for her. They were bound by no rules and regulations like her sister, Kate; no pretense like her mother was; no fears and phobias like her brother; no cold indifference like her father's touched their relationship. There was no bitterness and hate as there was in Rose's life.

So, for the first time in her spiral note-book the decisions had not automatically filtered one to the top.

She would accept none of these invitations.

She would stay instead in her own apartment.

She would decorate it with green leaves and red berries.

She would put up cards and silver bells.

She would play the old traditional songs of Christmas. She would sip good wine and watch the television programs showing how people all around the world were celebrating. She was not a woman whose life had been ruined. She was one whose life had been enhanced.

True, she would never be seen as one of the Sisters who led the fight for women's independence, but neither would she be looked on as a poor female who thought that youth and grooming were the only feminine traits which mattered. She was not like Rose, but neither was she like her mother.

She would sit in her own place and have her own Christmas. She believed that, despite his protestations that their love was over, Edward **would** come to see her as usual on Christmas Eve and she would be here for him.

She would ask nothing more than he was able to give and she felt in her heart that he would still be able to give the little he had given over the past two decades. It cost him so little and it meant so much.

He had once said she was the true spirit of Christmas. Wasn't that a wonderful memory to have, the man you loved paying such a compliment? What wife, what young loved girl ever heard words so full of meaning?

And, as the shops filled up their windows with seasonal gifts, as the fuss and excitement of the Christmas season began all over again, Janet Mills went through it calmly. Five people were disappointed that she would not join them at their invitation, or said they were disappointed. Heads were shaken, brows darkened, and tut-tuts were heard.

But Miss Mills, the calm Miss Mills, who knew where everything was in the office, and how everything was done, and how decisions were made, didn't seem to be aware of the head shaking and the tutting and the sighing about her.

None of these people had ever been called the Spirit of Christmas. None of **them** would ever know the happiness she had known—and since happiness was in the heart anyway, she knew she would have a better Christmas than all of them put together.

Catering for Love

Ronnie often thought that a degree in psychology might be a better training for a caterer than all those cookery courses she had done. True, it was a help to be able to make the food without any flap or fuss in the most awkward kitchens ever designed by humans. True, it was essential to have learned how to cost and budget and give a menu that would be competitive but still leave her with some profit. But really and truly, after three years in the job, Ronnie thought that she should have called herself a patter down, a soother, a consoler. She seemed to spend more of her time dealing with the nerves of the hostess than with food for the guests. She was so often placating people she wondered should she advertise that her service was placating rather than catering. It might be a better job description.

She didn't think it would be like that when she went to Dara Duffy's house. Everyone knew who Dara Duffy was. She was a Success. A very good-looking thirty-year-old, who had risen to the top of at least two jobs—she was on the board of this, on the committee for that, she was on television, she was at the races, she was at the theater and at gallery openings. She had a great big head of black, shiny hair, like an advertisement for shampoo, and a warm smile. Dara Duffy could have had any man, one assumed, but she was the regular, if not constant, companion of Tom O'Brien. That was Tom "High Flier" O'Brien, as the newspapers always called him, usually photographed with a brief-case in his hand, laughing and at ease wherever he went, the boy with the golden touch, the man who had everything. Everything except a wife and family, but then he was still far enough away from forty not to worry about that. People wondered about him and Dara Duffy; they said there would be a huge wedding in the summer, or a quiet one in Paris or New York, with a huge party afterwards while they laughed shamefacedly at what they had done.

Ronnie was impressed by Dara Duffy on the telephone—she was friendly and businesslike at the same time. She explained exactly what she wanted, a buffet supper for twelve, the main course hot, but one that wouldn't spoil if guests were late. She didn't want to pretend that she had done it herself; in fact, she would love it if Ronnie would come and help her serve it so that she could enjoy herself.

Ronnie could understand why this woman had been such a success; her manner was so pleasant, asking for advice and listening to it. She said she would confirm their arrangement in writing and send a deposit. Ronnie wished that all customers were so thoughtful. Only a week ago she'd had a woman who changed her mind so often about the menu that six totally different meals had been ordered and planned. It had been a house with a tiny old-fashioned kitchen and no space and it had not been an easy night. Ronnie felt sure that things would be different at Dara Duffy's place.

For one thing, Dara had asked her to call around and inspect the premises, to see if there was anything further that was needed. Ronnie always felt that it made a booking much easier if you knew the lay of the land. To some places you definitely needed to take an extra cooker, to others a bag of ice. Hostesses were renowned for telling you they had plenty of plates when in fact they hadn't nearly enough and nothing matching—they didn't realize that the presentation was a great part of it. In fact, some hostesses were insulted if Ronnie brought her plain white china with her.

Ronnie admired the window boxes and the climbing plants outside Dara Duffy's small house. How did this woman have the time to do all this as well as everything else?

Dara opened the door, smaller than she looked on television, and a little tired around the eyes, but the same warm, friendly smile and the sense of genuine pleasure that could not have been put on for the occasion.

She brought Ronnie into the house and poured a glass of wine. She was utterly unaffected, Ronnie thought, delighted with the praise of the house, enthusing herself at all the space that had been created and how quiet the street was. She talked eagerly about the party: it was a welcome home for a friend of hers, a man who had been in America for a month. He would fly in on Friday morning, rest all day, and be ready for a great gathering in the evening. Dara Duffy's big dark eyes looked bright and eager as she spoke of the man coming back from New York. She referred to him as Tom, and each time she said the name she seemed to smile more broadly.

Ronnie thought they must be very well suited, the whiz-kid businessman and this lovely girl. She sighed to herself about how clever some women were. Dara Duffy knew exactly how to handle this man: she was putting no pressures on him, making no demands, instead she had decided to give a supper for his friends. No wonder she had Tom O'Brien in the palm of her hand.

They walked into the kitchen, and as Ronnie had expected, everything was perfect: there was style and space, it had been well laid out. There was plenty of simple unfussy china, cutlery, and glassware.

By the time she left Ronnie thought of Dara Duffy as a friend, a friend she slightly envied. It was wonderful to have created that kind of life, to be content with your own company on the many, many evenings that Tom O'Brien would not be around. Ronnie had seen the books, the records, the well-thumbed cookery books. Dara Duffy could have done this party herself, it was just that she would be working late and wanted it to be extraspecial. Ronnie drove home, back to the flat she shared with two friends. She hoped that when she was as old as Dara Duffy she would be independent and confident like that and have a fantastic man like Tom O'Brien flying home to be with her.

Ronnie was determined that the supper was going to be perfect, not just because

she might get more jobs out of it—Tom
and Dara's friends would be the people
who could afford a caterer, people who
might take her card. After all, that was
how Dara had come across her, at a press
reception, and had quietly asked for a
brochure. But Ronnie wanted it to be
perfect because Dara deserved it. Sometimes you came across truly nice people.
She was one of them.

She went through the rest of her jobs
that week. A directors' lunch, where she
felt the food was ruined because they
smoked and drank so much, a prewed-
ding drinks party where the bride-to-be
and her mother had obviously had a major
row twenty minutes before Ronnie arrived.
A bridge party where four tables of serious
bridge players might as well have been
served slices of cardboard for all the
interest they took in the food, all sixteen of
them itching to get back to the table.

On the Thursday she had a small dinner,
a woman she didn't know very well who
often asked Ronnie to deliver and prepare
a meal for six, but to stay in the kitchen—
the meal was passed off as being home-

cooked. In fact, she had to use the woman's dishes to prepare it. Ronnie never minded this, people paid for a service and they got it; she didn't expect to be on stage and feted for everything she did.

Ronnie was getting the garnish ready for the soup when she heard the easy laugh of Tom O'Brien coming from the living room where the guests were having drinks. She had heard him so many times being interviewed, and this laugh was distinctive. But then he wasn't coming back until tomorrow, until Dara's party.

Ronnie peered through the hatch. Normally she had no interest in who was at these parties. They were not likely to employ her since they thought that the food was homemade—she was not meant to exist. Perhaps Tom had come home a day early and he and Dara were here. What a coincidence that she should see them from the kitchen.

But she saw that though Tom O'Brien was there, Dara most definitely was not, and Tom had his arm affectionately around the shoulder of the hostess.

Ronnie applied herself to chopping the

herbs and arranging the spoon of cream. She sprinkled the croutons and laid the six soup tureens on the tray while the hostess, flushed and happy, came to collect it.

She wouldn't think about it, it was none of her business, and there was bound to be an explanation. Ronnie knew that the first rule of catering work was not to get involved. People had to be regarded professionally as clients needing a service. She mustn't get caught up in their lives.

The dinner party was going well when Ronnie put on her coat quietly and let herself out. She peeped once more through the hatch before she left. Tom O'Brien, jacket off, tie loosened, was leaning back in his chair talking expansively; he felt at home in this house.

Dara Duffy's house was full of flowers and she looked very glamorous when Ronnie arrived. She put a finger on her lips.

"He's exhausted, poor love," she said, pointing upstairs to a room where Tom O'Brien must have been sleeping. "He never admits it, of course, but his flight was delayed and everything that could have gone wrong did."

Ronnie nodded grimly. She ferried the food in from her little van.

Together Ronnie and Dara set up the table, the plates here, the napkins, the little plates of hors d'oeuvres, and Dara was pretty and excited like a girl going to her first party, not a successful career woman of thirty-something.

"I want this to be enjoyable for him, I want him to feel that Dublin is his center," she confided.

Ronnie bit her lip and said nothing. She knew she sounded a little ungracious and lacking in response, but perhaps Dara Duffy would put it down to concentration and trying to get the work done properly. Dara was a professional; she knew that work was all-important and Dara must have seen nothing amiss.

"I'll let you in on a secret," she said to Ronnie. "I don't know why I'm telling you this, but you are so helpful and supportive, I think of you as a friend already...I'm going to ask him to come and live here." Dara paused to let the words sink in. Then she went on, "It's silly his keeping that expensive flat, he never uses it; I went around there last night to make it welcoming for him and it's like a suite of offices, mail on the floor, no personality. Men are hopeless! There's an extra room here he can use for an office, and, well, as for everything else..." Her eyes danced with the excitement of having Tom O'Brien live with her. She felt it was in her grasp.

Ronnie lifted her head from the canapé tray she had been decorating with edible flowers. With the nasturtiums clutched in her hand she looked at Dara Duffy pleadingly, willing her to have less confidence in this man, a man who had crept back to Dublin to the dinner party and bed of another woman last night.

But Dara showed no signs of being cautious about this man. If ever there was headlong devotion and trust and confidence, it was here.

Ronnie looked at her as you might look at a loved sister. She felt that something was telling her not to speak, but speak she did.

"I'm dying to meet him," she said. "I saw

him briefly last night—he was at this dinner party I did, in Sandymount..." She gave the name of the road and the woman who had held the party. Dara looked at her in amazement.

"No, it couldn't have been Tom, he's only just come back today!"

He was standing at the door, tall and handsome, fastening his cuff links, at ease with himself, with Dara, with the world. He had heard Ronnie.

She felt her stomach go cold; his eyes were hard as they looked straight at her.

"What's all this?" he asked pleasantly.

"I was just saying I served your dinner last night," she said.

"Not unless you are an Aer Lingus hostess," he said. "You must forgive me for not remembering everyone—it's old age, I greatly fear."

Ronnie went back into the kitchen, each step like lifting a lead weight. She had seen Dara Duffy's face, the first doubts and lack of certainty.

One way or another Dara would never ask her to come to this house again. She had lost the other woman too—no longer could Ronnie be trusted to do a dinner professionally and keep it confidential.

But worst of all, she wasn't sure she had done the right thing. Hurt hung in the air with the smell of garlic bread. When Ronnie had begun catering, someone had told her never to make her own mayonnaise, never to serve shellfish without offering an alternative, and always to bring slightly more food than was asked for. Ronnie had followed those instructions to the letter.

She had forgotten about minding her own business.

A Winter's Tale

Miss McCarthy always wanted to fall in love in winter. Not in spring, like everyone else.

It had started long ago when she used to be on the hockey team and they would cross the city after a match, steaming with energy and health, carrying bursting sports bags, and waving hockey sticks as weapons. She used to look around hopefully in case she might catch the eye of some young lounging fellow and have a bit of repartee.

And then, when she was in the secretarial college, it was the same. She never felt wistful about those who went off to court in the Dublin mountains on long sunny evenings, or who wandered hand in hand along a strand in the sunset. But she was filled with envy when she saw a little winter love. When she saw a couple buying the ring on Christmas Eve in the cold crisp air with all the excitement about the place. Or when she saw well-wrapped-up young lovers heading off on a freezing Saturday to some match.

Her pangs were sharpest when she thought of love by a dancing fire, full of warm burning briquettes where lovers sat on the rug and talked of the future.

Miss McCarthy's section in the service all seemed to get engaged with great regularity. Girls who had been talking about Sean one month, and Donal the next, produced small diamonds in unusual settings given to them by Michael the next.

Miss McCarthy had oohed and aahed over more rings in ten years than she would ever have believed possible. Young girls tossing their heads: "We'll have the deposit for the house in two years, we can live with his mother until then." Other girls: "Well, it's hard to explain, but it really is like something out of a book, we're so happy." More girls: "And it's going to be an evening wedding, much nicer really, there can be dancing and everything."

Mr. Blake used to admire Miss McCarthy a lot. She was so patient with these silly girls, she just had the right touch—a little enthusiasm, a bit of excitement over their nonsensical romancing and telling what they did last night and whether they would be in when the fella rang next—and then back to work.

Miss McCarthy never told them to stop wasting time; instead, she looked at the clock and gasped guiltily, as if it were she who had been distracting everyone. It worked every time. Peace and activity settled back in their accustomed hum, and Mr. Blake was full of admiration for that.

He was not a leader of people himself, and he saw a kind of authority in Miss McCarthy. She was a bit like a nun he knew back home, firm but never harsh.

She was a fine-looking woman too. Tall and slim with nice lacy blouses and soft cardigans, pink and blue and gray. He liked those nice brooches she wore at the neck of her blouse too. She was what would have been called a very nice girl, a superior kind of girl, back at home. Even his mother, who was fairly critical of almost anyone, would find it hard to say anything against Miss McCarthy.

It was when he started to wonder what his mother's view of Miss McCarthy might be that Mr. Blake realized, for the first time in six years of working in the same section, that he was actually thinking of Miss McCarthy as a woman, and what's more, as a woman for him. He was startled and not altogether pleased by this realization.

Mr. Blake's life was very well organized and it didn't need any complications. He lived in a grand house in Clonskeagh with a distant cousin of his. He paid for his room and breakfast there, and had been settled there for six years, since he came to Dublin.

His room was big enough for him to have a friend in for a chat, or a game of cards, and there was even an armchair in it to encourage the fiction that Mr. Blake had a bedsitter.

Miss McCarthy thought Mr. Blake a very nice man but that he was a bit put upon by everyone. Extra work was always arriving in his tray. Knotty, boring, endless problems were always given to him, the kind of thing there was actually no solution to. Then other people would sigh because Mr. Blake had found no solution.

He was a late entrant into the service. She heard that he had worked in the family business in Cork somewhere and there had been a row. He lived now in some cousin's place, and, from all she could ever gather, he hadn't much of a life. He never volunteered much but she thought that he had seen a lot of the television programs that they talked about in the office and none of the plays or the films.

Maybe he sat in every night and watched the television in a darkened room with his cousin and her two school-going children. The cousin was a deserted wife, Miss McCarthy had heard in some whisper, and it was nice for her to have the money coming in.

Mr. Blake wondered idly what Miss McCarthy did in the evenings. She was always businesslike and bustling about going home, not wedded to a desk like some of the lonely older women who were really sorry to leave the comforting life of the office at the end of the day. He knew she lived with her mother in Rathmines.

He knew that she must be about thirty, four years younger than himself. He knew she had no regular boyfriend, no love life. It would have been hard to hide a love life in that section. He knew that she always found him pleasant and agreeable, so he decided that he would ask her out for a meal. What Mr. Blake didn't know was how hungry Miss McCarthy was feeling for a little winter love.

It was a wet February evening and they felt awkward walking together down the street instead of separating with a wave as they normally did at six. Mr. Blake had suggested a drink first, since it wouldn't be worth their while going home just to come into town again.

Miss McCarthy had worn a dress and jacket to work instead of her normal blouse and skirt with a pastel cardigan over her shoulders.

When six o'clock came she put on more lipstick, a pair of earrings, and a cream chiffon scarf. She looked dressed up to go out.

They walked companionably past all the shops selling Valentine cards and into a lounge where there was music and thick carpets. Mr. Blake had two half pints of a fancy draft lager, Miss McCarthy had two glasses of white wine.

They talked about the office and about the likely changes and about the man in the section who was a troublemaker and about how they had spent Christmas. Mr. Blake had decided to stay in Dublin to avoid all the traveling, he said—which meant that Mr. Blake had been on such poor terms with his family over whatever it was that he didn't even go home to wherever it was in Cork for Christmas.

Miss McCarthy had said she and her mother had a lovely quiet time, very peaceful, which meant that she and her mother had had nowhere to go and, even more sadly, had had few people to ask in. But the loneliness that hung over both of them didn't seem sad. In the buzz and burr of a warm city pub in early evening it seemed companionable.

But they didn't admit anything even to themselves, and by no glance did they let the other know that this was something possible, something warm and nice that they might hold on to, and it might become big and developing and look after them. They were treading very delicately in case it would go away.

And it went away. It went away because it was blown away.

It blew away as they went to the restaurant. Mr. Blake had suggested one place and Miss McCarthy thought it sounded very nice. When they got there it had candlelit tables and red tablecloths. There was a pianist playing softly at the back. There would be no worry about how much it cost since the menu was on the door, but suddenly Mr. Blake's neck seemed to bristle about it.

He turned to Miss McCarthy, who was looking inside with her pale eyes shining and her head filled with two unaccustomed glasses of white wine and a wish to look after Mr. Blake and make sure he wasn't put upon too much by the world.

"I don't think this is the kind of place... do you?" he said hesitantly.

"What? I beg your pardon?" Miss

McCarthy was taken away from her vision, the windows wet and studded with raindrops, the warm, soft place with loving people inside. Every table seemed to have a couple at it.

"What?" she said again.

Mr. Blake looked around without any pleasure.

"I don't know about you, Miss McCarthy," he said, "but I like a place where you can see what you're eating, where you can get the hang of what's going on. A grill bar or something?" He looked at her, waiting for her quick, eager agreement, her pleasant easing of situations.

But she was not giving any.

"Whatever you say," she said in a clipped sort of voice.

Mr. Blake thought her face looked a little sharp and pinched, like that nun he remembered back at home.

Holidays

The Dream Holiday

They never missed a Saturday lunchtime, all four of them coming from different places and taking the corner table in Kriti, the Greek restaurant. They were well-established regulars now: Yanni would run up with the basket of bread and the dish of olives, and dust down the chairs for them.

They were nice people, he told his wife: two couples, longtime friends, easy to please, telling each other news, always happy.

Julie came from her shift in the florist's. It was a part-time job, just on Saturday mornings. Five hours, eight to one, nice extra cash, and at least it kept her out of the other shops, she would laugh. She liked it there, opening up the shop, waiting for the flowers to come in from the market. In a way she would have liked a full-time job there instead of at the cash desk in the butcher's shop. Everyone was in a hurry there, and there wasn't the same feel about taking money for fillet steak or lamb chops as there was for ten white carnations laid against ferns, or giving advice about how to keep a little cyclamen from flopping immediately.

But they didn't need her full-time, they said. There really wasn't the work. They had hoped that the new office block nearby would fill up and then there would be loads of customers. But it had been slow. It had been a fairly tough area once and businesspeople hadn't wanted to relocate to an area without a good name.

But because of supermarket shopping and hairdressers in the area they could offer her Saturday work—there were always lots of orders to fill on a Saturday morning. They came with messages saying "Thank you" and "I love you" as well as "Happy Birthday" or "Congratulations."

Once there had been a huge bouquet

with just a one-word message: **Sorry.** Julie had told the others and they spent the whole lunchtime wondering what anyone could have done that warranted fifty pounds' worth of roses.

Julie's husband, Bob, went to see Flora, his daughter from his first marriage. There was a problem every single Saturday morning. Either Flora's mother would call and say the girl hadn't got up yet, or Flora would arrive herself, in tears over something. It always upset Bob, and Flora had to be consoled by a visit to the shopping mall to buy a new CD.

It would take Bob an hour or so to unwind when he got to Kriti. He looked pale and tired. Julie's heart went out to him but she would pat his hand and say it would all be all right. It always was, anyway. Neither would she tell him that Flora was as devious a sixteen-year-old as anyone was ever likely to meet, who knew exactly how to manipulate her father. No, it was better that they should be with Brian and Carol, where nothing would be said but all would be understood. And soon Bob would be smiling again.

Carol came to Kriti direct from work. She ran a recruitment agency with two other women. Saturday was one of their busier days. Women who were working Monday to Friday but who wanted to change jobs liked to come in on a Saturday and see what else was on offer. Carol's two partners were women with small children and they often found it hard to work on Saturdays. Of course, Carol and Brian had small children too, but then Carol was a genius at getting people to look after them. She had such a support system organized that you would have to look at her with awe.

They all said that Carol could run the universe—and she agreed. Or she said she could have a fair shot at it anyway.

Brian's mother lived in a granny flat in their house. Well, that was the theory, but in reality she lived with them. Not a happy camper, Brian's mum. Every Saturday morning she liked to be taken out to the hairdresser, or the chemist, for a little look around the shops and for a coffee with two other old ladies. Then Brian would drive her home, serve her lunch, and head out for Kriti, where he would be more than ready for the one treat of the week which could not be interrupted by the sound of his mother's stick knocking on a wall.

The two young girls at the next table had a selection of holiday brochures and were debating where they should go.

"Doesn't it make you feel old?" Julie said. She wasn't remotely old, only mid-thirties, in fact. She had been to France on a grape-picking holiday once. And she had gone with her mother on a four-day coach tour of Belgium. But she had never really traveled for sheer pleasure, not like those two kids were planning. She had never got onto a charter flight for two weeks in the sun without a care in the world.

When she and Bob married, they went on a honeymoon to Cornwall, which was lovely; but they had to be back for Saturday so that Flora would know that she hadn't lost her daddy permanently just because he was married to someone else.

"I don't think I'd like that kind of holiday, even if we did have the time," Carol said. "You know, screaming teenagers, discos, wet T-shirt competitions..."

"I don't know—wet T-shirts..." Brian made a feeble joke. "Doesn't sound all that bad to me."

"It wouldn't have to be a big, high-rise place," Julie said. "It could be small and quiet, a villa near the sea maybe."

"A nice walk in the evening into some bar by a harbor and dinner in the open air," said Bob, who had just recovered after this morning's onslaught from Flora.

"And our own balconies to snooze on," Carol said thoughtfully. "With no sound of telephones ringing anywhere for miles!"

"And we could have a little bit of culture as well," Brian suggested.

"Just a little," the others agreed, and realized that they were actually planning their first holiday together. They had an extra bottle of wine to celebrate the decision. Yanni asked them what was the occasion.

"A holiday abroad," Julie explained. "I know it doesn't seem such a big thing—millions of people are setting out on them every day—but somehow we four didn't manage to." They were quiet for a moment looking back on all the years when they hadn't headed off for the airport like everyone else. And the reasons why. But that was behind them now. They knew this, and there was a great sense of excitement.

"And where will you go?" Yanni asked.

They had no idea.

"I hope very much that you go to my country. Greece is a beautiful place." He pointed to the pictures on the restaurant wall, pictures that now had a new significance. A ruined palace, a fishing village, white buildings covered with flowers. Anything was possible. They agreed to have the brochures next week and they went home in high good spirits.

Julie unpacked her shopping and stacked it in the kitchen; in the little basket where they put receipts she saw one from Bob's credit card. It was to a boutique for forty-nine pounds, seventy pence. She sat down on the kitchen stool to get over the shock.

More than she had earned all morning, standing in a drafty flower shop where the door was open letting in an east wind. Nearly fifty pounds he had spent on that monstrous girl. And judging from Bob's strained face when he had arrived in the restaurant, Flora had obviously not been sufficiently grateful even for this huge generosity. So her husband had bought something that cost fifty pounds in a shop where Julie would not even dare to **walk in** on account of the prices.

Could she really let them go on like this? Father and daughter caught in a love-hate trap that was bleeding their savings account dry, without bringing any happiness to either of them. Surely someone should put a halt to this before it drove everyone insane. But then, was she the right person to do it? Was it worth all the drama and confrontation that would be involved? Perhaps a wise woman would stay out of it.

Julie felt her hands shaking as she stored the detergent in its place on a shelf. She had walked to a discount store further away to save pennies on this packet—**pennies,** while her husband had spent fifty pounds to placate a selfish teenager whom nothing would please, not even the return of her father to be a full part of her life. Flora only wanted Bob on Saturday mornings, she just needed to make him feel guilty the rest of the time. This ceaseless attempt to buy her affection must stop.

Yet Julie was loath to bring the subject up. Bob worked so hard in that television center, with the house calls, and lugging huge boxes up and down stairs. She really wanted him to have some breathing space before going back to work on Monday morning. But then suppose that he gave Flora so much money there wouldn't be enough left for their holiday?

Julie picked up a fifty-pence coin and spun it. Heads she'd tackle him about the purchase. Tails she would let it pass.

Bob came into the kitchen, smiling at her warmly.

"You're a very good girl, Julie," he said. "Did I ever tell you how easy it is to live with you?"

"What brought this on?" she asked.

"Just to come in and see you spinning a coin like a child—I don't know, it's very endearing."

She let the coin fall and didn't look at

which side was up. Instead, she put her arms around his neck.

"It's dead easy being married to you too, my love," she said. And they went upstairs together.

Later on that evening, when she was getting the supper, Julie found the coin; it had landed head side up. Fate had meant her to confront him, tell him that these payments to his disaffected daughter must go on no longer. But then fate can come at us in different ways. Bob had just walked into the kitchen at that moment and said that he loved her. They had spent the afternoon in bed. Wasn't that much better than any confrontation? Julie was sure that it was.

Over in Brian and Carol's house, the supper of cold chicken salad had been placed on the table by Maria, the au pair. She had been with them for four years now and was part of the family. Carol always said that if you spent the money building a small bathroom and gave them a television in their own room, then there was no problem with au pairs. The real strains only came when they lay in your bath all day and sat in your sitting room looking at rubbish on television all night. It couldn't have been quite as simple as this, but anyway, for Carol it seemed to work.

There they were, Maria about to go out for the night, the seven-year-old twins, all clean and shiny in their dressing gowns, were going to hear their bedtime story. It was about a huge, good-tempered, vegetarian monster who loved eating nettles and thistles and playing with little boys and girls. Matt and Sara loved this story.

Brian had just begun to read in that slow, measured voice he used in the classroom, making sure every word was heard. Halfway through the first page, the knocking on the wall began.

"I'll go." Carol started to get out of her chair.

"She's my mother," Brian said, handing the book to Carol.

"Right, kids, you've got me," Carol said.

"Dad reads better," Matt complained.

"Will we play a game until Dad gets back?" Sara suggested.

"It might be very late though, might be

well past your bedtime," Carol said doubtfully to her daughter. That's exactly what Sara had hoped.

The children were asleep, and Carol had her papers all over the dining room table when Brian got back. She was lost in her work, and didn't seem at all annoyed that he had been gone for over an hour. She gathered the spreadsheets together.

"Sorry, love," he said.

"Not at all, gave me time to look at those figures," she said. Carol took a lot of work home with her—she had been thinking of building an extra little office area under the stairs. You saw such marvelous conversion jobs in the advertisements.

He didn't explain what his mother had wanted: it didn't matter anyway; it was always one thing or another, or just nothing at all. Brian took away the cloth that covered their chicken salad.

"Lucky it was cold," he said, trying to rescue something from the evening.

Carol pushed her glasses back on her head.

"It always is on Saturday nights, hadn't you noticed? She always calls you on a

Saturday around this time. That's why we have cold chicken." There was no complaint in her voice. It was just the way things were.

They all talked about the holiday at work the next day. At the butcher's shop they told Julie that she should go to the Munich Beer Festival, great fun and some of the finest sausages a body could ever want. Julie didn't tell them that she would be happy never to see meat again for the duration of the holiday and that the notion of seeking it out would be ludicrous.

In Brian's staff room they were amazed. "Two weeks without the kids? Brilliant, mate—no wonder you're looking forward to it." Brian felt it wouldn't be necessary to say that the children would be no problem; he might even have time to finish reading them that story. It was his mother that he was longing to escape.

Carol told her partners that she would definitely take two weeks off in August. "I'll believe that when you're actually sitting on the plane," said one of them. "Some holiday with your mobile phone tucked in the elastic of your bikini bottoms," said the other.

"I will not. I'll unwind totally," Carol insisted, stung at the accusation. Her partners looked at each other and her and laughed affectionately.

It was a busy Monday; everyone's television set seemed to be on the blink. When they paused for tea, Bob told them about the holiday. "Great thing, a holiday," one of his colleagues said. "The women always get turned on—I think it's the climate. My wife never feels like it here but it's different out foreign."

"That's good," said Bob. It would be just his little secret that he didn't have that problem at home at all.

They all brought brochures to Kriti next Saturday, but what they hadn't expected was that Yanni would join in too. On the table with the pita bread and the big juicy olives was a small photograph album with pictures of a white house by a magnificent sandy beach. The sand was white and the water a turquoise blue and green. Rich purple bougainvillea climbed the white walls. Scarlet and blue rugs were on the wooden floor and colorful plates and pottery around the walls.

There were two bedrooms, two bathrooms, a kitchen, a long wooden veranda that ran around the house, with a dining table. It was the villa of Yanni's brother, the great investment that would make their fortune. It was free for two weeks because of a cancellation, it could be theirs for very little money: their own home in Crete.

It wasn't only because it was Yanni and his brother: the place touched their hearts. It was exactly what they had dreamed of. And the bus passed the door six times a day, so they could go into the harbor town; they could spend a day at the ruins of Knossos; they could go to the museum in Heraklion or shopping in the touristy places. They could take a boat trip, learn to water-ski.

The other brochures remained unopened. This was where they would go.

Julie said she would collect the money. She would take so much a week every Saturday and put it all in the post office or a building society, whichever they preferred. This surprised the others: usually

Carol would make that kind of suggestion. They didn't know how desperately Julie wanted to make sure that her husband's quota was not spent foolishly on his daughter.

There were twelve whole weeks before they left. Time to lose seven pounds weight. Time to learn a few phrases of Greek conversation. Time to read about King Minos and the minotaur so they would understand it when they got there, time for anything to happen.

The first thing that happened for Carol was that they got three months' notice to quit on their premises. Her recruitment agency would be right in the middle of the move at the date of the planned holiday. That is, if they ever found suitable premises.

"I can't tell you how sorry I am," she said to Brian.

"Let's not make any decision yet," he began. He had become so excited by the holiday, reading the works of Kazantzakis, showing the children on the map where Crete was.

"But I have to make this decision, it's

only fair on the others to let them know in case they want to find another couple..."

"But you know they won't find another couple." His disappointment was naked on his face. "This is the four of us—we've been planning it, dreaming about it..."

"Brian, the agency is my **life,**" Carol said. "It's what I nearly killed myself setting up... it's my whole life."

"I suppose it is," Brian said bitterly.

The next thing that happened was that Flora took the news of the vacation very badly indeed. Flora's mother began calling during the week.

"She won't eat, she won't go to school. Really, Bob, I don't know what you're going to do."

"But what **can** I do?" Bob wailed down the phone. "It doesn't have anything to do with me."

"It has everything to do with you," his ex-wife snapped. "The girl is naturally upset that you're going off to Greece with that woman and giving no thought to her Saturdays, her needs."

"It will sort itself out," Julie said through gritted teeth. "Believe me it will, once she sees that you're not going to waver." But she didn't like the look on Bob's face.

"I did leave her, Julie, I did abandon her, there's no saying I didn't do that."

"Well, let's not say it to the others just yet," she pleaded. The florist's shop where Julie worked was doing excellent business these days. That new office block had, after all, meant a significant increase in customers. It had taken some time for the units to sell. They offered Julie a full-time position. But there was one problem: they didn't want her to have the two weeks off in August—in fact, that was when they needed her most. She said nothing to anyone. She still had a week to make up her mind.

Shortly after she heard that she was going to a home for two weeks of the Greek holiday, Brian's mother got chest pains.

The doctor said that it was most likely to be heartburn or indigestion. Brian's mother took up the words "most likely." It meant that the doctor just didn't know. She gravely doubted that she would be alive on their return if thrown into an old people's home at this critical time in her health.

They all met for Saturday lunch as usual in Kriti: there were now only three weeks to go.

Yanni knew that something was wrong. They were never like this, these people, his friends as he considered them. He had written to his family in Crete and asked them to be sure and look after them when they arrived; they were not like the greedy, selfish tourists who had so often spoiled their countryside. Now there was trouble.

He passed near their table to hear what they were saying. He could hear snatches of conversation about a teenage daughter crying down the phone, an elderly mother refusing the offer of two weeks being cared for in a home with the certain know-ledge that she was not going to be left there permanently. Yanni heard one of the women saying that there was no office space left anywhere you would want to go, and even if she did find somewhere, there wasn't a question that she could go on holiday just now.

The other woman, the one he had always liked best, stood up. She looked very pale.

"This morning I have had to quit the flower shop," she began, "because I couldn't accept the job I've wanted for years. They are going to take on a girl of nineteen instead. She can't do the displays like I do, she doesn't know how to bring in the greenery properly or make ribbons into lovely bows. But she **is** free to start because she doesn't have three people depending on her to go on a promised holiday." She looked at their stricken faces.

"It's all right. Really it is. It was only a job—it's not a mother like you have, Brian, or a daughter, Bob, or a Life as you have, Carol, it was only a job I would have liked and now I'll have to stay on at the butcher's, which I don't really like..." They were wordless as they saw Julie struggling to be fair about it. Then her face changed slightly.

"But it's not only the lost holiday. I think we've lost something else. I've lost some respect for your great business sense, Carol. The office block down by my florist's still has some empty units—you haven't tried there.

"You could have paid Maria extra to look after your mother and taken the twins in to see her every day, Brian, then she wouldn't have had this panic about the old people's home and thought it was the thin end of the wedge.

"And, Bob, you must know that even if she is your daughter, Flora is just as much a bully as anyone in a playground. By staying at home you are proving to her not only that she can get whatever she wants but that somehow she was right all along, that you **did** abandon her instead of breaking your heart to be there for her all the time." She wasn't in tears but her voice had a shake.

"I'll go down and start the business of getting the money back—no, please don't stop me; it's all I'm fit for really, to go and do errands. I'm the one who lost a good job this morning, a job I'd really have liked, and I lost it only because I was stupid enough to think we were going on holiday. I need to be alone for a bit anyway. I'll be back in about an hour."

She was relieved that she got to the door before the tears of self-pity and rage fell. It all took some time, the forms, the explanations, then Julie walked through a big store and stopped at the cosmetic counters.

"Want some sun cream?" the very well-groomed girl asked.

"No, the holiday's been canceled," Julie said flatly.

"Always a bit overrated holidays, I think," said the blond beauty.

"You're right, I'm sure," Julie agreed and held out her wrists for a spray of very expensive perfume instead.

She never knew what had happened in the restaurant while she was gone: what they had said, who they had phoned, what deals had been done. And she knew that she would never ask Bob when they were alone.

Whatever had happened stayed between those three. Close friends, distraught that they hadn't shared enough in the dream.

And it was never awkward, no unspoken words hung between them as they walked through the airport with the other holiday-makers. And when they danced the Greek dances under the moonlight with Yanni's cousins and friends, and climbed the mountain paths and swam in the turquoise sea, nobody said or needed to say how nearly they had lost this holiday—which would in so many ways alter the rest of their lives...

Sandra's Suitcase

Everyone said that Sandra was mad. All those countries in such a few days, overnight stops in cities that she would never remember. What a way to see Europe! But Sandra did not agree. All her life she had spent money on clothes and shoes—she had spent nothing on seeing foreign places.

She didn't know what Paris looked like, or Brussels, or Venice, Florence or Rome. She wouldn't waste her two weeks' holiday just in one place—after all, clothes were so expensive and so essential that she might never be able to afford to travel again.

Sandra knew you had to dress well to make a statement in life.

So that's what she did. Made expensive statement after statement with everything she bought.

She had read so many articles about how your clothes were a key to your character that she really believed it.

Now, at the age of twenty-seven, she wondered why on earth these messages that she was sending out hadn't borne more fruit. Beautifully dressed, perfectly groomed, she sat in a dead-end job day after day and her private life contained no husband, partner, or even long-term relationship.

But it would all change eventually, Sandra knew it would. After all, she was playing life by the rules.

Perhaps people might think she was dull because she hadn't traveled anywhere. After all, that silly girl in accounts who looked as if she had fallen out of a garden hedge had been to Russia and even went for weekends to Brittany.

And the girl in marketing who wore the same dreary suit with a collection of different-colored T-shirts for years had been to Australia and come home via Fiji.

Unfair as it was, people **did** seem to think they were more interesting to talk to than Sandra, who spent every waking moment reading fashion magazines and then scouring the stores to buy the latest recommendation.

So now she was going on this coach tour.

They were confined to one suitcase each, and Sandra spent six happy weeks wondering what to wear when being photographed outside the Louvre or in a gondola.

She packed them as all the fashion articles had instructed, with layers of tissue so they would not crush, but put in a travel iron just in case.

She chose a simple washable dress to travel in, and met all her fellow holiday-makers at the coach depot.

They seemed a nice enough crowd, nobody very stylish and some of the women looking positively frumpish. Sandra shuddered. How could they bear to travel like that? Hardly any makeup, jeans, anoraks—comfortable, certainly, but more suitable for doing the garden than for continental travel.

And, oddly, a lot of them seemed to be married or traveling with partners.

Extraordinary what some men would put up with; Sandra sniffed disapprovingly.

Their guide was a very fat man called Johnny. Johnny had a voice like a foghorn and a series of nonstop jokes.

But he also managed to give them quite a lot of information. There were thirty people on the bus and Johnny had learned all their names before they got to Belgium.

The coach whizzed them to the ferry, over the Channel, and then, for the first time, Sandra's eyes saw a land that wasn't her own.

People drove on the wrong side of the road, but she had expected that, and they had shutters outside their houses, and a lot of people on bicycles.

The traffic had been slower than the driver expected.

When they got to Brussels it was beginning to get dark.

"Now you're all to go into your rooms, open your suitcases, have the quickest shower ever known to humans and be back on the bus in fifteen minutes, then I'll take you to the Grand Place and show you the sights and we'll have our dinner."

Johnny's good humor was catching; the group was already looking forward to the night out.

They all pulled their suitcases from the row of bags waiting outside the hotel—all except Sandra. Her bag wasn't there.

She knew it had to be at the back of the bus somewhere, so she waited and waited.

Then Johnny told her what she could not accept. Her bag was in London.

"But when will they send it? Will it be here tomorrow morning?" Sandra was white with anxiety.

"They can't find it," Johnny said, glumly. "There'll be compensation, of course, but I'm very sorry."

He was unprepared for the sense of tragedy in Sandra's face.

"My life is over," she said simply. "My first and only trip abroad. I had brought everything to be photographed in so that I would always remember it, and now your company has lost everything I love."

"Oh, nonsense, Sandra, you'll go abroad lots, and if they can't find it then you'll get the money to buy new gear."

"But what will I do for this trip?" she wept.

"Leave it to me," said Johnny.

In the foyer, before they headed out for the Grand Place, he called a crisis meeting. "Small problem," he said cheerfully. "Now I want twenty-nine of you here to donate one item each to poor Sandra, whose case has gone missing."

As Sandra looked on, stricken, she heard generous, well-meaning women offering her used T-shirts, a sweater, panties, sandals a half size too big, nighties, jeans, and shorts. And from the men, short-sleeved shirts, a baseball cap, another sweater, an anorak four sizes too large.

Ashen-faced, Sandra tried to thank them for their kindness as they all went to their rooms and returned with the terrifying items, laying them proudly on Sandra's bed. She washed the dress that she was wearing, hoping that it would be dry in the morning, and put on a disgusting-looking green-and-white shirt with a crushed pair of jeans and a hooded anorak.

Glumly she went out to the big square in the center of Brussels and half listened as Johnny told them all about the buildings and led them to an inexpensive restaurant in a small street nearby.

For tonight, Sandra had planned to wear a sleeveless cream-colored shirt with a rose skirt. A cream- and rose-colored jacket would be on her shoulders for the photograph.

Instead, she was pictured looking like a freak with thirty people in a group photograph. The next morning, as the coach thundered on to Paris, a quiet man said to her, "That's my sweater you have on; it looks much better on you than on me."

Normally she would have told him that she didn't wear synthetic materials and that unless something was pure wool it was unwise to wear it at all. She might even have said that she didn't like that dull, gray-blue color and that she wanted something smarter that brought out the best in her complexion.

But she said nothing and he said that the color of his sweater was exactly the color of her eyes.

His name was Ken and he had never taken a coach tour either. He worked too hard and for his thirtieth birthday thirty of his friends had bought him this trip as a gift.

Sandra was pictured wearing this terrible shapeless, colorless garment in front of the Eiffel Tower.

The day they went to Geneva she wore the faded jeans of a woman called Lola, who had taken a course at the Open University and discovered that actually she was very interested in the history of modern art. Now she worked in a local gallery and was considered a sort of expert. She had married the gallery owner, who was minding the shop while she darted around Europe on a coach having a quick look at everything she could see in eleven days.

The day they got to Milan, Sandra was wearing a bright orange T-shirt, Lola's jeans—which were actually quite comfortable—and she had Ken's sweater tied around her shoulders.

"It's still the color of your eyes," he said. He asked Johnny the guide to take a picture of them arm in arm.

"Hope the T-shirt isn't the color of my face," Sandra said, and everyone laughed.

She was surprised; she hadn't really ever made a joke before.

In Florence, Sandra got up early and went to the Uffizi Gallery with Lola. They stood, staggered by the beauty of the paintings.

"But I thought you only liked modern art," Sandra said to Lola.

"We can all like everything beautiful," Lola said. "Isn't it wonderful that there's so much for us all to see?"

In Venice, Sandra wished that she and Ken could have taken a gondola together.

They might have, but foolishly she had said it would be a waste of money and she would prefer to spend her lire on shoes.

She would remember to keep her mouth closed about such things in future. That evening, in a crushed lilac skirt and a shrunken yellow sweater as she strolled around the beautiful streets of Florence hand in hand with Ken, Sandra said how much she was enjoying it all, such great people, such deep, satisfying things to see.

"I'd love to know about all these Renaissance painters," she admitted. "Like what kinds of lives they lived and were they special in themselves. It's all such a mystery."

"Maybe we could do a course when we got back to London...that's if you felt like meeting me again?" Ken said.

And Sandra thought it would be a great idea.

Sandra had intended to buy shoes in Rome, but what was the point if she was wearing these terrible clothes?

Instead she invited Ken to come out on an early evening tour, just the two of them, in a horse and carriage.

She could have got really good shoes for the money, but she had plenty of shoes at home.

That night the group went to supper in a beautiful piazza, all of them talking like old friends about the marvelous things seen and those still to come.

Johnny wasn't with them, he'd had to stay in the hotel because he was expecting a message.

He was such a good tour leader that they

were all deciding already what they would buy him as a gift.

Some were saying that they should get him a briefcase, one of those lovely soft leather cases. Others said a really expensive Italian silk tie. Ken thought he might like one of those embroidered waistcoats. He had heard him admiring them.

They were fiendishly expensive, but between thirty of them it would be easy to buy.

Sandra was about to open her mouth and say that for someone like Johnny to wear one of those elegant waistcoats would be ridiculous.

But she kept it closed.

She was becoming less and less sure of things on this trip.

The waistcoat would make Johnny look enormous. But then, if Ken had said that he admired them…

She handed over her contribution willingly and they all went silent because Johnny appeared with a message in his hand.

"I have wonderful news for you, Sandra. They've located your bag of all your smart clothes. It will be there to greet you when we get home." He looked at her, waiting for the delight in her eyes.

Instead, he saw gratitude and heard polite remarks.

This was the woman who had bitten his head off nine days ago and said that her holiday was ruined.

"I'll be able to wash and iron all your kind gifts to me," she said to the group, "and send them back to you."

They told her she must keep them—it would be their privilege.

Sandra remembered the fun she had in these jeans and that T-shirt, how well and easily she slept in that nightie.

She remembered the lilac skirt and the yellow sweater she had worn when Ken had said he would like to see her in London.

"I'd love to keep them all—and I'll never forget you," she said.

They smiled at Sandra in a way that she knew they would somehow never have smiled if she had not lost her suitcase.

The Canary Valentine

Annie was utterly lost when her best friend, Clare, got married. She had never expected to feel so beached. She had been delighted for Clare, she had been through all the excitements, the ups and downs of the romance, the drama of the engagement, the rows about the wedding, and had worn a hat for the first time in her life to be Clare's bridesmaid.

But now Clare and John had gone to live in the West, and even though she knew they would love her to stay with them on weekends, she couldn't go **every** weekend. And she had been so accustomed to spending every weekend with Clare she didn't really know how to have one without her.

Annie didn't feel the same enthusiasm about going to concerts or theaters on her own and there wasn't as much fun spending a morning trying on clothes you were never going to buy if you did it by yourself, and though she did have other friends, it wasn't the same.

It was only when they were making up the holiday list in the office that Annie remembered this would be her first holiday for years without Clare. Up to now they used to pore over the brochures and agree that since all they wanted was a small taverna or pensione right beside the sea, they didn't have to spend hours agonizing about the culture of this place versus that. Where was cheapest in off-peak times? That would be the criterion. Maybe somewhere near a harbor where Clare and Annie would sit in the evening and look at the people and laugh and be picked up sometimes and sometimes not, but it never mattered much either way. This year Annie would have to go on her own.

She decided not to go anywhere she

had been with Clare; it would point up too sharply that she was now alone, with few resources. No, she would have to try somewhere new. They were pressing her to choose her dates, after all she was twenty-six, one of the seniors in the office, she must have first pick. It had been a quiet Christmas, a lonely New Year, the weather was bad, and the holiday prospects wouldn't become any less gloomy by putting off the date. Annie decided she would take two weeks in February. The others were very pleased; this meant they could have more reasonable times to juggle around between themselves.

"You'll be away for St. Valentine's Day," said a giggling junior who was so immature Annie felt sure that she should be in school, not out earning a living. "That could be very romantic."

Annie looked at her grimly, confirming the girl's belief that Annie was indeed elderly and half mad. Then Annie wondered where she would go. Usually she and Clare would have a serious and wailing examination of their finances when it came to planning a holiday, but Annie found that she had plenty of money to spend. Without Clare she didn't spend anything in Grafton Street on a Saturday, she didn't drink so much wine, she went on fewer outings. It didn't cost much to sit in her flat and watch television or read books from the library, and since Clare got married in September that had been Annie's main entertainment. She could go anywhere within reason. Not the Far East or America or anything, but she could go on the kind of holiday they had always dismissed before as out of their reach.

It was very, very cold. Annie saw a woman with a warm, tanned face and a happy smile; she asked her where she had been, and the woman said she had been in the Canaries. Annie booked herself on the Sunday flight; so it appeared did half of Ireland, and she wondered mildly did everyone take their holidays on Sunday, February 10, but the man at the airport said it was like this every Sunday. Whenever a country was in crisis its citizens started flying out to the sun. It was a sure sign of desperate things ahead. Annie was annoyed about the discrimination against

people who travel on their own, and how
the single room supplements seemed to
jack up the cost of the holiday in a very
unfair way, and how the world of tourism
seemed to be devised for those who go
into the Ark two by two.

She noticed that she was the only
passenger traveling by herself. Everyone
else was in groups of even numbers. This
had never worried her in the past. In those
days she had been waiting for Clare or
going to meet her, not because she was
genuinely on her own. Now it was different
somehow.

She gave herself a brisk mental shake.
"I'm not going to be the only person on my
own when I get there," she told herself
firmly. "There's bound to be hundreds of
people who came from different lands by
themselves."

Well, if there were, Annie didn't meet
them. And she became self-conscious on
the beach. She felt people were looking
at her, and wondering why was she so odd
and friendless that she sat alone, rare in
the breed of sun-seeking humans. She sat
all by herself reading a book, rubbing on

suntan oil, smiling at the children playing, admiring the fashion parade that walked up and down. She didn't **feel** very lonely; she just thought that she looked lonely and a little eccentric. So Annie did something that **was** a little eccentric; she brought two towels out to the beach with her and spread one beside her as if her companion had just gone away for a while. She even took an extra pair of flip-flops to make it look more realistic. Once or twice she began a postcard to Clare and she was about to tell her of this idiotic subterfuge, but realized that it might sound pathetic and even verging on the insane, so she tore up the postcard and put it out of her mind.

There was a big notice in the hotel lobby announcing a St. Valentine's Day party. Everyone was to wear a big label shaped like a heart with their name on it and it would create great romance in honor of the saint, the hotel announcement said.

"I thought everyone here was romantic already! What would they want to know anyone else's name for?" Annie asked the man behind the desk out of genuine interest.

"Oh, a man is always searching for new romance," he said, smiling with thirty-two overwhite teeth. Annie thought this was probably true. But on Thursday it was either put on a red heart with "Annie" written on it, or else go up to her room and sit on the balcony. There was no middle course. She took her heart and pinned it on her dress and went into the big room.

There was a welcome cocktail, a very dangerous tasting drink, which was a bright, limpid purple and might have been cleaning fluid with some cassis added. Annie sipped it cautiously. Then a Swede asked her to dance at once and said that he would like her to come to his apartment later for some Good Loving Games and wine. Annie said she thought not, and he wanted to know did she think not or did she say not. When she said she was saying not, he shrugged, finished the dance with the air of a courteous martyr, and left her.

She danced with an Englishman, who said his wife was behaving like a tramp, and she spent the dance assuring him that he might be mistaken in this view;

then she danced with a man who didn't speak at all. The name on his heart was Sven, so she assumed he was another Scandinavian. He had a nice smile. She was sorry he didn't speak. She began to talk herself but it coincided with a very loud blast of "The Rivers of Babylon" as they were passing the band and he just smiled and pointed to his ears. There was a cabaret and there was a supper of aphrodisiac foods, oysters and straw-berries mainly, and a lot of wine. Sven came and filled her glass up once and Annie wished he would say something. If Clare had been here they would have made a joke and called him Sven the Speechless to each other, but on your own it's hard to make jokes and laugh at them.

The band, six lustful-looking fellows with flashing eyes, had managed to make con-nections with two groups of three equally lustful girls. It was safe to hunt in packs, Annie thought. If she had two friends with her she too might have gone off to what-ever was promised, but on your own it was inviting some kind of disaster. She watched the musicians packing up their guitars hastily before the mood of lust passed from them or before the girls had second thoughts. A group of cheerful Irish people who had what seemed to be a jeroboam of Baileys Irish Cream with them were in high form and hardly noticed the departure of the band. For a moment Annie was tempted to join them; they looked married and settled and as if they wouldn't object, in fact they seemed the kind who'd pull up a chair for her and give her a pint mug of Baileys, but something held her back. She took off her cardboard heart so as not to look silly in the lift and was walking to the door. She saw Sven taking off his heart too and smiling at it.

"I think I'll keep it as a souvenir," he said to her.

Annie wondered was she in fact very drunk; this Dane or Norwegian or whatever he was spoke with a Dublin accent.

"I beg your pardon?" she said, hoping to clear her head.

"They can never spell Sean properly so I wrote it down for them and then they couldn't believe it; they thought I was an illiterate Swede who couldn't spell his own name."

The false Sven had a lovely smile.

"Did you have a row with your friend?" he asked her.

"What friend?"

"The one that never turns up to collect his towel and his shoes on the beach."

"There's no friend," she said.

"That's great," said the false Sven. "Will we go out on the terrace and have a pint?"

Annie pealed with laughter. And as they sat in the moonlight with a lot of very cold lager and their two cardboard hearts on the table in front of them, she never once thought what a pity Clare wasn't here to share all the laughs. She never thought of Clare at all.

Half of Ninety

Kay woke up because the curtains in her bedroom were being pulled back. This hadn't happened for a long time, not for five long years, since Peter had left. It gave her a shock.

Then she heard a breakfast tray rattling and saw a big vase of flowers on a table. Her daughter, Helen, must have let herself into the house and was giving her a birthday treat.

"It's all from Nick as well," Helen explained, not wanting to take all the praise. "He delivered the flowers, reminded me to keep the half bottle of champagne cold, he would have been here if he could."

"Champagne!" Kay couldn't believe it.

She felt tears in her eyes. They were so

good to her, and always had been.

"Just a half bottle and fresh orange juice—you are going to have a Buck's Fizz or a Mimosa or whatever they call it." Helen was struggling with the cork.

Kay sat up in bed happily. There were fresh croissants on a warmed plate and a thermos flask of coffee. This breakfast could go on all morning if she wanted it to. And why not? Her day was her own until ten o'clock, when she went to work in a nearby antiques shop, and it wouldn't really matter if she were late. They didn't depend on her to run it, exactly.

But she wouldn't think of that now as she sipped the fizzy orange. Alcohol at eight in the morning—whatever next?

"I'll just have a sip then I must go to work." Helen was all busy and excited. "Anyway, tonight, Mum, it's the birthday present. Nick and I will be here at seven to pick you up and we'll all go to this restaurant and give you our present."

"But **this** is my present, this and the dinner, surely?" Kay protested.

"Nonsense. We have to do something special—after all, it's not every day that your mother makes it to half of ninety," said Helen, giving her a kiss, and was out the door.

The color went out of the spring morning, the fizz went out of the lovely fresh drink she had been enjoying so much, the coffee tasted bitter, and the crisp fresh croissants on the warm plate lost their appeal.

Kay Nolan was forty-five, half of ninety.

What a sad, lonely, terrible thought.

She got out of bed and looked at herself in the mirror.

She couldn't quite work out what she was looking at.

A small woman with red-brown hair, quite fit and trim from all that hard work lifting and moving things around the antiques shop where she worked and walking the dog over the common twice a day.

Did she **look** half of ninety?

Impossible to say.

But now that she realized this is what she was, she sure as anything felt it.

She sat at her dressing table, head in hands.

Only the young, happy Helen and Nick, convinced that she was doing fine, would say that as a sort of joke. They were twenty-four and twenty-two, strong and handsome.

Nick would marry Julia this autumn and Kay was already dreading the wedding day when she would have to be courteous to Peter and watch him doing his proud, concerned father bit.

Helen seemed to be talking rather a lot about a musician called Johnny, but assuring everyone that there was nothing in it, really.

How could they, young people who thought that thirty was over the hill, know what it was like to be given such a statement about being forty-five?

She sighed a great sigh and Sandy came in quivering and carrying his lead. He had been hoping it was time to go out and had viewed the breakfast in bed ceremony with displeasure.

"Okay. Come on, Sandy." Kay put on her tracksuit and took the dog for a run. She would shower and dress and be ready and smiling when the antiques shop opened at ten.

That was the thing about people her age, they were programmed to work and smile and they just go on with it.

The day seemed endless, as if things were in slow motion.

She thought about Peter; he would have been forty-five some six months ago. Kay wondered if Susie, his twenty-seven-year-old wife, had made any jokes about him becoming half of ninety. Very probably not.

She was not wistful and wishing that she could spend her birthday with Peter. She didn't love him anymore. That was an absolute. He had lied too much, hurt and humiliated her too often. There had been no dignity in their breakup.

She knew the children saw him from time to time but they never talked to her about it.

"Do you want to hear how Dad is?" Helen had asked once in the early days.

"Why should I want to hear?" she had countered, so now they said nothing about any visits.

A colleague had told her that Susie was pregnant. Kay never asked further.

It didn't upset her; the upset was all in the past.

She just wanted no part of it now, no interested discussions and phony friendship with a man who had betrayed her and made her feel so foolish for so long. She wanted none of this so-called civilized behavior. Peter had never been civilized before, not when he was sleeping with Susie in the mobile home that Kay had worked such long hours to save and pay for. She did not want to see, hear of, or meet this woman with whom he was making a new life and, from all accounts, a new family.

She went out at lunch hour to have her hair done and the girl in the salon asked her was she going on a holiday this summer.

"No, indeed, walking my dog around the common is my holiday. I've reached that time of life," Kay said, and she saw the naked pity in the girl's face.

Nick brought his fiancée, Julia, with him to the restaurant and Helen said that Johnny just **might** drop in at the coffee stage but no one was to read anything into it.

It was a nice Italian restaurant and the staff was friendly and welcoming.

More than once Helen and Nick said that they wished they had an Italian family.

As they had dinner they talked about their work, Nick and Julia in a High Street bank, Helen as a receptionist in a local radio station. Kay told them about the antiques shop and the wonderful little inlaid cabinet that had come in last week and how they all loved it so much they hoped it would never sell.

Enthusiasts, yes, they were definitely that, but businesswomen probably not, she laughed ruefully.

They talked about when Nick and Julia would get married, probably at the end of the summer. They were fixing a date and sending the invitations very shortly.

She thought she saw them looking at each other as if they wanted to ask her a question, but perhaps she only imagined that.

So instead she asked them questions.

Would it be a big wedding or a small one?

Secretly she hoped it would be a big one, less need to talk to Peter if they were to be submerged in crowds.

Julia's mother wanted the works; her father wanted half the works.

"And what do **you** want, Julia?" Kay wanted to know.

Julia shrugged. "I'm an only child, Kay, so it isn't really up to me because they'll have no other wedding. Nick agrees with me in this, that I should do whatever they want to do, it's only a day."

Johnny arrived for coffee, and, as instructed, they made no fuss and read nothing into it even though his hand never moved from Helen's knee.

There were more curious conversations beginning and ending, topics about wedding days being for everyone, about the need to forget the past.

Suddenly Kay realized that they were definitely preparing the path for Susie to be invited to the wedding.

She felt a wave of rage and resentment pass over her.

To please their father, they were going to ask this woman, barely older than themselves.

They were going to let him smirk even more as he propelled his young, pregnant wife around a family gathering.

It was beyond reason to ask her to accept this.

But she would not have a row now, instead she talked vaguely as if she hadn't understood where the conversation was leading.

Then she saw them all getting ready for the present giving. There were no wrapped parcels beside them, so she thought it might be a piece of jewely or a silk scarf.

She got her face ready.

It was indeed in a big white envelope, so it might be a scarf, but when she took it out it was a travel brochure and a page marked with a big yellow sticker. They had bought her a holiday in Italy.

Her son and daughter, who surely couldn't afford this, had paid for the present she would least like in the world. Two weeks in a small family-owned Italian hotel, where it said **ENGLISH SPOKEN** in very big letters.

Kay could hardly believe it.

There was no way she could refuse such a gift, such a misplaced generosity. And yet this was what she was now committed to. A punishing two weeks in a place where English couples would sit two by two at their tables and nod to the lonely woman aged half of ninety sitting at a table by herself.

"But I can't accept this..." she began. "It's far too generous."

They beamed with pleasure and assured her that it was all paid for, she wouldn't be stopped at the airport.

"I'm not sure if I can take the time off," she blustered.

They had been to the antiques shop and she could.

"But Sandy?"

"Is going to my parents for the two weeks and you **know** they'll look after him properly," said Julia.

And so she went.

Keeping up the appearance that she was delighted and that she had the two most generous children in the world.

Nobody would have known she was furious with them for not consulting her, for not asking her opinion, treating her as helpless to be packed off to wherever they thought "suitable."

Had Kay been given a choice she might well have gone to Italy, but for a one-week art tour to Venice or Florence, somewhere she would have been with people of similar interest, not sitting awkward and alone amongst middle-aged, middle-class, smug couples visiting Tuscany.

But it was too late, so she would go with a good grace.

It was exactly as she expected. A beautiful house with a long terrace overlooking a magical valley. A hardworking Italian family and seven English couples. They were polite and welcoming, her countrymen and women. But Kay, who had married at twenty and had never known the heady excitement of traveling alone, felt out of things. She did not want to intrude on these people's lives, she feared that she was boring them and becoming a hanger-on. So, for the first two evenings, after dinner she excused herself and said she liked to take a little walk before going to bed.

She didn't want to go down to the center of the little town with pavement cafés and the music coming from the bars. It reminded her too much of a life that was over. Instead, Kay would go out the back gate and up a windy road.

In the warm Italian evening she would walk and look into people's houses and then past fields and eventually up to a wonderful hill and sit under what she thought might be an old cedar tree and look down on the lights of the town.

A man walking a dog passed her on both nights and they exchanged a cordial good evening in both languages.

At first she was alarmed in case she looked vulnerable or available sitting alone like that, but he seemed to think she was perfectly entitled to be there and did not stay to interrupt her thoughts. Her thoughts were not very worthy; Kay realized they were mainly self-pitying, yet she would not welcome that woman to Nick and Julia's wedding.

They didn't need her there...

There was no reason for her to want to attend a celebration of the family that she had succeeded in breaking up. If this Susie had any style, class, or feeling she would not **want** to go.

It would be quite hard enough to meet Peter again, but that was all she would do, because every word he said would remind her of a betrayal, a lie.

If he were to mention his mother she would remember the number of times he was meant to be dealing with his mother's nerves when in fact he was in the mobile home with Susie...

Kay knew she had been foolishly naïve to believe everything he had said over the long months that he was involved with Susie. But you **do** believe things from someone you love and trust, so what was so foolish about that?

Except, of course, that it did mean that it took a long time to discover about Susie and the trips they had and the hotels in the Lake District and the meals in places that Peter and Kay couldn't afford.

And that was hard either to forgive or forget.

And she thought about the children and how they had supported her all through the separation and then the divorce, and though they moved out to live in flats they kept in touch, calling almost every day, visiting twice or three times a week.

She was so lucky in so many ways, so perhaps they deserved this "family" day they all seemed to crave so much.

It was very unfair that she should have to make this choice. She was the innocent party in all this—why must she be the one to extend the hand of friendship to a woman who had lied and lied and was now expecting Peter's child? And yet if Kay refused to do this, she was disappointing her son and daughter.

She shouldn't sit here under this tree and think only of the bad hand that she had been dealt. She should think of the many good things that also filled her life.

It was just that in this place, where people came for a two-week vacation, there seemed to be a spotlight saying Successful Marriage shining over the heads of every couple that she saw.

On her way back into the garden of the little hotel, Kay passed the open kitchen door and saw the Italian family sitting around the table; she waved and was about to pass by, but they called her in.

There was Liliana and her two brothers and her three children. They ran this place between them since their parents had died. Liliana must be about her own age, very different in style: tall, handsome, voluble, long dark hair tied back with a yellow ribbon. Her eyes never stopped moving, looking, seeing what had to be done, smiling at everyone.

They were all going to a funeral in a village at the other side of the valley the following morning. They would really like to go now, but they were trying to sort out how to serve tomorrow's breakfast here in the hotel. Lunch would be arranged in a local trattoria and the family would be back again by dinnertime. Nobody could agree on who they should ask in. There were people considered reliable by part of the family and totally unsuitable by others. Suddenly Liliana had said the quiet Signora Inglese might be willing to do it. It would only involve one morning, and mean making coffee and whatever eggs the English people wanted. The cold milk and hot bread would be delivered at seven. Could the Signora possibly consider it?

It would help them all so much.

Her face must have shown total shock. Kay hoped that it didn't show the annoyance she felt. They had only asked her because she was the single one, the person with nothing to stay in bed for in the morning, with nothing to talk about at breakfast.

Had she been here with Peter or any other partner, they would not have made such a request. It was just because they saw her walking alone and pitied her they felt they could ask.

Immediately they started to apologize.

Most of all Liliana.

"You must forgive us, such a thing to ask. Please forget we spoke. It's just that the funeral has distressed us, you see."

Kay rushed in to tell them she would love to help.

"Believe me, it's just a British thing. I never expected that you would let me loose in your kitchen, or even trust me to do it. It would be a great pleasure, and I can't really make too much of a mess out of coffee and eggs, can I?"

"Are you really sure?" Liliana said. "I thought of asking you because you have kind eyes."

Kay knew she meant it.

"I can't tell you how much I would like to do this very small favor for you, Liliana. Why don't you let everyone else get ready for the journey and you tell me exactly what's to be done?"

The two women sat and talked. Liliana said that only one couple was difficult: they had brought their own jar of marmalade and this is where it was kept. The young honeymoon couple only came down for coffee at ten and took it upstairs again.

The smart couple who dressed up as if they were going to a wedding were always very bad-tempered in the morning; it had something to do with their metabolism, they needed a lot of coffee to bring them up to normal communication level.

It was both exciting and reassuring to be allowed into the secrets of the hotel. Kay went to bed happier than since she had arrived.

The next morning she joked with the other guests as she served the breakfast and felt that they somehow envied her for being taken into the inner sanctum.

"I would have done it happily, I worked in catering for a while," said the bad-tempered, well-dressed woman.

Kay rushed to make sure that she had more coffee before she was allowed to become resentful.

She washed the dishes and put them away in the sunny kitchen and looked at the photographs around the wall. There was Liliana and her three children laughing and shielding their eyes against the Italian sun. In the early years there was a hand-some, laughing man with them all. It must have been Liliana's husband, the father of her children.

Not in evidence these days; possibly he was dead now and not aware that his wife, her brothers, and his children had made such a success of this little hotel. Maybe they had separated? Kay would probably never know. It wasn't the kind of thing you could ask someone you hardly knew.

She stayed around the house while they were gone to deal with callers. Many people came with sympathy cards in black-edged envelopes.

A local girl came in to make the beds at lunchtime as Liliana had explained she would. Kay sat on the terrace writing post-cards back home that it was wonderful and that she was very happy.

And for the first time she began to think that she really **was** fairly happy here and certainly not useless, friendless, and self-pitying, as she had felt up to now.

The tall dark man with the big dog, the man who always said good night to her when she sat under the tree, passed the house several times. As if he were watching it, guarding it even. But then possibly she was just being fanciful.

Kay felt they wouldn't want her around when they got back and had to set to making a dinner immediately after the journey.

She left her bedroom window open and could hear the noises in the kitchen, the smells too of the cooking wafted up to her, and she heard the doors of people's bedrooms opening and closing and the sound of running water as they showered for dinner on the terrace.

She wondered what the others would be doing back home. Eight-thirty here in Italy, seven-thirty back in England.

Nick and Julia would have come from work, they might be making a snack in their little house where the mortgage took up such a percentage of their bank salary, and then sitting down for more wedding chat and wondering how to include Susie in their plans.

Julia's parents were still debating the wedding, but they were serious dog lovers; they would have fed Sandy well and taken him on at least two walks.

Helen would be with Johnny and perhaps they were busy putting up posters in one of the clubs where he was playing tonight.

And her friends, the women from the antiques shop, they would have taken their trains and buses home, one to a difficult mother, one to a wordless husband, and one to an unreliable lover. They would all envy Kay out under the warm skies of Tuscany, and hope that she was having a good time.

Kay noticed that Liliana did not have her two sons to help her that evening as dinner was served, so afterwards she slipped into the kitchen to know if she could do anything to help.

"Please," she said to Liliana, "you can see I am on my own here and I like to talk, so the nights are often long for me."

The other woman looked at her for a long moment.

"My sons stayed with their grandmother. I would love now to send my brothers home to their wives. Signora Kay, if you were to help me with the washing-up, we will have a beautiful Italian brandy afterwards and talk through the night."

And it seemed to take no time to restore the kitchen to rights, and to take out the really good glasses that were never given to guests. And Kay sat and listened to the story of today's funeral. It was Paolo's father who had died. Papa Gianni. A kind old man who never did anyone any harm and who had cried when he heard that his son Paolo was leaving the hardworking Liliana for a rich woman who lived in the city far away in Milano.

Liliana didn't want to go to the funeral and see Paolo getting out of the big car that his rich wife had bought him. She did not want to see him holding his five-year-old twins by the hand and watch him moving around in his expensive leather jacket, accepting sympathy from old friends.

She did not want to raise her eyes to meet again those of the woman with money who had come here once on a vacation and who had bought Paolo and taken him away.

But she had done it for the children. For her children, who must go and say good-bye to their grandfather, and go with the knowledge that their mother too would mourn the kind old man, no matter what had happened in the past. And her children had a right to meet and know their little half brothers too. These were just innocent little boys—they must not grow up in a shadow, in fear of a household that could never be mentioned.

You didn't have to like it but you did it. That's how life and families went on. And oddly it got easier. This was the third time. And there would be more times, weddings, christenings, and funerals.

Maybe if Liliana got married again herself they would all come and dance at her wedding. The whole extended family.

"Speaking of that, do you think that man with the dog fancies you?" Kay asked. "He's always going past the house."

Liliana laughed until she cried. "No, he fancies **you,** Signora Kay. That's Pietro. He thinks you have beautiful eyes, but did not like to approach you, so he just admires from afar."

Kay telephoned Nick and Julia that night; Helen and Johnny were there, but no significance was to be attached to that.

"You sound great," Nick said. "Have you found a fancy man?"

"Well, yes, in a way. A man admires me—he keeps walking past the hotel with his dog."

They were delighted.

"You're not to make anything of it," she said, reacting to the way Helen went on. "We haven't exchanged more than a few good evenings. And I didn't call about that, it was something else."

They sounded alarmed.

"No, nothing wrong, just something I forgot when we were talking; you **have** included Susie, Dad's Susie, on your wedding list, haven't you?"

"Well, yes, no, I mean we didn't really know...you see she's sort of—"

"Pregnant, yes, I know...Even more important then that she should be included."

Kay went for her walk, she sat under the tree and waited for Pietro to pass by; she would ask him to sit down and they would talk in fractured Italian and English. Kay knew she wouldn't enjoy seeing Peter and Susie, but Liliana was right, it had to be done.

It was the way life and families went on.

A NOTE ABOUT THE AUTHOR

Maeve Binchy was born in County Dublin and educated at the Holy Child convent in Killiney and at University College, Dublin. After a spell as a teacher she joined **The Irish Times.** Her first novel, **Light a Penny Candle,** was published in 1982 and she went on to write more than twenty books, all of them best sellers, including **Maeve's Times: In Her Own Words.** Several have been adapted for cinema and television, most notably **Circle of Friends** and **Tara Road,** which was an Oprah's Book Club selection. Maeve Binchy received a Lifetime Achievement Award at the British Book Awards in 1999 and the Irish PEN/A.T. Cross Award in 2007. In 2010 she was presented with the Bob Hughes Lifetime Achievement Award at the Bord Gáis Energy Irish Book Awards for **A Week in Winter.** She was married to the writer and broadcaster Gordon Snell for thirty-five years. She died in 2012 at the age of seventy-two. Visit her website at www.maevebinchy.com.